Enderby

FAT, flatulent, middle-aged, Enderby the poet may or may not be the Milton of our age. But as the hero of Anthony Burgess's new novel he is certainly one of the great comic creations of modern fiction.

Enderby rising drunkenly after a poet's luncheon to refuse the honorary prize. . .

Enderby captured by Vesta Bainbridge to pen the "Poet's Corner" page for the women readers of slick, glossy *Fem*. . .

Enderby springing from his honeymoon bed to jot down a fleeting inspiration—and dismayed to find his bride gone when he returns. . .

Enderby pursuing his way through a world of charlatans, plagiarists and jackals, the innocent handservant of his Muse. . .

Out of dozens of magnificent scenes of catastrophe and comedy, Burgess has developed a character who will rank with Gully Jimson of *The Horse's Mouth*—a touching and hilarious portrait of an artist who is whisked from obscurity to the heights of pop fame but cannot cohabit with the bitch goddess, Success.

"A splendid, irresistible flood of the major novelistic virtues. Hurry to the store and buy it." —*Saturday Review Syndicate*

THE BOOKS OF
Anthony Burgess

Novels
*ENDERBY
*TREMOR OF INTENT
*THE DOCTOR IS SICK
*A VISION OF BATTLEMENTS
*THE LONG DAY WANES
*NOTHING LIKE THE SUN
*HONEY FOR THE BEARS
*THE WANTING SEED
*A CLOCKWORK ORANGE
*DEVIL OF A STATE
*THE RIGHT TO AN ANSWER

Nonfiction
LANGUAGE MADE PLAIN
*RE JOYCE
THE NOVEL NOW
URGENT COPY

*BALLANTINE BOOKS

ENDERBY

ANTHONY BURGESS

BALLANTINE BOOKS • NEW YORK

Copyright © 1968, 1963 by Anthony Burgess

All rights reserved.

Library of Congress Catalog Card No. 68-13483

This edition published by arrangement with
W.W. Norton and Company, Inc.

First Printing: September, 1969

Printed in the United States of America

Ballantine Books, Inc.
101 Fifth Avenue, New York, N.Y. 10003

TO *Deborah*

Book One

—Allons, dernier des poètes,
Toujours enfermé tu te rendras malade!
Vois, il fait beau temps, tout le monde est dehors,
Va donc acheter deux sous d'ellébore,
Ça te fera une petite promenade.

                    Jules Laforgue, *Dimanches*

I

1

One

Pffffrrrummmp.

And a very happy New Year to you too, Mr Enderby!

The wish is, however, wasted on both sides, for this, to your night visitors, is a very old year. We, whispering, fingering, rustling, creaking about your bedroom, are that posterity to which you hopefully addressed yourself. Congratulations, Mr Enderby: you have already hit your ball smack over the pavilion clock. If you awaken now with one of the duodenal or pyloric twinges which are, to us, as gruesome a literature-lesson spicer as Johnson's scrofula, Swift's scatophobia, or Keats's gallop of death-warrant blood, do not fancy it is ghosts you hear sibilant and crepitant about the bed. To be a ghost one has first to die or, at least, be born.

Perrrrrp.

A posterior riposte from Mr Enderby. Do not touch, Priscilla. Mr Enderby is not a *thing* to be prodded; he is a great poet sleeping. Your grubby finger out of his mouth, please, Alberta. His mouth is open for no amateur dental inspection but to the end that he may breathe. That nose is, at forty-five, past its best as an organ, the

5

black twitching caverns—each with its miniature arm-pit—stuffed and obtuse. The world of smell is visited by his early poems, remember (pages 1 to 17 of the Harvard University Press selection which is your set book). There we have washed hair, pickles, gorse, bath-salts, skin, pencil-shavings, tinned peaches, post offices, Mrs Lazenby at the corner-shop in his native slum, cloves, diabetes. But it has no existence in his maturer work; the twin ports are closed for ever. That gentle noise, Harold, is snoring. That is so, Christine; his teeth, both upper and lower, are removable: they have been re-moved to that plastic night-jar there. Child, child, you have spilt denture-fluid on to Mr Enderby's landlady's carpet. No, Robin, the carpet is neither beautiful nor rare, but it is Mrs Meldrum's property. Yes, Mr Enderby himself is our property, the world's property, but his carpet is his landlady's. Mrs Meldrum's.

Now. His hair goes a daily journey from head to brush, squad by tiny squad on a one-way ticket. Here on the dressing-table are the imitation-silver-backed brushes bequeathed by his father, the tobacconist. The bristles are indeed dirty, Mavis, but great poets have other things to do than attend to the calls of hygiene. See how the bristles have trapped their day's quota of Mr Ender-by's few remaining hairs. Holy relics, children. Do not rush. One each for everybody. There. Keep it safe, each of you, in your little diary of posterity's present year. Shed hairs, Henry, become the property of the picker. They are of no use to Mr Enderby, but they are already fetching, at classical auction-rooms, a pound or so each if nicely mounted. It is not proper, Audrey, that you should try to pick your hair *alive*. Such a rough tug at the scalp is enough to wake Mr Enderby.

Querpkprrmp.

You see? He's disturbed. Let him settle as one lets churned water settle. Right. A better view of Mr Ender-by, you will agree, children, as he flops on his back cruciform and sends the bedclothes sliding and plopping to the floor. His belly bulges in two gentle hills, one on either side of the cutting pyjama-cord. There is a wealth of hair, see. It is one of the abominable ironies of middle age that hair should march down from the noble summit, the eagle's lodge, to leave that bare as an eagle, in order that the camps and barracks and garrisons of the warm vulgar body be crammed with a growth that is neither useful nor pretty. The flabby chest too, see. Rich in hair, aflame with whorls and tendrils of it. And for good measure, chin and jowls bristling. Horrent, Milton might say.

Yes, Janice, I am constrained to agree that Mr Enderby does not make a pretty sight when sleeping, even in total darkness. Yes, remark again the scant hair, the toothless jaws, the ample folds of flesh rising and falling. But what has prettiness to do with greatness, eh? There is something for you all to ponder on. You would not like to have been married to him, Alberta? Might not the reverse also have applied, even more so, you stupid giggling silly thing? Who are you to think that you would ever be meet to mate with a great poet?

The extremities. The feet that trod Parnassus. Callosities on the intricate map of the sole, see. Torn toenails, though that of the great toe too rocky to be tearable. They could both do with a long sudsy soaking, agreed. The outstretched right hand, like a beggar's, really a king's. Gaze with reverence on those fingers that rest now from writing. Tomorrow they will write again, continuing the poem that he considers to be his masterpiece. Ah, what these fingers have produced! Each of you kiss the hand, more gently, though, than a fly crawling. I realise that the act of kissing needs an effort of will to overcome a certain natural revulsion. Here, however, is a little lesson for you in scholastic philosophy. The grubby knuckles, the nails with black borders, the deep stains of tobacco-tar (the cigarette was held interdigitally, forgotten, while the poet's mind soared above the smell of burning), the coarse skin—these are the accidents, the outer aspects of the hand, their concession to the ordinary world of eating and dying. But the essence of the hand—what is that? A divine machine that has made our lives more blessed. Kiss it, come on, kiss it. Althea, stop making that vomiting noise. Your

7

face, Charles, is ugly enough without contorting it to a rictus of nausea. That's right, kiss it.

It has hardly disturbed him at all. He scratches it gently in his sleep, the tickle of a questing alighting moth. Listen. In his sleep he is going to say something. Your kiss has prodded a sleeping inspiration. Listen.

> *My bedmate deep*
> *In the heavy labour of unrequited sleep.*

No more? No more. There, children, what a thrill! You have heard his voice, a mumbly sleepy voice, true, but still his voice. And now let us pass on to Mr Enderby's bedside table.

Books, children, Mr Enderby's bed-reading. *Blondes Like Bullets*, whatever that means; *Who Was Who in the Ancient World*, useful, no doubt; *Raffity's Deal*, with a brutish cover; *How I Succeeded*, by a tycoon who died of arteriosclerosis; *Little Stories of the Marian Martyrs*, sensational. And here, dears, is one of Mr Enderby's own: *Fish and Heroes*, his early poems. What a genius he had then! Yes, Denis, you may handle it but, please, with care. Oh, you stupid boy, you have sent a shower of things to the floor. What are these, that were hidden between the well-thumbed pages? Photographs? Don't touch, leave them, they are not for you! Merciful heavens, the weaknesses of the great. What shame we have unintentionally uncovered. Do not giggle, Brenda and Maureen, and hand that photograph back to me this instant. You will wake Mr Enderby with those obscene girlish noises. What, Charles, are they doing? The man and woman in the picture? They are minding their own business, that's what they're doing.

Bopperlop.

Rest, rest, perturbed spirit. That picture, please, Robin. I can see it in your blazer pocket. Thank you. Fellation, if you must know, is the technical term. And now, no more of that. Shall we tiptoe into Mr Enderby's bathroom? Here we are. This is where Mr Enderby writes most of his verse. Remarkable, isn't it? Here, he knows, he can be truly private. The bath is full of

8

manuscripts and dictionaries and ink-milked ballpoint pens. In front of the WC is a low desk, just the right height. There is an electric heater to glow on to his bared legs. Why does he choose this meagre chamber? Poetry, he has already said in an interview, is appropriate to it; the poet is time's cleanser and cathartiser. But, one may be sure, there is much more to it than that. Some childhood agony not yet to be uncovered by us. But Educational Time Trips are already talking of pushing further back into the past. Who knows? Before you leave school you may yet visit Shakespeare struggling, in the parish of St Olave, with verse quantities and a quill. Nigel, leave those rusty razor-blades alone, stupid boy. Softly, softly, now. To the room where he eats and, when not writing, lives is but a step. No, Stephanie, Mr Enderby lives alone through choice. Love, love, love. That's all that some of you girls can think about. Mr Enderby's love-life up to this point is obscure and shrouded. His attitude to women? You have his poems, though they, admittedly, mention the sex but little.

Porripipoop.

The horns of Elfland. We have left him to his poet's peace. There is one thing, though. The poems of this year—which, of course, he has not yet written—show a shy stirring of a more than photographic interest in woman. But we have no biographical evidence of an affair, a change of ménage. We have little biographical evidence of anything. He was essentially a man who lived inside himself. And this sandy seaside address is the only one we have. Can you hear the sea, children? It is the same sea that we know, cruel, green, corrupt.

And what of Mr Enderby do we find in this room? It is Mrs Meldrum, his landlady, who speaks out clear in all this ranged bric-à-brac. Yes, survey it with wonder: a geometrical series of baby ebony elephants, the sweetest of china shepherds flute-blowing to unseen lambs, a plaster toy toast-rack with ancient Blackpool gilding, a tea-caddy replica of tarnished Brighton Pavilion, an enmarbled papier-mâché candlestick, a china bitch and her china litter, a filigree sheet-iron button-box. Do you like the picture above the electric-fire mantelpiece? It shows men in rusty red preparing for the hunting morning, all men identical because, we presume, the pseudo-artist could afford only one model. And, on the opposite wall, British admirals of the eighteenth century unrolling maps of *terra incognita*, wine being poured for them in tankards that catch the fire's glow. Here, jolly monks fish on Thursday; there, they lap up their Friday feast. A pot head of a twentyish flapper, hatted and lipsticked, on that strip of wall past the kitchen door. Emily, leave your nostrils alone. To blow spittle-bubbles on your nether lip is, need I say, Charles, childish. The kitchen is hardly worth examining. Very well, if you insist.

What a strong stench of stale bread! See that fish glow in the dark. Pans on the high shelf. Do not touch, Denis, do not. Oh, you damnable young idiot. The whole blasted flaming lot clanking and clashing and ringing down. You bloody young fool. You will all laugh on the other sides of your faces when I get you back to civilisation. Oh God, a frying pan has knocked the kettle over. The gas-stove is full of water. What a filthy, damnable, metal noise! Who has spilt the pepper? Stop sneezing, blast the lot of you. Aaaaaarch! Howrashyouare! Out of here, quickly.

You can't be trusted, any of you. This is the last time I arrange such an expedition. Look down on all those Victorian roofs, fish-scaled under the New Year moon. You will never see them again. Nor any of this town, in whose flats and lodgings the retired and dying wheeze away till dawn. Very well, very well. I forgive you. It is all very much like a great hair-comb, isn't it?—the winking jewelled handle, the avenues of teeth combing the hinterland of downs, the hair-ball of smoke which is the railway station. Above us, the January sky: Scutum, Ophiuchus, Sagittarius, the planets of age and war and love westering. And that man down below, whom that clatter of cheap metal has aroused from dyspeptic and flatulent sleep, he gives it all meaning.

Two

Enderby awoke, aware of both noise and heartburn. Clamped to his bedhead was a lamp in a plastic shade. He switched this on, realised he was shivering and saw why. He picked up the tangle of bedclothes from the floor, covered himself roughly, and lay back again to savour the pain. It had an inexplicable note of raw turnip about it. The noise? The kitchen-gods fighting. Rats. He needed bicarbonate of soda. He must, he reminded himself for at least the seven-thousandth time, remember to keep it ready-mixed and handy by his bed. The stab of sharpened raw turnip shattered his breastbone. He had to get up.

He saw himself in the wardrobe mirror as he slapped stiffly out of the room into the tiny hallway of his flat, a rheumatic robot in pyjamas. He entered the dining-room, switching on, sniffing like a dog as for a craftily hidden presence. Ghosts had been whimpering around, he was sure, ghosts of the dead year. Or perhaps, he smiled wryly at the conceit, posterity had been shyly looking in. He was astonished at the mess in the kitchen. Such things happened, though: a delicate balance upset by a micrometric subsidence of the old house, an earth tremor, self-willed monads in the utensils themselves. He took a cloudy glass from the draining-board, saw with surprise that it already contained water, snowed in some sodium bicarbonate, stirred with two fingers, then drank. He waited thirty seconds, squinting at the glazed pane of the back door. A tiny hand hidden beneath his epiglottis gave a come-up signal. And then.

Delightful. Oh, doctor, the relief! I feel I must write to say thank you for the benefits I have obtained from your product. Aaaaaaarp. Almost immediately after the second spasm of release came a fierce and shameless hunger. He moved the three steps necessary from sink to food-cupboard and found himself freezingly sploshing in spilt water by the stove. He dried his feet in the dropped tea-towel and rearranged the fallen pans on their shelf, wincing with old man's bent pain as he picked them up. He then remembered that he needed his teeth, so he padded back to the bedroom for them, switching the living-room fire on on the way. He clacked a false gleam at the mirror when he returned to the living-room, then did a brief lumbering dance of rage at his reflection. In the food-cupboard were pellets of rocky cheddar, greasily wrapped. A lone midget cauliflower swam like a doll's brain in dense pickle. There was half a tin of sardines, soft plump knives in golden oil. He ate with fingers that he then wiped dry on his pyjamas.

Almost at once his bowels reacted. He ran like a man in a comic film, sat down with a sigh and clicked on the bathroom heater. He scratched his bare legs and read, thoughtfully, the confused draft he was working on. Pfffrumpfff. It was an attempt at allegory, a narrative poem in which two myths were fused—the Cretan and the Christian. A winged bull swooped from heaven in a howling wind. Wheeeeeee. The law-giver's queen was ravished. Big with child, called whore by her husband, she went incognita to a tiny village of the kingdom, there, in a cheap hotel, to give birth to the Minotaur. But the old gummy trot who tended her would keep no secret; she blazoned it about the village (and this spread beyond to the towns, to the capital) that a god-man-beast had come down to rule the world. Prrfrrr. In hope, the anarchic party of the state was now ready to rise against the law-maker: tradition had spoken of the coming of a divine leader. Civil war broke out, propaganda flashed in jagged lightnings from both sides. The beast was evil, said King Minos: capture it, kill it. The beast was God, cried the rebels. But, nobody, except the queen-mother and the toothless midwife, had ever seen the beast. Brrrrbfrrr. The baby Minotaur was growing fast, bellowing lustily, hidden away safely with its dam in a lonely cottage. But, by treachery, the forces of Minos were given knowledge of its whereabouts. Manifestly, thought Minos, when it was brought to his palace, though technically a monster it was no horror: its gentle eyes were twin worlds of love. With the talisman and mascot of the rebels in his power, Minos was able to

12

call for surrender. He had a labyrinth built, vast and marbly splendid, with the Minotaur hidden in its heart. It was a horror, unspeakable, reputedly fed on human flesh; it was the state's bogey, the state's guilt. But Minos was economical: the peripheral corridors of the labyrinth became a home of Cretan culture—university, museum, library, art gallery; a treasury of human achievement; beauty and knowledge built round a core of sin, the human condition. Prrrrf. (Enderby's toilet-roll span.) But one day, from the west, there flew in the Pelagian liberator, the man who had never known sin, the guilt-killer. Minos by now was long dead, along with his shameless queen and, long, long before, the midwife. Nobody living had seen the monster and survived, so it was said. Greeted with cheers, flowers and wine, the liberator went to his heroic work. Blond, bronzed, muscular, sinless, he entered the labyrinth and, a day later, emerged leading the monster on a string. Gentle as a pet, with hurt and forgiving eyes, it looked on humanity. Humanity seized it and reviled it and buffeted it. Finally it was nailed to a cross, where it died slowly. At the moment of giving up the ghost there was a sound of rending and crashing. The labyrinth collapsed; books were buried, statues ground to chalk-dust: civilisation was at an end. Brrrrp.

The poem was to be called, tentatively, *The Pet Beast*. Enderby realised that a great deal of work had to be done on it, symbols clarified, technical knots unravelled. There was the disinterested craftsman, Daedalus, to be brought into it, the antisocial genius with the final answer of flight. There was Pasiphae's pantomime cow. He tried out, in his deep woollily inept voice, a line or two on a hushed audience of hanging dirty towels:

> He, the cold king, judged cases in his dreams.
> Awake, lithe at his task,
> The other whistled, sawing pliant beams.
> Law is what seems;
> The craftsman's place to act and not to ask.

The words, resounding in that tiny cell, acted at once

13

like a conjuration. Just outside the flimsy door of Mr Enderby's ground-floor flat was the entrance-hall of the house itself. He heard the massive front door creak open and the hall seem to fill with New-Year revellers. He recognised the silly unresonant voice of the salesman who lived in the flat above, the stout-fed laugh of the woman who lived with him. There were other voices, not assignable to known persons but generic, voices of *Daily Mirror*-readers, ITV-viewers, HP-buyers, Babycham-drinkers. There were loud and cheerful greetings:

"Happy New Year, Enderby!"

"Prrrrrrrrp!"

The stout-fed woman's voice said, "I don't feel well. I'm going to be sick." She at once, by the sound of it, was. Some one called:

"Give us a poem, Enderby. 'Eskimo Nell' or 'The Good Ship Venus.'"

"Sing us a song, Enderby."

"Jack," said the sick woman weakly, "I'm going straight up. I've had it."

"You go up, love," said the salesman's voice. "I'll be after you in a minute. Got to serenade old Enderby first." There was the noise of a staggering fall against the door of Enderby's flat, a choirmaster's "One two three," and then the vigorous ragged strains of *"Ach Du Lieber Augustin,"* but with rude English words:

Balls to Mister Enderby, Enderby, Enderby;
Balls to Mister Enderby, ballocks to you.
For he keeps us waiting while he's masturbating, so—

Enderby stuffed moistened pellets of toilet-paper in his ears. Locked safely enough in his flat, he now locked himself safelier in his bathroom. Scratching a warmed bare leg, he tried to concentrate on his poem. The revellers soon desisted and dispersed. He thought he heard the salesman call out, "That's the enderby, Enderby."

Three

Cosily muffled against the sharp marine morning, Enderby walked down Fitzherbert Avenue towards the sea. It was ten-thirty by the Town Hall clock and the pubs were just opening. He passed Gradeleigh ("for Gradely Folk"), Kia-Ora (retired Kiwis), Ty-Gwyn (couple from Tredegar), Channel View, White Posts, Dulce Domus, The Laurels, Ithaca (former classics master and convicted pederast). Converted to flats, humbled as guest-houses, all were owned by foreigners from north and west of the downs, bemused by an image of the glamour of the south coast: France winked at night across the water; here the air had a fancied mildness. Not today, thought Enderby, smacking his woolly bearpaw palms together. He wore a scarf coloured like a Neapolitan ice; his overcoat was a tightly-belted Melton; he was shielded from heaven by a Basque beret. The house wherein he had a flat was, he thanked that same heaven, nameless. Number 81, Fitzherbert Avenue. Would there ever, some day, be a plaque to mark that he had lived there? He was quite sure not. He was one of a dying race, unregarded by the world. Hurray.

Enderby turned on to the Esplanade, joined a queue of old women in a cake-shop, and came out with a sevenpenny loaf. He crossed over to the sea-rail and leaned on it, tearing the loaf. The gulls wheeled screaming for the thrown bread, beady-eyed greedy creatures, while the sea whooped in, the green-grey winter Channel, then grumbled back, as at the lion-tamer's whip, grudgingly rattling many tambourines. Enderby tossed the last crumbs to the bitter air and its grey planing birds, then turned from the sea. He looked back on it before he entered the Neptune, seeing in it, as so often from a distance, the clever naughty green child which had learned to draw a straight line free-hand.

The saloon-bar of the Neptune was already half-filled with old people, mainly widows. "Morning," said a dying major-general, "and a happy New Year to you." Two male ancients compared arthritis over baby stouts. A bearded lady drank off her port and slowly, toothlessly, chewed the mouthful. "And to you too," said Enderby. "If I can live to see the spring," said the general, "that's as much as I can hope for." Enderby sat down with his whisky. He was at home with the aged, accepted as one of them, despite his ridiculous youth. Still, his recorded age was a mere actuarial cipher; his gullet burning as the whisky descended, his aches and pains, his lack of interest in action—these made him as old as the crocks among whom he sat.

"How," asked a gentle tremulous man made of parchment, "how," his hand shaking his drink like a dicebox, "how is the stomach?"

"Some quite remarkable twinges," said Enderby. "Almost visible, you know. And flatulence."

"Flatulence," said the major-general, "ah, yes, flatulence." He spoke of it as though it were a rare old vintage. "Many years since I've had that. Now, of course, I eat nothing. A little bread soaked in warm milk, morning and evening. I swear it's this rum that's keeping me alive. I told you, did I, about that contretemps over the rum ration at Bruderstroom?"

"Several times," said Enderby. "A very good story."

"Isn't it?" said the general, painfully animated. "Isn't it a good story? And true. Incredible, but true."

A plebeian crone in dirty black spoke from a bar-stool. "I," she said, "have had part of my stomach removed." There was a silence. The aged males ruminated this gratuitous revelation, wondering whether, coming from a female and a comparative stranger, it was really in the best of taste. Enderby said kindly: "That must have been quite an experience." The old woman looked crafty, gripped the counter's edge with papery hands that grew chalky at the knuckles, canted her stool towards Enderby and said, very loudly, "Pardon?"

"An experience," said Enderby, "never to be forgotten."

"Six hours on the table," said the woman. "Nobody here can't beat that."

"Crump," called the major-general in an etiolated

martinet's voice. "Crump. Crump." He was not reminiscing about the first World War; he wanted the barman to replenish his rum-glass. Crump came from behind the bar, seventyish, in a waiter's white jacket, with a false smile both imbecilic and ingratiating, his grey head cocked permanently to one side like that of a listening parrot. "Yes, General," he said. "Similar, sir? Very good, sir."

"I'm always telling him," said an ancient with the humpty-dumpty head of Sibelius, "about the use of the word. It's common among barmen and landlords. They say you can't have the *same* again. But it is, in fact, precisely the same again that one wants. One doesn't want anything *similar*. You deal in words, Enderby. You're a writer. What's your view of the matter?"

"It *is* the same," agreed Enderby. "It's from the same bottle. Something similar is something different."

"Professor Taylor used to argue that out very persuasively," said an old man mottled like salami, a dewdrop on the hook of his nose.

"What's happened to Taylor?" asked the major-general. "We haven't seen him for quite some time."

"He died," said the mottled man. "Last week. While drawing a cork. Cardiac failure."

"He'd just turned eighty," said a man just turned eighty. "Not all that old."

"Taylor gone," said the general. "I didn't know." He accepted rum from obsequious Crump. Crump accepted silver with an obsequious inclination of a broken and mended torso. "I thought I'd go before him," said the general, "but I'm still here."

"You're not all that old yourself," said the tremulous parchment man.

"I'm eighty-five," said the general in puffy indignation. "I call that *very* old."

Higher bids came from the corners. One woman confessed coyly to ninety. As if somehow to prove this, she performed a few waltz-twirls, humming from *The Merry Widow*. She sat down again to genteel shocked applause, her lips blue, her heart almost audibly thumping.

17

"And," asked the Sibelius-man, "how old might you be, Enderby?"

"Forty-five."

There were snorts of both contempt and amusement. One man in a corner piped, "If that's meant to be funny, I don't think it's in very good taste."

The major-general turned sternly and deliberately towards Enderby, both hands resting on the ivory bull-doghead of his malacca. "And what is it you do for a living?" he asked.

"You know that," said Enderby. "I'm a poet."

"Yes, yes, but what do you do for a living? Only Sir Walter made a living out of poetry. And perhaps that Anglo-Indian man who lived at Burwash."

"A few investments," said Enderby.

"What investments precisely?"

"I.C.I. and B.M.C. and Butlin's. And local government loans."

The major-general grunted, as though none of Enderby's replies was above suspicion. "What was your rank in the last war?" he asked, a last throw.

Before Enderby could give a lying answer, a widow in antique tweeds, a long thin woman with black-rimmed spectacles, fell from a low stool by a wicker table. Old men reached trembling for their sticks, that they might lever themselves up and help. But Enderby was there first. "Sho kind," said the woman genteelly. "Sho shorry to cauzhe all thish trouble." She had evidently been tanking up at home before opening-time. Enderby lifted her from the floor, as light and as stiff as a bundle of celery. "Thezhe thingzh," she said, "happen in the besht of familiezh."

His hands still hooked in her armpits, Enderby was shocked to see the image of his stepmother in the big Gilbey's Port mirror on the wall opposite. Shaken, he nearly dropped his burden to the floor again. The image nodded to him, as out of some animated painting in a TV commercial, raised its glass in New Year salutation, then seemed to hobble out of the picture, into the wings, thus disappearing.

"Get on with it, Enderby," said the peevish major-general. "Put her back on her seat."

"Sho very kind," said the woman, trying hard to focus on her gin-glass. Enderby looked in the room for a source of that mirror-image, but saw only a bent back hobbling to the Gents. That might be it, a trick of the light or the New Year. It was his stepmother, strangely enough, who had told him as a child that, on New Year's Day, a man walked the streets with as many noses on his face as there were days in the year. He had gone looking for this man, thinking of him fearfully as of the family of the Antichrist that walked the world before the day of judgment. Long after he had seen through the trick, New Year's Day still possessed for him an irritating macabre flavour, as a day of possible prodigies. His stepmother was, he was pretty sure, dead and buried. She'd done her work, as far as he was concerned. There was no point in her staying alive or coming back from the grave.

"Now," said the major-general, as Enderby sat down again with a new whisky, "what did you say your rank was?"

"Lieutenant-general," said Enderby. In speech a comma is as good as a hyphen.

"I don't believe you."

"Look it up." Enderby was almost sure he saw his stepmother leave the jug-and-bottle department, a quarter-bottle of Booth's in her bag. The Neptune was the sort of pub in which any of the three parts—saloon, public, outdoor—is visible from any other. Enderby spilt whisky on his tie. An old man who had not previously spoken pointed at Enderby with shaky care and said, "You've spilt whisky on your tie." Enderby felt that fear would possibly make worse happen. The outer world was not safe. He must go back home and closet himself, work at his poem. He finished the driblet in his glass, buttoned himself up and donned his Basque beret. The major-general said, "I don't believe you, sir."

"You must please yourself, General," said Ex-lieutenant Enderby. And, with a general salute, he left.

"He's a liar," said the major-general. "I always knew he

19

wasn't to be trusted. I don't believe he's a poet, either. A very shifty look about him this morning."

"I read about him in the public library," said the salami-mottled man. "There was a photograph, too. It was an article, and it seemed to think quite a lot of him."

"What is he? Where does he come from?" asked another.

"He keeps himself very much to himself," said the mottled man and, just in time, he snuffed up a perilous dewdrop.

"He's a liar, anyway," said the major-general. "I shall look up the Army List this afternoon."

He never did. A motorist, irritable and jumpy with a seasonal hangover, knocked him down as he was crossing Nollekens Avenue. Long before spring, the major-general was promoted to glory.

Four

Out in the gull-clawed air, New-Year blue, the tide crawling creamily in, Enderby felt better. In this sharp light there was no room for ghosts. But the imagined visitation had acted as an injunction to honour the past before looking, as at every year's beginning, to the future.

Enderby first thought of his mother, dead at his birth, of whom there had seemed to be no record. He liked to imagine a young woman of gentle blondness, sweetly refined and slenderly pliant. He liked to think of her swathed in gold, in a beeswax-breathing drawing-room, singing "Passing By" to her own accompaniment. The dying heat of a July day sang in sadness through the wide-open french windows from a garden that glowed with Crimson Glory, Mme. L. Dieudonné, Ena Harkness and Golden Sceptre. He saw his father, become bookish, wearing bookman's slippers, O-ing out smoke from an oval-bored Passing Cloud, nodding his head in quiet pleasure as he listened. But his father had never been quite like that. A wholesale tobacconist, ruling lines in the ledger with an ebony sceptre of a ledger-ruler, sitting in the office behind the shop in waistcoat and black bowler, always glad of opening-time. Why? To escape from that bitch of a second wife. Why in God's name had he married her? "Money, son. Her first one left her a packet. Her stepson will, we hope, reap the benefit." And, to some extent, it had turned out that way. Hence the few hundred a year from I.C.I., British Motors and the rest. But had it been worth it?

Oh, she had been graceless and coarse, that one. A hundred-weight of ringed and brooched blubber, smelling to high heaven of female smells, rank as long-hung hare or blown beef, her bedroom strewn with soiled bloomers, crumby combinations, malodorous bust-bodices. She had swollen finger-joints, puffy palms, wrists girdled with fat, slug-white upper arms that, when naked, showed indecent as thighs. She was corned, bunioned, calloused, varicose-veined. Healthy as a sow, she moaned of pains in all her joints, a perpetual migraine, a bad back, toothache. "The pains in me legs," she would say, "is killin' me." Her wind was loud, even in public places. "The doctor says to let it come up. You can always say excuse me." Her habits were loathsome. She picked her teeth with old tram-tickets, cleaned out her ears with hairclips in whose U-bend earwax was trapped to darken and harden, scratched her private parts through her clothes with a matchbox-rasping noise audible two rooms away, made gross sandwiches of all her meals or cut her meat with scissors, spat chewed bacon-rind or pork-crackling back on her plate, excavated beef-fibres from her cavernous molars and held them up for all the world to see, hooked out larger chunks with a soiled sausage-finger, belched like a ship in the fog, was sick on stout on Saturday nights, tromboned vigorously in the lavatory, ranted without aitches or grammar, scoffed at all books except *Old Moore's Almanac*, whose apocalyptic pictures she could follow. Literally illiterate all her life, she would sign cheques by copying her name from a prototype on a greasy piece of paper, drawing it carefully as a Chinese draws an ideogram. She provided fried meals mostly, ensuring first that the fat was tepid. But she brewed good tea, potent with tannin, and taught young Enderby the technique, that he might bring her a cup in the morning: three for each person and two for the pot, condensed milk rather than fresh, be lavish with the sugar. Enderby, sixth-form boy, would stand over her while she drank it in bed—tousled, wrinkled, puffed, ill-smelling, a wreck—though she did not really drink it: the tea seemed to soak into her, as into parched earth. One day he would put rat-poison in her cup. But he never did, even though there was rat-poison in the kitchen. Hate? You've just no idea.

When Enderby was seventeen, his father went off to Nottingham to be shown over a tobacco factory, was away for the night. July heat (she showed up badly in that) broke in monsoon weather, with terrifying lightning. But it was only the thunder that scared her. Enderby awoke at five in the morning to find her in his bed, in dirty winceyette, clutching him in fear. He got up, was sick in the lavatory, then locked himself in, reading till dawn the scraps of newspaper on the floor.

Her death was reported to him when he was in the Army, L. of C. troops in Catania. She had died after drinking a morning cup of tea, brought by his father. Heart failure. The night of hearing the news, Enderby went with a woman of Catania (one tin of corned beef and a packet of biscuits) and, to her almost concealed laughter, could do nothing. Also, on arriving back at his billet, he was sick.

Well, there it was. His stepmother had killed women for him, emerging in a ladylike belch or a matchstick picking of teeth from behind the most cool and delectable façade. He had got on quite nicely on his own, locked in the bathroom, cooking his own meals (ensuring first that the fat was tepid), living on his dividends and the pound or two a year his poems earned. But, as middle-age advanced, his stepmother seemed to be entering slyly into him more and more. His back ached, his feet hurt, he had a tidy paunch, all his teeth out, he belched. He had tried to be careful about laundry and cleaning the saucepans, but poetry got in the way, raising him above worry about squalor. Yet dyspepsia would cut disconcertingly in more and more, blasting like a tuba through the solo string traceries of his delicate creations.

The act of creation. Sex. That was the trouble with art. Urgent sexual desire aroused with the excitement of a new image or rhythm. But adolescence had prolonged its techniques of easy detumescence, normal activities of the bathroom. Walking towards the Freemason's Arms he felt wind rising from his stomach. Damn. Brerrrrp. Blast. He was, however, on the whole, taking all things into consideration, by and large, not to put too fine a point on it, reasonably well self-sufficient. Brrrrrp. Blast and damn.

Five

Arry, head cook at the Conway, was standing by the bar of the Freemason's with a pint tankard of brown ale and bitter mixed. He said to Enderby, " 'Ere yar." He handed over a long bloody parcel, blood congealed on a newspaper headline about some woman's blood. "A said ad get it an' a got it." Enderby said, "Thanks, and a happy New Year. What will you have?" He eased away some of the newspaper at one end, "Missing Persons" covered with blood, and the head of a mature hare stared at him with glass eyes. "Yer can joog it today," said Arry. He was in a brown sports-coat that reeked of old fat, a tout's cap on his head. His upper jaw had only two canines. These were gateposts between which his tongue, car-like, occasionally eased itself out and in. He came from Oldham. "Red coorant jelly," said Arry. "What a generally do is serve red coorant jelly on a art-shaped croutong. Coot out a art-shaped bitter bread with a art-cooter. Fry it in 'ot fat, quick. Boot, livin' on yer own, a don't suppose yer'll wanter go to that trooble." He drank down his brown ale and bitter and, on Enderby, had another pint. "Good job yer coom in when yer did," he said. " 'Ave to go now. Special loonch for South Coast Association of Car Salesmen." He swigged the pint in one lift of the tankard, had another, yet another, all in two minutes flat. Like most cooks he could eat little. He had ferocious gastric pains which endeared him to Enderby. "Seein' yer," he said, leaving. Enderby nursed his hare.

This bar was the haunt of all local lesbians over fifty. Most of them fulfilled the paradigms of marriage, a few were divorced, widowed or estranged. On a stool in the corner was a woman called Gladys, a peroxided Jewess of sixty with tortoise-shell spectacle-rims and leopard-skin jeans. She was kissing, more often and more passionately than seemed necessary, another woman in New-Year greeting. This woman wore a bristling old fur coat and was delicately cross-eyed. A fierce-looking thin woman in a dress as hairy and simple as a monk's habit, a nutria coat swinging open over it, crashed into the bar and greeted her too, long and gluily. "Prudence, my duck," she said. Prudence seemed to be a popular girl. The peculiar charm of strabismus. And then the fragments of a new poem came swimming with a familiar confidence into Enderby's head. He saw the shape, he heard the words, he felt the rhythm. Three stanzas, each beginning with birds. *Prudence, prudence, the pigeons call.* And, of course, that's what they did call, that's what they'd always called. *Act, act, the ducks give voice.* And that was true, too. What were the other birds? They weren't sea-gulls. The dyed-blonde Jewess, Gladys, suddenly, raucously, laughed. It was a bird like that. *Caution, caution.* Rooks, that was it. But why were they calling, giving voice, proclaiming?

He had a ballpoint pen, but no paper. Only the wrapping of the hare. There was a long empty stop-press column, two forlorn football results at the head. He wrote the lines he had heard. Also other fragments that he could hear dimly. The meaning? Meaning was no concern of the poet. *The widow in the shadow. The widow in the meadow.* A voice, very clear and thin, spoke as though pressed to his ear: *Drain the sacrament of choice.* Gladys began to sing, pop garbage composed by some teenager, much heard on radio disc-programmes. She sang loudly. Excited, Enderby cried, "Oh, for Christ's sake shut up!" Gladys was indignant. "Who the bloody hell do you think you're telling to shut up?" she called across, with menace. "I'm trying to write a poem," said Enderby. "This," said someone, "is supposed to be a respectable pub." Enderby downed his whisky and left.

Walking home quickly he tried to call back the rhythm, but it had gone. The fragments ceased to be live limbs of some mystical body that promised to reveal itself wholly. Dead as the hare, meaningless onomatopoeia; a silly jingle: *widow, shadow, meadow.* The big rhythms of the nearing tide, the winter sea-wind, the melancholy gulls. A gust shattered and dispersed the merging form of the poem. Oh, well. Of the million poems that beckoned, like coquettish girls, from the bushes, how very few could be caught.

Enderby stripped the hare of its bloody paper as he approached 81 Fitzherbert Avenue. There was a public litter basket attached to a lamp-post almost in front of the front-steps. He threw the crumpled mess of news, blood, inchote poetry in, and got out his key. A tidy town, this. Must not let our standards relax even though there are no holiday visitors. He entered the kitchen and began to skin the hare. It would give him, he thought, stewed with carrots, potatoes and onions, seasoned with pepper and celery salt, the remains of the Christmas red wine poured in before serving, enough meals for nearly a week. He slapped the viscera on to a saucer, cut up the carcass, and then turned on the kitchen tap. Hangman's hands, he thought, looking at them. Soaked in blood up to the elbows. He tried out a murderer's leer, holding the sacrificial knife, imagining a mirror above the kitchen sink.

The water flowing from the faucet cast a faint shadow, a still shadow, on the splashboard. The line came, a refrain: *The running tap casts a static shadow.* That was it, he recognised, his excitement mounting again. The widow, the meadow. A whole stanza blurted itself out:

> "Act! Act!" The ducks give voice.
> "Enjoy the widow in the meadow.
> Drain the sacrament of choice.
> The running tap casts a static shadow."

To hell with the meaning. Where the hell were those other birds? What were they? The cuckoo? The seagull? What was the name of that cross-eyed lesbian bitch in the Freemason's? Knife in hand, steeped in blood to the elbows, he dashed out of his flat, out of the house, to the rubbish-basket clamped to the lamp-post. Others had been there while he had been gutting and skinning and quartering. A Black Magic box, a Senior Service packet, banana-peel. He threw it all out madly into the gutter. He found the defiled paper which had wrapped the beast. Frantically he searched page after crumpled page. THIS MAN MAY KILL, POLICE WARN. NOW THIS BOY IS LOVED. *Most people stop Acid Stomach with Rennies.* Compulsive reading. He read: "The pain-causing acid is neutralised and you get that wonderful sensation that tells you the pain is beginning to go. The antacid ingredients reach your stomach gradually and gently—drip by drip. . . ."

"What's this? What's going on?" asked an official voice.

"Eh?" It was the law, inevitably. "I'm looking for these blasted birds," said Enderby, rummaging again. "Ah, thank God. Here they are. Prudence, pigeons. Rooks, caution. It's as good as written. Here." He thrust the extended sheets into the policeman's arms.

"Not so fast," said the policeman. He was a young man, apple-ruddy from the rural hinterland, very tall. "What's this knife for, where did all that blood come from?"

"I've been murdering my stepmother," said Enderby, absorbed in composition. *Prudence, prudence, the pigeons call.* He ran into the house. The woman from upstairs was just coming down. She saw a knife and blood and screamed. Enderby entered his flat, ran into the bathroom, kicked on the heater, sat on the low seat. Automatically he stood up again to lower his trousers. Then, all bloody, he began to write. Somebody knocked—imperious, imperative—at his front door. He locked the bathroom door and got on with his writing. The knocks soon ceased. After half an hour he had the whole poem on paper.

26

"Prudence! Prudence!" the pigeons call.
"Scorpions lurk in the gilded meadow.
An eye is embossed on the island wall.
The running tap casts a static shadow."

"Caution! Caution!" the rooks proclaim.
"The dear departed, the weeping widow
Will meet in you in the core of flame.
The running tap casts a static shadow."

The injunction of the last stanza seemed clear enough, privy enough. Was it really possible, he wondered, for him to follow it, making this year different from all others?

"Act! Act!" The ducks give voice.
"Enjoy the widow in the meadow.
Drain the sacrament of choice. . . ."

In the kitchen, he could now hear, the water was still flooding away. He had forgotten to turn it off. Casting a static shadow all the time. He got up from his seat, automatically pulling the chain. Who was this blasted widow that the poem referred to?

2

One

WHILE Enderby was breakfasting off reheated hare stew with pickled walnuts and stepmother's tea, the postman came with a fateful letter. The envelope was thick, rich, creamy; richly black the typed address, as though a new ribbon had been put in just for that holy name. The notepaper was embossed with the arms of a famous firm of chain booksellers. The letter congratulated Enderby on his last year's volume—*Revolutionary Sonnets*—and was overjoyed to announce that he had been awarded the firm's annual Poetry Prize of a gold medal and fifty guineas. Enderby was cordially invited to a special luncheon to be held in the banqueting-room of an intimidating London hotel, there to receive his prizes amid the plaudits of the literary world. Enderby let his hare stew go cold. The third Tuesday in January. Please reply. He was dazed. And, again, congratulations. London. The very name evoked the same responses as *lung cancer, overdrawn, stepmother.*

He wouldn't go, he couldn't go, he hadn't a suit. At the moment he was wearing glasses, a day's beard, pyjamas, polo-neck sweater, sports-jacket and very old corduroys.

In his wardrobe were a pair of flannel trousers and a watered-silk waistcoat. These, he had thought when settling down after demobilisation, were enough for a poet, the watered-silk waistcoat being, perhaps, even, an unseemly luxury of stockbroker-like extravagance. He had had it, by mistake, knocked down to him for five shillings at an auction.

London. He was flooded with horrid images, some derived from direct experience, others from books. At the end of the war, searching for William Hazlitt's tomb in its Soho graveyard, he had been abused by a constable and had up in Bow Street on a charge of loitering with intent. He had once slipped on the greasy pavement outside Foyle's and the man who had helped him up—stocky, elderly, with stiff grey hair—had begged five bob to 'elp aht a bit cos they was on strike that week, guv. That was just after he had bought the watered-silk waistcoat: ten bob down the drain. In the urinal of a very foggy pub he had, unbelievably, been invited to a fellation party by a handsome stranger in smart city wear. This man had become nasty at Enderby's polite refusal and threatened to scream that Enderby was assaulting him. Very unpleasant. Along with other memories that made him wince (including one excruciating one of a ten-shilling note in the Café Royal) came gobbets from *Oliver Twist*, *The Waste Land* and *Nineteen Eighty-Four*. London was unnecessarily big, gratuitously hostile, a place for losing money and contracting diseases. Enderby shuddered, thinking of Defoe's *Journal of the Plague Year*. And there he was—as he emptied his cold plateful back into the saucepan—with his stepmother again. At the age of fifteen he had bought off a two-penny stall in the market a duodecimo book of recipes, gossip and homilies, printed in 1605. His stepmother, able to read figures, had screamed at the sight of it when he had proudly brought it home. 1605 was "the olden days," meaning Henry VIII, the executioner's axe, and the Great Plague. She thrust the book into the kitchen fire with the tongs, yelling that it must be seething with lethal germs. A limited, though live, sense of history.

And history was the reason why she would never go to London. She saw it as dominated by the Bloody Tower, Fleet Street full of demon barbers, as well as dangerous escalators everywhere. As Enderby now turned on the hot-water tap he saw that the Ascot heater did not, as it should, flare up like a bed of pain. The meter needed a shilling and he was too lazy to go and look for one. He washed his soup-plate and mug in cold water, reflecting that his stepmother had been a great one for that (knives and forks wrapped in grease as if they were guns). She had been very lazy, very stupid, very superstitious. He decided, wiping the dishes, that he would, after all, go to London. After all, it wasn't very far—only an hour by electric train—and there would be no need to spend the night in a hotel. It was an honour really, he supposed. He would have to borrow a suit from somebody. Arry, he was sure, had one. They were much of a size.

Enderby, sighing, went to the bathroom to start work. He gazed doubtfully at the bathtub, which was full of notes, drafts, fair copies not yet filed for their eventual volume, books, ink-bottles, cigarette-packets, the remains of odd snacks taken while writing. There were also a few mice that lived beneath the detritus, encouraged in their busy scavenging by Enderby. Occasionally one would surface and perch on the bath's edge to watch the poet watching the ceiling, pen in hand. With him they were neither cowering nor timorous (he had forgotten the meaning of "sleekit.") Enderby recognised that the coming occasion called for a bath. Lustration before the sacramental meal. He had once read in some women's magazine a grim apothegm he had never forgotten: "Bath twice a day to be really clean, once a day to be passably clean, once a week to avoid being a public menace." On the other hand, Frederick the Great had never bathed in his life; his corpse had been a rich mahogany colour. Enderby's view of bathing was neither obsessive nor insouciant. ("Sans Souci," Frederick's palace, was it not?) He was an empiricist in such matters. Though he recognised that a bath would, in a week or two, seem necessary, he recoiled from the prospect of preparing the bathtub and evicting the mice. He would compromise. He would wash very neatly all over in the basin. More, he would shave with exceptional care and trim his hair with nail-scissors.

Gloomily, Enderby reflected that most modern poets were not merely sufficiently clean but positively natty. T. S. Eliot, with his Lloyd's Bank nonsense, had started all that, a real treason of clerks. Before him, Enderby liked to believe, cleanliness and neatness had been only for writers of journalistic ballades and triolets. Still, he would show them when he went for his gold medal; he would beat them at their own game. Enderby sighed again as, with bare legs, he took his poetic seat. His first job was to compose a letter of gratitude and acceptance. Prose was not his *métier*.

After several pompous drafts which he crumpled into the waste-basket on which he sat, Enderby dashed off a letter in *In Memoriam* quatrains, disguised as prose. "The gratitude for this award, though sent in all humility, should not, however, come from me, but from my Muse, or else the Lord ..." He paused as a bizarre analogue swam up from memory. In a London restaurant during the days of fierce post-war food shortage he had ordered rabbit pie. The pie, when it had arrived, had contained nothing but breast of chicken. A mystery never to be solved. He shrugged it away and went on disguising the chicken-breast of verse as rabbit-prose. A mouse, fore-paws retracted like those of a kangaroo, came up to watch.

Two

Enderby found Arry in white in his underground kitchen, brown ale frothing beside him, slicing pork into blade-thin shives. An imbecile-looking scullion in khaki threw fistfuls of cabbage on to plates. When he missed he picked up the scattered helping carefully from the floor and tried again. Massive sides of beef were jocularly being unloaded from Smithfield—the fat a golden fleece, the flesh the hue of diluted Empire burgundy. Enderby said:

"I've got to go up to London to be given a gold medal and fifty guineas. But I haven't got a suit."

"Yer'll be able to buy a good un," said Arry, "with that amount of mooney." He didn't look too happy; he frowned down at his precise task like a surgeon saving the life of a bitter foe. "There," he said, forking up a translucent slice to the light, "that's about as thin as yer can bloody get."

"But," said Enderby, "I don't see the point of buying a suit just for this occasion. I probably shan't want to wear a suit again. Or not for a long time. That's why I'd like to borrow one of yours."

Arry said nothing. He quizzed the forked slice and nodded at it, as though he had met its challenge and won. Then he returned to his carving. He said. "Yer quite right when yer suppose av got more than wan. Am always doin' things for people, aren't a? Boot what dooz any boogger do for me?" He looked up at Enderby an instant, his tongue flicking out between its gateposts as if to lick up a tear.

"Well," said Enderby, embarrassed, "you know you can rely on me. For anything I *can* do, that is. But I've only one talent, and that's not much good to you. Nor, it seems," the mood of self-pity catching, "to anyone else. Except a hundred or so people here and in America. And one mad female admirer in Cape Town. She writes once a year, you know, offering marriage."

"Female admirers," said carving Arry, pluralising easily. "Female admirers, eh? That's wan thing a 'aven't got. It's *me* oo admires '*er*, that's the bloody trooble. It's got real bad, that 'as." He became violently dialectal. "Av getten eed-warch wi' it," he said. Then, as an underling sniffed toward him with a cold, "Vol-au-vent de dindon's in that bloody coopboard," he said.

"Who?" said Enderby. "When?"

"Er oopstairs," said Arry. "Thelma as serves int cocktail bar. A knew it definite ender the moonth. Bloody loovely oo is boot bloody cruel," he said, carving steadily. "Oo's bloody smashin'," he said.

"I don't know," said Enderby.

"Don't know what?"

"Who's bloody smashing."

"Oo is," said Arry, gesturing to the ceiling with his knife. "Oo oop thur. That Thelma."

Enderby then remembered that two Anglo-Saxon feminine pronouns co-existed in Lancashire. He said, "Well, why don't you go in and win? Just put a few teeth in your mouth first, though. The popular prejudice goes in favour of teeth."

"What's pegs to do with it?" said Arry. "A don't eat. Pegs is for eatin'. Am in loove, that's bloody trooble, and what's pegs to do with that?"

"Women like to see them," said Enderby. "It's more of an aesthetic than a functional thing. Love, eh? Well, well. Love. It's a long time since I've heard of anybody being in love."

"Every boogger's in loov nowadays," said Arry, ending his carving. He drank some brown ale. "There's songs about it ont wireless. A used to laff at 'em. And now it's me oo's copped it. Loove. Bloody nuisanse it is an' all, what with bein' busy at this timer year. Firms given' loonches an' dinners till near the end of February. Couldn't 'ave come at a worse time."

"About this suit," said Enderby. He faced a vast carboy of pickled onions and his bowels melted within him. He wanted to be gone.

"Yer can do summat for me," said Arry, "if am to do summat for you." He tasted this last pronoun and then decided that his revelation, his coming request, called for *tutoyer* intimacy. "Summat for thee," he amended. "Al lend thee that suit if tha'll write to 'er for me, that bein' thy line, writin' poetry an' all that mook. A keep sendin' 'er oop special things as av cooked special, boot that's not romantic, like. A nice dish of tripe doon in milk, which were always my favourite when a were eatin'. Sent it down, oontooched, oo did. A reet boogger. What would go down best would be a nice loove-letter or a bitter poetry. That's where *you'd* coom in," said Arry, and his snake-tongue darted. "'Av a grey un, a blue un, a brown un, a fawn un an a 'errin-bone tweed.

Tha's welcome to any wan on 'em. Thee write summat an' sign it Arry and send it to me an' a'll send it oop to 'er."

"How shall I spell Arry?" asked Enderby.

"With a haitch," said Arry. "Two a week should do the bloody trick. Shouldn't take yer not more than a coopler minutes to write the sort of thing that goes down all reet with women. You and yer bloody female hadmirers," he said.

Before going back to his flat, Enderby used—long, lavishly and painfully—the gentlemen's lavatory on the ground-floor of the hotel. Then, shaken, he went to the cocktail bar for a whisky and to have a look at Thelma. It would not do if he dug up old poems, or wrote new ones, celebrating the glory of fair hair or pegs like margarite if she should chance to be black, grey, edentulous. The bar seemed full, today, of car salesmen, and these chaffed and mock-courted, with ha-ha-ha and obsolete pilot's slang, a quite personable barmaid in her late thirties. She had all her front teeth, black hair, naughty eyes, ear-rings that jangled tinnily—clusters of minute coins—a snub nose and a comfortable round chin. She was superbly bosomed and efficiently uplifted. She seemed to be a repository of old bar-wisdom, epigrams, radio-show catch-phrases. A car salesman bought her a Guinness and she toasted him with "May you live for ever and me live to bury you." Then, before drinking, she said, "Past the teeth and round the gums, look out, stomach, here it comes." She had a fair swallow. She had decorated her little bar with poker-work maxims: "Laugh and the world laughs with you; snore and you sleep alone." "Water is a good drink when taken with the right spirit." "When you're up to your neck in hot water be like the kettle and sing." There was also a Browningesque couplet (content if not technique) above the gin bottles:

For when the last great Scorer comes to write
against your name,
He writes not that you won or lost, but how you
played the game.

Enderby doubted whether he could achieve the same gnomic tautness in anything he wrote for her. Still, that wouldn't be called for, love being essentially imprecise and diffuse. He drank his whisky and left.

Three

Enderby's attitude to love-poetry was dispassionate, impersonal, professional. The worst love-poems, he had always contended, were the most sincere: the lover's palpitating emotions—all too personal, with an all too particular object—all too often got in the way of the ideal, the universal. A love-poem should address itself to an idea of a loved one. Platonism could take in ideal breasts, an ideal underarm odour, an ideal unsatisfactory coitus, as well as the smooth-browed intellectual wraith of the old sonneteers. Back in his bathroom, Enderby rummaged for fragments and drafts that would serve to start off the *Arry to Thelma* cycle. He found, mouse-nibbled:

> I sought scent, and found it in your hair;
>   Looked for light, and it lodged in your eyes.
> So for speech: it held your breath dear;
>   And I met movement in your ways.

That felt like the first quatrain of a Shakespearian sonnet. It wouldn't do of course; the sprung rhythm and muffled rhymes would strike Thelma's world as technical incompetence. He found:

> You were there, and nothing was said,
> For words toppled over the edge or hovered in air.
> But I was suddenly aware, in the split instant,
> Of the constant, in a sort of passionless frenzy:
> The mad wings of motion a textbook law,
> Trees, tables, the war, in a fixed relation,
> Moulded by you, their primum mobile,
> But that you were there really was all I knew.

He couldn't remember writing that. The reference to the war dated it within six years. The place? Probably some town with avenues, outdoor tables for drinking. Addressed to? Don't be so bloody stupid; addressed to nobody, of course; pure ideal emotion. He continued rooting, his arms deep in the bathtub. The mice scuffled up and out to their primary home, a hole. He found half of a priceless piece of juvenilia:

> You are all
> Brittle crystal,
> Your hands
> Silver silk over steel.
>
> Your hair harvested
> Sheaves shed by summer,
> Your repose the flash
> Of the flesh of a river-swimmer . . .

Then a jagged tear. He must have been, sometime, taken short. There was nothing in the bath that would do for Thelma, even an ideal Thelma. He would have to compose something new. Stripping his lower half for poetic action, he took his seat and got down to work. Here was a real problem, that of bridging the gap, of making something that should not seem eccentric to the recipient and at the same time not completely embarrass the author. After an hour he produced the following:

> Your presence shines above the fumes of fat,
> Glows from the oven-door.
> Lithe with the litheness of the kitchen cat,
> Your image treads the floor
> Ennobling the potato-peel, the lumps
> Of fallen bread, the vulgar cabbage-stumps.
>
> "Love!" cry the eggs a-whisk, and "Love!" the beef
> Calls from the roasting-tin.
> The beetroot blushes love. Each lettuce-leaf
> That hides the heart within

Is a green spring of love. Pudding and pie
Are richly crammed with love, and so am I.

But, after those first two painful stanzas, he found it
hard to stop. He was led on ruthlessly, horrified by a
growing facility, a veritable logorrhoea. At the end of
the ode he had emptied Arry's kitchen and filled ten
closely written sheets. One point, he thought he had
very clearly established, and that was that Arry was in
love.

Four

It was the day of the London luncheon. Tremulous
Enderby fell out of bed early to see snow staring
through the morning dark. Shivering, he snapped every
electric heater in the flat on, then made tea. Snow
gawped blankly at him through all the windows, so he
drew the curtains, turning raw morning into cosy
muffiny toast-toe evening. Then he shaved. He had
washed, fairly thoroughly, the night before the night
before last. He had almost forgotten what it was like to
shave with a new blade, having—for nearly a year now—
used the old ones stacked up by the previous tenant on
top of the bathroom cupboard. This morning he slashed
cheeks, underlip and Adam's apple: shaving-soap froth
became childhood ice-cream sprinkled with raspberry
vinegar. Enderby found an old poem beginning *And if
he did then what he'd said he'd do*, and with bits of this
he stanched the flow. He started to dress, putting on a
new pair of socks bought at a January sale and tucking
the ends of his pyjama-trousers well inside them. He had
a white shirt specially laundered, he had found a striped
tie—lime and mustard—in a suitcase, with the name
PADMORE in marking-ink on white rag attached to its
lining (who was, or had been, or might be in the unreal-
ised future, Padmore?) and had cleaned with care his
one pair of brown shoes. He had also, for show and blow
respectively, saved two clean handkerchiefs. He would
beat these city-slickers at their own game. The suit from

Arry was sober grey, the most Eliotian one in his whole wardrobe.

He was pleasantly surprised by the decent gravity of the figure that bowed from the wardrobe mirror. Urban, respectable, scholarly—a poet-banker, a poet-publisher, teeth a flashing two double octaves in the electric fire-light, spectacles drinking of the bedlamp's glow. Satisfied, he went to get his breakfast—a special breakfast today, for God knew what ghastly sauced muck he might be coldly given in the great hotel. He had bought a Cornish pasty but had, coming out of the shop, slipped on an icepatch. This had hurt him and flattened the pasty, but its edibility was hardly impaired. It was to be eaten with Branston pickle and, as an extra-special treat, washed down with Blue Mountain coffee. He felt an unwonted exultation as he prepared this viaticum, as if—after years of struggle—he had at last arrived. What should he buy with the prize-money? He couldn't think what. Books? He had done reading. Clothes? Ha ha. There was nothing he really needed except more talent. Nothing in the world.

The coffee was disappointingly cool and weak. Perhaps he had not made it properly. Could he take lessons in that? Were there teachers of such things? Arry. Of course, he would ask Arry. At nine-fifteen (train at nine-fifty-five, ten minutes walk to station) he sat with a cigarette, hypnotised by the gash-gold-vermilion of the electric fire, waiting. He suddenly caught another memory like a flea. Far childhood. Christmas Day, 1924. Snow came down in the afternoon, transfiguring the slum street where the shop was. He had been given a magic lantern and, after dinner, he was to project slides of wild animals on to the sitting-room wall. Powered by a candle, the lantern had been fitted with a candle—a new one, its flame much too high for the lens. His Uncle Jimmy the plumber had said, "We'll have to wait till it burns down. Give us a tune, Fred." And Fred, Enderby's father, had sat at the piano and played. The rest of that dim gathering—only the stepmother bright in memory, belching away—had waited for the candle to burn down to lens-level, the coloured animals suddenly to appear on the wall.

Why, wondered Enderby now, why had nobody thought to cut the candle? Why had they all, every single one of them, agreed to wait on the candle's convenience? It was another mystery, but he wondered if it was really a mystery of a different order from this other waiting—waiting on Shakespeare's time's candle to burn down to time to dress warmly, time to leave for the station. Enderby suddenly passionately wished he could cut the whole long candle to its end—have written his poetry and have done. Then he grinned as his stomach, having slyly engineered this melancholy, plaintively subscribed to it.

Pfffrrrp. And then Brrrrrrr. But that, he realised, after surprise at his stomach's achievement of such metallic ectophony, that, he heard with annoyance, was the doorbell. So early, whoever it was, and coming so inconveniently. Enderby went to his flat-door and saw, waddling down the hallway of the house itself, his landlady, Mrs Meldrum. Well. He paid her by post. The less he saw of her the better. "If I can trouble you for a moment, Mr E," she said. She was a woman of sixty, with pinched East Midland vowels. Her face was modelled on that of a tired but cheerful crescent moon in a bedtime-malted-milk-drink advertisement that even Enderby had seen often: Punch-nose meeting cusp-chin, but no jolly Punch plumpness. She had a full set of Tenniel-teeth of the colour of small chips of dirty ice, and these she showed to Enderby now as to a mirror. Enderby said:

"I've got to go up to town." He thrilled gently, saying that, a busy man of affairs.

"I shan't keep you not more than one minute," said Mrs Meldrum, "Mr E." She waddled in past Enderby as if she owned the place, which she did. "It's really to empty the shillings out of the electric meter," she said, "which is, in one way of speaking, why I called. In another way of speaking, it's about the complaints." She went ahead of Enderby into the living-room. At the table she examined minutely the remains of Enderby's breakfast, shook her head comically at them and then, picking up the pickle-jar, read from the label like a priest muttering the Mass: "Sugar cauliflower onions malt vinegar tomatoes carrots spirit vinegar gherkins dates salt marrow . . ."

"What complaints?" asked Enderby, as he was expected to.

"New Year's Eve," said Mrs. Meldrum, "being a special occasion as calls for jollifications, nevertheless Mrs Bates down in the basement has complained about loud singing when she couldn't go off to sleep with the backache. Your name came into it a lot, she says, especially in the very rude singing. On New Year's Day you was seen running up and down the street with a carving-knife and all covered with blood. Well, Mr E, fun's fun as the saying goes, though I must confess I'm surprised at a man of your age. But the police had a quiet word with Mr Meldrum, unbeknownst to me, and I could only get it out of him last night, him being shy and retiring and not wanting to cause trouble. Anyway, we've had a talk about it and it can't go on, Mr E."

"I can explain," said Enderby, looking at his watch. "It's all really quite simple."

"And, while we're on the subject," said Mrs Meldrum, "that nice young couple upstairs. They say they can hear you in the night sometimes."

"I can hear *them*," said Enderby, "and they're *not* a nice young couple."

"Well," said Mrs Meldrum, "that's all according as which way one looks at it, isn't it? To the pure all things are pure, as you might say."

"What, Mrs Meldrum, is this leading to?" Enderby looked again at his watch. In the last thirty seconds five minutes had gone by. Mrs Meldrum said:

"There's plenty as would like this nice little flat, Mr E. This is a respectable neighbourhood, this is. There's retired schoolmasters and captains of industry retired along here. And I wouldn't say as how you kept this flat all that clean and tidy."

"That's my business, Mrs Meldrum."

"Well, it may be your business, Mr E, but then again it might not. And everybody's putting the rents up this year, as you may as well know. What with the rates going up as well and all of us having to watch us own interests."

"Oh, I see," said Enderby. "That's it, is it? How much?"

"You've had this very reasonable," said Mrs Meldrum, "as nobody can deny. You've had this at four guineas a week all through the season. There's one gentleman as works in London as is very anxious to find respectable accommodation. Six guineas to him would be a very reasonable rent."

"Well, it's not a very reasonable rent to me, Mrs Meldrum," said Enderby angrily. His watch-hand leapt gaily forward. "I have to go now," he said. "I've a train to catch. Really," he said, shocked, "do you realise that that would be eight guineas more a month? Where would I get the money?"

"A gentleman of independent means," said Mrs Meldrum smugly. "If you don't want to stay, Mr E, you could always give a week's notice."

Enderby saw with horror the prospect of sorting out the bathful of manuscripts. "I'll have to go now," he said. "I'll let you know. But I think it's an imposition."

Mrs Meldrum made no move. "You go off then and catch your train," she said, "and think about it in your first-class carriage. And I'll empty the shillings out of the meter, as has to be done now and again. And if I was you I should stack those plates in the sink before you leave."

"Don't touch my papers," warned Enderby. "There are private and confidential papers in that bathroom. Touch them at your peril."

"Peril, indeed," scoffed Mrs Meldrum. "And I don't like the sound of that at all, continental papers in *my* bathroom." Meanwhile Enderby wrapped his muffler on and fought his way—as if towards the light—into his overcoat. "I never heard of such a thing, and that's a fact," said Mrs Meldrum, "and I've been in the business a fair amount of time. I've heard of coals in the bath with some of them slummy people, though I thank the Almighty God I've never harboured any of them in *my* bosom. You're going out like that, Mr E, with bits of paper stuck all over your face. I can read a word there, just by your nose: *epileptical,* or something. You're not doing yourself or me or any of the other tenants any good at all, Mr E, going out in that state. Peril, indeed."

Enderby dithered out, doubtful. He had not reckoned on having to search for new lodgings, not in the middle of *The Pet Beast.* And this town was becoming more and more a dormitory for bald young men from London. In one pub he had met the head of a newsreel company, a lavish gin-man with a light, fast voice. And there had been a processed-cheese executive heard, loud and unabashed, somewhere else. London was crawling southward to the Channel.

Enderby crawled northward to the station, picking off odd words from his razor-cuts. The snow had been trodden already, by people rushing earlier with insincere eagerness to get to work in London. Enderby teetered in tiny gavotte-steps, afraid of slipping, his rump still aching from last night's fall. Work-trains, stenographer-trains, executive-trains. Big deals over the telephone, fifty guineas nothing to them. Golfball-money. But, thought Enderby, that would provide for half a year's rent increase.

Looking up at the zinc sky he saw a gull or two flapping inland. He had neglected to feed the gulls for two days now; he was becoming careless. Perhaps, he thought vaguely, he could make it up to them by buying some special treat at the Army and Navy Stores. He passed a block of bright posters. One of them extolled domestic gas: a smiling toy paraclete called Mr Therm presided over a sort of warm Holy Family. Pentecostal therm; pentecostal sperm. Two men in dyed army overcoats marched, as in retreat, from the station, with demoralised thug faces. One said to the other, "Can't make up its bleeding mind. Rain one day, snow the next. Be pissing down again tomorrow." Enderby had to stop, short of breath, his heart martelling away as though he had just downed a half-bottle of brandy, his left hand clutching a snowcapped privet-hedge for support. *The pentecostal sperm came pissing down.* No, no, no. *Hissing down.* The line was dealt to him, like a card from a weighing-machine. He had a sudden image of the whole poem like a squat evil engine, weighing, waiting. The Holy Family, the Virgin Mary, the pentecostal sperm. He heard a train whistle and had to rush.

Panting, he entered the little booking-hall and dug out his wallet from his right breast. There was still a Christmas tree by the bookstall. That was wrong: Twelfth Night was over, St Distaff's Day had set the working year spinning again. Enderby approached the stern shirt-sleeves behind the *guichet*. "A day return to London, please," he begged. He picked up his change with his ticket and sent a shilling over the floor. "Don't lose that, mister," said a lively old woman in black. "Need that for the gas." She cackled as Enderby chased the shining monocycle to the barrier. The ticket-collector flapped a heavy boot on to it, trapped. "Thank you," said Enderby. As he arose from picking it up his eyes misted, and he saw a very clear and blue picture of the Virgin Mary at a spinning-wheel, a silver queen set in baby blue. This had nothing to do with *The Pet Beast* and its Mary-Pasiphae. This had something to do with his stepmother.

> In this spinning womb, reduced to a common noun,
> The pentecostal sperm came hissing down . . .

That was not it, the rhythm was wrong, it was not couplets. The couplets came from the doves in the Queen's speech in *Hamlet*. Doves, loves, leaves. Enderby clomped down the steps and up the steps to the up-train platform. The train was just arriving. There was an -*eave* rhyme somewhere. Enderby boarded the train. There were few passengers at this hour—women going up to fight in the January sales, a scholarly-looking police-inspector with a briefcase, two men looking much, Enderby thought distractedly, like himself—smart, normal, citified. Doves came from dove, dove meant paraclete. A dove in the leaves of life. Eve, leave, thieve, achieve, conceive.

"I beg your pardon?" said a woman sitting diagonally

opposite to Enderby. They were the only two in the compartment. She was thin, blonde, washed-out, fortyish, smart with a mink cape-stole and a hat like a nest. "Peeve," said Enderby the city-man. "Believe. Weave." The train began to pant north-east with urgent love of London, a sperm to be swallowed by that giant womb. "Swallowed," announced Enderby, with loud excitement, "by the giant stomach of Eve. I knew Eve came somewhere into it." The woman picked up her foliosized handbag and silver-grey couplet of gloves and left the compartment. "Eve leaves," said Enderby. Where was paper? None. He had not expected this to be a working day. Inkpencil he had. He rose and followed the woman out to the corridor. She scampered, with a kitten-scream, to the next compartment, which held a trio of talking and nodding wives drably dressed for salesbattle. Enderby, a homing dove, went straight to the lavatory.

Five

In this spinning room, reduced to a common noun,
　　Swallowed by the giant stomach of Eve,
The pentecostal sperm came hissing down.

Enderby sat, fully dressed, on the sea of the WC, swaying as on a father's rocking knee, a cock-horse to Charing Cross. No, London Bridge. No, Victoria. An electric sperm plunging towards Our Lady of Victories, Enderby astride. He had removed the toilet-roll from its holder and scratched away on panel after panel of paper with his inkpencil. The poem was definitely a song for the Blessed Virgin.

Whence this Marianism? Enderby knew. He remembered his bedroom with its devotional pictures by Italian commercial artists: Pius XI with triple tiara and benedictory gesture; Jesus Christ with radioactive heart exposed and—for good measure—indicated by a divine delicate index-finger; saints (Anthony, John the Baptist,

Bernadette); the Virgin Mary with tender smile and winsome wimple;

> I was nowhere, for I was anyone—
> The grace and music easy to receive:
> The patient engine of a stranger son.

Outside the bedroom door had been a holy-water stoup, dried up with the drought of Enderby's boyish disbelief. All over the house, as far as the frontier of the shop's neutral or Protestant territory, there had been other stoups, also crucifixes, plaster statuettes, withered Holy-Land palm-leaves, rosaries blessed in Rome, an Angnus Dei or two, decorative pious ejaculations (done in Dublin in pseudo-Celtic script) as brief as snarls. That was his stepmother's Catholicism, imported from Liverpool—relics and emblems and hagiographs used as lightning-conductors; her religion a mere fear of thunder.

The Catholicism of the Enderbys had come from a small Catholic pocket not far from Shrewsbury, a village which the Reformation had robbed only of its church. Weak in the tobacconist-father (his pan scraped on Holy Saturday, a drunken midnight Mass at Christmas—no more), it had died in the poet-son, thanks to that stepmother. It had been too late now for more than twenty years to look at it afresh—its intellectual dignity, its cold coherent theology. He had struggled out of it with bitter tears in adolescence, helped by Nietzsche, Tolstoy and Rousseau, and the struggle to create his own myths had made him a poet. He couldn't go back to it now, even if he wanted to. If he did, he would be seeking the converts who wrote thrillers out of a sense of damnation or who, forming an exclusive club out of the converts of Oxford and pretending that that was the Church, would not let Enderby join. Publicly known as an apostate, Enderby would have to be bracketed along with various wild Irish. It was best, therefore, to be quiet about his faith or loss of it (asked for his religion when joining the army, he had said "Hedonist" and been made to attend parades of the United Board); the only trouble seemed to be that his art refused to be quiet.

His laughter was fermenting in the cell,
   The fish, the worm were chuckling to achieve
The rose of the disguise he wears so well.

Ultimately religious belief didn't matter; it was a question of what myths still carried enough emotional weight to be used. So the Virgin Mary now spoke her final triplet, smiling faintly in elegant blue at the distaff:

And though, by dispensation of the dove,
   My flesh is pardoned of its flesh, they leave
The rankling of a wrong and useless love.

There was too much love in the air, worried Enderby, as he read over this poem with displeasure. He saw that, apart from the obvious surface myth, there was something there about the genesis of the poet. He wrote on a final panel of toilet-paper: *Every woman is a stepmother*, then committed it to the lavatory-pan. That, he thought, has general validity. And now, judging from the loud darkness outside the cell where his poem had been an hour fermenting, they had arrived. Roars of seals in a circus, collapse of crates, high heels on the platform, a hiss, shudder and recoil as the train, in Elizabethan locution, died.

3

One

SOME hours later Enderby sat under a magnificent ceiling, bemused by food and drink and insincere laudations. A not very choice cigar shook between fingers which, he now saw, he had neglected to pumice. In a winter afternoon's dream he failed to register many of the words of orating Sir George Goodby. Across the table and at either side twenty-odd fellow-writers were suspended from the ceiling by cigarette-smoke, their faces flapping before Enderby's eyes like two lines of drying smalls. Very solid in his stomach there pawed and pranced a sort of equestrian statue that symbolised both Time and London. He desired to pick his nose. A Hangman's Blood cocktail of all the liquids he had so far taken that day was swiftly mixed in a deep visceral shaker and then shot up to his mouth for tasting. There had been an oily mock turtle with very fresh rolls and rose-shaped butter-pats. Roast duck, of which Enderby had been served with one of the greasier segments, peas and *sauté* potatoes, acid orange sauce and a thick warmish gravy. Cranberry pie, the pastry soggy, with rich whipped cream substitute. Cheese.

Cheese. Enderby smiled across back at some woman who had smiled at him. I have always admired your poetry but to see you in the flesh is a revelation. I bet it bloody well is. Perrrrrp.

"A revelation," said Sir George, "of the purest beauty. The magical power of poetry to transmute the dross of the everyday workaday world into the sheerest gold." Sir George Goodby was an ancient man whose visible parts were made mostly of sewn bits of well-tanned skin. He had founded the firm which bore his name. This firm had become rich mainly by selling rude books which other firms had been too squeamish to handle. Knighted by Ramsay MacDonald for services to the cause of mass-literacy, Sir George had always desired to serve literature otherwise than by selling it: he had aspired from youth to be a starving poet recognised only after death. Starved poetry he had continued to write long after fate had condemned him to the making of money, and this he had blackmailed one small miserable firm into publishing, brandishing the threat of a chain-boycott of all its publications. He had paid all costs of printing, publicising, and distributing, but the firm's reputation had been ruined. The volumes of Sir George's doggerel most memorable for badness were *Metrical Yarns of a Pipeman, A Dream of Merrie England, Roseleaves of Memory* and *An Optimist Sings.* He could not, of course, force people into buying or even reading these atrocious collections, but once a year, presenting a cheque and medal to, as he coyly termed him, a brother-singer, he would lard his speech richly with gobbets of his own work and render his auditors sick with embarrassment.

"The giants of my youthful days," Sir George was saying, "Dobson, Watson, Sir Edwin Arnold the mystic, Bridges the revolutionary, Calverley for laughter, Barry Pain for the profounder sigh." Enderby took a shallow draught of his cigar and felt it bite rawly. A childhood image again: the woman teacher in the elementary school explaining the soul and sin's carious effect upon it. She had chalked on the blackboard a big whitish shape like a cheese (the soul) and then, using a spit-wet finger, had spotted it like a Dalmatian (sins). For some reason, Enderby had always been able to taste that chalk-soul—a sharp vinegary raw potato—and he could taste it strongly now. "The soul," said Sir George appropriately, "which is a fair field for the poet's wandering, the sea whereon he sails his barque of rhyme, his mistress of whom he sings. The soul, which is the parson's Sunday concern, is the poet's daily bread." His daily raw potato. Enderby felt a borborygm rising.

Brrrrfffp.

"I shall inflict," twinkled Sir George, "one of my own sonnets on you, on a theme appropriate to the occasion." He read out, with a voice pitched high and on one tuning-fork note, a poem of fourteen lines which was certainly no sonnet. It had verdant meads in it and a sun with effulgent rays, also—for some reason—a rosy-bosomed earth. Enderby, preoccupied with the need to suppress his body's noises, heard only fragments of an exquisitely bad poem and he nodded approvingly to show that he considered Sir George to have made a very good choice of an illustrative example of very bad poetry. As the last line scrannel-piped wretchedly out, Enderby felt a particularly loud noise coming, so he covered it with a laugh.

Ha ha (perrrpf) ha.

Sir Gorge was rather surprised than displeased. He gaped down at Enderby for five seconds and then scanned his typescript tremblingly, as if fearful that something scatological had stolen ambiguously in. Reassured, he frowned on Enderby, his patches of skin shaking, and then took breath for the peroration. As he opened his mouth, Enderby, with infelicitious timing, gave vent.

Brrrbrrrpkrrrk.

Shem Macnamara said, "And as good and succinct a piece of criticism as ever I heard." He had a double-chinned stormy Irish face and was shag-haired and black-shirted (to save laundry). Enderby, in his daily poet's garb, was seedy-looking, but this man was a barn-sleeping hedge-dragged sturdy beggar. The white tired faces of the other guests—which Enderby could see but dimly—moved in titters. And suddenly Sir George himself seemed to grow tired. He smiled weakly, frowned, opened his mouth as in silent joy, frowned, swallowed, said in *non sequitur*:

"And it is for this reason that it gives me pleasure to bestow on our fellow singing-bird here, er er Enderby, the Goodby gold medal." Enderby rose to applause loud enough to drown three cracking intestinal reports. "And a cheque," said Sir George, with nostalgia of poet's poverty, "that is very very small but, one trusts, will stave off pangs for a month or two." Enderby took his trophies, shook hands, simpered, then sat down again. "Speech," said somebody. Enderby rose again, with a more subdued report, then realised that he was unsure of the exordial protocol. Did he say, "Mr Chairman"? Was there a chairman? If Sir George was the chairman should he say something other than "Mr Chairman"? Should he just say, "Sir George, ladies and gentlemen"? But, he noticed, there seemed to be somebody with a chain of office gleaming on his chest, hovering in the dusk, a mayor or lord mayor. What should he say—"Your Worship"? In time he saw that this was some sort of menial in charge of wine. Holding in wind, a nervously smiling Aeolus, Enderby said, loud and clear:

"St George." There was a new stir of tittering. "And the dragon," Enderby now had to add. "A British cymbal," he continued, seeing with horror that orthographical howler in a sort of neon lights before him. "A cymbal that tinkles in unsound brass if we are without clarity." There were appreciative easings of buttocks and shoulders: Enderby was going to make it brief and humorous. Desperately Enderby said, "As most of us are or are not, as the case may be. Myself included." Sir George, he saw, was throwing up wide face-holes at him, as though he, Enderby, were on a girder above the street. "Clarity," said Enderby, almost in tears, "is red wine for yodellers. And so," he gaped aghast at himself, "I am overjoyed to hand back this cheque to St George for charitable disposal. The gold medal he knows what he can do with." He could have died with shock and embarrassment at what he was saying; he was hurled on to the end in killing momentum, however. "Dross of the workaday world," he said, "as our fellow-singer Goodby so adequately disproves. And so," he said, back in the Army giving a talk on the British Way and Purpose, "we look forward to a time when the world shall be free of the shadow of oppression, the iron heel with its swastika spur no longer grinding into the face of supine freedom, democracy a reality, a fair day's pay for a fair day's work, adequate health services and a bit of peace hovering dovelike in the declining days of the aged. And in that belief and aspiration we move forward." He found that he could not stop. "Forward," he insisted, "to a time when the world shall be free of the shadow of oppression." Sir George had risen and was tottering out. "A fair day's work," said Enderby feebly, "for a fair day's pay. Fair play for all," he mumbled doubtfully. Sir George had gone. "And thereto," ended Enderby wretchedly, "I plight thee my truth."

The party broke up at once. Two men turned bitterly on Enderby. "If," said Shem Macnamara, "you didn't want the bloody money you might at least have remembered that there's others as do. Myself included," he mocked. He breathed, bafflingly, onions on Enderby, for onions had not formed any part of the meal. "I didn't mean it," said Enderby, nearly crying. "I didn't know what I was saying." Enderby's publisher said, "Want to ruin us you do?" in a sharp rising intonation. He was a young bright man from Newport. "Put your foot in it you have bloody nicely, man, make no mistake about it." A small man moustached like Kipling, with the same beetle-spectacles and a heavy watch-chain, came up to Enderby and took him firmly by Arry's lapels. "I'm Rawcliffe," he announced. He dragged Enderby away from the table in short dance-steps, lapels still held hard. Rawcliffe nodded many times, stopped, nodding, cocked an ear, nodded in satisfaction, then just nodded, chewing. "Very fibrous duck," said Rawcliffe. "You know me. I'm in all the anthologies. Now then, Enderby, tell me, tell me in all sincerity what you're doing at the present time."

"Just writing, you know," said Enderby. He was trying to think who Rawcliffe was. Uneasily he heard behind him debates in small groups on his speech and its consequences for the retail book trade.

"One would have supposed," said Rawcliffe, tugging Arry's lapels like cow-teats, "mildly supposed, I suppose, that you would be writing." He chuckled, swallowed, and nodded. "Now then, Enderby, what? What are you writing? Tell me, elm," he laughed. "Tale told of stem or stone, eh? James Joyce, that is. Myth-maker, what?"

"Well," said Enderby, and with babbling nerves, he blurted out a detailed synopsis of *The Pet Beast*.

"And the beast is really Original Sin, eh?" saw Rawcliffe. "Without Original Sin there is no civilisation, is that it? Good, good. And the title, let's have that title again." He released the lapels, found a short pencil in a waistcoat pocket, licked the point, took out a cigarette-packet, shook it ruefully, then block-lettered Enderby's title on its bottom flap. "Good," he said again. "Infinitely obleeged." And he made off nodding. Enderby sadly watched him join a group of important poets who had not been above cynically taking a free meal—P. S. ffolliott, Peter Pitts, Albert Death-Stabbes, Rupert Tombs, or some such names. They had mostly murmured "Well done" to him at the pre-prandial sherry-bibbing. Now he was left alone with his wind, companionless. Medalless also, and chequeless. Rather a wasted trip, really.

Two

"Mr. Enderby?" The lady panted slightly and very prettily. "Oh, thank goodness I was in time."

"I knew," said Enderby, "that Sir George would realise it was all a joke. Do, please, convey my apologies to him."

"Sir George? Oh yes, I know who you mean. Apologise? I don't understand." She was perhaps thirty, with fashionable stallion-flared nostrils and a model-girl's swan-neck. She wore with grace a Cardin sugar-scoop hat of beige velours, and, from the same master, a loose-jacketed suit with only a hint of flare to the peplum. An ocelot coat swung open over this. Chic shone from her demurely. Such cleanness and fragrance. (*Miss Dior*), thought Enderby with deep regret, such slender and sheer-hosed glamour. A face, he decided, devoid of all obvious sensuality—no lusciousness of the underlip, the cat-green eyes very cool and intelligent, a calm high forehead shaded by the sugar-scoop brim. Enderby tightened his tie-knot and smoothed his side-pockets, saying: "I'm sorry." And then, "I thought. That is to say." She said:

"Oh." They stood looking at each other under the glowing glass-slab signs of the hotel passage, their feet sunk in burgundy carpet. "Well. I would like, before anything else, to tell you that I genuinely admire your work." She spoke with the intonation of one expecting an incredulous snort. The voice was quiet, though the consonants had the sharpness of some speaker too close to a microphone, and there was the faintest tang of educated Scots. "I wrote to you care of your publishers, ages ago. I don't think the letter could ever have reached you. If it had reached you I'm sure you would have replied."

"Yes," said flustered Enderby. "Oh yes, I would. But perhaps that was forwarded by them to my old address because I'd forgotten to tell them about my new address and also, for that matter, the Post Office. Cheques," said blabbing Enderby, "are normally paid straight into my bank. I don't know why I'm telling you all this." She stood in a model pose, listening coolly with lips parted, handbag hanging from right forearm, gloved left hand's thumb and index-finger lightly ringing ungloved right hand's ring-finger. "I'm terribly sorry," said humble Enderby. "That may explain why I never got it."

She finished her quiet listening and suddenly became brisk. "Look," she said, "I had an invitation to that luncheon-party but I couldn't make it. Could we, do you think," she suggested, with a kind of movement on the fringe of non-movement which was a sort of apotheosis of a working-girl's jigging up and down in a winter-day bus-queue, infinitely feminine, "sit down somewhere for a few minutes, if you can spare the time, that is? Oh," she said, "I'm so stupid," the gloved hand striking the lips in *mea culpa,* "not telling you who I am. I'm Vesta Bainbridge. From *Fem.*"

"From what?"

"*Fem.*"

"What," asked Enderby, with great and suspicious care, "is that?" He had heard it as, though hardly believing it possible, something like *Phlegm,* and wondered what could be the purpose of an organisation (if it was an organisation) so named.

"Yes, of course. I see, of course you probably wouldn't know about that, would you? It's a magazine for women. And I," said Vesta Bainbridge, "am the Features Editress. Could we then, do you think? I suppose it's too early to have tea, isn't it, or is it?"

"If you would care for some tea," said gallant Enderby, "I should be only too happy, I should be only too delighted."

"Oh, no," said Vesta Brainbridge, "you have to have it with me, you see, because it goes on my expense account. And this is a business thing, you see, connected with *Fem.*"

Enderby had once, as a poor soldier, been treated to a tea of poached egg on haddock and shortbread by a kind old lady in an Edinburgh restaurant. But by anyone so glamourous, so alluring as this, he had never thought, never dreamed. He was both shocked and awed. "Do you, by any chance, come from Edinburgh?" he asked. "Something in your voice—"

"Eskbank," said Vesta Bainbridge. "How remarkable! But, of course, you're a poet. Poets can always dig out things like that, can't they?"

"If," said Enderby, "you really like my poetry, which you said you did, I should really ask you to have tea with me, not you me with you. The least I could do," said generous Enderby, fingering a half-crown in Arry's trouser-pocket.

"Come," said Vesta Bainbridge, and she made the wraith of a gesture of taking Enderby by the arm. "I *do* admire your work, really," she insisted. She led him on sure high heels past the dainty boutiques that sold flowers and jewelry, the air-travel kiosk where there was busy telephoning about flights to New York and Bermuda, past the ugly and rich cocooned in an enchantment of wine-coloured snow underfoot, perfumed air all about, light drifting, dust-soft, from unseen sources in the delicate golds of fine white bordeaux. Here every breath, every footfall, thought thrifty Enderby, must cost at least a tanner. Vesta Bainbridge and he entered a vast room of huge scooped cubes of biscuit-coloured softness in which people lounged warmly cushioned. Laughter tinkled, teatrays tinkled. Enderby felt with horror his bowels prepare to comment on the scene. He looked up at a baroque ceiling with many fat-arsed cherubim in evidence. This did not help. They sank down, Vesta Bainbridge exhibiting the delicacy of exquisite shin-lines, a fine moulding of ankle. A Roman waiter, lantern-jawed, took her order. Scots, she asked for a substantial spread: anchovy toast, egg sandwiches, pikelets, cakes, China tea with lemon. "And," said Enderby, "do you manage to eat dinner after a tea like that?"

"Oh, yes," said Vesta Bainbridge. "I can't put on weight, however hard I try. The lemon tea's because that's the way I like tea, not for slimming reasons. Obviously," she added.

"But," said Enderby, drawn to the obvious weary compliment, "you're surely perfect as you are." Suddenly he saw himself, boulevardier Enderby, witty with women, graceful in flattery, roguish eyes atwinkle, taking tea. At the same time wind fought, as a picked-up naughty kitten fights, to be free. Tea free. A free tea. "And," he said, "if I may ask, what precisely is this business with *Phlegm?*"

"Oh," she said, "isn't that funny? That's what Godfrey Wainwright calls it. He does covers, you know. *Fem.* Not, perhaps, a very good choice of name. But, you know, the market's saturated with magazines for women—*Feminocrat, Goodwife, Lilith, Gamourpuss.* The straightforward names with Women in them were worked out long ago. It's so difficult for them to think of anything new, as you'll appreciate. But *Fem* isn't too bad, is it? It's short and sweet, and it sounds Frenchified and a bit naughty, wouldn't you agree?"

Enderby eyed her warily. Frenchified and a bit naughty, eh? "Yes," he said. "And where would I come in with something like that?" Not very good, she'd said, and not too bad—both in the same breath. Perhaps not a very sincere sort of woman. Before she could answer his question the tea arrived. The Roman waiter laid it down gently on the fretted claw-footed low table—silver dish-covers steaming, tiny cakes oozing cream. He rose, bowing with sneering jowls, retiring. Vesta Bainbridge poured. She said:

"I thought somehow you'd prefer your tea like this—sugarless, milkless, lemony. Your poems are a little, shall we say, astringent, if that's the right word." Enderby looked down sourly at the sour cup. He preferred stepmother's tea really, but she'd ordered without consulting him. "Very nice," he said. "Just right." Vesta Bainbridge began to eat with great appetite, showing fine small teeth as she bit into her anchovy toast. Enderby's heart warmed to this: he liked to see women eat, and this gusto mitigated, somehow, her lean perfection. But, he thought, she had no right, with such a figure, to have such an appetite. He felt a desire to invite her out to dinner, that same evening, to see how she would tuck into minestrone and pork chops. He feared her.

"Now," said Vesta Bainbridge, and a rosy tongue-point darted out, picked up a toast-crumb, then darted in again. "I want you to know that I admire your work, and what I propose now is entirely my own idea. It's met with some opposition, mind you, because *Fem* is essentially a popular magazine. And your poetry, as you'll be proud to admit, is not exactly popular. It's not unpopular either, of course; it's just not known. Pop-singers are known and TV interviewers are known and disc-jockeys are known, but you're not known."

"What," asked Enderby, "are these things? Pop-singers and so on?" She looked askance at him and noticed that his bewilderment was genuine. "I'm afraid," said Enderby, "that since the war I've rather shut myself off from things."

"Don't you have a radio or a television set?" said Vesta

Bainbridge, her green eyes wide. He shook his head. "Don't you read newspapers?"

"I used to read certain Sunday papers," said Enderby, "for the sake of the book reviews. But it made me so very depressed that I had to stop. The reviewers seemed so," he frowned, "so very *big*, if you see what I mean. They seemed to *enclose* us writers, so to speak. They seemed to know all about us, and we knew nothing about them. There was one very kind and very knowledgeable review of a volume of mine, I remember, by a man who, I suppose, is a very good man, but it was evident that he could have written my poems so much better if only he'd had the time. Those things make one feel very insignificant. Oh, I know one *is* insignificant, really, but you've got to ignore that if you're to get any work done at all. And so I've tended to cut myself off a bit, for the sake of the work. Everybody seems to be so *clever*, somehow, if you see what I mean."

"I do and I don't," said Vesta Bainbridge, smartly. So far she had eaten all the anchovy toast, five egg sandwiches, a couple of pikelets and one squelchy little pastry, and yet contrived to look ethereal, mountain-cool. Enderby, on the other hand, who, because of his heartburn, had only nibbled mouse-like at a square inch of damp bread and an egg-ring, was aware of himself as gross, sweating, halitotic, his viscera loaded like a night-soil-collector's bucket. "I don't feel insignificant," said Vesta Bainbridge, "and I'm just nothing compared with you."

"But you don't *have* to feel insignificant, do you?" said Enderby. "I mean, you've only to look at yourself, haven't you?" He said this dispassionately, frowning.

"For a man," said Vesta Bainbridge, "who's cut himself from the world, you're not doing too badly. I should have thought," she said, pouring more tea, "that it was very unwise for a poet to do that. After all, you need images, themes, and so on, don't you? You've got to get those from the outside world."

"There are quite enough images," said Enderby, speaking with firm authority, "in half a pound of New Zealand cheddar. Or in the washing-up water. Or," he added, with even greater authority, "in a new toilet-roll."

"You poor man," said Vesta Bainbridge. "Is that how you live?"

"Everybody," said Enderby, with perhaps diminishing dogmatism, "uses toilet-paper." A man in spectacles, very tall and with an open mouth, looked across from his chair as if to dispute this assertion, thought better of it, then returned to his evening paper. *Poet Refuses Medal,* said a tiny headline which Enderby caught sight of. Some other bloody fool shooting his mouth off, some other toy trumpet singing to battle.

"Anyway," said Vesta Bainbridge, "I think it would be an excellent thing for you to have a wider audience. Would you try it for, say, six months, a poem every week? Preferably set in the form of prose, so as not to offend anyone."

"I thought people didn't actually find verse *offensive,*" said Enderby. "I thought they just despised it."

"Be that as it may," said Vesta Bainbridge, "what do you say to the proposal?" She shattered a sort of macaroon with a fork and, before eating, said, "The poems would have to be, shall I say, and I hope this is the right word, ephemeral. You know, dealing with everyday th‍ ‍gs that the average woman would be interested in."

"The dross of the workaday world," said Enderby, ͏‍ ‍‍d to sheere ͏‍ ‍‍‍ I suppose I could do that. ͏‍ ‍‍ow all about household chores and dishcloths and so ͏n. Also lavatory brushes."

"Dear me," said Vesta Bainbridge, "you *have* got a cloacal obsession, haven't you? No, not that sort of thing, and not too much of this sheerest gold, either. Woman-kind cannot bear very much reality. Love and dreams are wanted, also babies without cloacal obsessions. The mystery of the stars would come in quite nicely, especially if seen from the garden of a council-house. And marriage, perhaps."

"Tell me," said Enderby. "Are you Miss Cambridge or Mrs?"

"Bainbridge, not Cambridge. *Fem,* not *Phlegm.* Mrs. Why do you want to know?"

"I have to call you something," said Enderby, "don't I?" She seemed at last to have finished her meal, so Enderby offered his crumpled cigarette-packet.

"I'll smoke my own," she said, "if you don't mind." She took from her handbag a packet of ship's Woodbines and, before Enderby could find an unused match in his matchbox (he saved used matches, a long unfathomable habit), she had flicked her pearl-faced lighter on and then off. Her wide nostrils walrussed out two pretty blue jets.

"I take it," said Enderby, "that your husband's in the navy."

"My husband," she said, "is dead. It shows how cut off you are, really, doesn't it? Everybody else seems to have heard of Pete Bainbridge."

"I'm sorry," said Enderby. "Very sorry."

"What for? Because he's dead, or because you've never heard of him? Never mind," said Widow Bainbridge. "He died in a smash four years ago, in the Monte Carlo Rally. I thought everybody knew that. It was a great loss, the papers said, to the motor racing world. He left behind a beautiful young widow, a bride of only two years," she said, her tone half-mocking.

"He did," said Enderby gravely. "He most certainly did. Beautiful, I mean. How much?"

"How much what? How much did he leave, or how much did I love him?" She seemed suddenly tired, perhaps from overeating.

"How much do I get for doing these poems?"

"Mr Dick sets us all right," said Vesta Bainbridge, sighing and sitting up straighter. She brushed minimal crumbs off her lap and said, "Two guineas a poem. It's not much, but we can't manage more. We're featuring the memoirs of a pop-singer, you see—not very long memoirs, of course, because he's only nineteen—but those are costing us a pretty penny, believe me. And the memoirs have to be written for him as well. Still, the effect on the circulation should be, to say the least, stimulating. If that princely fee is all right by you I'll send you a contract. And some back numbers of *Fem*, to

59

show you what it's like. Please remember that the vocabulary of our readers isn't very extensive, so don't go using words like 'oriflamme' or 'ineluctable'."

"Thank you," said Enderby. "I'm really most grateful that you should have thought of me like this. You're really being most kind." He had been poking into the ashtray with a matchstick, breaking up cigarette-ends; this had necessitated a sort of crouching on the chair's edge, his bald crown presented to Mrs Bainbridge. Now he looked up sincerely, his eyes rather wet behind their glasses. She smiled.

"Look," she said, "you don't believe me about my liking your poetry, do you? Well, I even know one or two of them by heart."

"Say one," begged Enderby. She took breath and recited, quite clearly but with few nuances of tone:

"A dream, yes, but for everyone the same.
    The thought that wove it never dropped a stitch;
    The Absolute was anybody's pitch
For, when a note was struck, we knew its name."

"Good," said Enderby. "This is the first time I've ever actually heard—"

"——That dark aborted any urge to tame
    Waters that day might prove to be a ditch
    But then were endless growling ocean, rich
In fish and heroes, till the dredgers came."

"Excellent," said Enderby. "And now the sestet." It excited him to hear his own verses. She went on confidently:

"*Wachet auf!* A fretful dunghill cock
    Flinted the noisy beacons through the shires;
A martin's nest clogged the cathedral clock,
    But it was morning (birds could not be liars).
A key cleft rusty age in lock and lock;
    Men shivered by a hundred kitchen fires.

There," she said, taking breath. "But I've no real idea what it means."

"Oh," said Enderby, "the meaning doesn't matter all that much. I'm surprised at your liking that. It's not what I'd thought of as a woman's poem." Suddenly the poem seemed to find its place in the real world—overseas businessmen reading financial papers, the scent of *Miss Dior* or whatever it was, the noise of London waiting to pounce outside the hotel. Spoken by her, it seemed suddenly to have a use.

"And what exactly do you mean by a woman's poem?" asked Mrs Bainbridge.

"For you," said Enderby with disarming candour, "something softer and yet more elegant, something with less harshness and thought and history in it. That, you see, is about the Middle Ages and the coming of the Reformation. In the sestet you get Martin Luther and the beginning of dissolution, everybody beginning to be alone, a common tradition providing no tuning-fork of reference and no way of telling the time, because the common tradition has been dredged away. Nothing sure and nothing mysterious."

"I see," said Vesta Bainbridge. "I take it you're a Catholic, then."

"Oh, no, no," protested Enderby. "I'm not, really I'm not."

"All right," said Vesta Bainbridge, smiling. "I heard you the first time." Protestant Enderby smirked and shut up. The Roman waiter came along, chewing gently but mournfully, with a bill. "For me," she said, and notes rustled in her bag like pork crackling. She paid the bill and, womanly, tipped the waiter merely adequately. Enderby said:

"I'd ask you to dine with me this evening, but I've just realised that I didn't bring very much money. I expected, you see, that I'd go straight back after lunch. I'm awfully sorry."

"Don't be," smiled Vesta Bainbridge, "I'm invited out. Somewhere in Hampstead. But it was nice of you to offer. Now," she said, looking at her tiny oyster watch, "goodness, the time, where do I write to?" She took out a small notebook and poised a pencil to record what Enderby dictated. Somehow, the address seemed vulgar and even comic, edited primly by that slim hand. 81 Fitzherbert Avenue. He tried to hide from her the sound of the lavatory's flush, the crusted milk-bottles on the doorstep, the mice scampering through the manuscripts. "Good," she said, closing the book. "Now I must go." She settled the ocelot over her shoulders, clipped her bag shut. Enderby stood. She stood. "It's been awfully nice," she said. "Oh, that's inadequate. But it's been quite a privilege, really it has. Now I really must fly." She gave him an unexpected handshake, straight from the elbow. "Don't bother to come to the door," she said. Then she was off, trimly and swiftly walking a tightrope across the carpet. For the first time Enderby caught a hint of colour of her hair, upswept at the nape, a sort of penny-colour. He sighed, and turned to see the waiter looking at him. The waiter made a gesture—quick frog-mouth, shrug—to indicate (a) that she was certainly elegant but much too thin, (b) that she was off to meet somebody handsomer than Enderby, (c) that women were fundamentally ungenerous, (d) that this was a hell of a life but there were always the consolations of philosophy. Enderby nodded, the poet at ease with all classes of men, then realised with joy that he was once more alone and free. The wind that blew through him celebrated this fact.

Three

Enderby was late returning home that evening. Though his perversely independent soul—the conscious Enderby shocked and gaping—had rejected the sweets of recognition, he felt that he and London had achieved more of a rapprochement than he could have thought possible, scratching paper and bared legs, the day before. A smart and worldly woman admired his work and had said so frankly. Lips that had been kissed by a prominent racing-driver and, Enderby presumed, by others whose teeth habitually gleamed at cameras, had recited from the *Revolutionary Sonnets* in a rich-smelling place whose denizens had passed beyond the need for the solace of poetry. Enderby, wandering the streets, was restless and had an obscure longing for adventure. Here the snow had long disappeared, but the tang of snow on the air bit sharply from the furthermost stretch of the river. London yearned back to gasflares and geese sold cheap at the end of the trading day amid raucous Cockney voices, Sherlock Holmes in Baker Street, a widow at Windsor, all's right with the world. That was from *Pappa Pisses*. Enderby grinned sadly to himself, standing outside a music-shop, as he remembered the disastrous lecture he had once given to a Women's Institute. Victorian Literature. That was one spoonerism that his audience had passed over. But *A Sale of Two Titties* had struck Lady Fennimore as something like calculated insolence. Never again. Never, never again. He was safer in retirement, shut away in his creative lavatory. But still, this one evening, the desire for adventure was strong. Yet what did one mean by adventure these days? He gazed at the shop-window, as if for an answer. Various pictures of young louts sneered out at him from song-covers and record-sleeves—simian-foreheaded, prehensile fingers on guitar-strings, lips twisted in a song of youth. Enderby had heard of secondary modern schools and now assumed that these flat-eyed little monsters must represent their end-product. Well, for two guineas a week he was going to serve the world that these loose-lipped leerers served. What was the name of the magazine again? *Flim* or *Flam* or something. Not *Phlegm*, that was quite certain. Within the consonantal frame he tried out various vowels. And there, next door but one, outside one of Sir George Goodby's own shops, a poster put him right: "Exclusive to *Fem*, FOR YOU, Lenny Biggs tells his own personal life story. Order your copy NOW." And there was a picture of Lenny Biggs—a face hardly distinguishable from others of the pantheon Enderby had just viewed, though perhaps more particularly baboon-like than generally simian, with teeth as manifestly false as those of Enderby himself, sniggering with confidence at the world.

Enderby saw a man in a peaked cap dump a couple of parcels into a van lettered GOODBY'S FOR GOOD BOOKS. This van then started up contemptuously and insolently pierced the traffic. "So," thought Enderby, "Sir George has already started his reprisals, has he? All copies of Enderby's poems to be withdrawn from sale, eh? Petty, a very petty-minded man." Enderby entered the shop and was depressed to see people buying gardening books. Display studio-portraits of groomed youthful bestsellers topped piles of their bestselling novels. Enderby felt that he wanted to flee; this was as bad as reading Sunday reviews. And, to brim his misery, he realised that he had maligned Sir George: two soiled Enderby volumes sulked there on the unvisited poetry shelves. He was beneath the notice of that wealthy knight, too mean for the meanness of retaliation. Oh, well. The name Rawcliffe suddenly hurled itself, along with a pang of dyspepsia, at Enderby's breastbone. In all the anthologies, did he say? Enderby would see.

Enderby looked through *Poetry Now, A Tiny Garner of Modern Verse, Best Poets of Today, They Sing for You, Soldier's Solace* (an anthology of verse by Lieutenant-General Phipps, V.C., D.S.O., etc., sixtieth thousand), *Voices Within,* and other volumes, and found that in all of them Rawcliffe was represented by the following artless lyric:

> "Perhaps I am not wanted then," he said.
>   "Perhaps I'd better go,"
> He said. Motionless her eyes, her head,
>   Saying not yes, not no.
>
> "I will go then, and aim my gun of grief
>   At any man's or country's enemies,"
> He said. "Slaughter will wreak a red relief."
>   She said not no, not yes.
>
> And so he went to marry mud and toil,
>   Swallow in general hell his private hell.
> His salts have long drained into alien soil,
>   And she says nothing still.

Enderby looked up bitterly from the tenth selected anthology, his tenth reading of the poem. And in none of these books was there anything by Enderby.

Enderby pulled out a spilling palmful of coin from Arry's right trouser-pocket. Snorting, he counted it: twelve and ninepence. In his wallet there was, he knew, one pound note. He muttered to himself as he moved doorwards, head down to count again. He bumped into a young salesman who said, "Whoops, sir. See nothing you fancy, sir?"

"Books," said Enderby, with proleptic drunken thickness. "Waste of time and bloody money." He left, saying a soldier's good-bye to Goodby's, not one of Goodby's good boys. There was a pub almost directly opposite, shedding cosy Christmas-card lights through its old-time bottle-glass windows. Enderby entered the public bar and ordered whisky.

Four

Enderby entered the public bar and ordered whisky. This was some hours later, a different pub. Not the second or third pub, but somewhere well on in the series, the xth pub or something. On the whole, benevolent and swaying Enderby decided, he had had not too bad an evening. He had met two very fat Nigerians with wide cunning smiles and many blackheads. These had cordially invited him to their country and to write an epic to celebrate its independence. He had met a Guinness-drinker with a wooden leg which, for the delectation of Enderby, he had offered to unscrew. He had met a chief petty officer of the Royal Navy who, in the friendliest spirit in the world, had been prepared to fight Enderby and, when Enderby had demurred, had given him two packets of ship's Woodbines and said that Enderby was his pal. He had met a Siamese osteopath with a collection of fighting fish. He had met a punch-drunk bruiser who said he saw visions and offered to see one then for a pint. He had met a little aggressive chinny chewing man, not unlike Rawcliffe, who swore that

Shakespeare's plays had been written by Sir William Knollys, Controller of the Queen's Household. He had met a cobbler who knew the Old Testament in Hebrew, an amateur exegetist who distrusted all Biblical scholarship after 1890. He had met, seen, or heard many others too: a thin woman who had talked incessantly to a loll-tongued Alsatian; a man with the shakes who swallowed his own phlegm (*Fem, Fem,* remember that, *Fem*); a pair of hand-holding lesbians; a man who wore flower transfers on a surgical boot; callow soldiers drinking raw gin. . . . Now it was nearing closing time and Enderby was, he thought, fairly near to Charing Cross. That meant two stops on the Underground to Victoria. There must be a nice convenient after-closing-time train to the coast.

Enderby, paying fumblingly for his whisky, saw that he had very little money left. He estimated that he had managed to consume this evening a good dozen whiskies and a draught beer or so. His return ticket was snug in Arry's left-hand inside jacket-pocket. He had cigarettes. One more drink and he would be right for home. He looked round the public bar smiling. Good honest British working-men, salt of the earth, bloodying and buggering their meagre dole of speech, horny-handed but delicate with darts. And, on a high-backed settle at right angles to the bar counter, two British working-women sat, made placid with the fumes of stout. One said:

"Starting next week, it is, in *Fem*. With free gift picture in full colour. Smashing, he is." Enderby listened jealously. The other woman said:

"Never take it, myself. Silly sort of a name it is. Makes you wonder how they think of them sometimes, really it does."

"If," said Enderby, "you are referring to the magazine to which I myself am to be a contributor, I would say that that name is meant to be Frenchified and naughty." He smiled down at them with a whiskified smirk, right elbow on the counter, left fingers on right forearm. The two women looked up doubtfully. They were probably about the same age as Vesta Bainbridge, but they had an aura of back kitchens about them, tea served to shirt-sleeved men doing their pools, the telly flicking and shouting in the corner.

"Pardon?" said one, loudly.

"Naughty," said Enderby, with a great clarity. "French-ified."

"What's French frieds to do with it?" said the other. "My friend and me was just talking, do you mind?"

"Poetry is what I shall write for it," said Enderby, "every week." He nodded several times, just like Rawcliffe.

"You keep your poetry to yourself, do you mind?" and she took a sharp draught of Guinness. A man came from the dart-playing part of the room, a single dart in his hand, saying:

"You all right, Edie?" He wore a decently cut suit of poor serge, but no collar or tie. His gold-headed collar-stud caught the light and dazzled Enderby. He had a gaunt quick face and was as small and supple as a miner. He inspected Enderby as if invited to give an estimate on him. "You saying something to her that you shouldn't?" he said. "Mate?" he added, provocatively.

"He was saying," said Edie, "about naughty poetry. French, too."

"Was you saying naughty poetry to my wife here?" said the man. Like Milton's Death, he shook a dreadful dart.

"I was just saying," said smirking Enderby, "that I was going to write for it. What they read, I mean. That is to say, Edie here, your wife, as I take it to be, doesn't read, but the other one does, you see."

"We'll have less of that about doesn't read, do you mind?" said Edie. "And less of using my name familiar, do you mind?"

"Look here," said Edie's husband. "You want to keep that for the saloon bar, where they pay a penny extra for the privilege, do you mind? We don't want your sort in here."

"Doing no harm," said Enderby huffily. He then poured over the huff a trickle of sweet sauce of ingratia-tion. "I mean, I was just talking." He leered. "Just passing the time of day, if you see what I mean."

"Well," said the dart-man, "don't you try to pass the time with my missis, do you mind?"

"Do you mind?" said Edie, in near-unison.

"I wouldn't want to pass the time with her," said Enderby, proudly. "I've other things to do, thank you very much."

"I'll have to do you," said the man, sincerely. "Too much bloody hoot altogether, mate, to my way of thinking, that's what you've got. You'd better get out of here before I get really nasty. Been smelling the barmaid's apron, that's your trouble."

Prrrfffp.

"Look," said Enderby, "that wasn't intended, I really had no intention, that was not meant in any way to be a comment, I assure you that is the sort of thing that could happen to any man, or woman too, for that matter, even Edie here, your wife, that is to say, yourself included." Prrrfffp.

"Do you mind?" said Edie.

"This here's my fist," said the man, pocketing his dart. The other customers quietened and looked interested. "You'll get it straight in the moosh, straight up you will, if you don't get out of my bleeding sight this instant, do you mind?"

"I was just going anyway," said dignified swaying Enderby. "If you will allow me the privilege of finishing my drink here."

"You've had enough, you have, mate," said the man, more kindly. From the saloon bar came the call of "Last orders." "If you want to drown your secret sorrows don't do it where me and my wife is, see, because I take the sort of thing you've been saying very hard, see." Enderby put down his glass, gave the dart-man a glassy but straight look, then eructed strongly and without malice. He bowed and, pushing his way courteously through the long-swallowers anxious to get one last one in, made an exit that was not without dignity. Outside in the street the heady air of a Guinness-sharp refrigerated night hit him and he staggered. The dart-man had followed him out and stood there, gauging and weighing. "Look, mate," he said, "this is not for me really, because I've

68

been like that myself often enough, God knows, but my wife insists, see, do you mind, and this is like for a keepsake." He bowed, and while bowing swerved his torso suddenly to the left as though listening to something from that side, then he brought left fist and torso right and up and let Enderby have one, not too hard, straight in the stomach. "There," he said, somewhat kindly, as if the blow had been intended purely therapeutically. "That'll do, won't it?"

Enderby gasped. The procession of the evening's whiskies and beers passed painfully through a new taste-organ that had been installed specially for this occasion. They grimaced in pain, making painful obeisance as they passed. Gas and fire shot up as from a geyser, smiting rudely the crystalline air. Premonitions of the desire to vomit huddled and fluttered. Enderby went to the wall. "Now then," said the man, "where is it you want to go, eh? Do you know where you are now, eh? Kennington you are now, see, if you didn't know."

"Victoria," said Enderby's stomach-gas, shaped into a word by tongue and lips. He had, at the moment, no air.

"Easy," said the kind man. "First to the right second to the left keep straight on brings you to Kennington Station, see. Get a train to Charing Cross, that's the second stop, Waterloo's the first, change at Charing Cross, see, Circle Line. Westminster St James's Park and then you're there, see. And the very best of luck and no hard feelings." He patted Enderby's left shoulder and re-entered the public bar.

Enderby still gasped. This sort of thing had not happened since his student-days when he had once been beaten up by a pub pianist and his friend for being bloody sarky about the sort of pseudo-music the pub pianist had been playing. Enderby filled his coughing lungs in draught after draught, then wondered whether he really wanted to vomit. He thought, for the moment, not. The punch in the stomach still glowed and smouldered, and the name LONDON fluttered in fearful flames, a warning, as in the trailer of some film about call-girls or the end of the world. He saw himself safe in his own lavatory, at work on his poems. Never again.

Never never again. Women's Institutes. Gold medals. London pubs. Traps set for poor Enderby, gins waiting for him to trip.

He reached Kennington Station without much difficulty and booked to Victoria. In the train, sitting opposite a cross-eyed man who spoke Scots to a complacent terrier on his knee, Enderby felt a shipboard motion and knew that soon he must dash to the rails. Further along on the side where he was sitting, he had the illusion that a couple of gum-chewing teenagers were discussing a play by Calderon. He strained to listen and nearly fell on his right ear. At Waterloo he was sure that the Scotsman with strabismus said *"morne plaine"* to his dog. A drum beat and a bugle brayed in Enderby's stomach; here, perhaps, he must admit defeat, stagger off, be sick in a fire-bucket. Too late. The train and time marched on from Waterloo, under the river, and, thank God, there was Charing Cross. The charing-cross-eyed man got out here too, with terrier. "A drop taken," he said confidentially to Enderby and then marched off to the Bakerloo Line, dog trotting with twinkletoes behind, fat rump, joyous tail. Enderby now felt decidedly unwell and bewildered. He had a confused notion that the southbound platform of this Northern Line would take him whither he wanted. He staggered over and sat on a bench. Across the rail a poster showed an outdoor man draining a milk stout, his fine muscular throat corded with stout-drinker's strength. Next to that was a colour-wash sketch, vivid with steam and laughter, of a confident young man wrestling with a delighted girl for a portion of pie made with meat-extract. Next to that a ginger child, macrocephalic, went "Oooool" with pleasure, his cheek gumboiled with a slab of extra-creamy toffee. Enderby retched, but memory saved him with four lines of a drinker's poem he had written in his drunken youth:

> And I have walked no way I looked
> And multitudinously puked
> Into the gutter, legs outstretched,
> Holding my head low as I . . .

That threw his present queasiness back into the past and also depersonalised it. The solace of art. And now the distant Minotaur roar of the tube-train alerted the others waiting on that platform. One man folded his evening paper and stuck it into the side-pocket of his greatcoat. *Poet Speaks Out for Fair Play*, read Enderby. Field-day for poets, this. The tube-train slammed itself into the clearing, bringing a fine gale of Arctic air which did Enderby good. He stood and felt giddy but steeled himself to travel to Victoria, seeing that, in his muzzy state, as a very large and desirable lavatory of blasts and sulphuretted hydrogen. He straddled before a not-yet-opened double-door of the train, trying to hold the unquiet platform steady, while the passengers waiting to alight stood as though for a curtain-call. Then a panic of doubt clouted Enderby as the doors slid open and the alighters flooded off. "Is this," he called, "all right for Victoria?" Many of the emergent did not speak English and made apologetic gestures, but a cool woman's voice said:

"This, Mr Enderby, is most certainly not all right for Victoria." Enderby blinked at this apparition. Mrs What's-her-name of *Fem*, racing ace's widow, in semi-formal pale apple-green taffetas, sheathed at the front, and three-quarter-length Persian lamb jacket, marcasite clip as single fine dress-embellisher, tiny hoop ear-rings of marcasite, marcasite-coloured glacé kid high-heels, penny-coloured hair cleanly glowing. Enderby's mouth opened sheepishly. "If you got this train," she said, "you would be travelling to Waterloo and Kennington, Tooting Bec, ultimately Morden. From the look of you, you would probably be awakened at Morden. You wouldn't like Morden very much."

"You," said Enderby, "should not be here. You should be at dinner somewhere."

"I *was* at dinner," she said. "I've just come back from Hampstead." The train-doors slid together and the train moved off into its tunnel, its wind stirring her hair and making her raise her voice, so that the Scots intonation became clearer than before. "And," she said, her sober green eyes appraising swaying Enderby, "I'm on my way

71

home to Gloucester Road. Which means we can take the same train and I can make quite sure that you alight at Victoria. From Victoria on you must be commended to the protection of whatever gods look after drunken poets." She had in her something of the thin-lipped Calvinist; in her tone was no element of amused indulgence. "Come," she said, and she took Enderby's arm.

"If you don't mind," said Enderby. "If you'll excuse me just a moment—" Green looked at green. Enderby managed to trap the brief flow in his show handkerchief. "Oh, God," he said. "Oh, Jesus, Mary and Joseph."

"Come on," she said. "Walk. Take deep breaths." She led him firmly towards the Circle Line. "You are in a bad way, aren't you?" All her perfume could not sweeten Enderby's shame.

Five

Enderby was back in 81 Fitzherbert Avenue, thoroughly sobered at last by two slips on to his bottom on the frozen way from the station. On that same sore bottom he sat on the stairs, crying. This flight ran up, starting at the side of Enderby's flat's front door, to a landing with mirror and potted palm. Then came a dark and sinister stairway, uncarpeted, to the flat above, the home of the salesman and his woman. Enderby sat crying because he had forgotten his key. He had neglected, perhaps because flustered by Mrs Meldrum's visit that morning, to transfer the key from his sports-coat pocket to the corresponding pocket of the jacket of Arry's suit. It was now after one in the morning, too late to call on Mrs Meldrum to open up for him with her master. He had no money for a hotel room; it was too cold to sleep in a shelter on the esplanade; he did not fancy begging a cell at the police station (there were criminal-looking coppers there, with wide-boy tashes.) It was best to sit here on the third step up, overcoated and muffled, crying and smoking alternately.

Not that he had much left to smoke. Mrs Whatever-her-name-was of *Fem* had taken his remaining packet of ship's Woodbines (she was out of them and smoked nothing else) as a reward for her stoic Scots toleration of his wanting to be sick on the deck of the train all the way to Victoria. Enderby had five Senior Service to last him till the late winter dawn. He cried. He was weary, far beyond sleepiness. It had been a long and eventful day, excruciatingly attritive. Even on his homeward coastward train journey the entire coach had seemed to be full of wet-mouthed Irishmen singing. And now the cold stair, the long vigil. He howled like a moon-bemused hound-dog.

The door of the flat above opened creakily. "Is that you, Jack?" whispered the woman's voice, huskily. "Have you come back, Jack?" Her vowels were not unlike Arry's: uvyer coom buck juck. "I'm sorry, Jack," she said. "I didn't mean what I said, love. Come on to bed, Jack."

"It's me," said Enderby. "Not him. Me. Without a key," he added.

"Who are you?" asked the woman. The bulb of the landing light had long burnt out, months ago, unreplaced by Mrs Meldrum. Neither could see the other.

"Him from downstairs," said Enderby, falling easily into demotic. "Not him as you live with."

"He's gone off," came the voice down the stair-well. "He's always said he would and now he's done it. We had a bit of a barney."

"That's right," said Enderby.

"What do you mean that's right? We had a bit of a barney and now he's gone off. I bet he's gone to that bitch down by the Ornamental Gardens."

"Never mind," said Enderby. "He'll come back. They always do."

"He won't. Not tonight he won't. And I'm frightened up here on my own."

"What are you frightened of?"

"Of being on my own. Like I said. In the dark, too. It went out while we was having this barney and I couldn't see to hit him. Have you got a bob you can let me have till first thing tomorrow morning?"

"Not a sausage," said Enderby proudly. "I blued it all on booze in town. I think I'd better come up there," he

73

added, bold. "I could sleep on the couch or something. I forgot my key, you see. It's a damn nuisance."

"If you come up here you'd better not let Jack get hold of you."

"Jack's gone off with this bitch down by the Ornamental Gardens," said Enderby.

"Ah. So you seen him, did you? I thought as much. You can see the black at her roots, bitch as she is."

"I'm coming up now," said Enderby. "Then you won't be frightened of being on your own. You've got a couch up there, have you?" said Enderby, rising in pain and crawling up the stairs.

"If you think you're going to get in bed with me you've got another think coming. I've finished with all men."

"I've no intention of getting into bed with you," said indignant Enderby. "I just want to lie down on the couch. I don't really feel all that good."

"You needn't be so bloody well on your bloody high horse. I've been in bed with better men than what you'll ever hope to be. Careful," she said, as Enderby kicked the metal pot of the palm on the landing. He clambered blind up the second flight, hugging the banister. At the top he collided with a warm bosomy shape. "You can cut that out for a start," she said. "A bit too forward you are for a start." She sniffed briskly. "That scent's very expensive," she said. "Who you been with, eh? Still waters run deep, if you're really who you say you are, meaning him that lives down there."

"Where is it?" groped Enderby. "I just want somewhere to lie down." His hands felt the softness and width of a sofa, the continuum broken by bottle-shapes (they clanked) and a half-full chocolate box (rustled). "Lay down," he corrected himself, to be more matey.

"Make yourself comfortable," she said, bloody sarky. "If you want anything don't hesitate to ring. At what hour of the morning would you like your morning tea?" she said, in a hot-potato chumble. "Men," she said, going, apparently, to her bedroom. She made a contemptuous noise worthy of Enderby himself, leaving him to the dark.

4

One

HE awoke with first light to the xylophone of milk bottles and impotent rasping of self-starters. He smacked his lips and clacked his tongue on his hard palate, feeling his mouth like—the vulgar simile swam up from his vulgar pub-crawl—an all-in wrestler's jock-strap. The vulgar simile put fingers to its nose in the gesture his stepmother had called "fat bacon," made the old Roman sign, raspberried, and clambered off up the wall like a lizard. Enderby in his overcoat felt cold and grubby, matching the room that now emerged like a picture on a television screen when the set has at last warmed up. With the picture, noise: that woman's snoring from the next room. Enderby listened, interested. He had never realised that women could snore so loud. His stepmother had, of course, been able to blast a roof off, but she had been unique. Unique? He remembered some lavatorial writing or other about all stepmothers being women or all women stepmothers or something, and then the whole day came back, certainly not a dull day, and he caught quite clearly the name of the widow who had given him tea and taken him to the Victoria tube-stop:

Vesta Bainbridge. Shame warmed all Enderby's body and then hunger hammered at him, as at a door. The shameful day marched by briskly, its nostrils widened in a silly smirk, and it carried a banner of St George. It noisily tramped off to stand at ease behind the gimcrack sideboard. Enderby put on his spectacles, seeing beer bottles and old *Daily Mirrors* with painful clarity, then creaked, groaning, to the kitchenette. This was full of small square platters that had held TV meals, also empty milk-bottles with crusty archipelagoes inside them. Enderby drank water from the tap. He opened the cupboard, wiping his mouth on a dish-cloth, and found gherkins. He ate some of these crisp slugs and soon felt better.

Before leaving he called on his hostess, but she lay sprawled over the double bed, uncovered, working hard at sleep. Her bubs, like blancmanges not properly set, shivered gently under the translucent night gown as a lorry went by. Black smoke of hair over her face lifted and fell, obedient to her snore. Enderby covered her with the eiderdown, bowed, and left. She was not so old, he decided. A fat stupid girl not really capable of ill-nature. She had given Enderby shelter: Enderby would not forget.

As Enderby went downstairs he met his own milkman: a pint for Enderby's door, a half-pint for the foot of the stairs. The milkman leered and double-clacked his tongue. So many dawns, so many betrayers. Enderby had an idea. "Had to sleep up there," he said. "Locked myself out. Do you know anything about locks?"

"Love laughs at locksmiths," said the milkman sententiously. "I'll just see if I've got a bit of wire."

A minute later the postman came with Littlewood's coupons for upstairs, nothing for Enderby. "That's not quite the way," he said critically. "Let me have a try." He breathed heavily over the lock, probing and fiddling. "Coming," he panted. "Half a tick." The lock sprang, Enderby turned the knob, the door opened.

"Very much obliged," he said, "to both you gentlemen." He had not relished the prospect of going to see

Mrs Meldrum. He gave them his last coppers and entered.

Ah, but it was a relief to be back. Enderby stripped off his overcoat and hung it by its left shoulder on the hook in the tiny hall. He took off, with slighty greater care, the suit he had borrowed from Arry and rolled it neatly in a ball. He placed this, pending the returning of it, on the unmade bed, and then he put on his turtle-neck sweater. He was dressed now for work. His bare legs twinkled into the living-room and at once he scented change. There was a letter on the table, unstamped, and the table itself had been cleared of yesterday morning's dirty dishes. Enderby kicked on the electric fire and sat down to read, his brow troubled. The letter was from Mrs Meldrum.

Dear Mr. E,

You will forgive me taking a look round when you was out, as I have every right being the landlady when all said and done. Well, you have got the place disgraceful no two ways about it, what with the bath full of pieces of pottery which was never the intention of them who make baths and have them fitted in. And the carpets not swept neither, I would be ashamed to have to show anybody round it. Well, what I said still hold water, that the rent goes up from next month and you been lucky to have it so cheap for so long, what with prices of things going up everywhere. If you dont like it you know what to do, I have others who will *keep the place proper* only too anxious to move in next week. You need somebody to look after you and no mistake, it is not natural for a man of your age and with your education as you say you have, living on his own and nobody to look after the house. To be blunt about it and not to shut up about what needs to be spoke out loud you need to get married before you sink to rack and ruin, which is the true opinion of many as I have spoke to.

Yours respctfly
W. MELDRUM. (Mrs)

So. Enderby scratched his knee bitterly. That's what they wanted, was it? Enderby looked after, the dishes washed properly, the beds made regularly, the bathroom a pretty dream of a place with glaucous curtains and brushes for back and nails, nylon bristles with plastic fish-shape handles, the bath always waiting for a pink healthy tubber singing la-la-la through the steam. And, for hubby Enderby, a den to write his precious poetry in, a hobby for hubby. No. Bird-voices started in his head: prudence-preaching pigeons, cautioning rooks: beware of meadows, widows. Act act act, called the ducks: drain the sacrament of choice. "This is my choice," said Enderby firmly, as he went to the kitchen to get breakfast (that bitch Mrs Meldrum had washed his dishes!) and brew up stepmother's tea. He would be true to that archetypal bitch, his father's second wife. She had made his life a misery; he would give no other woman that privilege.

And yet. And yet. Enderby had his breakfast of dry bread, strawberry jam, and tea, then went to his workshop. His papers lay untouched by Mrs Meldrum; his table with its legs specially shortened awaited him by the hollow seat. *The Pet Beast* was growing slowly; the volume of fifty poems, planned for the autumn, was nearly complete. The first job to be cleared out of the way was the composing of a new love lyric for the *Arry to Thelma* sequence. Enderby felt guilty about the state of Arry's suit. It had, inexplicably, collected mud round the knees; a lapel had been incontinently soiled; the knife-crease had, with incredible speed, become blunted. Arry should be mollified with something really good. He had been complaining about the subject-matter of Enderby's offerings: too many kitchen similes, the appeal to her hard heart too indirect. She had, Arry swore, been reading these poems aloud to the car salesmen, and they had been yak-yakking at them. Enderby must write something very direct, not crude, mind, but direct, telling her what Arry desired to do with her, something that she would keep under her pillow and blush when she drew it (scented with her scent) out. Enderby thought, sitting on his throne, that he might have something suitable in stock. He rummaged in the bath and found certain very early lyrics. Here was one he had written at the age of seventeen. "The Music of the Spheres," it was called.

78

I have raised and poised a fiddle
  Which, will you lend it ears,
Will utter music's model:
  The music of the spheres.

By God, I think not Purcell
  Nor Arne could match my airs.
Perfect beyond rehearsal
  My music of the spheres.

Not that its virtue's vastness—
  The terror of drift of stars.
For subtlety and softness
  My music of the spheres.

The spheres that feed its working,
  Their melody swells and soars
On thinking of your marking
  My music of the spheres.

This musing and this fear's
  Work of your maiden years.
Why shut longer your ears?
  Look, how the live earth flowers!
The land speaks my intent:
  Bear me accompaniment.

That, addressed to a supposed virgin, was manifestly
absurd for Thelma. And was not that spherical imagery
perhaps too gross for a barmaid brought up, one presumed, respectably? Dirty jokes in the bar were one
thing, but dirty literature, even the most factitious suggestion of its presence, was another. His stomach, still
sore, attested this.

Seventeen. The date of composition was at the foot of
the manuscript. To whom had he written that? He
brooded, scratching. To nobody, he decided glumly. But
had he not dreamed, at that romantic age, of some
willow-wand creature who, though of infinite refinement
and smelling sweet as May, would not be offended by
this all too decipherable symbolism of importunacy? He

had shaped this girl in his heart, as mystics shape God, in terms of what she should not be, namely his stepmother; then her positive image had arisen by dint of long brooding on her negative attributes. She had come in a dream then, slender and laughing and, above all, *clean. Not* a widow: he refused to allow this re-issue of the image to take on the colours and scents of Mrs Bainbridge.

He sighed, then began, very deliberately and coldly, as a pure poetic exercise, to write a very erotic poem from Arry to Thelma, full of breasts and thighs and panting longing. When he had finished he set it aside to cool, then he went on with his building of the labyrinth, home of the Pet Beast.

Two

This was the order of a usual Enderby day: he would rise at dawn or just after, winter and summer alike; he would breakfast, defecate, and then work, sometimes beginning his work while actually defecating; at ten-fifteen he would shave and prepare to go out, sometimes with a shopping reticule; at ten-thirty he would leave the flat, walk seawards, buy a loaf, feed the gulls; immediately after that he would take his morning whisky with the aged and dying or, if Arry were not at work, with Arry in the Freemason's Arms; sometimes he would visit Arry in his kitchens, and Arry would give him scraps for his larder—a turkey carcass, a few slices of fat pork, a bit of scrag-end for Sunday's meal; Enderby would then do such shopping as was needed—a loaf for himself, potatoes, ten cigarettes, pickles, a small meat-pie, a fourpenny custard; back home he would prepare his meal, or, if something cold was left over from the day before, eat at once, working while he ate; he would then loll somnolent in a chair or even, rolling dressed into bed, deliberately sleep. Then back to the lavatory for the last long stint of the day; after that the remains of his earlier meal, or bread with some cheap relish; stepmother's tea as a nightcap; bed. A way of life which harmed no one. Sometimes the caprices of the Muse would disrupt this pattern by hurling poems—fragmentary or fully-formed—at Enderby; then, in mid-whisky, in bed, cooking, toiling at the structures of non-lyrical works, he would have to write down at once to her hysterical or coldly vatic or telegraphic dictation. He respected his Muse but was frightened of her whims: she could be playful kitten or tiger fully-clawed, finger-sucking idiot child or haughty goddess in Regency ball-gown; her moods, like her visits, were unpredictable. More predictable were his other visitants—dyspepsia in its various forms, wind, hiccoughs. Between dispensations of celestial and visceral afflation he lived his quiet days, a solitary man, harmless. Letters and visitors rarely disturbed his door, news from the dangerous world never intruded. His dividends and tiny royalties were paid straight into the bank; the bank he visited once a month only, humbly waiting with his cash cheque made out neatly for twenty-odd pounds behind bull-necked publicans and ascetic-faced butchers who paid in, inexplicably, dull mounds of copper that took long to count. He envied nobody except the great proved dead.

His routine, already disturbed by the disastrous London trip, was further disturbed by a consequence of that trip, namely the arrival of a big parcel. The address-panel had *Fem* printed on it and the picture of a well-groomed though moronic-faced young woman, evidently a typical *Fem*-reader. Enderby, who had been deep in his poem, received the parcel trouserless and open-mouthed, then ran into the living-room with a thudding heart to open it up. There was a contract for him to sign and a brief letter from Mrs Bainbridge telling him that here was a contract to sign and here were copies of past issues of *Fem*. She wrote in thick long strokes, was formal and business-like, but had allowed her scent to inspissate, most delicately, the writing-paper. Enderby had little nose, but he caught her very feminine image very clearly. So.

Enderby knew little of magazines. As a boy he had read *Film Fun* and *Funny Wonder*. As a young man he had known poetry periodicals and waspish left-wing week-end reviews. In the Army he had seen such things as the troops read. In professional waiting-rooms he had sat stony-faced over *Punch.* He was aware of a post-war rash of cheap journals and wondered at their range of specialisation and at the number of cults they seemed to serve. There were two or three, he knew, wholly devoted to some dead film-star who had become a sort of corn-god; he had seen others which, severally, glorified young living louts with guitars—presumably what Mrs Bainbridge had called pop-singers. There was evidently a strong religious hunger among young girls which these poor simulacra and their press-priests alone seemed available to feed. There was also, among these same young girls, money crying to be spent, for it seemed that in this age of specialists only the unskilled and witless were at a premium. But the dreaming wives had money also. *Fem* fought screaming for their sixpences, trying to elbow out *Womanly,* kick *Lovely* in the teeth, rip the corsets off *Wifey* and tear out the hair of *Blondie* by its black roots.

He sat down eagerly to read *Fem.* Time passed, lost for ever, never to be redeemed, as he snorted adenoidally over its contents. The cover had a girl's face, generically and boringly lovely. The cover of each issue, he noted, flicking through the pile on his knees, had a young woman's face, probably always the same one, though he could not be certain. The covers of magazines for men, he fancied, preferred to exploit woman from the neck down. A fair division. Enderby read readers' letters: somebody's little girl asked if God lived in an aeroplane; how to turn an old jam-jar into an elegant vase by using four different shades of nail-varnish (total cost 8s. 6d.); that sweet grateful smile was all the reward she could ask for her act of charity; the budgerigar of Mrs F. (Rotherham) could say "Dolly loves Mummy"; how stupid men could be, couldn't they, wanting to keep potatoes in a kitchen-drawer! (Enderby read this gravely puzzled: why was that stupid?) There was a serial story called "For Ever and a Day," illustrated opulently with a ravishing but doubtful bride. A five-page article demonstrated that it did not cost *very* much more to make your own disc-cabinet (or to get husband or boyfriend to make it) than to buy it in a shop. There were short stories called "Heart Afire," "Why Did You Leave Me?," "I Thee Wed," "Hello, Romance," mostly garnished with pictures of couples glued together, upright. A vital-warming religious column by a popular young pop-singing parson was followed by a feature on "Our Queen's Dogs." There was a chilling clinical chat on tumours, there were articles on stiletto heels, marmalade-making, being a radiant bride. Enderby sat absorbed for a long time in a Special Cookery Supplement, seeing at last a means of improving his diet (he would try Orange Goody tomorrow). He was shocked and touched by letters sent to Millicent Goodheart, a blue-haired lady with sharp red talons and a gentle smile; "He said it was artificial respiration, but now I find I am to have his child"; "I have only been married three months but I have fallen in love with my husband's father." Enderby nodded approvingly at the good sense of the replies. She should not have done it; I'm terribly sorry for you, my dear, but you must remember marriage is for keeps.

Dusk fell while he was still reading, with much more reading still to do. He stole to the light-switch, feeling guilty, excusing himself for this long soaking: after all, he was going to write for them, he had to know their tastes. His belly growled its neglect. Enderby had nothing in the flat except bread, jam, pickles; he must go out and buy something. He rather fancied a dish concocted by Gillian Frobisher, Head of *Fem's* Cookery Department: Spaghetti Fromaggio Surprise.

Enderby went out with his shopping-net and returned with a pound of spaghetti, a quarter of cheese, and a large garlic for fourpence. (The recipe gave the alternative of two large onions, but Enderby had an obscure repugnance to entering a green-grocer's just to ask for two onions; garlic was a different matter, being exotic.) Panting with excitement, he took the relevant issue of *Fem* into the kitchen and followed the instructions slavishly. "Enough for four," he read. He was but one man alone, himself, he, hungry Enderby. He must divide ev-

83

erything, then, by four. He took the pound of spaghetti and broke the brittle sticks into small pieces. He took his frying pan (pity that the recipe asked for a large deep one; still, never mind) and poured one tablespoonful of olive oil. (He had about a cupful of this in his cupboard, saved from sardine tins.) He threw in about a quarter of the spaghetti, lit the gas, and cooked it slowly, turning and stirring. He then added two cupfuls of water, remembered that he was to divide by four, so threw some of the water out again. He turned, breathing heavily, to *Fem*, while the pan gently simmered. Grated cheese. He grated some with Mrs Meldrum's nutmeg-grater and threw it into the mixture. Now this question of onion or garlic. "Two large onions chopped," said Gillian Frobisher, or "garlic to taste." Enderby looked at his garlic, stronger, he knew, than onions; perhaps this one would be equivalent to two of those. Should he skin it? No. The goodness was in the skin: potatoes, for instance. He sliced the garlic warpwise, then woofwise, then threw the bits into the simmering pan. And now. A greased dish. He found a cloudy Pyrex on the shelf, and he liberally coated its inside with margarine. He now had to transfer the stuff from the pan into the Pyrex. He had some difficulty in turning it out: it had stuck to the pan for some reason, and he had to gouge vigorously to detach what was willing to be detached. He flopped the mixture into the dish. "Top with sour cream," said Gillian. There was no sour cream, but plenty of sour milk, greenish on top. He crowned the dish with generous curds, then lit the oven. It had to cook to a slow heat therein, about twenty minutes. Groaning, he placed the dish on the oven shelf, kicked the black door shut, wiped one hand on the other. There.

Damn. He had not, he realised, consistently divided by four. Never mind. And perhaps the spaghetti was meant to turn black. He had heard of smart restaurants where things were deliberately burned before one's eyes, as one sat cool and well-dressed at table. He went back to the electric fire to continue his reading of yet another issue of *Fem*. After gazing transfixed at a soup advertisement showing a cup of cold blood, and an egg advertise-

ment in which a pallid yolk hung over the edge of the
fish-slice that lifted it aslant from the pan, ready to flop
in pale yellow, Enderby settled to a story called "You're
Not My Darling." This was about an air-hostess who fell
in love with the captain of her aircraft, a theme new to
Enderby. He gawped on long past Gillian Frobisher's
twenty minutes of cooking-time, came to with a hiccoughing start, then drew his Spaghetti Fromaggio Surprise out of the oven. Its name was not inept. He sat
down to it, and savoured mingled hues of burnt farinaci-
ty and shouting brutal garlic, loud and hot as an acety-
lene blast; the tone of these hues was a tired tepidity. He
had not quite expected this; still presumably Gillian
Frobisher knew what she was doing. He ate dutifully,
with many draughts of cold water. He must learn the
tastes of his prospective readers.

Three

Enderby awoke in the middle of the night, jerked with
sergeant's roughness out of an odd dream about pokers.
The pain was ghastly though it did not feel dangerous.
Enderby's head was clear enough as he crawled out; he
even remembered the name of the bloody woman. Gillian Frobisher. There was a photograph of her in one of
the Cookery Supplements: a crisp handsome Jewish girl
with an impossibly clean frying pan. If he ever got hold
of her, Enderby vowed, he would dirty that frying pan
and no mistake. He had been taken advantage of.

Bicarb shattered the pain and sent its fragments flying
on the wind. Enderby sat down in his living-room and
switched on the electric fire. It was, said his watch,
three-ten. A ghastly hour. There was noise upstairs, a
woman's voice shouting as through a muslin strainer,
"Get out, do you hear? Get out, you pig." Then the
rumble of a man's voice and the tread of heavy shoes.
Jack was, apparently, back. Soon the woman's abuse grew
fainter and was curiously articulated, as though from the
side of the mouth, in brief bursts. Later the springs
began to bounce. Enderby picked up the contract from

the sofa, wondering whether he ought to sign or not. To produce a block of rhymed clichés weekly, sententious vapourings about the stars so far away, the feel of chubby baby's arms round mummy's neck, being kind to those in trouble—was not this prostitution? The poems he was writing to Thelma from Arry were not that, whatever they were. Where they were not straightforwardly sensual they were gently ironical: he needn't be ashamed of them. But this proposal of Mrs Bainbridge—was it not the fiend luring him away from proper art with the chink of guineas that, anyway, would be all for Mrs Meldrum? Enderby walked into the bathroom to survey all the tumbled years' work in the bath. He had moved, over the last decade and a half, from town to town and flat to flat, but he had thought that here he could settle. It was not good to change one's workshop in the middle of a major creation. The mood altered under the subtle influence of a new place, the continuity was broken. And then the thought of packing all this bathful into suitcases—mice, breadcrusts and all. One lost things, one was tempted to throw things away. But Enderby, standing in bare feet, thinking hard, wondered whether perhaps he ought to make the sacrifice, move on up or down the coast, away from Mrs Meldrum and—a much more dangerous person, the widow to be enjoyed in the meadow—Mrs Bainbridge, coolly elegant, self-confessed admirer of his poems.

He saw that to some extent he was rationalising his fear of a relationship with a woman, the possibility that what was now finishing upstairs might soon start downstairs. And yet a worry that had often nagged him —especially after scurrying away from the verge of other relationships—was that this very desire to remain uncommitted might impair his work. Love of woman had always, traditionally, played a large part in the lives of the poets. Look at Goethe, for instance, who had to have a new love affair before he could begin a new lyric. Enderby, in so far as German culture had played any part in his development, had chosen to be influenced by a much dourer personality—Schopenhauer. Spengler, too, with his promise of the undergoing of evening lands, had had something to say to him. He had needed to invoke both philosophers before writing a poem about sex and other people. He remembered the typical evening of wartime, blackout in the garrison town, horny hands groping for giggling bodies in the dark.

> Nymphs and satyrs, come away.
>   Faunus, laughing from the hill,
> Rips the blanket of the day
>   From the paunch of dirty Will.
>
> Each projector downs its snout,
>   Truffling the blackened scene,
> Till the *Wille's* lights gush out
>   *Vorstellungen* on the screen.
>
> Doxies blanch to silverwhite;
>   All their trappings of the sport,
> Lax and scattered, in this light
>   Merge and lock to smooth and taut.
>
> See! The rockets shoot afar!
>   Ah! The screen was tautest then.
> Tragic the parabola
>   When the sticks reel down again.

That was no romantic attitude to sex. Love, Schopenhauer had seemed to say, was one of the perpetual cinema performances or *Vorstellungen* organised by the evil Will, projectionist as well as manager, and these slack bodies of gum-chewing gigglers were made into stiff shining screens for the projection of what looked like reality, value. But the deflation, the reeling to earth after coitus, was frightful, and one saw the inflated words of desire—so soon after their utterance—for what they really were. The casual images of onanism could not be hurt, could not be lied to.

Enderby went back to the living-room. Heartburn, like labour pains, had started again. There was plenty of bicarbonate solution still in the glass, so, in less than half a minute, Enderby was able to growl it away hollowly:

Grerrbrogharrrgawwwwwpfffffh.

There was an immediate response from upstairs: a shoe of admonition was banged three times. Enderby looked up to the noise meekly, as to chiding God. It was time that he left. He heard what sounded like, "Shut up, Enderby," and then the woman's voice said, "Leave him alone. He can't help it." A row of indistinguishable words then began, ending with Jack shouting, "Oh, he did, did he? And whose idea was that? False little bitch, aren't you?" The sadness, see, after coition. Enderby shook his head sadly and went back to bed. He would give a week's notice to Mrs Meldrum; he would sign no contract with Mrs Bainbridge. Mrs Meldrum could have her smiling bald bath-taking young man on an expense account; if there was no weekly poem from Enderby it was not likely that the strong-stomached readers of *Fem* would pine away.

Four

That settled it. Morning brought a letter from Vesta Bainbridge:

Dear Mr Enderby,

Well, you do seem to have been beating it up pretty tidily on your visit to London. I have only now managed to get hold of an evening paper of that memorable day which, albeit briefly, makes it reasonably clear that you went out of your way to antagonize a certain knightly patron of your art. I must confess that, in some ways, I admire your independent attitude, though God knows how any poet nowadays can afford that Byronic luxury. Sir George, I hear, is very angry and hurt. What came over you? I just don't understand, but then I'm only a very ordinary person with no great claim to intellect, and I would never be so presumptuous as to think myself capable of fathoming a poet's brain. The fact is, and I daresay you'll hear this from your own publisher fairly soon, that your name smells to heaven with Goodby's for Good Books, so watch out.

In the circumstances, I think it would be a good plan to print your weekly effusion under or over a pseudonym. This would also give us a chance to prettify the feature with a photograph of some long-haired male model with a quill in his hand and his dreamy eyes up to heaven—you know what I mean: *The Poet:* what every housewife thinks a poet ought to look like. Can you suggest a pseudonym? Do sign that contract and return it. I *did* enjoy our tea together.

Yours,
VESTA BAINBRIDGE

Enderby trembled with rage as he crushed the good quality writing-paper. His heart out-thumped the thumping that seemed to be going on upstairs, the regular morning row. He hurled the letter into the lavatory-pan and then pulled the chain, but the thing was too thick to flush down. He had to pick it out wet and then take it into the kitchen and put it in an old cardboard rubbish-box along with condensed-milk tins, fishbones, potato peelings and tea-leaves. After an hour of brooding and trying to carry on with his work, he felt a compulsion to read it again and did so, all smothered with tea-leaves as it was. Beating pretty tidily London memorable day albeit briefly independent attitude Byronic what every housewife thinks Vesta Bainbridge. He stood frowning, reading it in the tiny hallway, squinting at the words because it was dark there. There was a sudden double-beating on the door, as on a gorilla's chest, and Enderby looked up, surprised. "Come out, Enderby," cried the voice of Jack. "I want a word with you, Enderby, you bloody poet."

"For cough," snarled Enderby, with much of his stepmother's spirit and intonation.

"Come out of there, Enderby. Come and out and fight like a man. Open that door and let me bash you, you bastard."

"No," said Enderby, "I won't. If I opened that door I'd regret it. I know I would. I don't want your blood on my hands."

"Enderby," shouted Jack, "I'm giving you fair warning. Open up there and let me do you in, you fornicating poet. I'll give you sleeping with my wife, you false sod."

"It's not your wife," said Enderby. "And I slept on the couch. Somebody's been telling lies about me. Now you clear off before I get angry."

"Open that door, Enderby, please," pleaded Jack's voice. "I want to do you in, it's only right and fair as I should, you bastard, and I'm already late for work. Open up and let's get it over." And he thumped with both hands on the door. From above the woman's voice could be heard, and there was something about it to show clearly the image of a woman in nightdress and curlers. "Stop it, Jack," she cried. "You're only making a fool of yourself."

"Fool of myself, eh? We'll soon see. Now you shut up. You've had your turn and now it's going to be Enderby's turn." He renewed the thundering. Enderby went to the kitchen and came back with his hare-eviscerating knife. "Open up, Enderby. Time's getting on, you bastard," Enderby opened up.

Jack was a youngish tough man with lined cheeks and eyes the colour of urine. If hairs be wires, black wires grew in his head. He had both fists ready, with the thumbs pitiably tucked inside. Enderby had been punched in London; he was not going to be punched here. He raised his knife. "For cough," he said.

"That's playing unfair," said Jack. "I meant clean bashing. That's not right when you get on to that stabbing lark. All I'm saying is, you leave her upstairs alone, see, and one bloody good bash in the chops and call it a day. You've no call to go fornicating with what's mine, as you ought to be first to admit. Now put that knife down like a man and take what's coming to you."

"For cough," said Enderby, in a murderer's stance. "I hadn't got my key, that was all, and she let me sleep on the sofa. If you don't believe that you'll never believe anything."

"I'll believe what I want to believe," said Jack with great candour. "I'm coming back to see you again. Don't think you've got away with this, because you haven't, Enderby, poet, or no poet. I tell you that straight. I'm off to work now and late too, which is your fault and makes things worse." With a sudden brisk jerk and stylish follow-through he wrested the knife from the grasp of Enderby. "There," he said proudly. "Now you've had it." Enderby swiftly slammed the door. "I'll be back, Enderby," called Jack. "Make no mistake about it. You'll be done, no two ways about that, as you'll see." He kicked

Enderby's door and then thumped out of the house, crashing the great outer portal shut.

Enderby locked himself in the lavatory, trembling. *Canaille, canaglia,* with their bloody sex and blasted jealousy. Well, the time had come; all things pointed to it: out, out, out. Where to now? He sat on the seat and began to scribble: (a) Draw cash from bank; (b) Get map of south coast; (c) Send cheque and week's notice Mrs M.; (d) Write to Mrs B.; (e) see Arry. With this need to plan and the thought of the nightmare of packing still to come, he grew flustered. He tried to calm himself by writing a final consummatory poem for Arry, the end of the whole cycle. It reeked with hot hands, white flesh, hoarse desire, love, love, love. It had a certain cathartic effect on Enderby, like loud blasphemous obscenities.

> ... And in that last delirium of lust
> Your image glows. Love is a blinding rain,
> Love crow all the cocks, love lays the dust
> Of this cracked crying throat whose thirst is pain. ....

He wrote out a cheque for Mrs Meldrum, composed the curtest of farewells: "Thank you for your unwanted solicitude. Take a week's notice. Your etc." To Mrs Bainbridge he wrote a courteous acknowledgment of her communications and regetted that, on maturer consideration, he found himself unable to find it in himself to meet the meagre poetic needs, if even these existed, of the readers of *Fem.* His compliments to Miss or Mrs Frobisher, if Mrs Bainbridge would be good enough to pass them on, and congratulations on possessing so tough-stomached a gang of followers of her culinary columns. He, Enderby, had, if it was of any interest to anyone, suffered greatly from her Spaghetti Fromaggio Surprise. He proposed to destroy the contract and distribute the copies of *Fem* to the poor. He was hers sincerely. P.S. He was moving from the above address forthwith, whither he knew not yet. No point in her replying. Calmer now, Enderby shaved and prepared to

91

go out. He would be safe so long as that shouter Jack was still at work.

Five

Arry, in grubby cook's white, complete with white necktie and white mushroom hat, stood at the bar of the Freemason's Arms, taking time off from his kitchens. He greeted Enderby with no enthusiasm but, without asking or being asked, ordered a double whisky for him. "That suit," he said, "were a right bloody mess. Ad to send it tert cleaner's." He drank off a good three-quarters of a pint of brown ale mixed with bitter.

"I'm sorry," said Enderby. "It won't happen again. I shan't have to borrow from you again. I'm leaving."

"Leavin'? Goin'? Not coomin' back 'ere naw mawr?"

"That's right."

Arry looked solemn, but that stiff crust of his expression seemed to be hiding a tiny feeling of relief; a whiff of relief escaped, as through a steam-hole in the crust. He said:

"Where to?"

"I don't know," said Enderby. "Somewhere else along the coast. It doesn't matter where, really."

"Thee get as far aweeeeeh," advised Arry, prolonging his vowels, as in some primitive language, "far aweeeeeh," to emphasise the distance, "far aweeeeeh," by onomatopoeic suggestion, "as tha can bloody get. That's naht 'ere, naht for nobody. Coom back 'ere," he said, "never naw mawr." He looked with gloom at the lesbians in the corner—Gladys in glasses and leopard-skin pants sly-cuddling cross-eyed Prudence—and then with compasson at Enderby.

"This is to say good-bye, really," said Enderby, "and to hope that your suit prospers."

"It'll be aw right when it cooms back fromt cleaner's."

"I meant the other suit," said Enderby, "the Arry to Thelma suit. I've brought one more poem for you, the very last of the cycle. If this doesn't do the job, nothing will." He took the folded sheet from his pocket.

Arry shook his head. "Naht doin'," he said, "naht doin' at all. It were a bloody wester mah tahm."

"My time, too," said Enderby.

"Wan' and int till," said Arry, "and toother betwinner legs. No good to man nor flamin' beast that Thelma. Oo's tecken no notice er naht av doon forrer."

"Well," sighed Enderby, "that's how it is. Nobody wants poetry nowadays. All wasted." He prepared to rip up his final fiery offering.

"Weren't wested," said Arry. "Ot stooff, wan or two were. *Ah* lakhed 'em. Boot oo," he said, "didn't 'ave bloody intelligence." He put out a clean cook's hand to rescue Enderby's poem. He took the folded sheet and unfolded it with wan interest. He pretended to read it, then put it into his trouser-pocket. Enderby bought him a pint of brown ale and bitter. Enderby said:

"Since I've lived here you're the only one I've been in any way friendly with. That's why I wanted to shake hands with you before I go."

"All sheck 'ands wi' thee," said Arry, and did so. "When will yer be clearin' off?"

"I've got to pack," said Enderby. "And then I've got to decide where I'm going to. Tomorrow, I should think. While Jack's out at work."

"Oo's Jack?"

"Oh, yes, sorry. The chap who lives upstairs. He thinks I've been carrying on with the woman he lives with."

"Ah," said Arry, shaking his head, then looking at Enderby with renewed compassion. "Get away as soon as yer can," said Array. "Shoove yer things in a bag and then get to Victoria Station. On Victoria Station there's nameser places stoock oop on indiketters. Teck thy choice, lad. There's plenty on 'em. You choose wanner them and go straight to it. All places is the same nowadays," he said. "The big thing to do is to kip movin'. And," he asked, "what will yer do when yeu've getten wherever yer goin'? Wilt kip on wi' same game?"

"It's all I can do," said Enderby. "Writing verse is all I'm cut out for."

Arry nodded and finished his pint, the fourth since Enderby's entrance. "Dawn't write too mooch abaht spaghetti, then," he said, frothily. "Leave spaghetti to them as knaws summat abaht it." He shook hands with Enderby once more. "Moost get back now," he said, "tert bloody job. Special loonch for Daughters Of Temperance." He spaced out the words like a poster. "Luke after yerself," said Arry. He waved a white cook's arm from the door and then went out. Spaghetti coiled, puzzled, in Enderby's brain. Then a horrid thought struck him. He finished his whisky palpitating but then calmed down. He might have sent it to Mrs Meldrum. But no, he distinctly remembered pinning a cheque to a quarter-sheet of writing-paper. But that made no difference, did it? That might still have got into the wrong envelope. He'd better get out of here very very quickly.

As he panted towards his packing down the esplanade, the gulls wheeled and wailed and climbed the blue wall of the marine winter day. For two days now he had forgotten to feed them. They planed, complained. Greedy beady eyes. Ungrateful birds. They mewed no farewell to Enderby; they would be there, waiting for his doles of bread, further up or down the coastline.

5

One

Of what the world would call essentials, Enderby
had few to pack. It was the bathful of verse that was
the trouble. Kneeling in front of it, as though—and
here he laughed sardonically—he worshipped his own
work, he began to bundle it into the larger of his two
suitcases, separating—with reasonable care—manuscripts
from sandwich-crusts, cigarette-packets, and the cylinders
of long-used toilet-rolls. But he found so many old poems
which he had quite forgotten that he could not resist
reading them through, open-mouthed, as afternoon
ticked on towards dusk. He had modified drastically his
original plan of departure, his aim now being to catch
some evening train (Jack permitting) to Victoria, spend
the night in a hotel, and then, about midday, follow
some new spoke to the south coast. He had, he felt, to
live near the sea, this being a great wet slobbering
stepmother or green dogmatic Church which he could
keep his eye on; nothing, at least, insidious about it.

It was amazing what things he had written, especially
in his youth: pastiches of Whitman, Charles Doughty, an
attempted translation of the *Duino Elegies*, limericks,

even the beginning of a verse-play about Copernicus. There was one sonnet in sprung rhythm and Alexandrines which dated from the days of his love and envy of the proletariat. He read the sestet with horror and wonder:

> When the violet air blooms about him, then at last
>   he can wipe
>   His hands sheerfree of swink, monarch of hours
>   ahead;
> Hearty he eats and, full, he sits to pull at his pipe,
>   Warm at the kitchen glow. The courts- and sports-
>   news read,
> He argues, sups, in the Lion vault; to a plate of tripe
>   Or crisp chips home returns, then climbs to a
>   dreamless bed.

Dead on this homecoming cue Jack came home, his hands sheerfree of salesman's swink, ready for Enderby. Enderby was aroused from the past by the gorilla two-fist beat on the door.

"Come on, Enderby, out of it. On the job, Enderby. Come and be bashed, you poetic bloody nuisance."

"Have you got my knife?" asked Enderby, standing now behind his punished door.

"Your knife, eh? That's been put in a refuse-bin, you dirty mess as you are, you. There's going to be clean bashing only, you nasty deceitful thing. I'm giving you fair warning, Enderby. If you don't open up I'm going to get old Ma Meldrum's key. I'll say that you lost yours, lying like you lied, you nasty liar. Then I'll come in and do you. So open up like a sportsman and play the game and be bashed, you bugger, you."

Enderby shivered with rage and immediately began to roam the flat, trembling, looking for some weapon. Meanwhile Jack, who should, by rights, have been fatigued by his work, hammered at the door and execrated nastily. In the bathroom Enderby cast around and his eyes momentarily softened as they lighted on his old friend, the lavatory-seat. It had always been somewhat loose; it was not difficult to wrench it from the pin that had held it to the pedestal. "Coming," called Enderby. "Shan't be a minute." He apologised to the wooden O as he pulled it roughly away, promising that soon he would write it a small ode of reparation. Armed with it he went to the door, pulled the door open and saw Jack's cunny-thumbed fists ready for a fierce double-bang at the empty air.

"That's not fair," he said, backing. "You're not playing the game, Enderby. All I ask is a fair apology for ill-treating me as regards my own property." ("Is that you back, Jack?" came the voice from above. "Don't hurt him too hard, love.")

"There's nothing to apologise for," said Enderby. "If you don't believe what I told you you must take the consequences of your disbelief. I'm going to clonk you on the head with this seat here."

"Not that," said Jack, trying, on dancing feet, to get in odd punches. "That's comic, that is, that's not decent. That's making a farce out of the whole thing." Enderby parried the weak blows, slamming Jack's wrists hard with his wooden weapon. He drove him down the hall-way towards the front door of the house, past the two spotted pictures on the wall, both of Highland scenery in wretched weather. Enderby raised the seat high, intended to hit Jack's wiry head with its hard border. He misjudged somewhat, and the seat came down to encircle Jack's face, so that Jack was framed like a most animated portrait in a bottom-shaped ring. His hands clawed at it, forgetting to chop at Enderby's own, which tugged down and down, Enderby's obscure aim being to pull Jack to the floor and then stamp on him. "You bastard, you," cried Jack. "This isn't funny, this isn't, you sod." He tried to lift off the wooden lei of bottom-polished smoothness, but Enderby's weight pulled down and down. "All I ask," panted Jack, "is an apology for what you done, did. Give me that and I'll let you go." Enderby swung round, still clinging to Jack's round pillory, and saw Jack's woman at the foot of the stairs. She was dressed like Hamlet in black tights, a black sweater above, inside which her bubs danced still from her descent.

"You," sobbed Enderby, at his last gasp with all this effort, "started all this. Tell him the truth."

"He bashed me," she said, "and I did nothing wrong. Now it's only right that you get bashed."

"Tell him the truth," cried Enderby's dying voice.

"That won't make no difference to Jack," she said. "You've got to get done by Jack. Jack's like that, you see."

"I want him to apologise," cried Jack, still framed.

"There's nothing to apologise for," gurgled Enderby's fading ration of air.

"Apologise for what you're doing now, then."

"I'll stop it," said Enderby. He let go of the wooden seat, and Jack, now pulling at nothing, went hurtling back to the hallstand, crashing into it and sending it over, still horse-collared. The little inlaid mirror tinkled; from the glove-drawer, suddenly opened, there issued letters, unforwarded, for people long shadily departed, and also highly coloured coupons representing, each, a fivepence rebate off a packet of soap-powder.

"Call it," Enderby, bent double as though air were something to be sucked up from the floor, tried to say, "Call it," seeing Jack on the floor with lavatory collar still on lying beside, as a wooden mate, the crashed hallstand, "a day."

"You come upstairs, love," said the woman to Jack. "You'll be tired after your hard day's work. I'll make you a nice cuppa."

Jack got up, removed the collar and, panting still, handed it to Enderby. "You got what was coming to you," he said. "I'm not one of those vindictive buggers, Enderby. Fair's fair's what I stand or fall by." He dusted himself down with the hallstand brush, still in his overcoat which was of a dull plum colour. "Don't do it again, that's all I'm going to say now, and let it be a warning." The woman, soothing, put her arms about him and began to lead him upstairs. Enderby, exhausted, entered his own flat, holding the lavatory-seat like a victor's wreath. It was a long long time since he'd exerted himself so much. He lay down for at least an hour on the floor of the living-room, seeing how dirty the carpet was.

Under the couch were walnuts and bits of paper. He lay until the town-hall clock struck, from afar, over the chill evening air of late January, the hour of seven. There was now no hope of leaving tonight.

When he felt better he got up from the floor and went into the kitchen to examine his store-cupboard. There was little point in, and little room for, taking these half-empty jars and bits of lard in paper, potatoes, cut spaghetti-sticks, mustard. He took down Mrs Meldrum's largest saucepan and prepared a stew of meat-paste, Oxo cubes, spaghetti, olive oil, spuds in jackets with dirt and all, pickled onions, cheese-heels, breadcrusts, dripping, half a meat pie, Branston sweet pickle, margarine, celery salt, water. At the back of the fast-emptying cupboard he found a neglected chicken carcass, a gift from Arry, which would go well. He left the stew to bubble, thrifty Enderby, and went back to the sorting and packing of his papers.

Two

Enderby, fagged out by fighting, packing, and the thin and oversavoury stew he had cooked, slept later the following morning than he had intended. The work of packing and clearing-up was not yet finished. Both suitcases were crammed, but there were still many manuscripts to bundle together and put safe somewhere. Enderby, yawning, creased, and with hair in sleepy spikes, made tea with the remaining half-packet of Typhoo and coffee with the last few spoons of Blue Mountain. Taking in the milk he left a note of farewell for the milkman, several empty bottles, and a cash cheque for five shillings and fourpence. He then drank one cup of tea and emptied the rest down the lavatory, feeling the sense of virtue he always felt when he knew he had used what another man might well have wasted. Then he heated up last night's stew and felt further virtue when the gas failed half way through the process. No waste there either. He switched on all the electric fires in the flat, ate breakfast, drank coffee, smoked.

Then, in shirt and underpants (last night's nightwear, his pyjamas having been packed) he emptied the rubbish out of its cardboard box into a small dustbin outside the backdoor. (Sunny, piercingly cold, gulls high-screaming.) He cleaned out this box with a copy of *Fem*, finding difficulty in dislodging corner-hugging mush of decayed peel and odd tea-leaf hieroglyphics, then lined it with two or three copies of the same magazine, collected handfuls of poems from the bath and packed them in tightly, covered with further *Fems*, then tied the box about with a discarded pair of braces and a long knotty link he made out of odd pieces of string that were lying around. He washed all dishes in (necessarily) cold water and packed them on their shelves. Then he had a cold and excruciating shave, washed quickly, and dressed in his daily working garb with corduroy trousers and a tie. The time was eleven-thirty. He could, he thought, soon now be off. The keys, of course. He went out into the hallway of the house, found that someone, probably Jack, had righted the crashed hallstand, and then he put the keys in the glove-compartment. On a letter addressed to a long-left Mrs Arthur Porceroy (postmark 8.VI.51) he wrote, in inkpencil, KEYS ENDERBY, and leaned this notice upright on the hallstand. While he was doing this the front door opened. A man looked in. He seemed to play an elaborate game of looking for someone everywhere except where someone was, his sad eyes roaming the entire hallway and then appearing at last to find Enderby. He nodded and smiled bleakly, as in modest self-congratulation on his success, and then said, "Would I be addressing one of the name of Enderby?" Enderby bowed. "Could I have the pleasure of a word with you?" the man asked. "A question of poetry," he added. He had a thin Uriah Heep voice. He was of less than medium height, had a long face and a fluff of whitish hair, wore a raincoat, was about Enderby's age.

"Who are you from?" asked Enderby sharply.

"From?" repeated the man. "From nobody except me. Me being of the name of Walpole. And coming to see you on a question of poetry. It's cold here in the hall," he said. Enderby led the way into the flat.

Walpole sniffed the warm dry air, the lingering sour stew-smell, the raised dust, and then noticed Enderby's packed bags. "Leaving, eh?" he said. "Well, I only just got you in time, didn't I?"

"I've got to catch a train," said Enderby, "any minute now. Would you—?"

"Oh, I'll be quick," said Walpole, "very quick. What I want to say is that I won't have you writing poetry to my wife."

Enderby saw rush and then fade a quite unreasonable possibility. Then he smiled and said, "I don't write poetry to anybody's wife."

Walpole drew from his raincoat pocket a carefully folded and smoothed sheaf of sheets. "This poetry," he said. "Look at it carefully and then tell me whether or not you wrote it."

Enderby looked at it quickly. His handwriting. The Thelma poems. "I wrote these, yes," he said, "but not on my own behalf. I wrote them at the request of another man. I suppose you could call him a client, really. You see, poetry is my profession."

"If it's a profession," said Walpole in all seriousness, "does it have what you might call rules of professional etty kwett? More important than that in a way of speaking, does it have a union?"

Enderby suddenly saw that he had been made a party to a proposed bed-breach. He said that he saw, ignoring Walpole's questions, saying, "I see, I see. I'm really very sorry about all this. I knew nothing about it. I'm even more innocent than Arry. It just never crossed my mind—and I take it that it never crossed Arry's—that Thelma was a married woman."

"Mrs Walpole," said Walpole tautologically, "is my wife. Thelma may or may not be her name, all according to whether she is on duty or not. At the moment she is not on duty. And this question of *Harry*"—he stressed the aitch pedantically—"is a question that brings you in as a hypocrite and a liar, if you don't mind me saying so." Walpole held up his hand as if taking the oath. "I make use of those terms," he said, "out of reference to the conventionalities you yourself, as a boor Joyce, probably

101

uphold. To me, in one manner of speaking, they have no proper revelance, being relics of boor Joyce morality."

"I," said Enderby warmly, "object very strongly to being called a hypocrite and a liar, especially in my own house."

"Clear your mind of cant," said Walpole, whose reading was evidently wide. He straddled comfortably, raincoat-tails spread, in front of the electric fire. "You are just leaving this place which is not a house and not, I presume, your property, and, moreover, what difference should it make to the effect of certain words on the individual brain whether those words are spoke in a church or in a lavatory, if you'll pardon the term, or, as it might be, here?" He made the knees-bend gesture of freeing a trouser-seat stuck in a rump-cleft.

The mention of church and lavatory went straight to Enderby's heart, also the invocation of logic. "All right, then," he said. "In what way am I a hypocrite and a liar?"

"A fair question," admitted Walpole. "You are a hypocrite and a liar"—he pointed a *j'accuse* finger with forensic suddenness—"because you hid your own desires under another man's cloak. Ah, yes. I have spoke to this man Harry. He admits to having sent up to Mrs Walpole plates of stewed tripe and, on one occasion, eels—both dishes to which she is not partial—but it was clear that that was in the way of colleagual friendliness, them both working in the same establishment. Both are workers, even though the place of their work is boor Joyce. Can you say the same for yourself?"

"Yes," said Enderby, "no."

"Well, then," continued Walpole, "I have it on the word of Harry, who is a worker, that he had no adulterating intention in mind. To him it came as a shock, and I was there and I saw the shock as it came, that another man should be sending poetry to a married woman and signing it with another man's name, the name of a man who, still living in a capitalist society, is not in the same position to hit back as what *you* are." Again the accusatory finger darted out like a chameleon's tongue.

"Why," said stunned Enderby, aghast at such treachery on Arry's part, "should not *he* be the liar and hypocrite? Why should you not believe me? Damn it all, I've only seen this woman once, and that was only to order a single whisky."

"Single or double makes no difference," said Walpole sagely. "And there have been occasions when men, especially poets, have only seen a woman once (and I will thank you not to use that term in connection with Mrs Walpole) or even not at all, and yet they have written reams and reams of poetry to her. There was the Italian poet who you may have heard of who wrote about Hell, and there again it was a married woman. He wrote about Hell, Mr Enderby, and not what you wrote in those shameful verses you have there and I would trouble you to hand back. There you have wrote about buttocks and breasts, which is not decent. I spent some time reading those poems, putting aside my other reading work to do so." Enderby now detected, surfacing from the thin starved East Midland accent, the stronger tones of Anglo-Welsh. "Indecencies," said Walpole, "that any man using to a married woman should be heartily ashamed of and should fear a judgment for."

"This is absurd," said Enderby. "This is bloody nonsense. I wrote those poems at Arry's request. I wrote them in exchange for the loan of a suit and a few gifts of chicken and turkey carcasses. Does that not sound reasonable?"

"No," said Walpole reasonably. "It does not. You wrote these poems. You wrote of breasts and buttocks and even navels in connection with Mrs Walpole and nobody else. And there the sin lies."

"But damn it," said angry Enderby, "she's got them, hasn't she? She's the same as any other woman in that respect, isn't she?"

"I do not know," said Walpole, stilling Enderby's rage with a choir-conductor's hand. "I'm no womaniser. I have had to work. I have had no time for the fripperies and dalliances of poetry. I have had to work. I have had no time for the flippancies and insincerities of women. I have had to work, night after night, after the labours of the day, reading and studying Marx and Lenin and the other writers who would lead me to a position to help my fellow-workers. Can you say as much? Where has your poetry led you? To this." He swept a hand round Enderby's dusty living-room. "Where have my studies led me?" He did not answer his own question; Enderby waited, but the question was definitely established as rhetorical.

"Look," said Enderby, "I've got to catch a train. I'm sorry that this has happened, but you can see it was all a misunderstanding. And you must take my assurance that I've had nothing to do socially with Mrs Walpole and very little more professionally. By "professionally"; added Enderby carefully, spying a possible misinterpretation, "I mean of course, in connection with her profession as a barmaid."

"That," said Walpole, shaking his head, "is not salaried. It is not a profession. Well," he said, "the question of punishment arises. I think, to some extent, that should be a matter to let rest between you and your Maker."

"Yes, yes," said Enderby, too eagerly, with too much relief, "I agree."

"You agree, do you?" said Walpole. "A more intelligent and more well-read man and who follows political theories would there be tempted to ask a certain simple question. What would that certain simple question be, Comrade Enderby?"

The chill honorific, with its suggestion of brainwashing and salt-mines, made Enderby's bowels react strongly: they seemed to liquefy; at the same time a solid blast prepared itself for utterance. Nevertheless he said bravely, "People who accept dialectical materialism don't usually accept the proposition of a divine first cause."

"And very well put, too," said Walpole, "though a bit old-fashioned in its circumloquaciousness. God is what you mean, Comrade Enderby, God, God, God." He raised his eyes to the ceiling, his mouth opening and shutting on the divine name as though he were eating it. "God, God, God," said Walpole. As in response to a summons there was a knock on the flat-door. "Ignore it," said Walpole sharply. "Here we have important things on hand and not the fripperies of visitors. I have done it," he said more softly, his eyes shining with bright dementedness. "I have discovered the sin thesis." The knock came again. "Ignore it," said Walpole. "Now then, Comrade Enderby, you should now by rights ask the question 'What sin thesis?' Go on," he said, with clenched fierceness, "*ask it.*"

"Why aren't you at work?" asked Enderby. Again the knock.

"Because," said Walpole, "today is Saturday. Five days shalt thou labour, as the Bible says. The seventh day is the Lord thy God's. The sixth day is for football and spreading the word and punishing and suchlike. Go on. *Ask it.*"

"What sin thesis?" asked Enderby.

"A sin thesis of *everything*," said Walpole. "The others left God out, but I put him in. I found a place for Him in the universe."

"What place?" asked Enderby, fascinated despite his bowels, his fear, the knock at the door.

"What place could it be," said Walpole, "except *His own place?* God's place is God's place, and you can't say fairer than that. Now," he said, "on your knees, Comrade Enderby. We're going to pray together to this same God, and you're going to ask for forgiveness for all sins of fornication." The knock came again, louder. "QUIET!" bawled Walpole.

"I won't pray," said Enderby. "I've committed no fornication."

"Who hasn't," said Walpole, "in his heart?" And, like Enderby's boyhood picture of the Saviour, he pointed to his own. "On your knees," he said, "and I shall pray with you."

"No," said Enderby. "I don't accept the same God as you. I'm a Catholic."

"All the more reason," said Walpole. "THERE IS ONLY ONE GOD, COMRADE!" he suddenly bawled. "On your knees and pray and you will be let off by me, if not by the Comrade Almighty. If you don't pray I shall be the Hound of Heaven and get some of the lads from the works on the job, and bloody quick, too, even if

105

you do think you're going off this morning. ON YOUR KNEES!" he ordered.

Enderby sighed and obeyed. His knees were stiff. Walpole knelt with the stage-fall ease of more practice. He didn't close his eyes; he kept them full on Enderby. Enderby faced the electric fire's tabernacular gold. Walpole prayed:

"Comrade God, forgive the boor Joyce transgressions of Comrade Enderby here, who has been led astray by the lusts of his own body into writing phonographic poetry to Mrs Walpole, who You know, though she is stiff-necked and not one of Thy chosen. Let Your light shine upon him to make him a decent worker and good member of his union, when, him being a poet, such shall be formed. Better still, make him stop writing filthy poetry altogether and take up some decent trade at correct union rates and live in Godly righteousness, if that be Thy holy will, with some decent woman of Thy choosing in the state of holy matrimony, till such time as this boor Joyce institution is replaced by something better and more in keeping with what the proletariat will require." Enderby now saw Walpole smile winningly at some apparition to his left, behind Enderby, at about picture-rail level. Enderby, presuming that this was God, felt no new fear. "Just a tick," said Walpole. "Marvellous what prayer can do, innit? A bloody miracle, that's what it is. To finish up with, then," he prayed, eyes now back on Enderby, "stop this Thy comrade servant womanising and messing about and bring him back to Your holy ways in the service of the classless society which Thou has promisedest in the fullness of the workers' time. Thank you, Comrade God," he said finally. "Amen."

Enderby, with much groaning and a posterior blast or two, got creaking to his feet. At that moment the electric fire, like some Zoroastrian deity now, having been prayed at, done with, went out. Enderby, standing, turned, blowing, and saw Mrs Bainbridge. She dangled Enderby's key in explanation of her entrance without Enderby's more direct agency, saying, "Well, I never in all my life knew a man more capable of surprises." She was a dream of winter bourgeois elegance: little black town suit with tiny white jabot of lace-froth; pencil skirt; three-quarter-length coat with lynx collar; long green gloves of suède; suède shoes of dull green; two shades of green in her leafy velvet hat, slim, clean, lithe-looking, delicately painted. Walpole, Marx-man of God, was clearly entranced. He handed her a small yellow throwaway poster and then, as a second thought, gave one to Enderby as well. "GOD OR CAPITALISM?" it read. "You Can't Have Both. H. Walpole will speak on this VITAL topic at the Lord Geldon Memorial Hall, Thursday, February 11th. All Welcome."

"You come to that, lady," said Walpole, "and bring him along. There's good in him if only we can get at it, as you yourself will know well enough. Work on him hard, make him a decent man and stop him sending poetry to women, that's your job, I would say, and you look to me capable of tackling it."

"Poetry to women?" said Vesta Bainbridge. "He makes a habit of that, does he?" She gave Enderby a hard-soft green womanly look, holding her large shovel handbag in front of her, legs, as in a model pose, slightly astride.

H. Walpole was, for all his theophanic socialism, a decent man of bourgeois virtues, who, now that Enderby had been thoroughly prayed for, did not want to put him in the bad with this fiancée of his here. "That's only in a manner of speaking, as you might say," he said. "A very sexual man, you might say Mr Enderby is, with strong desires as must be kept down, and," he said, "you look to me like the one capable of doing it."

"Thank you very much," said Vesta Bainbridge.

"Look here," said Enderby. The other two waited, listening. Enderby had really nothing to say. Walpole said:

"Right. In his poetry if not in his private life, if you see what I mean. That's where you'd come in, comrade madam, and would give him a bigger sense of reality. May the blessings of the God of all the workers bless your union till such times as society makes something better come abuut."

"Thank you very much," said Vesta Bainbridge.

"And now," said Walpole cheerfully, "I take my leave. I've enjoyed our little dialectical conversation together and hope to have many more. Don't show me out, I know the way. God keep you in His care," he said to Enderby. "You have nothing to lose but your chains." He blessed Enderby and his putative betrothed with a clenched fist, smiled once more, then went out. Enderby and his putative betrothed were left together, listening to Walpole's marching footsteps and cheerful whistle recede.

"This," said Enderby, "is where I live."

"So I see. But if you live here why are you moving?"

"I don't quite get that," said Enderby. "Would you say that again?"

"I don't quite get *you*," said Vesta Bainbridge. "You send me what I suppose you'd call a verse-letter, straining at the leash with quite unequivocal suggestions, then you take fright and decide to run away. Or is it as simple as that? Obviously you thought I wouldn't get the letter till Monday morning, so it seems as though you planned to attack and retire at the same time. Actually, I always go into the office on Saturday mornings to see if there's any mail, and there I found the letter-rack practically sizzling with your little effort. I got a train right away. I was puzzled, intrigued. Also worried."

"Worried?"

"Yes. About you." She sniffed round the living-room with a wrinkle of distaste. "I can see one would have cause to be worried. This place is absolutely filthy. Does nobody come in to clean it?"

"I do it myself," said Enderby, suddenly and shamefully seeing the squalor of his life more clearly against the foil of her frightful wholesomeness. "More or less." He hung his schoolboy head.

"*Exactly*. And what, Harry, if I may call you that— indeed, I *must* call you that now, mustn't I?—were you proposing to do? Where were you proposing to go?"

"Harry's not my name," said Not-Harry Enderby. "It's just the name at the end of the poem."

"I know, of course, it can't really be your name, because your initials don't have an aitch in them. Still, you

108

signed yourself Harry and Harry seems to suit you." She surveyed him with a cocked parrot head, as though Harry were a hat. "I repeat, *Harry*, what are you going to do?"

"I don't know," said pseudoharry wretched Enderby. "That was all to be thought out, you see. Where to go and whatnot. What to do and so on and so forth."

"Well," said Vesta Bainbridge, "a few days ago I gave you a tea and you offered me a dinner which I couldn't accept. I think it would be a good idea if you took me out to lunch somewhere now. And after that—"

"There's one place I shan't take you," said Enderby, betrayed and angry. "That's quite certain. It would poison me. It would choke me. Every mouthful."

"Very well," soothed Vesta Bainbridge. "You shall take me wherever you choose. And after that I'm taking you home."

"Home?" said Enderby with sudden fear.

"Yes, home. Home, home, home. You know, the place where the heart is. The place that there's no place like. You need looking after. I'm taking you home, Harry."

II

1

One

Errrrrrrrp.

Enderby was in a very small lavatory, being sick. He was also married, just. Enderby the married man. A vomiting bridegroom.

When his forehead was cooler he sat, sighing, on the little seat. All below him was June weather, June being the month for weddings. Alone in this buzzing and humming tiny lavatory he had his first leisure to feel both gratified and frightened. The bride, though only in a severe suit suitable for a registry office, had looked lovely. Sir George had said so. Sir George was friendly again. All was forgiven.

Almost the first thing she had insisted on was an apology to Sir George. Enderby had written: "So sorry I should seem to rate your sirship as a stupid dolt, but thought you would appreciate that feeble gesture of revolt. For you yourself have tried, God wot, the awful agonising art, and though, as poet, you are not worth the least poetaster's fart, yet you're equipped to understand what clockwork makes the poet tick and how he hates the laden hand below the empty rhetoric. . . ." That, she had said, was not really suitable, so he had tried something briefer in genuine prose, and Sir George had only been too delighted to accept the formal creaking apology.

Oh, she had begun to reorganise his life, that one. From the start, taking breakfast together in the large dining-room of her large flat, February Gloucester Road sulking outside, it was clear that things could only go one way. For what other relationship could be viable in the world's eyes than this one they were beginning now? Enderby had been forced to reject that of landlady and tenant, for he had paid no rent. The step-relationship was, with women, practically the only other one he had experienced. She was, he knew, and for this he valued her, antipodeal to a stepmother, being clean and beautiful. His father's remarriage had introduced brief squibs of step-aunts-in-law and the fable of a paragon stepsister, too good for this world and hence soon dead of a botulism, whom Enderby had always visualised as a puppet doll-dangling parody of his stepmother. Vesta was not, he had felt, a stepsister. A Female Friend? He had rung that on his palate several times, upper case and all, and savoured a melancholy twilit aquarelle of Shelley and Byron, with chorusmen's calves as if limned by Blake, holding reading-parties in a moored boat with high-waisted rather silly ladies, lovers of Gothic romances, while midges played fiddles in the sad air. Epipsychidion. Epithalamion. Ah God, that word had really started things off, for it had started off a poem.

The cry in the clouds, the throng of migratory birds,
The alien planet's heaven where seven moons
Are jasper, agate, carbuncle, onyx, amethyst and
    blood-ruby and bloodstone.
Or else binary suns
Wrestle like lions to a flame that we can stand,
Bound, twisted and conjoined
To an invertebrate love where selves are melted
To the primal juice of a creator's joy,
Before matter was made,
Two spheres in a single orbit. ...

They had drunk Orange Pekoe with breakfast and she, in a rust-coloured suit with a heavy clip of hammered pewter on the left lapel, had just gone off to work. Enderby, in the kitchenette whose pastel beauty made him feel particularly dirty and gross, had put on the kettle for stepmother's tea, and the word "epithalamion," like the announcement of a train's approach, had set the floorboards trembling with thunder. Panting at the dining-table, he had set down words, seeing his emergent poem as a song for the celebration of the consummation of the passion of the mature—Gertrude and Claudius in *Hamlet*, red bearded lips on a widow's white neck. The leafy tea had cooled beside him. Mrs Opisso the daily woman had come in, dusky, hippy, bosomy, garlicky, moustached, leering brilliantly, a wartime Gibraltarian evacuee in whose blood seethed Genoese, Portuguese Jewish, Saracen, Irish and Andalusian corpuscles, to say, interrupting sweeping, "What are you in this house, eh? You not going out, not doing work, true? What are you to her, eh? You tell." It had not been easy to tell; it was not enough to say that it was none of her business.

> .... Swollen with cream or honey,
> The convalescent evening launches its rockets,
> Soaring above the rich man's gala day,
> In the thousand parks of the kingdom
> Which radiate from this bed. ....

Vesta would not necessarily think that this epithalamion was intended for her and her guest-Male Friend-protégé, for she had already said sardonically, "If you intend to write any love poetry this morning make sure you don't send it to Sir George by mistake. This carelessness of yours will land you into big trouble one of these days, you mark my words." Enderby had hung his head. She had been irritable that morning, tired, rubbing her brow tiredly, as in a TV commercial for some quack analgesic, under her green eyes delicate blue arcs of tiredness. She had stood by the door, in neat rust, a chiffon scarf in two tones of green, a minute brown beret

115

aslant, brown suède gloves to match her shoes, slender, elegant and (so Enderby had divined) menstruating quietly. Enderby had said:

"Menstruation hits some women more than others, you know. Try gin and hot water. That's said to work wonders."

She had blushed faintly and said, "Where did you learn that?"

"In *Fem.*"

Sighing, she had said, "It's all very confusing. I must work out, when I have time, the precise nature of our relationship."

> Anoint the ship with wine! On ample waters,
>   Which always wear this ring, that the earth be
>   humbled
> Only away from cities, let it dance and ride. . . .

And again, another time, the precise nature still not worked out, "The question is, what's to be done with you?"

"Done with me?"

"Yes, that's the question."

"Nothing is to be done with me." He had looked across at her in fear, over the shattered fragments of toast which he had been feeding, as to a pet bird, to his mouth. "I am, after all, a poet." A lorry had backfired the world's answer.

"I want to know," Vesta had said, chill morning hands round her breakfast-cup, "exactly how much money you've got."

"Why do you want to know that?" cunning Enderby had asked.

"Oh, please. I've got a busy day ahead of me. Let's not have any nonsense. Please." Enderby had begun to tell out the contents of his left trouser-pocket. "Not that sort of money," she had cut in, sharply. Enderby had said, with care:

"Ten thousand pounds in local government loans at five and a half per cent. For dividends. Two thousand pounds in I.C.I., B.M.C., Butlin's. For capital appreciation."

"Ah. And what income does all that yield?"

"About six hundred. Not a lot, really, is it?"

"It's nothing. And I suppose your poetry brings in less than nothing."

"Two guineas a week. From *Fem*, God bless it." For he had at last signed the contract and already seen in print, over the name of Faith Fortitude, hogwash beginning, "A baby's cheeks, a baby's limbs are prayers to God and holy hymns; a little baby's toothless smile does the holy saints beguile. . . ."

"An income like yours isn't worth having, really it isn't. So we've got to work out what's to be done with you."

"Done with me?" prompt Enderby had flashed.

"Look," she had said, "I know you're a poet. But there's no need to regale us with poetic drama in the style of early Mr Eliot, is there? Not at breakfast there isn't."

"Stichomythia," had been learned Enderby's comment. "But it's you who keep starting it off."

Well, that was something not yet started off: useful employment, a *deuxième métier* for a poet. From Valentine to Pentecost he had been allowed, though not in the lavatory, to work at *The Pet Beast* peaceably. But after the honeymoon things would have to be different.

> And you whose fear of maps
> Set buzzing the long processes of power,
> Resign your limbs at length to elements
> Friendly or neutral at least,
> Mirrors of the enemy. . . .

His own bit of money had not, even before they'd started on capital purchases, been going very far ("Call in at the Lion, will you, and buy a couple of bottles of gin. Pay Mrs Opisso; I'm clean out of cash."). And the greedy maws of Fortnum and Mason and the Army and Navy Stores. And a new wardrobe for himself, London not really favouring the casual valetudinarian garb of the seaside. Enderby's capital was going now. She, a thriftless Scot, did not believe in money, only in things. Hence the seven-thousand-pound house in Sussex on her name, this being his marriage settlement, also furniture, also a bright new Velox for Vesta to drive, Enderby when most sober managing a car like the drunkest drunk. And a mink coat, a wedding present.

Who had proposed mariage, and when? Who loved whom, if at all, and why? Enderby, in thinker's pose on the lavatory seat, frowned back to an evening when he had sat finishing his epithalamion in her trim dining-room, facing a piece of furniture he admired—a sideboard, massive and warped, proclaiming its date (1685) among carved lozenges and other tropes, fancies of the woodworker signifying his love of the great negroid ship-oak he had shaped and smoothed. Above that sideboard hung a painting of Vesta done by Gideon Dalgleish, she pearly-shouldered and haughty in a ballgown, seeming about to fly off, centrifugally, back into waiting but invisible paint-tubes. Above open bookshelves was a photograph of the late Pete Bainbridge. He grinned handsomely in a helmet, seated at the wheel of the Anselm 2.493 litre (six-cylinder; 250 b.h.p. Girling disc brakes; Weber 58 DCO carburettors, etc.) in which he had met his messy death. Enderby had started his last stanza:

> And even the dead may bring blue lips to this banquet
> And twitter like mice or birds down their corridors
> Hung with undecipherable blazons. . . .

He had felt a sudden and unwonted surge of personal, as opposed to poet's, strength: he, unworthy and ugly as he was, was at least alive, while this bright and talented handsome one had been blown to pieces. He had grinned, borrowing the shape of the grin from the dead man, in a sort of triumph. Vesta, reading some new brilliant novel by an undergraduate, had looked up from her Parker-Knoll and caught the grin. She had said:

"Why are you grinning? Have you written something funny?"

"Me? Funny? Oh, no." Enderby had covered his manuscript with clumsy paws, as one protects one's dinner-plate from an importunate second scooping of mashed potato. "Nothing funny at all."

She had got up, so graceful, to see what he was writing, asking: "What are you writing?"

"This? Oh, I don't think you'd like it. It's—Well, it's a sort of——"

She had picked up the sheet of scrawled lines and read aloud:

"... For two at least can deny
That the past has any odour. They can witness
Passion and patience rooted in one paradigm; in this
    music recognise
That all the world's guilt can sit like air
On the bodies of these living."

"You see," Enderby had said, over-eagerly, "it's an epithalamion. For the marriage of two mature people." Inexplicably she had lowered her head with its sweet-smelling penny-coloured hair and kissed him. Kissed him. Him, Enderby.

"Your breath," she had said, "is no longer unhealthy. Sometimes it's hard for the body and mind to come to terms. You're looking better, much better." What could he say but, "Thanks to you?"

Airsick, seated in this aerial lavatory, he had to admit that a new Enderby had emerged out of the spring and early summer—a younger Enderby with less fat and wind, new teeth imperfect enough to look real, several smart suits, hair cunningly dressed by Trumper's of Mayfair and breathing delicately of Eucris, less gauche in company, his appetite healthier with no dyspeptic lust for spices and bread-and-jam, more carefully shaven, his skin clearer, his eyeballs glassy with contact lenses. If only Mrs Meldrum could see him now!

Who had mentioned love? Had anybody mentioned love? They had lived under one roof chaste, vestal, phoenix and turtle, with Pete Bainbridge grinning from some Elysium of racing-drivers at the strange ménage of Friends. But one had only to chuck and see spin that worn coin on the polished floor for it to chink louder and louder music and revolve into a world. Had it been pocket or handbag? Enderby could not remember, but he was sure that one evening one of them had spoken the word in some connection or other, perhaps denouncing its inflation in popular songs or in the hoarse speech of immediate need, perhaps discussing its personified identification with, in seventeenth-century religious poetry, the Lord. Then, by a swift process too subtle and irrational for analysis, one or other of them had whistled down the dove-hawk from safe heights of speculation to perch, blinking, on a pair of joined hands.

"I've been so lonely," she had said. "I've been so cold at night."

Enderby, potential bedwarmer, still potential on his brief flight to the honeymoon, for they had been chaste till now. Till tonight. Tonight in the Albergo Tritone on the Via Nazionale. Something, gulped Enderby, to look forward to.

"Look," said a voice, meaning "Listen." Enderby started from the tiny seat, listening. "Your ticket does not entitle you to undisputed monopolisation of the john." That, Enderby considered, was well put. The voice was American and authoritative and Enderby hastened to give place, fairly sure now that he felt better. Outside the folding doors he breathed deeply, taking in a large touristy man who nodded at him, edging past. He had a steak complexion and two cameras—still and movie respectively—on his stomach at the ready. Enderby wondered if he would photograph the john. Through a porthole summer cloud shone up. Enderby walked down the aisle to his bride who sat, cool and lovely, gazing at summer cloud beneath. She looked up and smiled, asking if he felt better. She gave her hand to him as he sat. It seemed to be a new life beginning.

Two

As if he were in a well-appointed bath, Enderby was struck by various liquid sensations as they descended to Rome (going down. Eternal City: pasta, old junk, monumental remnants, figleaved stone stalwarts, veal, Vatican, staircases to basement and bones of martyrs. The whole roofed in ringing silver and refreshed by fountains. And the very best of luck). He felt cold sweat as his stomach, tardy in descending, encouraged its master to view Rome in a sort of stepmother-context (Pope in picture on bedroom wall, blessing seven hills; translucent image of St. Peter's embedded in cross of blancmange-coloured rosary; missal bookmark of Holy Family as middle-class spaghetti-guzzlers, printed in Rome). Then he was warmed by thrilling gushes, the chicken-skinned hand that held the hand of the bride growing smooth again, as there swam up from the *News of the World* a picture of a heavy-breasted starlet sploshing, for a lark, in the Trevi fountain. There were also weary handsome princes in sordid divorce cases and Cinecittà was greater than the Vatican. It was all right really, it would be all right, sensual, thrilling. He looked with pride on his bride and, like a distant rumour of war, felt a prick of desire, legitimate desire; she was, in a flash, identified with this new city, to be, all so legitimately, sacked and pillaged. He said to her, a few words coming back from his L. of C. days, "*Io ti amo.*" She smiled and squeezed his hand. Enderby, Latin lover.

The warmth, the excitement, the sense of rejuvenation, survived the landing (the stewardess smirked at the exit as though she herself, after the aerial gestation, had given birth to the airport; the American who had ousted Enderby from the john began clicking away desperately). In the ragged procession to the buildings, Ciampino stretching in hot honeymoon weather, Enderby felt the barren flat airfield express, like a blank page, his new freedom, this being a freedom from his old freedom. A Cassius-lean and Casca-sullen Roman customs-man zipped open roughly the overnight bag of Vesta and held up for the whole shed to see a new nightdress. He winked sullenly at Enderby, and this to Enderby was a good omen, even though the man was starved-jawed and hence untrustworthy. The fat bus-driver sang some plangent oily aria with *amore* in it, jolting up the Appian Way, thus inspiring confidence. And then, whoosh, came the cold water again as the sun clouded over above a mossy aqueduct growing in ruins out of the dry grass, over an old plinth lying like a large merd under a comic-strip-coloured petrol poster. The American from the john fed his cameras like lapdogs. Meanwhile Enderby grew oppressed with a sense of travelling through a butcher's shop of mean history, be-tween the ribs of carcasses, already being force-fed with chunks of the carrion empire. Rostra were quietly set up just beyond his line of vision and on them settled a sort of Seneca chorus of smirking noseless ancient Romans, fat on Sicilian corndoles and gladiator's blood. They would be present at the honeymoon; it was their city.

The sun suddenly exploded, a fire in a syrup factory, as they arrived at the airline terminal on the Via Na-zionale. A dwarf porter of great strength carried their cases the few doors down to the hotel, and Enderby gave him a tip of over-light suspect coins. They were bowed at and greeted with insincere golden smiles in the hotel lobby. "Signor Enderby," said Signor Enderby, "and Signora Bainbridge." "No, no, no," said Signora Enderby. Enderby smiled. "Not used to it yet, you see. Our honeymoon," he explained to the receptionist. He, a dapper Roman elf, said:

"Honeymoon, eh? I maker sure everythinger quiet forer honeymoon. A longer time since I have a honey-moon," he said regretfully. Vesta said:

"Look, I don't feel all that well. Do you think we could be taken to our——?" There were immediate calls and dartings and hoistings of bags.

"Darling," said Enderby, concerned. "What is it, dar-ling?"

"Tired, that's all. I want to lie down."

"Darling," said Enderby. They entered a lift that was

all rococo filigree-work, an airy frail cage that carried them up to a floor paved with veiny marble. Enderby saw, with interest, an open Roman lavatory, but he waved the interest away. Those days were over. They were shown into their room by a young man in a wine-coloured coat, his nose squashed flat as in desperate contradiction of the myth of Roman profiles. Enderby gave him several worthless slips of metal and asked for *vino*. (Enderby in Rome, ordering *vino*.) The young man shook hands with himself fiercely, then tensely raised the upper hand, teeth clenched as though lifting a killing weight, showing the space between to Enderby— a bottle of air with a hand-bottom and hand-top. "Frascati," he nodded direly, and went out, nodding. Enderby turned to his wife. She sat on the window-side of the double bed, looking out at the Via Nazionale. The little room was full of its noise—tram-clanks, horse-clops, Fiats and Lambrettas. "Tired, tired, tired," said Vesta, blue arcs back under her eyes, her face weary in the sharp Roman light. "I don't feel at all the thing."

"It's not——?" asked Enderby.

"No, of course it's not. This is our wedding-day, isn't it? I'll be all right when I've had a rest." She kicked off her shoes and then, as Enderby gulped, swiftly un-hitched her stockings. He turned to the dull sights of the street: metropolitan dourness, no flashing Southern teeth, no song. Across the road a shop, as though for Enderby's own benefit, had a special display of holy pictures going cheap, ill-painted hagiographs festooned with rosary-beads. When he turned back towards the bed Vesta was already in it, her thin arms and shoulders uncovered. Not a voluptuous woman; her body pared to a decent female minimum. That was as it should be. Enderby had once caught his stepmother stripped off in the bathroom, panting with the exertion of one of her rare over-all washes, flesh shaking, fat tits swinging like bells. He shuddered at the memory, his burring lips becoming, for the moment, those of his stepmother flinch-ing at the cold sponge. There was a knock. Enderby had read Dante with an English crib; there was, he knew, a line which contained the word for "come in". He delved for it, and it came up just as the door opened. "All hope abandon," he called in fine Tuscan, "you who —" A long-faced waiter peered in, doubtful, then entered with his tray, leaving without waiting (a non-waiting waiter) for a tip. Enderby, a mad Englishman, sighed and poured wine. He shouldn't have said that. It was a bad omen. It was like Byron waking on his wedding-night and thinking that the bedroom fire was hell. He said:

"Darling. Would you care for a glass of this, darling?" He gulped some thirstily. A very nice little wine. "Help you to sleep if you're going to sleep." She nodded tiredly. Enderby poured another glass, the urine-gold flashing in the clear light, belching as it left the bottle. He gave the glass to her and she sat up to sip it. Fair down on her upper lip, Enderby noticed in love and pity, his arm round her shoulders to support her sitting up. She drank half a glassful and at once, to Enderby's shock and horror, reacted violently. Pushing him and the glass away, she fought to leave the bed, her cheeks bulging. She ran on bare feet to the wash-bowl, gripped its side, groaned and started to vomit. Enderby, much concerned, followed and stood by her, slender, defenceless in her minimal unalluring summer underwear. "That's your lunch coming up," said Enderby, watching. "A bit fatty, wasn't it?" With a roar more came up. Enderby poured water from the water-bottle.

"Oh God," she groaned. "Oh Jesus." She turned on both taps and began to retch again.

"Drink this," said Enderby. "Water." She gulped from the proffered glass and vomited again, but this time mostly water, groaning between spasms blasphemously. "There," said Enderby, "you'll be better now. That was a nasty sort of pudding they served up. All jammy."

"Oh Jesus Christ," retched Vesta (All jammy). Enderby watched kindly, a past master on visceral dysfunctions, as she got it all up. Then weak, wet, limp, spent, she staggered back to the bed. "A good start," she gasped. "Oh God."

"That's the worst of meals on aircraft," said Enderby, sage after his first flight. "They warm things up, you see.

Have some more wine. That'll settle your stomach." Fascinated by the near-rhymes, he began softly to repeat, "That'll settle, that'll settle," pacing the room softly, one hand in pocket, the other holding wine.

"Oh, shut up," moaned Vesta. "Leave me alone."

"Yes, darling," said Enderby, accommodating. "Certainly, darling. You have a little sleep, darling." He heard himself wheedling like a foreign whore, so he straightened up and said, more gruffly, "I'll go and see about traveller's cheques." Saying that, he was standing up against the door, as if challenging it or measuring himself against it. When a knock came he was able to open it at once. The long-faced boy looked startled. His arms were full of roses, red and white. *"Fiori,"* he said, *"per la signora."*

"Who from?" frowned Enderby, feeling for an accompanying card. "Good God," he said, finding it. "Rawcliffe. And Rawcliffe's in the bar. Darling," he called, turning. But she was asleep.

Three

"Ah," said Rawcliffe. "You got the message, got the flowers? Good. Where," he said, "is Mrs Enderby?" He was dressed as when Enderby had last seen him, in an old-fashioned heavy suit with a gold watch-chain, Kipling-moustached, beetle-goggled, drunk.

"Mrs Enderby," said Enderby, "is dead."

"I beg your pardon," said Rawcliffe. "Already? Roman fever? How very Jamesian!"

"Oh, I see what you mean," said Enderby. "Sorry. She only became Mrs Enderby today, you see. It takes some getting used to. I thought you meant my stepmother."

"I see, I see. And your stepmother's dead, is she? How very interesting!" Enderby shyly examined the bar, the shelves massed with liquors of all countries, the silver tea-urn, the espresso apparatus. Behind the bar a short fat man kept bowing. "Have some of this Strega," said Rawcliffe. "Dante," he said, and the fat un-Dantesque man came to attention. Rawcliffe than spoke most intricate Italian, full, as far as Enderby could judge, of subjunctives, but with a most English accent. "Strega," said Dante. "Are you," said Enderby nastily, "in all the Italian anthologies, too?" He was given, with flourishes, a glass of Strega.

"Ha, ha," said Rawcliffe, without much mirth. "As a matter of fact, there's a very good Italian translation of that little poem of mine, you know. It goes well into Italian. Now, tell me, tell me, Enderby. What are you writing at the moment?"

"Nothing," said Enderby. "I finished my long poem, *The Pet Beast*. I told you about that."

"You most certainly did," said Rawcliffe, bowing. Dante bowed too. "A very good idea, that was. I look forward to reading it."

"What I'd like to know," said Enderby, "is what you're doing here. You don't look as though you're on holiday, not in those clothes you don't."

Rawcliffe did something Enderby had read about but never before seen: he placed a finger against his nose. "You're right," he said. "Most certainly *not* on holiday. At work. Always at work. Some more Strega?"

"With me," said Enderby. Dante bowed and bowed, filling their glasses. "And one for you, too," said Enderby, expansive, on his honeymoon. Dante bowed and said to Rawcliffe, "*Americano?*"

"*Inglese*," said Rawcliffe.

"*Americani*," said Dante, leaning forward, confidential, "fack you. *Mezzo mezzo.*"

"*Un poeta*," said Rawcliffe, "that's what he is. *Poeta.* Feminine in form, masculine in gender."

"I beg your pardon," said Enderby. "Did you by any chance mean anything by that?"

"As a matter of fact," said Rawcliffe, "it's my belief that all we poets are really a sort of a blooming hermaphrodite. Like Tiresias, you know. And you're on your honeymoon, eh? Have some more Strega."

"What exactly do you mean by that?" said Enderby, wary.

"Mean? You are a one for meaning, aren't you? The meaning of meaning. I. A. Richards and the Cambridge

126

school. A lot of twaddle, if you ask my opinion. All right, if you won't have more Strega with me I'll have more Strega with you."

"Strega," said Enderby.

"Your Italian's coming along very nicely," said Rawcliffe. "A couple of nice vowels there. A couple of nice Stregas," he said, as these appeared. "God bless all." He drank. He sang, "Who would an ender be, let him come hither."

"How did you know we were here?" asked Enderby.

"Air terminal," said Rawcliffe. "Today's arrivals from London. Always interesting. Here, they said honeymoon. Remarkable, Enderby, in a man of your age."

"What do you mean by that?" asked Enderby.

"You gentlemen ave Strega on the ouse," said Dante, pouring.

"*Tante grazie*," said Rawcliffe. "There you go, Enderby, worrying about meaning all the time." He sang, standing to attention, "Would you a spender be, would you a mender be, God save the Queen. No meaning there, is there? Would you a fender be. That's better still. Too much meaning in your poetry, Enderby. Always has been." His words rode over a few drinker's belches. "Pardon, as they say." He drank.

"Strega," said Enderby. "*E uno per Lei, Dante.*"

"You can't say that," said Rawcliffe, hiccoughing. "What bloody awful Italian you speak, Enderby! Bad as your poetry. Pardon. Fair criticism. But I will say that the monster idea of yours was a bloody good one. Too good to make a poem out of it. Ah, Rome," he said, lyrically, "fair, fair, Rome. Remarkable place, Enderby, no place like it. Listen, Enderby. I'm going to a party tonight. At the house of the Principessa Somebody-or-other. Would you like to come? You and your missus? Or does it behove you to retire early this fair nuptial night?" He shook his head. "La Rochefoucauld, or some other bloody scoundrel, said you mustn't do it on the first night. What did he know about it, eh? Homosexuals, the lot of them. All writers are homosexuals. They have to be. Stands to reason. To hell with writing." He poured his last few drops of Strega on to the floor. "That," he said, "is for the Lares and Penates to come and lap up. A potation, that is to say a libation. They come to lap it up like bloody big dogs. More Strega."

"Don't you think?" said Enderby cautiously. "I mean, if you're going to a party—"

"Not for hours yet," said Rawcliffe. "Hours and hours and hours. Plenty of time for you to get it over and done with several times over before it starts. If you can, that is. Shellfish are bloody good, you know. Magnificent augmenters of male potency. Scampi. Dante," he cried, "send for some scampi for this here signore. He is a newly married man, God bless him." Rawcliffe swayed on his stool. Dante said:

"Today you are married? Very good. You ave Strega on the ouse." He poured. "*Salute*," he toasted. "*Molti bambini*," he winked.

"Lovely grub," said Rawcliffe, drinking. Enderby drank and said:

"What you've been saying is very indelicate. You ought by rights to be bashed."

"Oh dear dear dear me, no," said Rawcliffe, shaking his head, his eyes shut. "Not on a day like this. Much too warm. *Pace, pace,* this is a city of peace." He began to fall asleep.

"*Troppo*," confided Dante. "Too mash. You get im ome."

"No," said Enderby. "Damn it all, I'm on my honeymoon. I don't like him, anyway. Nasty bit of work."

"Jealous," mumbled Rawcliffe, eyes still shut, head drooping to the counter. "I'm in all the anthologies. He's not. Popular poet, me. Known and loved and respected by all." He then neatly, as in a professional tumbling act, collapsed with the stool on to the deep carpet of the bar, falling, it seemed, quite slowly, in a rotary figure. The noise, though muffled, was loud enough to summon men in skimpy suits from the hotel lobby. These spoke very fast Italian and looked with hate upon Enderby. Enderby said:

"Nothing to do with me. He was drunk when I met him." Surlily he added, "Damn it all, I'm on my honeymoon." Two men bent over Rawcliffe and Enderby was afforded an intimate, non-tourist's glimpse of the city, for one man had dandruff and the other boil-scars on his nape. Rawcliffe opened one eye and said, very clearly:

"Don't trust him. He's a spy pretending to be on his honeymoon. Made me drunk to shteal official shecretsch. Overthrow of Italian government plot dishcovered, alleged. Bombs shecreted in Foro Traiano and Tempio di Vesta."

"You leave my wife out of this," threatened Enderby.

"Ah, wife," said one of the men. "*Capito*". All was clear. Enderby had knocked Rawcliffe down in wronged husband's legitimate anger. A matter of honour. Rawcliffe now snored. The two men returned to their lobby to see about a taxi for him. Dante said to Enderby, tentatively: "Strega?"

"*Si*," said Enderby. He signed the chit and counted the number of other chits he had signed, all for Strega. Amazing. He would have to go easy, he hadn't all the money in the world. But, of course, he reflected, after this honeymoon he would start *earning* money. The capital was there to be spent; Vesta had said so.

Rawcliffe ceased snoring, smacked his lips, and said: "Thou hast wrongedst me, O Enderby." His eyes did not open. "I wished no harm. Merely desired to crown your nuptials in appropriate manner." He then gave a loud snore. A taxi-driver with a square of moustache dead under his nose entered, shook his head tolerantly, and started to lift Rawcliffe by the shoulders. Members of the hotel staff appeared, including menials in off-white jackets, and Dante struck a pose behind the bar. All were waiting for Enderby to lift Rawcliffe's feet.

Enderby said: "I know he's *Inglese* and I'm *Inglese*, but it bloody well stops there. I can't stand him, see? *Io*," he said, piecing the sentence together painfully, "*non voglio aiutare*." Everybody inclined, with smiles, to show that they appreciated this attempt on the part of an Englishman to use their beautiful language, but they ignored the meaning, perhaps having been well schooled by this snoring Rawcliffe. "I won't help," repeated Enderby, picking up Rawcliffe's feet. (There was a hole in the left sole.) "This is no way to be spending a bloody honeymoon," said Enderby, helping, very awkwardly, to carry Rawcliffe out. "Especially in Rome." As he passed, now panting, the ranked officials of the hotel, these bowed fully or gently inclined, all with smiles.

The Via Nazionale was afire with sun and brilliant with people. The taxi throbbed, waiting, by the kerb. Enderby and the driver sweated as they pushed their way, Rawcliffe still snoring. A sort of begging friar rattled his box at Enderby. "For cough," said Enderby. An American, not the john one, poised his camera to shoot. "For cough," snarled expiring Enderby. The driver, raising his knee to support the snoring body, freed his hand to open the passenger-door. Rawcliffe, like six months' laundry, was bundled in. "There," said Enderby. "All yours."

"*Dove?*" asked the driver.

"Oh, God, yes, where to?" Enderby manhandled, still panting, the loud, still Rawcliffe, trying to shout, "Where do you live, you bastard? Come on, tell us where."

Rawcliffe came awake with startling briskness, as though he had merely pretended to pass out so that he might be carried. His blue eyes, quite clear, flashed patches of Roman sky at Enderby. "Tiber, Father Tiber," he said, "on whom the Romans prey. The Via Mancini by the Ponte Matteotti."

The driver eagerly drank that in. "O world, O life, O time," intoned Rawcliffe. "Here lies one whose name was *not* writ in water. In all the anthologies." He returned to a heavy sleep with louder snores than before. Enderby hesitated, then, since the whole waiting world seemed to expect it of him, roughly made room next to Rawcliffe. They drove off. The driver honked down the Via Nazionale and turned abruptly into the Via IV Novembre. Then, as they sped north up the Via del Corso, Rawcliffe came quite alive again, sat up sedately, and said:

"Have you such a thing as a cigarette on you, my dear Enderby? An English cigarette, preferably."

"Are you all right now?" asked Enderby. "Can I get out here and let you go home on your own?"

"Over there on the left," pointed Rawcliffe, "you'll find

130

the Pantheon if you look carefully. And there"—his hand swished right, striking Enderby—"down the street of humility, at the end, is the Fontana di Trevi. There you will throw your coin and be photographed by touts in berets. Do give me a cigarette, there's a good fellow." Enderby offered a single crushed Senior Service. Rawcliffe took it steadily without thanks, lighting up as firm as a rock. "We come now, Enderby, to the Piazza Colonna. There it is, the column itself, and at the top Marcus Aurelius, see."

"I could get off here," suggested Enderby, "and go back to the hotel. My wife isn't too good, you know."

"Isn't she?" said Rawcliffe. "Not too good at what? A great admirer of poets, though. I'll say that for her. She always liked my little poem in the anthologies. It's quite likely, you know, Enderby, that you're going to be a great man. She likes to back winners. She backed one very good one, but that was in the field of sports. Poets don't get killed as racing-drivers do, you know. Look, the Piazza del Popolo. And now we're coming up to the Via Flaminia and there, you can just see, is Father Tiber himself, into whom the Romans spit."

"What do you know about my wife?" asked Enderby. "Who told you I'd married Vesta Bainbridge?"

"It was in the popular papers," said Rawcliffe. "Didn't you see? Perhaps she kept them from you. Pete Bainbridge's widow to remarry, they said. The popular papers didn't seem to know very much about you. But when you're dead there'll be biographies, you know. There haven't been any biographies of Pete Bainbridge, so there's a lot to be said for not being known to the readers of the *Daily Mirror*. Ah, here is the Via Mancini." He banged the glass partition and made grotesque boxing gestures at the driver. The driver nodded, swerved madly, and came to rest before a small drinking-shop. "This is where I have my humble lodging," said Rawcliffe. "Above here."

"Do you really believe that?" asked Enderby. "I thought perhaps I appealed to a sort of protective instinct in her. And I'm very fond of her. Very, very fond. In love," said Enderby. Rawcliffe nodded and nodded, paying the driver. He seemed to have recovered completely from his Strega-bout. The two poets stood in the warm street, cooled by river air. Enderby let the taxi go and said, "Damn. I've let that taxi go. I ought to get back to my wife." He reminded himself that he disliked Rawcliffe because he was in all the anthologies. "It strikes me," said Enderby, "that you were swinging the bloody lead. I needn't have come with you at all."

"Strega," said Rawcliffe, nodding, "passes through my system very quickly. I think, now we're here, we'll have some more. Or perhaps a litre or so of Frascati."

"I must get back. She may be all right now. She may be wondering where I am."

"There's no hurry. The bride's supposed to wait, you know. Supposed to lie in cool sheets smelling of lavender while the bridegroom gets drunk and impotent. The Toby night, you know. That's what it used to be called. After Tobias in the Apocrypha. Come on, Enderby, I'm lonely. A brother poet is lonely. And I have things to tell you."

"About Vesta?"

"Oh, no. Much more interesting. About you and your poetic destiny."

They entered the little shop. It was dark and warm. On the walls were vulgar mosaics, pseudo-Etruscan, of prancing men and women in profile. There were glass jars of wine and cloudy tumblers. An old man from the age of Victor Emmanuel sucked an ample moustache; two sincere-eyed rogues, round-faced and, despite the heat, in overcoats, whispered roguery to each other. A champing old woman, each step an effort, brought a litre of urine to two English poets. "*Salute,*" said Rawcliffe. He shuddered at the first draught, found the second blander. "Tell me, Enderby," he said, "how old would you say I am?"

"Old? Oh, about fifty."

"Fifty-two. And when do you think I stopped writing?"

"I didn't know you *had* stopped."

"Oh, yes, a long time, a long, long time. I haven't written a line of verse, Enderby, since I was twenty-seven. There, that surprises you, doesn't it? But writing verse is so difficult, Enderby, so so difficult. The only people who can write verse after the age of thirty are the people who do the competitions, you know, in the week-end papers. You can add to that, of course, the monkey-gland boys, of whom Yeats was one, but that's not playing the game, by God. The greatest senile poet of the age, by God, by grace of this bloody man Steinach. But the rest of us? There are no dramatic poets left, Enderby, and, ha ha, certainly no epic poets. We're all lyric poets, then, and how long does the lyric urge last? No bloody time at all, my boy, ten years at the most. It's no accident, you know, that they all died young, mainly, for some reason, in Mediterranean lands. Dylan, of course, died in America, but the Atlantic's a sort of Mediterranean, when you come to think of it. What I mean is, American civilisation's a sort of sea-board civilisation, when you come to think of it, and not a river civilisation at all." Rawcliffe shook his head in a fuddled gesture, the Frascati having wakened the sleeping Strega. "What I mean is, Enderby, that you're bloody lucky to be writing poetry at all at the age of—what is your age?"

"Forty-five."

"At the age of forty-five, Enderby. What I mean is, what are you looking forward to now? Eh?" He let more Frascati stagger into his glass. Outside, the Roman daylight flashed and rippled. "Don't kid yourself, my dear boy, about long bloody narrative poems, or plays, or any of that nonsense. You're a lyric poet, and the time is coming for the lyric gift to die. Who knows? Perhaps it's died already." He looked narrowly at Enderby over the glass flask of Frascati swimming and dancing in his grip. "Don't expect any more epiphanies, any more mad dawn inspirations, Enderby. That poem of mine, the one in the anthologies, the one I'll live by if I'm going to live at all, I wrote that bugger, you know, Enderby, at the age of twenty-one. Youth. It's the only thing worth having." He nodded sadly. As in a film, an easy symbol of youth orchestrated his words, passing by outside, a very head-high girl of Rome with black hair and smoky sideburns, thrust breasts, liquid waist like Harry Plough-man's, animal haunches. "Yes, yes," said Rawcliffe, "youth." He drank Frascati and sighed. "Haven't you felt, Enderby, that your gift is dying? It's a gift appropriate to youth, you know, owing nothing to experience or learning. An athletic gift, really, a *sportif* gift." Rawcliffe dropped his jaw at Enderby, disclosing crooked teeth of various colours. "What are you going to do, Enderby, what are you going to do? To the world, of course, all this is nothing. If the world should enter and hear us mourning the death of Enderby's lyric gift, the world, Enderby, would deem us not merely mad. They would consider us, Enderby, to be, Enderby"—he leaned forward, hissing—"really talking about something else in the guise of the harmless. They would think us, perhaps, to be *Communists*."

"And," said Enderby, frightened by this vision of coming impotence, impotence perhaps already arrived, "what do *you* do?"

"I?" Rawcliffe was already drunk again. He shoulder-jerked spastically and munched the air like spaghetti. "I, Enderby, am the great diluter. Nothing can be taken neat any more. The question is this: do we live, or do we partly live? Or," he said, "do we," and he was suddenly blinking in the killing lights, before the cranking cameras, jerking upright to stand against the wall, as against, with spread thin arms, a rockcliff, a rawface, "die?" He then collapsed on the table, like a Hollywood absinthe-drinker, but none of the Romans took any notice.

Four

"And," said Vetsa, "what exactly do you think you've been doing? Where exactly do you think you've been?" Enderby felt a sort of stepson's guilt, the only kind he really knew, looking at her, head hung. She was brilliant in a wide-skirted daffodil-yellow dress, penny-coloured hair smooth and shining, skin summer-honeyed, healthy again, her eyes green, wide, nasty, a most formidable and desirable woman. Enderby said, mumbling: "It was Rawcliffe, you see."

She folded her bare arms. "You know Rawcliffe," chumbled Enderby and, a humble and hopeful attempt at palliation of his crime or crimes, "he's in all the anthologies."

"In all the bars, most likely, if I know anything about Rawcliffe. And you've been with him. I'm giving you fair warning, Harry. You keep out of the way of people like Rawcliffe. What's he doing in Rome, anyway? It all sounds very suspicious to me. What did he say? What was he telling you?"

"He said that being a lyric poet was really like being a racing motorist and that you've only lowered yourself to marry me because you'll be in all the biographies and will share in my eternal fame and glory, and he said that my poetic gift was dying and then what was I going to do? Then he passed out and I had to help carry him upstairs and that made me very thirsty. Then I couldn't find a taxi for a long time and I couldn't remember the name of the hotel. So that's why I'm late. But," said Enderby, "you didn't say anything about what time to be back, did you? You didn't say anything at all."

"You said you were going to cash traveller's cheques," said Vesta. "It was your duty to stay here, with me. A fine start to a honeymoon this is, isn't it, you going off with people like Rawcliffe to get drunk and listen to lies about your wife."

"What lies?"

"The man's a born liar. He was always trying to make passes at me."

"When? How do you know him?"

"Oh, he's been a journalist of sorts," said Vesta. "Always messing round on the fringes of things. He's probably here in films, I should think, just messing round. Look," she said very sternly, "in future you're not to go anywhere without me, do you understand? You just don't know the world, you're just too innocent to live. My job is to look after you, take charge of things for you."

"And *my* job?" said Enderby.

She smiled faintly. Enderby noticed that the bottle of

Frascati, three-quarters full when he had left the bed-room, was now empty. She had certainly recovered. Outside was gentle Roman early evening. "What do we do now?" asked Enderby.

"We go and eat."

"It's a bit early for that, isn't it? Don't you think we ought to drink a little before eating?"

"You've drunk enough."

"Well," said Enderby, looking again at the empty Frascati bottle, "you haven't done too badly yourself. On an empty stomach, too."

"Oh, I sent down for some pizza and then a couple of club sandwiches," said Vesta. "I was starving. I still am." She took from the wardrobe a stole, daffodil-yellow, to cover her bare shoulders against evening cold or Italian lust. She had unpacked, Enderby noticed; she couldn't have been ill for very long. They left the bedroom and went down by the stairs, mistrusting the frail filigree charm of the lift. In the corridors, in the hotel lobby, men frankly admired Vesta. Bottom-pinchers, suddenly realised Enderby, all Italians were blasted bottom-pinchers; that raised a problem. And surely duels of honour were still fought in this backward country? Out on the Via Nazionale, Enderby walked a pace behind Vesta, smiling sourly up at the SPQR shields on the lamp standards. He didn't want any trouble. He hadn't before quite realised what a responsibility a wife was. "I was told," said Vesta, "that there's a little place on the Via Torino. Harry, why are you walking behind? Don't be silly; people are looking at you."

Enderby skipped to her side, but, invisible to her, his open hand was spread six inches behind her walking rump, as though warming itself at a fire. "Who told you?"

"Gillian Frobisher."

"That," said Enderby, "is the woman who nearly killed me with her Spaghetti Surprise."

"It was your own fault. We turn right here."

The restaurant was full of smeary mirrors and smelt strongly of cellar-damp and very old breadcrumbs. Enderby read the menu in gloom. The waiter was blue-jawed, lantern-jawed, untrustworthy, trying to peer, sly-ly, into Vesta's *décolletage*. Enderby wondered why such glamour surrounded the Italian cuisine. After all, it consisted only of a few allomorphs of paste, the odd sauce or so; the only Italian meat was veal. Nevertheless Enderby read "bifstek" and, with faint hope, ordered it. Vesta, starving, had worked through minestrone, a ravio-li dish, some spaghetti mess or other, and was dipping artichoke leaves into oily vinegar, Enderby had begun to glow on a half-litre of Frascati when the alleged steak arrived. It was thin, white, on a cold plate. Enderby said to the waiter:

"Questo é vitello." He, who had, before his life with Vesta, subsisted on ghastly stews and dips in the jampot, now became steak-faced with thwarted gastronome's an-ger.

"Si, é vitello, signore."

"I ordered beefsteak," cried furious Enderby, uncouth Englishman abroad, "not bloody veal. Not that it is bloody veal," he added, with poetic concern for verbal accuracy. "Fetch the manager."

"Now, Harry," rebuked Vesta. "We've had enough naughtiness for one day, haven't we? See, people are looking at you." The Roman eaters all round were shov-elling away, swollen-eyed, sincerely voluble with each other. They ignored Enderby; they had seen his type before. The manager came, fat, small, shiftily black-eyed, breathing hard with suppressed indignation at Enderby.

"I ordered," said Enderby, "a steak. This is veal."

"Is a same thing," said the manager. "Veal is a cow. Beef is a cow. Ergo, beef is a veal."

"Are you," said Enderby, enraged by this syllogism, "trying to teach me what is a beefsteak and what is not? Are you trying to teach me my own bloody language?"

"Language, Harry, language," said Vesta ineptly.

"Yes, my own bloody language," cried Enderby. "He thinks he knows better than I do. Are you going to stick up for him?"

"Is a true," said the manager. "You not a eat, you pay a same. What a you a order you a pay."

Enderby stood up, saying, "Oh, no. Oh, most certainly bloody well no." He looked down at Vesta, before whom frothed a zabaglione. "I'm not," he said, "paying for what I didn't order, and what I didn't order was that pallid apology down there. I'm going to eat somewhere else."

"Harry," she ordered, "sit down. Eat what you're given." She pinged her zabaglione glass pettishly with her spoon. "Don't make such a fuss over nothing."

"I don't like throwing money away," said Enderby, "and I don't like being insulted by foreigners."

"You," said Vesta, "are the foreigner. Now *sit down.*"

Enderby grumpily sat down. The manager sneered in foreigner's triumph, ready to depart, having resolved the stupid fuss, meat being veal anyway, no argument about it. Enderby saw the sneer and stood up again, angrier. "I won't bloody well sit down," he said, "and he knows what he can do with this bloodless stuff here. If you're staying, I'm not."

Vesta's eyes changed from expression to expression rapidly, like the number-indicator of a bus being changed by the conductor. "All right," she said, "dear. Leave me some money to pay for my own meal. I'll see you in fifteen minutes in that open-air café place."

"Where?"

"On the Piazza di what's-its-name," she said, pointing.

"Repubblica," said the waiter, helpful.

"You keep your bloody nose out of this," said Enderby. "All right, then. I'll see you there." He left with her a large note for several thousand or million lire. From it the face of some allegorical lady looked up at Enderby in mute appeal.

Fifteen minutes later Enderby, gazing glumly at the colour-lit fountain, watching the Vespas and the Fiats and the sober crowds, sat near the end of a bottle of Frascati. It had come to him warm, and he had said to the terrace waiter, "*Non freddo.*" The waiter had agreed that the bottle was *non freddo* and had gone off smiling. Now the bottle was less *freddo* than ever. It was a warm evening. Enderby felt a sudden strong longing for his old life, the stewed tea, the poetry in the lavatory, onanistic sex. Then, wanting to blubber, he realised that he

138

was being very childish. It was right that a man should marry and be honeymooning among the fountains of Rome; it was right to want to be mature. But Rawcliffe had said something about poetry being a youthful gift, hence immature, cognate with the gifts of speed and alertness that made a man into a racing-driver. Was it possible that the gift was already leaving him, having stayed perhaps longer than was right? If so, what was he, what would he turn into?

Vesta arrived, a *Vogue* vision of beauty against the flood-lit fountain. Fluttered and suddenly proud, Enderby stood up. She sat down, saying, "I was really ashamed of you in there. You behaved absolutely disgracefully. Naturally, I paid for the meal you ordered. I hate these petty wrangles over money."

"My money," said Enderby. "You shouldn't have done it."

"All right, your money. But, please remember, *my* dignity. I don't allow you or any man to make a fool out of me." She softened. "Oh, Harry, how could you, how could you behave like that? On the first day of our honeymoon, too. Oh, Harry, you upset me dreadfully."

"Have some wine," said Enderby. The waiter inclined with a Roman sneer, bold eyes of admiration for the *signora*. "That last lot," said Enderby, "was bloody *caldo*. This time I want it *freddo*, see? Bloody *freddo*." The waiter went, sneering and leering. "How I hate this bloody town!" said Enderby, suddenly shivering. Vesta began to snivel quietly. "What's the trouble?" asked Enderby.

"Oh, I thought things would be different. I thought you'd be different." Suddenly she stiffened, staring straight ahead of her, as though waiting for some psychic visitation. Enderby looked at her, his mouth open. Her mouth opened, too, and, as from the mouth of a spiritualistic medium, there was emitted what sounded like the greeting of a Red Indian "control":

Haaaaooooo.

Enderby listened in silent wonder, his mouth open wider. It was a belch.

"Oh," she said, "sorry. I couldn't help that at all, really I couldn't."

"Let it come," said Enderby kindly. "You can always say excuse me."

Barrrrrp.

"I *do* beg your pardon," said Vesta. "You know, I don't think I feel frightfully well. I don't think this change of food is agreeing with me." Rorrrrp. Auuuuu.

"Would you like to go back to the hotel?" asked Enderby eagerly.

"I think I'll have to." Borrrrphhh. "We're having the most unfortunate day, aren't we?"

"The Toby night," said Enderby with relief. "Like Tobias in the Apocrypha." He took her arm.

2

One

"PIAZZA San Pietro," said the guide. "St Peter's Square." He was a young Roman with a crewcut, insolent, bold eyes for the ladies. "Place Saint Pierre. St Peter's Platz." Vulgar, decided Enderby. Pretentious. The guide saw Enderby's sourness, saw that he was not impressed. "Plaza San Pedro," he said, as though playing a trump card.

It was a real scorcher, and Vesta was dressed for a real scorcher in beige linen, something austere and expensive by Berhanyer. She had amazing powers of recuperation. Last night her stomach upset had jabbered and frothed away like an idiot child even when, eventually, she had got to sleep. Enderby had lain in clean pyjamas listening tolerantly, her slim back and haunches visible through the diaphanous nightdress, neat but unseductive, heaving occasionally with new accessions of wind, the bedclothes having been kicked away by Enderby because of the warmth of the night. The bedside lamp out, she had become a mere parcel of noises which had filled Enderby with weak nostalgia for his single days, so that he had gone to sleep to dream of stewpans and the

141

craft of verse, the sea. At three-thirty by his luminous wristwatch (a wedding-present), he had awakened with his heart punch-balling desperately because of Strega and Frascati to hear her still fizzing and pooping healthily away. But, waking at nine o'clock to the peevish traffic of the Via Nazionale, he had seen her at the window, eating.

An essential task had not yet been accomplished. Enderby, blinking and squinting, noting that he had slept with his teeth in, wondering where he had put his contact lenses, was emboldened by morning chordee to say, "Oughtn't you to come back to bed for a while? What I mean is you ought really." Impromptu verses, wittily gross, came into his head to give the lie to Rawcliffe's raised finger of doom; the Muse was still very much with him:

> The marriage contract was designed,
>   Despite what all the notaries think,
> To be by only one pen signed,
>   And that is mine, and full of ink.

Enderby hesitated about saying these verses aloud. Anyway, Vesta said:

"I've been up for hours. I had a ham omelette in the restaurant and now I'm eating the breakfast I ordered for you. But it's only *croissants* and jam and things. Look, we're going on a little excursion. I thought it might be fun. We're going to see Rome. The coach calls here at nine-thirty, so you'd better hurry." Waving the excursion tickets in a shaft of Roman sun, then cracking a kind of hard bread: "You don't seem very enthusiastic. Don't you want to see Rome?"

"No." Ask a straight question and you get a straight answer.

"You call yourself a poet. Poets are supposed to be full of curiosity. I don't understand you at all."

Anyway, here they were, stepping out of the coach in full noon, to inspect the Obelisk of Nero's Circus. The guide, who had decided that Enderby was a Spaniard, said ingratiatingly, "Obelisco del Circo de Nerón." "*Sí,*" said Enderby, unenticed. "Look," he said to Vesta, "I'm parched. I must have a drink." It was all the solids they'd been forced to eat—the Pincian Gate and the Borghese Gallery and the Pincio Terrace and the Mausoleum of Caesar Augustus and the Pantheon and the Senate House and the Palace of Justice and the Castle of St Angelo and the Via della Conciliazione. Enderby remembered what the great poet Clough had said about Rome. Rubbishy, he had called it. Enderby was always ready to defer to the judgment of a great poet. "Rubbishy," he quoted.

"You know," said Vesta, "I do believe you're really quite a philistine."

"A thirsty one."

"All right. It's nearly the end of the tour, anyway." Enderby, who had developed in less than a day a sightless instinct for drinking-shops, led Vesta down the Road of Conciliation. Soon they were sitting very cool and drinking Frascati. Vesta sighed and said:

"Peace."

Enderby choked on his wine. "I beg your pardon?"

"That's what we all want, isn't it? Peace. Peace and order. Certitude. Certainty. The mind quiet and at peace in the presence of order." Her skin was so clear, so youthful, under the wide-brimmed hat (also from the Madrid workshop of the crafty young Berhanyer), and her body so elegantly decked; exquisitely the stallion-flared nostrils and honest and yet clever the green eyes. "Peace," she said again, then sighed once more. "Och."

"What was that word?" asked Enderby.

"Peace."

"No, no, the one after."

"I didn't say anything after. You're hearing things, Harry boy."

"What did you call me then?"

"Really, what is the matter with you? Rome's peculiar magic seems to be having a curious influence. . . . And you're drinking far far more than you drink in England."

"You cured my stomach," said Enderby ungrudgingly. "I find I can down any quantity of this stuff without any ill effects. That diet you put me on certainly worked wonders." He nodded cheerily at her and poured more wine from the flask.

Vesta looked slightly disgusted; she flared her nostrils further, saying, "I talk about peace and you talk about stomachs."

"One stomach," said Enderby. "Poets talk about stomachs and *Fem* editors talk about peace. That seems a fair division."

"We can look forward to so much peace," said Vesta, "the two of us. That beautiful house in Sussex, overlooking the downs. It breathes peace, doesn't it?"

"You're too young to want peace," said Enderby. "Peace is for the old."

"Och, we all want it," said Vesta fiercely. "And I feel it here, you know, in Rome. A big big peace."

"A big piece of peace," said Enderby. "*Pax Romana*. Where they made a desolation they called it a peace. What absolute nonsense! It was a nasty, vulgar sort of civilisation only dignified by being hidden under a lot of declensions. Peace? They didn't know what peace was. The release of the vomitorium after field-fares in syrup and quail's brains in aspic and a go at a little slave-boy between courses. They knew that. They knew the catharsis after seeing women torn apart by mangy starved lions in an arena. But they didn't know peace. If they'd been quiet and reposeful for thirty seconds they'd have heard too many voices telling them that the Empire was all a bloody swindle. Don't talk to me about the bloody *pax Romana*." Enderby snorted, not quite knowing why he was so moved.

Vesta smiled in tolerance. "That's not real Rome. That's Hollywood Rome."

"Real Rome *was* Hollywood Rome, only more so," said Enderby. "And what's really left of it now? Mouldering studio-lots. Big vulgar broken columns. The imperial publicity of P. Virgil Maro, yes-man to Augustus and all his triumphal arches, now dropped. Boots boots boots boots marching up and down again. Rome." Enderby made, appropriately but vulgarly, the old Roman sign. "A big maggoty cheese, with too many irregular verbs."

Vesta was still smiling, somewhat like Our Lady in the

vision Enderby had had that slippery day, travelling to London with a poem to give birth to. "You just don't listen, do you? You just don't give me a chance to say what I want to say."

"Bloody Roman peace," snorted Enderby.

"I didn't mean that Empire. I meant the other one being nourished in the catacombs."

"Oh God, no," murmured Enderby.

Vesta drank some wine and then, quite gently, belched. She did not say excuse me; she did not seem to notice. Enderby stared. She said, "Doesn't it seem to you to be a bit like coming home? You know—the return of the prodigal? You opted out of the Empire and have regretted it ever since. It's no good denying it; it's there in your poems all the time."

Enderby breathed deeply. "In a way," he said, "we all regret the death of a universal order. A big smile of teeth. But that smile is a smile of dead teeth. No, not even just dead. False. It never began to be alive. Not for me, anyway."

"Liar."

"What do you know about it?" said Enderby, truculent.

"Oh, more than you think." She sipped her Frascati as though it were very hot tea. "You've never been much interested in me, have you? Not really. You've never troubled to find out anything about me."

"We haven't known each other very long," said Enderby, somewhat guiltily.

"Long enough to get married. No, be honest. To Enderby, Enderby's always been the important thing. Enderby the end of Enderby."

"That's not really true," said Enderby doubtfully. "I've regarded my work as important, I suppose. But not myself. I've not cared very much for my own comfort or honour or glory."

"Exactly. You've been too interested in yourself to be interested in those things. Enderby in a void. Enderby spinning round and round in an eternal lavatory."

"That's not fair. That's not true at all."

"You see? You're getting really interested. You're

prepared for a good long talk about Enderby. Supposing we talk about me instead."

"Gladly," said Enderby, settling himself in resignation. Vesta pushed her wine-glass away and, with slim hands folded on the table, said:

"How do you think I was brought up?"

"Oh," said Enderby, "we know all about that, don't we? Good Scottish home. Calvinist. Another authoritarian dream to be opted out of."

"Oh, no," said Vesta, "not at all. Not Calvinist. Catholic. Just like you." She smiled sweetly.

"What?" squawked Enderby, aghast.

"Yes," said Vesta, "Catholic. There are Catholics in Scotland, you know. Lots and lots of them. It was intended that I should be a nun. There, that's a surprise for you, isn't it?"

"Not really," said Enderby. "Granted that original premise, which I'm still trying to digest, not at all a surprise. You wear your clothes like a nun."

"What a very odd thing to say!" said Vesta. "What, I wonder, do you mean by that?"

"Why didn't you tell me before?" asked Enderby, agitated. "I mean, we've lived under the same roof for, oh, for months, and you've never breathed a word about it."

"Why should I have done? It never seemed relevant to anything we ever talked about. And you never showed any curiosity about me. As I've already said, you have, for a poet, surprisingly little curiosity."

Enderby looked at her, definitely curiously: by rights, this revelation should have modified her appearance, but she still seemed a slim Protestant beauty, cognate with his adolescent vision, an angel of release.

She said, "Anyway, it makes no difference. I left the Church when I was, oh, when I married Pete. He, as everybody but you knows, had already been married and divorced. I was drifting anyway; I didn't believe any more. Pete believed in motor engines, I'll say that for him, and he used to pray before racing, though I don't know what to; perhaps to some archetypal internal combustion engine. Pete was a nice boy." She drained her glass.

"Have some more wine," said Enderby.

"Yes, I will, just a little. Rome has a peculiar atmosphere, hasn't it? Don't you feel that? It makes me, somehow, feel that I'm empty, empty of belief and so on."

"Be careful," said Enderby, very clearly, leaning across. "Be very careful indeed of feeling like that. Rome's just a city like anywhere else. A vastly overrated city, I'd say. It trades on belief just as Stratford trades on Shakespeare. But don't you start thinking that it's a great pure mother calling you home. You can't go home, anyway. You're living in sin. We were only married in a registry office, remember."

"And are we living in sin?" asked Vesta coolly. "I haven't noticed particularly."

"Well," said Enderby, confused, "that's what the world would think if the world happened to know and to be Catholic. We're not, of course, really, as you say, living in sin at all."

"You've contracted out of everything in your time, haven't you? Out of the Church, out of society, out of the family—"

"Damn it all, I am, after all, a poet—"

"Everything goes into the lavatory, everything. Even the act of love."

Enderby flushed flea-coloured. "What do you mean by that? What do you know about that? I'm just the same as anybody else, except that I'm not accustomed, except that it's been a long time, except that I'm ugly and shy and—"

"Everything's going to be put right. You just wait. You'll see." She gave him, forgiving, a kind cool hand. Anything he might then have wanted to say was snatched from his very lungs by a massive silver plunging of claws, swallowed, as all sounds of angelic noontime were swallowed, by a sudden boisterous revelry of bells, huge throats of white metal baying, snarling, hurling, fuming at the sky, the heavens of Rome a nickel and aluminium flame of bells.

Two

After sauced pasta and a straw-harnessed globe of Chianti, Vesta's proposal seemed reasonable enough. Because she spoke of the process rather than the end: cool breezes stirred by the fan of the moving coach; the stop for tasting the wines of the Frascati vineyards; the wide sheet of lake and the *albergo* on its shore. And then the rolling back to Rome in early evening. It was more than a proposal, anyway. When Enderby said yes she promptly pulled the tickets out of her handbag. "But," said Enderby, "are we to spend all our time in Rome riding in coaches?"

"There's a lot to see, isn't there? And you'd better see it all just so you can confirm that it's rubbishy."

"It is rubbishy, too." And Enderby, in after-lunch somnolence, thought particularly of that ghastly Arco di Costantino which was like a petrified and sempiternal page of the *Daily Mirror*, all cartoons and lapidary headlines. But a lake would be, especially in this cruel mounting heat, different altogether. Rome was really best taken in liquid form—wine, fountains and Aqua Sacra. Enderby approved of Aqua Sacra. Charged with a wide selection of windy chemicals, it brought the wind up lovely and contrived a civilised evacuation of the bowels. In these terms he recommended it seriously to Vesta.

Enderby was surprised that this lake was to be visited by so many. Boarding the coach at the hotel, he had immediately prepared for sleep; almost at once they, and the jabbering polyglot others, had been told to get out. They were at some nameless piazza, sweltering and bone-dry, mocked by a fountain. There, their metal blistering in the sun, stood a fleet of coaches. Men with numbered placards stuck on sticks yelled for their squads, and obedient people, frowning and wrinkling in the huge light, marched on to markers. "We're Number Six," said Vesta. They marched.

Heat was intense in the coach; it had cooked to a turn

in a slow oven. Even Vesta glowed. Enderby became a kind of fountain, his bursting sweat almost audible. And a worried man came on to the coach, calling, "Where is Dr Buchwald?" in many languages, so that a kind of fidgety sense of responsibility for this missing one pervaded the coach and engendered scratchiness. In front of Enderby a Portuguese snored, his head on the shoulder of a Frenchman, a stranger; Americans camerarecorded everything, like the scene of a crime; there were two chortling Negroes; a large ham-pink German family spoke of Rome in serious and regretful cadences, churning the sights and sounds into long compound sausage-words. Enderby closed his eyes.

Vaguely, through the haze of his doze, he was aware of comforting wind fanned in by the movement of the coach. "A very popular lake," he said sleepily to Vesta; "must be. All these people." The convoy was rolling south. Through the coach loud-speaker came the voice of the guide, in Italian, French, German and American, and the intermittent drone was finneganswaked by lightly sleeping Enderby into a parachronic lullaby chronicle, containing Constantine the grandgross and battlebottles fought by lakes which were full of lager. He awoke, laughing, to see villas and vineyards and burning country, then slept again, carrying into deeper sleep a coin-image of Vesta looking on him protectively with the protectiveness of a farmer's wife carrying a pig to market.

He was awakened, smacking dry lips, to a small town of great charm and cleanliness, napkin-carrying waiters waiting on a wide terrace full of tables. Stiff stretching coach-loads got out to drink. Here, Enderby understood, they were very near to Frascati, and that wine that was so shy of travel had travelled the least possible distance. White dust, heat, the shimmering flask on the table. Enderby felt suddenly well and happy. He smiled at Vesta and took her hand, saying:

"Queer that we're both renegade Catholics, isn't it? You were right when you said that it's a bit like coming home. What I mean is, we understand a country like this better than the Protestants. We belong to its traditions."

149

He indicated, with a kind smile, a couple of hungry-eyed children at the foot of the terrace steps, the elder of the two solemnly nose-picking. "Even if you don't believe any longer," said Enderby, "you're bound to find England a bit strange, a bit inimical. I mean, take all the churches they stole from us. I mean, they can keep them for all I care, but they ought to be reminded occasionally that they're really still ours." He looked round the full drinking terrace happily, soothed by the jabber of alien phonemes.

Vesta smiled somewhat sourly and said: "I wish you wouldn't talk in your sleep. Not in public, anyway."

"Why, what was I saying?"

"You were saying, 'Down with the Pope,' or words to that effect. It's a good thing that not many people on this trip can understand English."

"That's funny," said Enderby. "I wasn't even thinking of the Pope. That's very curious. Amazing what the subconscious mind can get up to, isn't it?"

"Perhaps you'd better stay awake on this leg of the journey," ordered Vesta. "It's the last leg."

"I mean, it isn't as though anybody mentioned the Pope, or anything, is it?" puzzled Enderby. "Look, people are climbing aboard."

They followed the chatter, smiling faintly at their fellow-passengers as they moved down the aisle of the coach. There had been some changing-round of seats, but that didn't matter: at the very furthest, you could not be more than one seat away from the window. A paunched small cocky Frenchman, however, linen-suited and with panama as though resident in a colony, hurled and fluted sharp words at a German who, he alleged, had taken his seat. The German barked and sobbed indignant denial. A tipsy lean Portuguese, thus encouraged by a fellow-Latin, started on an innocent red cheese of a Dutchman: a claim had, at the outset, been staked to that seat nearest the driver and renewed at this stop for refreshment—see, your fat Dutch arse is sitting on it, my map of Rome and environs. Europe now warred with itself, so that a keen-eyed Texan called, "Aw, pipe down." The guide came aboard and spoke French, saying that as a little infant at school he had been taught to keep to the first seat allotted to him. Enderby nodded; in French that sounded reasonable and civilised. The guide translated into American, saying, "Like you were in school, stick to your own seat and don't try and grab somebody else's. Okay?"

Enderby felt himself growing instantly red and mad. He cried: "Who the hell do you think you are—the Pope?" It was an Englishman's never-never-never protest against foreign overbearingness. Vesta said, "Why don't you keep your big mouth—" The words of Enderby were translated swiftly into many tongues, and faces turned to look at Enderby, some wondering, others doubtful, yet others fearful. But one elderly man, a grey and dapper *raisonneur*-type, stood to say, in English, "We are rebuked. He reminds us of the purpose of our journey. Catholic Europe must not be divided." He sat down, and people began to look more warmly on Enderby, one wizened brownish woman offering him a piece of Belgian chocolate. "What did he mean by that?" asked Enderby of Vesta. "The purpose of our journey, he said. We're going to see this lake, aren't we? What's a lake got to do with Catholic Europe?" "You'll see," soothed Vesta, and then, "I think, after all, it might be better if you *did* have a little sleep."

But Enderby could not now doze. The countryside slid past, brilliant distant townships on high sunlit plateaux, olive, vine and cypress, villas, browned fields, endless blue sky. And at length came the lake, a wide white sheet of waters in laky air, the heat of the day mitigated by it, and the little inn close by. The guide, who had sulked and been silent since Enderby's blast of brash Britishry in rebuke, now stood up to say, "We stay here two hours. The coach will be parked in the parking-place for coaches." He indicated with a sketchy squizzle of his Roman fingers roughly where that might be. He frowned at the Enderbys as they came down the coach-aisle, a blue-jawed lean Roman's frown despite Enderby's "No hard feelings? Eh?" He was even stonier when Enderby said, "*Ma é vero che Lei ha parlato un poco pontificalmente.*" "Come on," said Vesta.

151

The wide silver water breathed coolness. But, to Enderby's fresh surprise, nobody seemed anxious to savour it. Crowds were leaving coaches and toiling up a hill towards what seemed to be a walled township. Coach after coach came up, disgorging unfestive people, grave, some pious with rosaries. There were carved Africans, a gaggle of Chinese, a piscatorium of Finns, a rotary chew of Americans, Frenchmen haussing their *épaules*, rare blond Vikings and their goddesses, all going up the hill. "We," said Vesta, "are also going up there."

"What" asked Enderby carefully, "lies up that hill?"

"Come on." Vesta took his arm. "A little poetic curiosity, please. Come and find out."

Enderby now half-knew what lay at the top of the hill-street they now began to ascend, dodging new squealing arriving coaches, but he suffered himself to be led, passing smiling sellers of fruit and holy pictures. Enderby paused for a moment aghast, seeing a playing-card-sized portrait repeated more than fifty-two times: it seemed at first to be his stepmother in the guise of a holy man blessing his portrait-painter. And then it was not she.

Panting, he was led up to massy gates and a courtyard already thronged and electric. Behind himself and Vesta crowds still moved purposefully up. A trap, a trap: he would not be able to get out. But now there was a holy roar, tremendous, hill-shaking, and an amplified voice began to speak very fast Italian. The voice had no owner: the open ecstatic mouths drank the air, their black eyes searching for the voice above the high stucco buff walls, the window-shutters thrown open for the heat, trees and sky. Joy suffused their stubbled faces at the loud indistinct words. The cry started—"*Viva, viva, viva!*"—and caught up. "So," said Enderby to Vesta, "it's him, is it?" She nodded. And now the French became excited, ear-cocking, lips parted in joy, as the voice seemed to announce fantastic departures by air: Toulon, Marseilles, Bordeaux, Avignon. "*Bravo!*" The vales redoubled to the hills, and they to heaven. "*Bravo, bravo!*" Enderby was terrified, bewildered. "What exactly is going on?" he cried. Now the voice began to speak

American, welcoming contingents of pilgrims from Illinois, Ohio, New Jersey, Massachusetts, Delaware. And Enderby felt chill hands clasp his hot body all over as he saw the rhythmical signals of a cheerleader, a young man in a new jersey with a large blue-woven P.

"Rhode Island," said the voice. "Kentucky, Texas."

"Rah, rah, rah!" came the cheers. "The Pope, the Pope, the Pope!"

"Oh God, no," moaned Enderby. "For Christ's sake let me get out of here." He tried to push, with feeble excuse-mes, but the crowd behind was dense, the eyes up to the hills, and he trod on a little French girl's foot and made her cry. "Harry," said Vesta sharply, "you just stay where you are."

"Mississippi, California, Oklahoma." It was like something from a sort of holy Walt Whitman.

"Rah, rah rah! The Pope, the Pope, the Pope!"

"Oh Christ," sobbed Enderby, "please let me get out, please. I'm not well, I'm ill, I've got to get to a lavatory."

"The Church Militant is here," said Vesta nastily, "and all you want is a lavatory."

"I do, I do." Enderby, his eyes full of tears, was now grappling with a redolent Spaniard who would not let him pass. The French child still cried, pointing up at Enderby. Suddenly there was a sort of exordium to prayer and everybody began to kneel in the dust of the courtyard. Enderby became a kind of raging schoolmaster in a sea of stunted children. She too knelt; Vesta knelt; she got down on her knees with the rest of them. "Get up!" bawled Enderby, and, like a sergeant, "Get off your bloody knees!"

"Kneel down," she ordered, her eyes like powerful green poisons. "Kneel down. Everybody's looking at you."

"Oh my God," wept Enderby, praying against the current, and he began to try to get out again, lifting his legs as though striding through treacle. He trod on knees, skirts, even shoulders, and was cursed roundly even by some who prayed with frightening sincerity, their eyes dewy with prayer. Stumbling, himself cursing, goose-stepping clumsily, laying episcopal palms on heads, he cut through the vast cake of kneelers and reached, almost vomiting, blind with sweat, the gate and the hill-road. As he staggered down the hill, past the smiling vendors, he muttered to himself, "I was a bloody fool to come." From the top of the hill came the sound of a great Amen.

Three

"*Cefil Uensdi*," said the man. "*Totnam Otispar. Cardiff Siti*." He had a surprised lion-face, though hairless, with a few wavy filaments crawling over his otherwise bare scalp. Staring all the time at Enderby as though convinced Enderby wished to mesmerise him and too polite (a) to object that he did not wish to be mesmerised and (b) to announce that the mesmerism was ineffectual, he ever and anon brought, with a bold arm gesture, a cigarette-end to his lips, drawing on this with a desperate groan as if it were a sole source of oxygen and he dying.

"*Tutti buoni*," nodded Enderby over his wine. "All football very good."

The man gripped Enderby's left forearm and gave a mirthless grin of deep deep blood-brotherhood's understanding. They were sitting at rough trestle-tables in the open air. Here Frascati had reached its last gasp of cheapness—golden gallons for a few bits of tinkly metal. "*Ues Bromic*," the man went on in his litany. "*Mancesita Iunaiti. Uolveramiton Uanarar*." This though more heartening than the geographical manifests up the hill, was beginning to weary Enderby. He wondered vaguely if perhaps that was what Etruscan had sounded like. Up on the main road, beyond the dark and nameless trees that were a wall to this sky-roofed tavern, the pilgrims could be heard coming back to their buses, walking slowly and with dignity now after the comic free-wheeling down the hill. If Vesta had any sense at all she would know where to find him. Not that, in his present mood, he cared much whether she found him or not. Next to the lion-faced man with the football litany lolled

154

a patriot who did not believe that Mussolini was really dead: like King Arthur he would rise with unsheathed sword to avenge his country's new wrongs. This man said that the English had always been the friends of Mussolini; Italian and Briton together had fought to expel the foul Tedesco. He bunched one side of his face often at Enderby, raising his thumb like an emperor at the games, winking in complicity. There were other drinkers on the periphery, some with bad unsouthern teeth, one carrying on his shoulder an ill-kempt parrot that squawked part of a Bellini aria. There was also a very buxom girl, a country beauty called Bice, who brought round the wine. Enderby did not, would not, lack company. He only wished his Italian were better. But "Blackburn Rovers" he fed to the litanist and "Newcastle United"; to the patriot "Addis Ababa" and "La Fanciulla del Golden West." Meanwhile thunder flapped with extreme gentleness on the other side of the lake. "Garibaldi," he said. "Long live Italian Africa!"

When Vesta at last arrived the pleasant dirty drinking-yard at once was disinfected into a background for a *Vogue* fashion pose. She looked tired, but her calm and elegance fluttered all present, making even the roughest drinkers consider removing their caps. Some, remembering that they were Italian, said dutifully, *"Molto bella"* and made poulterer's pinching gestures to the air. Without preamble she said to Enderby, "I knew I'd find you in some such place as this. I'm fed up. I'm sick to death. You seem to be doing your utmost to make a farce out of our honeymoon and a fool out of me."

"Sit down," invited Enderby. "Do sit down. Have some of this nice Frascati." He bowed her towards a dry and fairly clean part of the bench on which he had been sitting. The litanist, grasping that she was *Inglese*, assuming a passion for football in her accordingly, said, ingratiatingly, "Arse an all," meaning a football team. Vesta would not sit. She said:

"No. You're to come with me and look for this coach. What I have to say to you must wait till we get back to Rome. I don't want to risk breaking down in public."

"Peace," mocked Enderby. "Peace and order. You

played a very mean trick on me, and I shan't forget it in a hurry. A really dirty trick."

"Come on. Some of the coaches are going already. Leave that wine and come on." Enderby saw that there still remained a half-litre of this precious golden urine. He filled his glass and said, "*Salute.*" His swallow excited cries of "*Bravo,*" as enthusiastic as those heard up the sacred hill, though not then for Enderby. "Right," said Enderby, waving farewell. "We're late," said Vesta. "Late for that coach. We wouldn't have been late if I hadn't had to come looking for you."

"It was a mean trick," repeated Enderby. "Why didn't you tell me that we were being taken to the Vatican?"

"Oh, don't be so stupid. That's not the Vatican; that's his summer residence. Now where on earth is this coach?"

There was a bewildering number of coaches, all looking alike. The pilgrims had nestled snugly and smugly in them; some of them were impatiently roaring off. Coaches had settled everywhere—by the roadside, down small hilly streets—like big bugs in bed-crevices. Vesta and Enderby began to examine coaches swiftly but intently, as though they proposed to buy them, passengers and all. None looked familiar, and Vesta made noises of distress. Listening through his thick curtain of wine, Enderby thought he heard the veneers and inlays of Received English stripped roughly off, so that something like raw Lallans became audible, as spicy as home-pickled onions with its gutturals and glottal stops. She was really worried. Enderby said:

"Damn it all, if they do leave us behind there's no great harm done. There must be a bus service or trains or taxis or something. It's not as though we're lost in the jungle or anything."

"You insulted him," complained Vesta. "It was blasphemous, too. These people take their religion very seriously, you know."

"Nonsense," said Enderby. Stealthily the sky had, above their searching heads, been clouding over. There was a greenish look in the atmosphere as though the atmosphere proposed, sooner or later, to be sick. From beyond the lake came renewed gentle drummings, as of finger-tips on timpani. "It's going to rain," wailed Vesta. "Och, we'll be caught in it. We'll be drenched." But Enderby, in impermeable of wine, said not to worry, they would catch that blasted bus.

But they did not catch it. As soon as they approached a coach, the coach skittishly started up, its gears grinding a derisive expletive all for Enderby. Faces looked down, grinning pilgrims, and some hands waved. It was as though Vesta and Enderby were host and hostess after some huge party, seeing off loads of quite unappreciative guests. "He's done it deliberately," cried Vesta. "He's getting his own back. Oh, you *are* a nuisance." They hurried towards another coach and, like a kitten in chase-me play, it at once began to move off. There were very few left now, but Enderby was fairly sure that, from one of these few, a Roman face, the ignoble face of a Roman guide, leered and Roman fingers made a complicated gesture of mean triumph.

The timpanists across the lake picked up their felt sticks and rolled for a few bars, while the coaches, as though they could thus escape from bad weather, sang off to the city. The lake underwent complex metallurgical changes and the sky, cloaking hot and fearsome lights, began to sweat, then cry. "Oh Jesus," called Vesta, "here it comes." And indeed there it came while they were still half a mile from shelter other than that of trees: the sky cracked open like a waterbutt, and the air became vertical glass down which pail after pail was poured. They dashed blindly towards the lakeside inn, Vesta tottering on her smart spikes, Enderby gripping her elbow as though her arm were a pair of blackboard dividers, already too wet really to be all that urgent about seeking shelter. The deluge made Enderby's scalp prickle with dandruff, and his fawn summer suit was soaked. But she, poor girl, was already a wreck: hat comically flopping, hair in rat-tails, mascara running, her face that of a crying old crone as though she wept over the disintegration of her *chic*. "In here," gasped Enderby, steering her straight into a room smelling of size and new paint, empty chairs and tables in it, a sleek boy-waiter admiring the free show of the rain. "I think," panted Enderby, "that we'll have to take a room, if they have one. The first thing to do is to get dry. Perhaps they'll—" The waiter called a name, then turned his young empty face back on these two wet ones. Enderby said, *Una camera. Si é possible.* The boy called again, an unbroken boy's yelp under the drumming water. A woman came, creamily fat in a flowered frock, clucked commiseration, took in in a swift look Vesta's ringed finger, said there was a *camera* with one *letto.* Beside her smiling hugeness Vesta looked a snivelling waif. *"Grazie,"* said Enderby. Lightning cracked momentarily the lake-sky, the timpanists counted half a bar and came in with a fine peal, rolling cosmic Berlioz chords. Vesta made the sign of the cross. She was shivering.

"What," asked Enderby, "did you do that for?"

"Oh God," she said, "it scares me. I can't stand thunder." Enderby felt his stomach turn over when she said that.

Four

Up in the bedroom they confronted each other naked. Somehow, for some reason, Enderby had not expected that, when they had stripped off their drenched clothes and dumped them outside the door, they would confront each other naked. Naked confrontation was supposed to come about otherwise: deliberately, in desire or duty. Enderby had been trying to digest too many other things to foresee this prelapsarian picture (and there up the hill, so neatly fitting into the pattern, was a great postlapsarian witness), for the room was very much like his own as a boy—pictures of St John the Baptist, the Sacred Heart, the B.V.M., a melodramatic Golgotha; a smell of unclean bedclothes, dust, boots and stale holy water; a stringy unbeaten carpet; a narrow bed. This reproduction of the main stage-set for so many adolescent monodramas, here in Italy under rain, did not depress him: that bedroom had always been an enclave

158

of revolt in stepmother country. Very clearly, lines of an unpublished poem came back to him:

... There were times, misunderstood by the family,
    When you, at fifteen, on your summer evening bed
Believed there were ancient towns you might an-
    ciently visit.
    There might be a neglected platform on some sta-
    tion
And a ticket bought when the clock was off its guard.
    Oh, who can dismember the past? The boy on the
        friendly bed
Lay on the unpossessed mother, the bosom of history,
    And is gathered to her at last. And tears I suppose
Still hunger for that reeking unwashed pillow,
    That bed ingrained with all the dirt of the past,
The mess and lice and stupidity of the Golden Age,
    But a mother and loving, ultimately Eden. ...

He nodded several times, standing there naked in rainy Italy, thinking that it was a mother he had always wanted, not a stepmother, and he had made that mother himself in his bedroom, made her out of the past, history, myth, the craft of verse. When she was made she became slimmer, younger, more like a mistress; she became the Muse.

Lightning again shivered the firmament and then, after a careful count, the laughing drummers knocked hell out of their resonant membranes. Vesta gave a little scream, put her arms round Enderby's trunk, and then seemed to try to push herself inside him as though he were a deviscerated rabbit of great size and she a mound of palpitating stuffing. "There, there," said Enderby, kindly but disturbed: she had no right to bring these stepmother terrors into his adolescent bedroom. Then he sweated, seeing more than a mere fear of thunder. Still, he clasped her to him and soothed her shoulder-blades, thinking how such naked contacts had an essential unalluring core of *heartiness:* the slap of palm on buttock; the jelly sound of two moist segments of flesh drawing apart. She shivered: the air had cooled considerably.

"You'd better," said Enderby, "get into bed."

"Yes," she shuddered, "yes. Into bed." And she pulled him towards bed, her grip on him unrelaxed, so that they shambled to it as though clumsily dancing. As soon as they were in it, a skein of lightning lay an instant against the sky, like a stunned man against a cliff, and then the drums whammed out from hi-fi loudspeakers all over the heavens. She again seemed to try to enter him in fear, a rather soft rock of ages, and he smelt her terror, as familiar a smell as that faintly oily one of the coverlet.

"There," he said again, clasping her, stroking and soothing. It was a very narrow bed. This, he kept reminding himself, was his bride, an intelligent and desirable young woman and it was time, under the thunder and rain, to be thinking of performing, that is to say consummating, that is to say. He stealthily felt his way down to find out what was his body's view of this constatation, but all was quiet there, as though he were calmly reading Jane Austen.

The rain eased and the thunder was trundled, grumbling, off. Enderby felt her body relax and seem, somehow, to grow moister and more expectant. She gripped him still, though there was no more thunder to fear. Enderby's engines, rusty and sluggish, tried to wake up and respond to various quite unoriginal ganglionic stimuli, but there were certain difficulties which were secret and shameful. Enderby had been spoiled by too many pictures; it was a long time since he had held a real woman in his arms like this; he had possessed in imagination houri after houri of a beauty, passivity, voluptuousness no real woman could ever touch. Perhaps, he now felt, if this body he held could become—just for twenty or thirty seconds—one of those harem dreams of his, pampered, pouting, perfumed, steatopygous, he could, he was sure, achieve what it was a plain duty, apart from all questions of gratification, to achieve. But the body of his bride was spare, barely cushioned. With a desperate effort he conjured a gross tit-swinging image, saw whose image it was, then, making the retching noises of a child trying to disgust, he swung out of the bed with unwonted agility and stood shivering on the worn mat. "What's the matter?" she called. "What is it? Don't you feel well?" Forgetting that he was naked, Enderby dashed out of the room without replying. Two doors down the corridor was the sign *Gabinetto*, and Enderby, re-living the past, entered it and locked its door. To his horror he found that the lavatory was not a sane comfortable English WC but a Continental crouch-hole with a right-hand hand-rail and a toilet-roll-fitting on the same side. Once, many years ago, he had fallen into one of these holes. He almost cried for the security of his old seaside lavatory but, unlocking the door to leave, the tears froze as he heard two female Italian voices on the corridor. One of these, saying loud passing greetings to the other, was now right up against the *gabinetto* door and trying the handle. Enderby swiftly re-locked himself in. The voice spoke urgently, saying, for all Enderby knew, that its owner was in a bad way, desperate, and couldn't wait too long. Enderby seated himself on the edge of the low crouch-hole dais, saying, "Go away. Go away," and, as an afterthought, "*Io sono nudo, completamente nudo,*" wondering if that was correct Italian. Correct or not, the voice was silenced and apparently carried back down the corridor. Enderby the completely naked sat on, in thinking pose, feeling at his lowest ebb.

Five

Like an Arab thief, though not so slippery, Enderby darted back to the bedroom. Vesta was sitting up in the bed, smoking a ship's (or export) Woodbine through a holder and, because of that, looking more naked than she was, though this, reflected Enderby, was not really possible. "Now then," she said. "We're going to have the whole thing out."

"No," mumbled Enderby. "Not like this." He sat shamefacedly down on the cane chair in the corner, wriggling and wincing as odd prickly cane-thorns assaulted his bottom. "Not," said Enderby, "with no clothes on. It's not right." He joined his hands as for prayer and, with this frail cage of fingers, hid his genitals from the smoking woman in the bed. "I mean," said Enderby, "one can't really talk about anything naked."

"Who are you to say that?" she said fiercely. "What do you know about the world? My first husband and I once belonged to a nudist camp—" (Enderby whimpered at the sudden formality of "first husband") "—and there used to be *really* prominent men and women there, and they didn't have any *pudeur* about talking. And they, I might add," she added acidly, "could talk about rather more than lavatories and stomachs and how rotten the Roman Empire must have been." Enderby gazed glumly out of the window, seeing that the rain had stopped and the June warmth, encouraged, was creeping back into the Italian evening. Then he was granted a brief image of a fat sack-bellied middle-aged female nudist don, breasts hanging like tripe, discoursing on aesthetic values. This cheered him up a little, so he turned boldly on Vesta to say:

"All right, then. Let's have it out, the whole damned thing. What exactly do you think you're playing at?"

"I don't understand you," she said. "I'm playing at nothing. I'm working hard, with absolutely no cooperation from you, to try and build a marriage."

"And your idea of building a marriage is to try to drag me back into the Church, is that it?" said Enderby, half-uncovering his genitals so as to gesticulate with one hand. "And in a nasty sly way, too. Not saying anything about being a Catholic yourself, and even being quite ready to have a registry office wedding, even though you know that sort of wedding means nothing at all."

"Oh," she said, "you admit that, do you? You admit that it means nothing at all? In other words, you admit that a Catholic wedding is the only valid one?"

"I don't admit anything," cried Enderby. "All I'm saying is that I'm confused, completely confused about what's supposed to be going on. What I mean is, we've only been married a couple of days, and everything seems to have changed. You weren't like this before, were you? You weren't like this when we were living in your flat in London, were you? Everything was all right then. You were on my side, and you were getting on with your job and I was getting on with mine, and it was all nice and pleasant and not a care in the world. But now look at things. Since we got married, and that's only a couple of days ago, mind you, only a couple of days—" (two fingers held up, five on his genitals) "—you've been doing your damnedest to turn into my stepmother."

Vesta's mouth opened and smoke wandered out. "To what, did you say? To turn into what?"

"My stepmother, bitch as she was. You're not fat yet, but I suppose you soon will be. You keep belching away all the time and saying "Och" and going on at me—natter and nag, nag and natter—and you're scared of the bloody thunder and you're trying to get me to go back into the Church. Why? That's what I want to know. Why? What's your motive? What are you getting at? What are you trying to do?"

"This," she said heavily, "is fantastic. This is the most incredible—this is the most incredible fantastic—" She started to get out of bed. Enderby, seeing this, saw that there would be too much visible nakedness about the room, so he lunged across from the cane chair, genitals swinging, and pushed her back into bed and pulled the clothes over her. He said:

"We'll have less frivolity, if you don't mind, and less nonsense. Before we got married—listen to me, I'm talking—before we got married you were what I'd dreamed of, ever since I was a boy. You were everything she wasn't; you were a release; you were a way out. You were something that would kill her for good and all. And now look at you." He pointed sternly. She, as though he were a stranger who had just broken in, pulled the grey sheet over her bosom and looked fearful. "You're trying to drag me back into that old world, aren't you? Back to the bloody Church and female smells all over the place——"

"You're drunk," she said. "You're mad." There was a knock at the door and Enderby, gesticulating, went to answer it, now wearing his nakedness as unconsciously as if it were a suit. "Drunk, eh?" he said. "Mad, eh? You've made me drunk, that's what it is." He opened the door, and the lady of the house presented a pressed pile of dried clothes. "*Tante grazie,*" said Enderby, and then, turning back on his wife, he presented his bottom to the *signora;* she slammed the door and went off speaking loud Italian. "Things," said Enderby, "already," dumping the clothes on the bed, "have not worked out at all as I expected. It's been a bloody big mistake, that's what it's been."

She reached over for her clothes, angrily fussily trembling, saying, "A mistake, you say? That's gratitude, I must say, gratitude." She paused, one hand on her clothes, breathing deeply as if a stethoscope had begun to wander down her back, eyes downcast, seeking self-control. Then she said, calmly, "I'm keeping my temper, you notice. Somebody has to be rational." Enderby began, in a sort of hopping dance, to put on his underpants. "Listen to me," she said, "listen. You're like a child, you know so little about life. When I first met you, it looked horrible that a man of so much talent should be living the way you did. No, let me speak, let me keep my temper." Enderby, from inside his shirt, was mumbling something. "You had nothing to do with women," she continued, "and no faith in anything, and no sense of responsibility to society. Oh, I know you had substitutes for all those things," she said bitterly. "Dirty photographs instead of flesh and blood." Enderby repeated the hopping dance, this time with his trousers, scowling and blushing. "Society," she said, with loud eloquence, "shrunk to the smallest room in the house. Is that any life for a man?" she asked strongly. "Is that any life for a poet? Is that the way you expect to make great poetry?"

"Poetry," said Enderby. "Don't you start telling me about poetry. I know all about poetry, thank you very much," he said with a bull-snort. "But let me tell you this. There's no obligation to accept society or women or religion or anything else, not for anyone there isn't. And

164

as for poetry, that's a job for anarchs. Poetry's made by rebels and exiles and outsiders, it's made by people on their own, not by sheep baaing bravo to the Pope. Poets don't need religion and they don't need bloody little cocktail-party gossip either; it's they who make language and make myths. Poets don't need anybody except themselves."

Vesta picked up her brassière and wearily dropped herself into it as though it were some necessary instrument of penance. "You seemed," she said, "to like going to parties. You seemed to think it was a good thing to wear a decent suit and talk with people. You said it was civilised. You gave me, one evening you may have forgotten, a long dull lecture on the Poet and Society. You even went to the trouble of thanking me for having rescued you from your old life. Some day," she sighed, "you'll make it absolutely clear to people what exactly you *do* want."

"Oh," said Enderby, "it was all right, I suppose. It made a nice change. It was nice to be clean and smart, you see, and hear educated accents. It was, you see, so different from my stepmother." Now fully dressed, he sat with greater confidence on the cane-bottomed chair in the corner. "But," he said, "if society means going back to the Church, I don't want anything to do with society. As far as I'm concerned, the Church is all tied up with that bitch, superstitious and nasty and unclean."

"Oh, you're so stupid," said Vesta, having put on her dress swiftly and neatly. "You're so *uneducated*. Some of the best modern brains are in the Church—poets, novelists, philosophers. Just because a silly illiterate woman made a nonsense out of it for you doesn't mean that it *is* a nonsense. You're a fool, but you surely aren't such a fool as all that. Anyway," she said, clicking her handbag open and rummaging for a comb, "nobody's asking you to go back into the Church. The Church, presumably, can get on very well without you. But if I'm going back, you might at least have the courtesy and decency to go through the form of going back with me."

"You mean," said Enderby, "that we'll have to get properly married? By a priest in a church? Look," he said, folding his arms and crossing his legs, "why didn't you think about all this before? Why did you have to wait till our honeymoon before you decided to baa back to the fold? Don't answer, because I know the answer. It's because you want to go down to posterity as the woman who reorganised Enderby's life, faith and works. It's what Rawcliffe said, and I hadn't thought of it before, because I really believed that you had some affection for me, but, looking at it more soberly, I can see now that was impossible, me being ugly and middle-aged and, as you're kind enough to say, stupid. All right, then; now we know how we stand."

She was combing her hair, gritting her teeth at the tangles, and the penny-colour shone out, crackling, renewed after its rat-tailed dullness. "Fool, fool," she said. "My idea was that we could make a go of marriage. We still can. Of course, if you think that Rawcliffe's more trustworthy than I am (and remember that Rawcliffe's jealous as hell of you) then that's your own affair and you can get on with it. The fact is that, for all your stupidity, I'm very fond of you and, at the same time, I feel that I can make you happy by making you more normal, more sane."

"There you are, you see," said Enderby in triumph.

"Oh, nonsense. What I mean is this: an artist needs a place in the world, he needs to be committed to something, and he needs to be in touch with the current of life. Surely the trouble with all your work is that it reads as though it's cut off from the current?"

"Very interesting," said Enderby, his arms still folded. "Very, very fascinating."

"Och," she said, drooping as though suddenly very weary. "What does it matter? Who's going to care whether you write great poetry or not? The feeblest teenage pop-singer is a million times more regarded than you are. You sell only a handful of copies of every book you write. There's going to be a nuclear war and the libraries will be destroyed. What's the use? What good can it all possibly be if one doesn't believe in God?" She sat on the bed, quite dispirited, and began to cry softly. Enderby came softly over to her and said:

"I'm sorry. I'm terribly sorry. But I think I'm too old to learn really, too old to change. Perhaps we'd better admit it's all a mistake and go back to things as they were before. No real harm's been done, not yet, has it? I mean, we're not even properly married, are we?"

She looked up sternly and said, "You're like a child. A child who doesn't like his first morning at school so says he doesn't think he'll go back in the afternoon." She wiped her eyes and became hard, self-possessed again. "Nobody makes a fool of me," she said. "Nobody throws me over."

"You could have the marriage annulled," said Enderby. "On the grounds of non-consummation. Because it won't ever be consummated, you know."

"You think," said Vesta, "that you'll go back to living on a tiny but adequate income, writing your poetry in the lavatory. But you won't. What little bit of capital you've got left I shall have. I'll make sure of that. And the things you've bought are on my name. Nobody makes a fool out of me."

"I can get a job," said Enderby, growing angry. "I'm not reliant on anybody. I can be independent." Then he felt tears of self-pity coming. "The poet," he said, whimpering, "is best left to live on his own." Through his tears he had confused images of Dantesque eagles flitting round lightning-shot peaks. He left the edge of the bed and went to stand in a corner. "The poet," he said, blubbing like that seven-year-old Elizabethan bridegroom who had cried to go home with his father.

3

One

"My main purpose," said swaying Rawcliffe, "was to present you with—" He swayed and fumbled in various pockets, drawing out filthy old papers decaying at their folds, two half-used tubes of stomach tablets which were dust-fluffy, a referee's whistle, a dry rattle of ballpoints, finally a quite clean envelope. "—These. Tickets for a première. I think, my dear old Enderby, you should be reasonably amused. I have no further interest in the film in question, having been so closely involved in it. And, let me tell you, Enderby, it is a cheap film, a film made on a shoestring, a film made very quickly, with bits borrowed—quite without permission, you know—from other films. Strega," he said suddenly to Dante behind the bar. The bar was, as at their first meeting in it, empty except for them. Enderby felt worn and old, his mouth seeming to taste of cascara-coated motoring chocolate. It was mid-morning, the day after the day of their return from the papal township by the lake, and Vesta had gone to see a woman called Princess Irene Galitzine, a Roman lady famed for her boutique models or couture designs or something. Vesta was spending money fast. "And," said Rawcliffe, "there are, of course, for this the world expects of Italy, several *sfacciate donne Fiorentine*, except that they're not Florentine but Roman, *monstrado con le poppe il petto*. There, Enderby, you see: brazen-faced bitches showing breasts with paps. Dante was a great prophet; he foresaw the Italian film industry. Dante."

Dante behind the bar bowed. "Same a name," he said confidentially to Enderby.

"Bloody big coincidence, eh?" swayed Rawcliffe. "You'll find everything in Dante, Enderby, if you look long enough. Even the film you're going to see derives its title from the *Purgatorio*. I found that title, Enderby, I, an English poet, for none of these unholy Romans has even so much as glanced at Dante since leaving school, if any of them ever went to school." Enderby took from the envelope the cards of invitation and saw that the film was named *L'Animal Binato*. It meant nothing to him. He turned to the bottle of Frascati on the counter and poured himself a tumbler. "Drinking hard, I see, Enderby," said Rawcliffe. "If I may make so lewd a guess, it is because you are using muscles you never used before. Venus catches cold without Bacchus and Ceres, although you can leave out that goddess of breakfast foods for all I care. Strega," he called again, nodding vigorously.

"Look," said Enderby, "I'm not taking you home again. You were a damned nuisance last time, Rawcliffe, and you made a real fool out of me. If you're going to pass out here, you can stay passed out, is that clear? I've got worries of my own without having to look after—"

"He talks in rhyme," said Rawcliffe in exaggerated wonder. "He is still very much the poet, is he not? But for how much longer now, eh?" he said sinisterly, slitting his eyes. "The Muse, O Enderby. Has the Muse yet been in to tell you that she has booked her one-way flight to Parnassus or wherever Muses live? She has done her long stint with Enderby and the time has come for Enderby to abjure this rough magic and pack it in, the Muse, unlike Ariel, being no airy slave of indeterminate sex but a woman, very much a woman." Rawcliffe now

169

made himself look shrunken and very old. "Perhaps, Enderby, I was destined never to be much of a success with that particular woman because of—you know, because of—that is to say, a certain, shall I say, indeterminate attitude towards sex." He sighed in a litre or so of Roman bar air. He drank down a centilitre or less of Strega. "And now, you see, Enderby, I'm on the move again. This afternoon, to be precise. So, you see, you won't have to carry me home or anywhere. The BEA men will come and collect me, excellent fellows. They will get me on that plane. Where am I going, Enderby?" He leered roguishly, wagging a finger. "Ah, I'm not telling you. I am, suffice it to say, on my way further south. I have picked up my little packet here." He tapped, winking, the right breast of his coat. "And now little Marco and Mario and that bloody Piedmontese, to quote Milton, can go and stuff themselves. I have finished, Enderby, with the lot. Finish, Enderby," he said loudly and with emphatic fists on the counter, "with the lot. You, I mean. Get wise to yourself, as they say. Wake up. A poet must be alone."

Enderby pouted, pouring himself the last of his bottle. He felt that it was not up to Rawcliffe to tell him that he must be alone. He took from his inside jacket-pocket a piece of paper on which he had been doing sums. "Did you know," he said, "how much mink costs? Mink," he repeated. "I have it here," he said carefully. "One Black Diamond mink coat: one thousand four hundred and ninety-five pounds. One hip-length jacket: five hundred and ninety-five pounds. One pastel milk bolero: three hundred and ninety-five pounds. We leave out of account," said Enderby, "as being too inexpensive for serious consideration, a pastel stole at two hundred pounds. That's a frippery, a mere nugacity." He smiled sillily. "What," he asked, "can a poet do with no money, eh? How does a poet live?"

"Well," said Rawcliffe, both hands round his new Strega as if it were something to be strangled, "there are jobs, you know. All sorts of jobs. Only the very luckiest of poets can be professional poets. You could teach or write for the papers or do film scripts or advertising slogans or lecture for the British Council or get unskilled work in a factory. Lots of things to be done."

"But," objected Enderby, "suppose one is no good at anything except writing poetry? Suppose one makes a bloody fool of oneself at anything else?"

"Oh," said Rawcliffe reasonably, "I don't think that anybody could make such a bloody fool of himself that it would really matter. Now, if I were you, I should leave everything in the hands of Auntie Vesta. She'll fix you up with something nice and easy."

"But," protested Enderby, "only a minute ago you were telling me that I've got to be alone."

"I see," said Rawcliffe seeing into his Strega. "Well, in that case it's all a bit of a mess, isn't it, Enderby? But don't worry me with your worries, Enderby, because I've got worries of my own, you see. You sort out things for yourself." He seemed suddenly sober and rather cold despite the June warmth. He downed his Strega and shivered exaggeratedly, as if he had taken a wholesome but bitter medicine. "Perhaps," he said, "I should have started this heavy drinking business earlier. I might possibly be dead by now instead of having putatively fathered or foster-fathered or helped with the illegitimate fathering of *L'Animal Binato*, alive and healthy and almost impervious to the more deadly effects of alcohol. I should, by rights, Enderby, have considered seeing myself off when I found that the lyric gift had departed from me. I could at least have contrived to be careless crossing the road, couldn't I? And, instead of that propaganda job during the war, I could perhaps have volunteered for something more genuinely lethal."

"What," asked Enderby morbidly, "did it feel like? I mean, when the lyric gift departed?" Rawcliffe looked up so morosely, fixing Enderby with an eye so baleful, that Enderby began to smile nervously. Rawcliffe said:

"Blast your mean little soul, it's no laughing matter, even in retrospect." Then he came nearer to Enderby and gave him a close-up of bad teeth and worse breath. "It was like everything going all dead," said Rawcliffe. "It was like going dumb. I could see quite clearly what had to be said, but I couldn't say it. I could perceive

171

that an imaginative relationship existed between disparate objects, but I couldn't tell what the relationship was. I used to sit for hours with paper in front of me, hours and hours, Enderby, and then I would at last get something down. But what I got down somehow—don't laugh at me—had a smell of decay about it. What I got down was *evil*, and I used to shudder when I crumpled it up and threw it in the fire. And then, at night, in bed, I used to wake up to hear mocking laughter. And then," tottered Rawcliffe, "one night there was the sound of an awful *click*, and then everything in the bedroom seemed cold, somehow, cold and obscene. I knew, Enderby, it was all over. Thenceforward I should be outside the Garden, useless to anyone, a mess, and, moreover, Enderby, in some indefinable way *evil*. Like an unfrocked priest, Enderby. The unfrocked priest does not become a mere neuter harmless human being; he becomes *evil*. He has to be used by something, for supernature abhors a supervacuum, so he becomes *evil*, Enderby." He swigged more Strega and staggered, as it were, against the ropes saying, "And all that is left for the poet, Enderby, when the inspiration is departed, Enderby, is the travesty, the plagiarism, the popularisation, the debasement, the curse. He has drunk the milk of paradise, but it has long passed through his system, Enderby, and, unfortunately for him, he remembers the taste." Rawcliffe shut weary eyes, saying, *"Ara vos prec,"* and then "be mindful in due time of my pain. I translate, Enderby, because you would not understand the original Provençal. That is the poet Arnaut Daniel in Purgatory. He was a lucky bugger, or is, Enderby, a lucky bugger to be in Purgatory. Not like some of us." At this point, Rawcliffe went quite gently to sleep standing up, his head reposing on arms he had folded on the counter. Dante said: "Better e slip." There was a plum-plush settee against the wall; to this Dante and Enderby carried, led, pushed, dragged Rawcliffe. "Too mash fackin Strega," diagnosed Dante. Sighing, Enderby sat next to Rawcliffe, a fresh bottle of Frascati and a tumbler on the table in front of him, and he continued to do sums on bits of paper. At intervals Rawcliffe gave gnomic utterance, often obscure, from his sleep; reports from the first crazed space-traveller:

"No expense of breath in falling downstairs."

"Mario, put that bread-knife away."

"You are a naughty boy, but not undelectable."

"In all the antholololologies."

"This will make Enderby feel very sick."

Indeed, Enderby felt very sick when he had worked out his sums and found that his credit balance in the bank stood at, taking the most liberal computation, little more than four hundred and ninety pounds. It was pointless asking himself where the money had gone to, for he knew all too well: it had flowed back to its source: his stepmother had given and his stepmother had, in a youthful, well-spoken, dove-soft, spring-smelling, highly improbable disguise, taken away again. From his sleep Rawcliffe called:

"Aha! Man not the boats, but woman-and-child them. I'll shoot all else. Back, you brute, back. The rash, smart, poet. Very wise of him to pack up."

Enderby spoke sternly to this dark voice. "I am not packing up," he said. This silenced Rawcliffe's sleep-persona temporarily. To himself, Enderby said, "If I can keep the relationship on the most superficial of levels, for superficially I am quite fond of her, then it should be possible to contrive some sort of satisfactory coexistence. But I will not be ordered about. And she has, after all, a good job and I could, at a pinch, refuse to get a job of my own or have a job found for me. The Sussex house has many rooms. My stomach is better." Rawcliffe's sleeping voice spoke again from outer space:

"You will do as I say, Vincent. I will not have you calling Reggy an old queen. He is not old." And then, "God should feel highly flattered that we have invented Him." And finally, before falling into serious speechless sleep, in the voice of Yeats speaking with the voice of Swift speaking with the voice of Job: *Let the day perish wherein I was born.*" Enderby shuddered, the wine seeming sharper than usual.

Two

They arrived late for the film première. The cinema was in an obscure street somewhere off the Viale Aventino, and the taxi-driver had difficulty in finding it. He at first denied, in the manner of taxi-drivers, the existence of what he himself did not know existed, until Enderby waved a ticket of invitation in his moustached face. The façade of the cinema rather let down the rest of Rome, thought Enderby, as he helped Vesta out of the cab.

Sculpturally and architecturally, the rest of Rome was rubbishy, yet rubbishy on a baroque and hypnotic scale, like the delusions of grandeur of some gibbering G.P.I. patient. But here was authentic fleapit, from the look of it, epitome of every bughouse that Enderby had, as a child, queued outside on Saturday afternoons, sticky paw clutching twopence, filthy-jerseyed other children clinging to him aromatically lest they lose him in the scrimmage of entrance, Enderby being the only one of their lot who could read. The old silent film had, Enderby reflected, been, in one facet, an extension of literature. He said now to Vesta, "This is one of those places where you go in with a blouse and come out with a jumper." He tweaked her elbow jocularly, but she looked queenlily blank. "Blouse?" she said. "I'm not wearing a blouse." She was, in fact, wearing black silk from her Roman-lady *couturière*, sleeveless, the back *décolleté*, the skirt slim, tails of mink dripping from her shoulders against the night's cool. Enderby was in white tuxedo, black silk in breast pocket to match tie. But it looked as though he needn't have taken so much trouble: there were no adoring crowds, no gleaming stars' mouths of coral and ivory in maniacal abandon to the flashbulbs, no jostle of Cadillacs and Bentleys. There were a few decent Fiats, unattended, evidently owner-driven; a painted banner across the deplorable rococo façade said, in the midst of cheap coloured bulbs, L'ANIMAL BINATO. The man who took their cards of invitation chewed something morosely and his lantern-jaw was ill-shaven. It let down Vesta as much as it let down Rome. Little, of course, thought Enderby, could let down Enderby.

They were flashlamped to their seats. Enderby felt torn cheap plush beneath him and smelt a strong citrus tang through the dark. Orange, too, bloodless orange, was the light which warmed the worn stage curtains. These now, as if they had been waiting only for Enderby and his wife, parted to the noise of loud cinema music, banal, conventionally sinister. Enderby peered through the dark: there did not, by the feel and sound of things, seem to be a very large audience. The screen said L'ANIMAL BINATO and followed this with jerkily dissolved frames of the names of the conspirators: Alberto Formica; Giorgio Farfalla; Maria Vacca; A. F. Corvo; P. Ranocchio; Giacomo Capra; Beatrice Pappagallo; R. Coniglio; Giovanni Chiocciola; Gina Gatto. Rawcliffe's name appeared near the end, Italianised to, as far as Enderby could tell, something like Raucliffo. "Serve him right," thought Enderby, and told Vesta so. She said shhhhh. The film began.

Night, very much night, with tortured cypresses lit by lightning. Thunder (Vesta dug her nails into Enderby's hand). Tempestuous wind. Camera tracks to steps of terrace, handsome woman standing thereon, much of Italian bosom exposed to lightning. She raises arms, cornily, to stormy heavens in crash of thunder. Camera swings up towards sky. Another stock shot of lightning cracking cloud like teacup. Thunder (Vesta's nails). New camera angle shows a something speeding down the firmament, a white flashing something. Cut to wooden effigy of cow, lightning-lit. Handsome bosomed woman seen walking through tempest, statelily, towards wooden cow. Lightning shows her doing something obscure, pulling some lever or other, then creaking music accompanies shot of wooden cow opening, two hollow half-cows, woman climbing into upright half, cow closing up, woman imprisoned in cow. Cut to white bull, snorting against the thunder, tearing down the sky, bull-lust from heaven.

"You know," said Enderby with wonder, "this is really an astonishinging coincidence."

"Shhhhh," said Vesta. Enderby, his eyes now accustomed to the dark, looked round to find the cinema half-empty, but next to him was a huge man, jowled and bag-eyed in lightning from the screen, a cigar slowly burning towards his fingers, already asleep and snoring slightly.

Day. Ruritanian palace, moustached handsome king in late middle age conferring with deferential bearded (false-bearded) counsellors. Fanfare. Palaver is ended. One counsellor stays behind, ingratiating Iago-type, to talk to the king. The king's eyes cornily cloud with suspicion. Odd Italian words that Enderby can understand snap out from the sound-track; queen, cow, Dedalo. Dedalo ordered to be brought in. Cut to Dedalo's workshop. Dedalo and Icaro, Dedalo's crisp-haired son, are building aeroplanes. Dedalo very old skinny man. Summoned by servant, he pulls down shirt-sleeves, dons jacket period 1860, follows down labyrinthine corridors, a kind old man with clever eyes and deep face-furrows. He enters royal presence. Long unintelligible Italian colloquy with much eloquent arm-waving. Dedalo struck on aged face by angry king. Iago-type goes off, bowing, oily, leaving royal face in royal hands. Dedalo hauled off for torture.

Enderby now began to feel an emotion other than wonder; his stomach heaved and pricked with apprehension: this was more than coincidence. "Don't you think," he said to Vesta, "this is just a little too much like my poem? Don't you think—"

"Shhhhh," she said. The snoring man next to Enderby said, in his sleep, "*Tace*." Enderby, reminded of the sleep-talking Raucliffo, said, "*Tace* your arse." And to Vesta, "This is just like *The Pet Beast*." He then remembered that she hadn't yet read it, had not, in fact, yet shown any desire to read it. He grimly watched the screen, the further unwinding of Raucliffo's infamy.

Day. Pregnant queen in exile, sitting in mean cottage with old crone. Colloquy. Labour-pains. Then dissolve to shot of doctor galloping in from afar. He enters cottage.

From bedroom door come bellowing noises. He enters bedroom. Close-up of doctor's face. Horror, incredulity, nausea, syncope. Close-up, with foul discord, of what doctor sees: head of bull-calf on child's body.

"That's mine," said Enderby. "It's mine, I tell you. If I find that blasted Rawcliffe—"

"It's nobody's," said Vesta. "It's just a myth. Even I know that."

"*Tace*," snored Enderby's pone.

Calf-child, in montage series, grows to bull-man, hideous, muscular, fire-breathing, gigantic. Having stolen piece of raw meat from kitchen, bull-man makes discovery of carnivorous nature. Kills old crone and eats her. Tries to kill mother, too, but mother escapes, falls over cliff screaming but uneaten. Good clean fun. Bull-man totters, tall as ten houses, to capital city, leaving bone-trail behind. Cut to palace gardens where Princess Ariadne, with sizeable bosom-show, is playing ball with giggling bosom-showing alleged maidens. Close-up of beast drooling through thicket. Screams, scatter, Ariadne carried off on beast's back. Beast, drooling, carries her, screaming, to cellars of metropolitan museum. Shots of priceless pictures, rare books, stately sculptures, sounds of great music as bull-man bellows his-its way to hideout deep beneath eternal monuments of culture. Ariadne shows more bosom, screams more loudly. Bull-man does not, however, wish to eat her, not yet anyway.

Enderby clenched his fists tight, their knuckles gleaming in the light that flashed, intermittently, from the screen.

Dénouement. Alpine-Italian hero, Mussolini-headed, crashes into deep cellars, wanders through dark, hears bull-bellow and princess-scream, finds monster and victim, shoots, finds bullets of no avail as bull-man is, on sire's side, thing from outer space. Ariadne escapes, screaming, showing allowable limit of Roman bosom, as howling chest-beating beast advances on hero. Hero, like Count Belisarius, has pepper-bag. He hurls its contents, temporarily blinding beast. To sneezes-bellows-howls, hero escapes. Lo, a prodigy: Dedalo and Icaro in flying-machine some decades ahead of its time drop bomb on metropolitan museum. Howls of dying bull-man, crash of statuary, flap and rustle of books caught alight, Mona Lisa with burnt-out smile, harp-strings pinging as they crack. Death of culture, death of the past, a rational future, embracing lovers. Dedalo and Icaro have engine-trouble. They crash in sea against glorious sunrise. Heavenly voices. End.

"If," trembled Enderby, "I could lay my hands on that bloody Rawcliffe—"

"Stop it, do you hear?" said Vesta very sharply indeed. "I can't take you anywhere, can I? Nothing satisfies you, nothing. I thought it was quite a nice little horror film, and all you can do is to say that it's been stolen from you. Are you getting delusions of grandeur or something?"

"I tell you," said Enderby, with angry patience, "that that bastard Rawcliffe—" The house-lights, all sick sweet orange, came gently up, disclosing applauding people crying *bravo, brava*, and *bravi*, as for the Pope's whole family. The fat man next to Enderby, now radiantly awake, lighted his long-gone-out cigar and then openly laughed at Enderby's clenched fists. Enderby prepared twelve obscene English words as a ground-row (variations and embellishments to follow), but, like a blow on the occiput, it suddenly came to him that he had had enough of words, obscene or otherwise. He smiled with fierce saccharinity on Vesta and said, so that she searched his whole face for sarcasm, "Shall we be going now, dear?"

Three

Late at night, thought Enderby, meant in England after the shutting of the pubs. Here there were no pubs to shut, so it was not yet late. He and Vesta picked up a horse-cab or *carrozza* or whatever it was called on the Via Marmorata, and this clopped along by the side of the Tiber while Enderby fed sedative words to his wife, saying, "I'm honestly going to make an effort, really I am. My maturity's been much delayed, as you realise.

178

I'm really terribly grateful for everything you've done for me. I promise to try to grow up, and I know you'll help me there as you've helped me in everything else. That film tonight has convinced me that I've got to make a real effort to live in public." Vesta, beautiful in the June Roman aromatic night, her hair stirred but gently by the bland wind of their passage, gave him a wary look but said nothing. "What I mean is," said Enderby, "that it's no use living in the lavatory on a tiny income. You were quite right to insist on spending all my capital. I've got to *earn* a place in the world; I've got to come to terms with the public and give the public, within reason, what it wants. I mean, how many people would want to read *The Pet Beast*? A couple of hundred at the outside, whereas this film will be seen by millions. I see, I see it all." He reminded himself of the main protagonist of a drink-cure advertisement in *Old Moore's Almanac:* the medicine cunningly mixed with the drunkard's tea; the immediate result—the drunkard's raising a hand to heaven, wife hanging, sobbing with relief, round his neck. Too much ham altogether. Vesta, still with the wary look, said:

"I hope you mean what you say. I don't mean about the film; I mean about trying to be a bit more *normal.* There's a lot in life that you've missed, isn't there?" She gave him her hand as a cool token. "Oh, I know it must sound a little pretentious, but I feel that I've got a duty to you; not the ordinary duty of a wife to a husband, but a bigger one. I've been entrusted with the care of a great poet." The horse should, rightly, have neighed; massed trumpets should have brayed from the Isola Tiberina.

"And you were quite right," said Enderby, "to bring me to Rome. I see that too. The Eternal City." He was almost enjoying this. "Symbol of public life, symbol of spiritual regeneration. But," he said, slyly, "when are we going back? I'm so anxious," he said, "to go back, so we can *really* start our life together. I long," he said, "to be with you in our own home, just the two of us. Let's," he said, bouncing suddenly with schoolboy eagerness, "go back tomorrow. It should be possible to get a couple of seats on some plane or other, shouldn't it? Oh, do let's go back."

She withdrew her hand from his, and Enderby had a pang of fear, not unlike heartburn, that perhaps she was seeing through this performance. But she said:

"Well, no, we can't go back. Not just yet. Not for a week or so, anyway. You see, I have something arranged. It was meant to be a surprise, really, but now I'd better tell you. I thought it would be a good idea for us to be married, here in Rome, married properly. I don't mean a nuptial mass or anything, of course, but just the plain ceremony."

"Oh," gleamed Enderby, swallowing bolus after bolus of anger and nausea, "what a very good idea!"

"And there is a very good priest, Father Agnello I believe his name is, and he'll be coming to see you tomorrow. I met him yesterday at Princess Vittoria Corombona's." She trilled the name with relish, dearly loving a title.

False Enderby breathed hard with the effort of pushing True Enderby back into the cupboard. "What," he asked, "was a priest doing in a dress-shop?"

"Oh, silly," smiled Vesta. "Princess Vittoria Corombona doesn't run a dress-shop. She does film-gossip for *Fem*. Father Agnello is very intellectual. He's spent a lot of time in the United States and he speaks English perfectly. Strangely enough, he's read one of your poems—the blasphemous one about the Virgin Mary—and he's very anxious to have a couple of good long talks with you. Then, of course, he'll hear your confession."

"Well," smiled Enderby, "it's good to know that everything's being taken care of. It's such a relief. I am really, you know, most grateful." He squeezed her hand as they turned into the Via Nazionale: lights, lights; the Snack Bar Americano; the Bank of the Holy Spirit; shop after shop after shop; the air terminal, alight and busy; the hotel. The fat horse clomped to a ragged halt and snorted, not specifically at Enderby. The driver swore that his taximeter was wrong, a mechanical fault hard to repair, it showed too little. Enderby would not argue. He gave five hundred lire more than the clocked amount,

180

saying "Sod you too" to the driver. Rome; how he loved Rome!

Enderby watched and waited carefully in the hotel bar. There were late coffee-drinkers at the little tables, voluble speakers of fast foreign tongues, ten or a dozen all told, and Enderby would have given them all for Rawcliffe. He wished yesterday morning could be shunted back for just five minutes, he and Dante and Rawcliffe alone in the bar, one damned good crack on the proleptically bloody nose. *L'Animal Binato*, indeed. The Muse would be very annoyed now, fuming, a harpy, with all that work wasted. Enderby watched Vesta, lovely over her glass of Pernod, waited till his third glass of Frascati, then writhed in simulated stomach-ache. "Uggggggh," said Enderby, "blast it. Arrrrgh." Vesta said: "You've been drinking too much, that's your trouble. Come on, we're going to bed." Enderby, artist to the end, made a harrowing borborygm, just like old times. Grerrrrkhrapshhhh. She rose in concern. Enderby said: "No, you wait here. There's a lavatory on the ground floor. Really, it's nothing." He smiled, the liar, through his agony, motioning her to sit down again. He gargoyle-bulged his cheeks, nodded vigorously to show that this showed what it seemed to show, then left the bar smartly, urrping and arrrkhing to the surprise of the coffee-drinkers, into the lobby. To the insincerely gold-grinning dapper receptionist, framed in tubes of light at his desk, Enderby said urgently, "I have to return to London. Just for a couple of days. Business. My wife will stay on here. I don't want you to think," added Enderby guiltily, "that I'm running away or anything like that. If you wish, I'll pay my bill up to date. But I'm leaving my luggage. All except one small overnight case. I take it that that will be all right, will it?" He almost prepared to give the receptionist a thousand-lire note of hush-money but, in time, thought better of it. The receptionist, with a graceful head-inclination as of one bending to hear the tick of a watch in an invisible man's waistcoat pocket, said that everything would be quite all right, but Signor Enderby must understand that there could be no rebate in respect of the time that Signor Enderby would be away. Signor Enderby gladly understood. "I want," he said, "to ring up the air terminal, the one on this street. Could you give me the number?" The receptionist would be only too pleased to ring up for him; he could take the call in one of those boxes over there.

From the box Enderby could just see Vesta eating a ham sandwich. It must be ham, because she was stroking each sliver with what must be, from the shape of the jar, mustard. Enderby tried, which was not difficult, to look very ill in case she should glance up and see him. If she came over he would have to pretend that he had blindly dashed in here because it had the outward appearance of a lavatory; if she saw him urgently mouthing into the telephone he would have to pretend he was calling a doctor. A voice now spoke in English to Enderby, and Enderby said furtively, "Enderby here." The name, understandably, meant nothing to the suave clerkly voice. Enderby said, "I want to travel to London by the next possible plane. Very urgent. I already have a first-class ticket, but my booking, you see, is for the twenty-fifth or twenty-sixth or something—I can't quite remember the exact date. This is very very urgent. Business. And my mother's dying." There was no cluck of condolence: hard bastards these Romans. The voice said, above the rustle of ledger-pages, that it thought there might be empty seats on the BOAC plane from Cape Town, due at Rome at five-thirty in the morning. The voice would ring back to confirm or deny. "A matter of life and death," said Enderby. The voice, however, seemed to know that Enderby was about to run away from his wife.

Vesta had finished her sandwiches and was picking her front teeth with a grubby London bus ticket she had taken from her bag. The bag was open, very untidy, but in it Enderby saw a bunch of keys. Those keys he would require: in the Glouchester Road flat were certain things he needed. Seeing the teeth-picking, Enderby nodded: another thing marshalling him the way that he was going. "How do you feel now?" she asked.

"A good deal better," smiled Enderby. "I got a lot of it up." With what was still in the bank, with what he thought he could legitimately filch from her (mink, chiefly) he considered it was possible for him to return for a year or two to something like his old life: the lone poet in some sordid attic or other with thin stews and bread, trying to make it up to his Muse. He did not repine at the loss of his capital. Not any longer. It was, after all, his stepmother's money, and here, now pulling a ham-fibre from her molars, though with grace and without ostentation, sat his stepmother, all too able to use that money. The interest, of course, was another matter. The Church had always condemned the lending out of money at interest, so no good Catholic had a right to claim the increment it had earned when the return of the loan was made. Enderby, though determined to be just, was also determined to be strictly Protestant here. As he smiled to himself he was suddenly jolted by the calling of his name over a loudspeaker.

"Who on earth," said Vesta, "can be ringing you up at this hour of the evening? You stay there, I'll take it. You're still looking a bit pale." And she rose.

"No, no, no," protested Enderby, pushing her roughly back into her cane armchair. "It's something you're not supposed to know about. A surprise," he tried to smile. She grimaced and, taking a hair-clip from her bag, began to clean her left ear. Enderby was delighted to see that.

The clerkly voice was pleased to be able to confirm a booking on the plane from Cape Town. Enderby was to report at the terminal at four; the clerk then on duty would alter his ticket for him. "*Deo gratias*," breathed Enderby, meaning *grazie*. But only that liturgical gratitude, he reflected, could express his relief at the prospect of getting out of, with its denotations and connotations, Rome.

"It's arranged," he smirked at Vesta. "Don't ask me what, but it's all arranged." As they rose to go to their room he saw on the table a hairclip; its bend of bifurcation was stuffed with earwax. He took Vesta's arm with something like love.

Four

Staying awake till three-thirty was not really difficult. Really difficult was getting the packing done on a night when Vesta, normally a good solid Scots sleeper, had decided to be restless and somniloquent. Enderby watched her warily as she lay prone, having kicked the clothes off the bed, her nates silvered by the Roman moonlight to the likeness of a meringue. Delectable, yes, but from now on for somebody else's delectation. Enderby stole about the silvered room in his socks, suddenly stiffening as in a statue dance each time she burbled in her sleep, rushing to the dark corner by the window to stand as if for his height to be taken when she pettishly whisked from the prone to the supine. Supine, she uttered strange words to the ceiling and then chuckled, but Enderby would not permit himself to be scared. Taking his passport and air ticket from the top drawer of the chest of drawers he also, after a few seconds of ethical thought, decided to take hers. Thus, if she woke to a realisation of Enderby's desertion, she would not be able to follow at once. But he placed several thousand or million lire on the mantelpiece, and he knew that she had traveller's cheques of her own. Although she and Rome went so beautifully together, he could not, in all decency, condemn her to too long an enforced stay; he hoped he still had enough humanity not to wish that on his worst enemy.

One suitcase was enough for Enderby's clothes and shaving gear. The lotions and creams and sprays she had made him buy—these he decided to leave behind: no one would ever want to smell him any more. Now there was the question of that key to the flat; he had left a couple of boxes there, stuffed with drafts and notes. The typescript of *The Pet Beast* was locked in the drawer of her own escritoire, and there it could stay. Its interest, he admitted glumly, was one of content more than form, and the content had been filched and distorted. Let that be a lesson to him. Enderby now squinted in the moonlight for Vesta's bag, a flat silver envelope into which, that evening, she had poured the entire load of rubbish from a black bag from a grey bag from a white bag from a blue bag, a woman who, with residual Scots thrift, could not bear to throw anything away. Enderby saw this silver bag, further silvered by the light, lying on her bedside table. He stalked over for it, like some clumsy ballerina on her points, and, as he made to pick it up, Vesta swiftly pronated, diagonal across the bed, and a bare slim arm flopped over the table to hold the bag down like a silver bar. Enderby hesitated now, standing with breathing suspended, wondering whether he dare risk. But then she, with the same swiftness, lurched her body to the supine, though with her left arm still across the table, and began to speak out of some profound dream. She said:

"Pete. Do it again, Pete. Och, Pete, that was bloody marvelous." It was a coarse accent, suggesting the Gorbals rather than Eskbank, and, to match it, the sleeping Vesta began to use coarse terms suggesting an extremity of abandon. Enderby listened horrified, at last calming his nerves by reflecting that anything, even necrophily, was allowed to the dreamer. He did not now try to extract the bag from under her silver arm; he could perhaps get into the flat without a key. Effect an entrance, as they say. He now wished to effect an exit, and quickly.

As he fumbled at the door-handle, hidden under the mink coat that hung from the door-hook, he had the impression that she was about to lift herself out of sleep, some warning bell having shrilled at the end of one of the long corridors of the cerebral cortex. He calmed her with words and a noise:

"Brarrrkh. Just going to the lavatory." His last words to her as he softly folded the mink over his arm. She grunted, smacked her lips, then, seeming satisfied, started to lower herself into deeper levels of sleep. Enderby opened the door and went out. Standing an instant to quieten his loud heart, he felt cautiously elated that soon, on the aircraft, he would be able to feel fully and uninhibitedly elated.

A poem began to twitch as he weighed his suitcase and paid his embarkation fee and bought his bus ticket:

Stepmother of the West . . .

Enderby waited with excitement for the images to come into focus—Emperor and Pope the same pantomime dame, no more red meat since spate of it in snarling arena, old bitch she-wolf with hanging dugs, the big backyard of broken columns for the refuse-collector; Enderby waited with impatience for the rhymes to line up. City, titty. Beyond that was nothing.

> Stepmother of the West, of venal cities
> Most venal something something she-wolf bitch
> Romulus Remus something something titties
> Something something something something rich
> which ditch pitch.

On the bus to Ciampino Enderby, frowning, called on his Muse to do something about this ragged *donnée*. On the aircraft, placed next to a Negro clergyman, Enderby muttered and grimaced so that the stewardess came up to ask if everything was all right. A suspicious character, muttering and frowning, a mink coat on the luggage rack overhead, Enderby looked down on Rome. He had forgotten all about Vesta already. He had expected that he would be able to recite, under his breath, at least a stanza of his poem in valediction. Thwarted and somewhat apprehensive, remembering the prophecy of the traitor Rawcliffe, he could only devise a farewell that went beyond words but which the Negro clergyman apparently took to be an adverse comment on his colour.
Fffffrrrrrerrrrrpshhhhhh.

III

1

One

"You've got absolutely nothing to worry about there,"
said Dr Preston Hawkes. "The plates are negative: no TB,
no carcinoma, nothing." He held up a couple of cloudy
portraits of the inner Enderby. "That's the lot, then." He
had a loud Northern voice, some of the vowels homemade approximations to Received Standard. "You can go
away with a contented mind." He was young and highly
dentate, tanned and tousled as though to advertise, for a
side-line, the healthful properties of the resort where he
practised. "If bicarb helps that dyspepsia, you just stick
to bicarb. But fundamentally your stomach and guts are
perfectly sound."

"You would say, would you," said Enderby, "that I'm
quite unlikely to die in the near future?"

"Oh, my dear fellow," said Dr Preston Hawkes, "none
of us can ever know that. Apart from the normal hazards
of living—getting run over or electrocuted or slipping in
the bathroom—there must always be some unknown
factor that doesn't yield to examination. We know a lot,"
he confided, "but we don't know everything. But, as far
as I can see, you're physically sound and likely to live

for many years." He glowed at Enderby like a frying slice of potato. "Of course," he said, "your tone isn't as good as it might be. Take exercise: tennis, golf, walks. You could do with paring yourself down a bit. Keep off fried things; don't eat too much starch. You're a sedentary worker, aren't you? A clerk or something?"

"Perhaps in the older sense," said Enderby. "I am," he explained sadly, "a poet."

"You mean," said Dr Preston Hawkes incredulously, "that's your job?"

"It was," said Enderby. "That's really why I came to see you. You see, I'm not writing any more poems."

"Oh." Dr Preston Hawkes became agitated; he tapped contrary-motion five-finger exercises on his desk, his smile fixed and nervous. He spoke now slackly, bubbling. "Well, I hardly think—I mean, that's nothing to do with me, is it? I mean, I should have thought—That is to say, if you don't propose writing any more poetry, well, good luck to you. The very best of luck and all that sort of thing. But that's entirely your own affair, isn't it? That's what I'd say, anyway." He now began to perform, though ineptly, the ritual of a man whose time is valuable: a syndrome of nervous grubbing among papers, looking at his watch, peering exophthalmically above Enderby's head as though the next patient was due to squeeze in between door and lintel.

"No," said Enderby, "you've got that wrong. What I mean is that I can't write poetry any more. I try and try, but nothing happens, nothing will come. Can you understand what I mean?"

"Oh, yes," said the doctor, smiling warily. "I quite see that. Well, I shouldn't worry too much about it if I were you. I mean, there are other things in life, aren't there? The sun is shining, the children are playing." That was literally true; Dr Preston Hawkes lifted a hand as if he himself were conjuring the warm evening shaft through the window, the noise of an infant squabble on the road to the beach. "I mean, writing poetry isn't the whole of life, is it? You're bound to find something else to do. Life is still all before you. The best is yet to be."

"What," asked Enderby, "is the purpose of life?"

The doctor brightened at this question. He was young enough to have answers to it, answers clearly remembered from pipe-puffing student discussions. "The purpose of life," he said promptly, "is the living of it. Life itself is the end of life. Life is here and now and what you can get out of it. Life is living by the square inch and the round minute. The end is the process. Life is what you make it. I know what I'm talking about, believe you me. I am, after all, a doctor." He smiled towards something framed on the wall, his duly certified twin baccalaureate.

Enderby shook his head in vigorous gloom. "I don't think Keats would have given you that answer. Or Shelley. Or Byron. Or Chatterton. Man," said Enderby, "is a tree. He bears fruit. When he stops bearing fruit life cuts him down. That's why I wanted to know whether I was going to die."

"Look," said the doctor sharply, "this is all a lot of morbid nonsense. It's everybody's duty to *live*. That's what the National Health Service is for. To help people to live. You're a healthy man with years of life ahead of you, and you ought to be very glad and very grateful. Otherwise, let's face it, you're blaspheming against life and God and, yes, democracy and the National Health Service. That's hardly fair, is it?"

"But what do I live for?" asked Enderby.

"I've told you what you live for," said the doctor, more sharply. "You weren't paying attention, were you? You live for the sake of living. And, yes, you live for others, of course. You live for your wife and children." He granted himself a two-second smirk of fondness at the photograph on his desk: Mrs Preston Hawkes playing with Master Preston Hawkes, Master Preston Hawkes playing with teddy-bear.

"I had a wife," said Enderby, "for a very short time. I left her nearly a year ago. In Rome it was. We just didn't get on. I'm quite sure I have no children. I think I can say that I'm absolutely sure about that."

"Well, all right then," said the doctor. "But there are lots of other people who need you, surely. Friends and so on. I take it," he said cautiously, "that there are still people left who like to read poetry."

"That," said Enderby, "is written. They've got that. There won't be any more. And," he said, "I'm not the sort of man who has friends. The poet has to be alone." This platitude, delivered rhetorically in spite of himself, brought a glassy look to his eyes; he got up stiffly from his chair. The doctor, who had seen television plays, thought he descried in Enderby the lineaments of impending suicide. He was not a bad doctor. He said:

"You don't propose to do anything silly, do you? I mean, it wouldn't do anybody any good, would it, that sort of thing? I mean, especially after you've been to see me and so on. Life," he said, less certainly than before, "has to be lived. We all have a duty. I'll get the police on to you, you know. Don't start doing anything you shouldn't be doing. Look, I'll arrange an appointment with a psychiatrist, if you like." He made the gesture of reaching at once for the telephone, of being prepared to tap, at once, all the riches of the National Health Service for the benefit of Enderby.

"You needn't worry," said Enderby soothingly. "I shan't do anything I'd consider silly. I promise you that."

"Get around a bit," said the doctor desperately. "Meet people. Watch the telly. Have the odd drink in a pub, all right in moderation. Go to the pictures. Go and see this horror film round the corner. That'll take you out of yourself."

"I saw it in Rome," said Enderby. "The world première." Here in England *L'Animal Binato* or *The Two-Natured Animal* had become *Son of the Beast from Outer Space*. "As a matter of fact," said Enderby, "I wrote it. That is to say, it was stolen from me."

"Look," said Dr Preston Hawkes, now standing up. "It would be no trouble at all for me to fix up an appointment for you. I think you'd feel a lot happier if you talked with Dr Greenslade. He's a very good man, you know, very good, very sympathetic. I could ring up the hospital now. No trouble at all. He could probably see you first thing in the morning."

"Now," said Enderby, "don't worry. Take life as it comes. Live it by the square yard or whatever it was you said."

"I'm not at all happy about what you might do," said Dr Preston Hawkes. "It wouldn't be fair for you to go back home and do yourself in straight after coming to see me. I'd feel happier if you'd see Dr Greenslade. I could ring up now. I could get a bed for you straight away. I'm not sure that it's right for you to be going off on your own. Not in your present state of mind, that is." He stood confused and young, mumbling, "I mean, after all, we've got a duty to each other——"

"I'm perfectly sane," soothed Enderby, "if that's what you're worrying about. And I promise you again not to do anything silly. You can have that in writing if you like. I'll send you a letter. I'll write it as soon as I get back to my digs." Dr Preston Hawkes bit his lip from end to end and back again, as though testing it for durability. He looked darkly and uncertainly at Enderby, not liking the sound of "letter" in this context. "Everything," said Enderby, with a great smile of reassurance, "is going to be all right." They had exchanged roles. It was with a doctor's jauntiness that Enderby said, "Nothing to worry about at all." Then he left swiftly.

He passed through a waiting-room full of people who, from the look of them, could not write poetry either. Some were in sporting kit, as if prepared to be tried out at the nets by Dr Preston Hawkes, wearing their ailments as lightly as a blazer-badge; others, dressed more formally, saw disease as a kind of church. Enderby had to squint his way out. He had lost his contact-lenses somewhere; the glasses he had formerly worn were, he supposed, still in the Gloucester Road flat. Unless, of course, she had thrown out all that was his. Walking through the rich marine light he regurgitated the word "police." If this doctor proposed to put the police on to him it would be necessary to act quickly. In imagination he heard what the world called sanity as something in heavy clumsy hoofing boots. He remembered the boots that chased him when, just back from Rome, he had tried to break into the flat by the window and been suddenly transfixed in the beam of a copper's lantern. He could have stayed to explain, of course, but the police might well, with their professional tendency to suspicion, have held him till the eventual arrival of Vesta. That mink coat, left behind in the scamper, would have taken some explaining away. So he had swung his suitcase into the constable's groin and, between a starting-line and finishing-tape of whistles, dodged about till—to his surprise, for he had thought such things only possible in films—he had managed to escape by skidding down a sidestreet and into an alley, waiting there till the whistles peeped, like lost tropical birds, forlornly in the distance.

The May sun whizzed over the sea, and spread over the sea was a sort of blinding silver-shred marmalade. It was not the sea near to whose roar he had laboured, to so little purpose, at *The Pet Beast,* but its north-western brother. It fed a louder and more vulgar resort than Enderby's former Channel home: there was more gusto in the pubs, the vowels were broader, jugs of tea could be bought to take on the sands, a pleasure-beach was hysterical with violent machines of pleasure, an open-air concert party had a comedian who told his feed that if his brains were elastic he wouldn't have enough to make a canary a pair of garters. "I've got blue blood in my veins," said the feed. "What do you think I've got in mine?" said the comedian. "Dandelion and burdock?" It was an odd place, so posterity might think, in which to choose to die.

On this lovely evening there were queues, Enderby peeringly noticed, for *Son of the Beast from Outer Space.* Next door but two to the cinema was a cool cavern of a chemist's, full of the smell of soap, holiday laughter in a place of medicines, the prints of beach snapshots being collected, sunburnt arms and necks. Enderby had to wait till a holiday woman had been served with hair-clips, skin-scream, hydrogen peroxide and other life-enhancers before he could ask for the means of death. At last the white-coated girl put her head on one side to him:

"Yes, sir?"

He felt as embarrassed as if he were buying condoms. "Aspirin, please."

"Which size, sir?" There were, it seemed, various sizes. Enderby said:

"Fairly small ones, please. I have to take rather a lot." She opened her mouth at him so he said, "Not a lethal dose, of course." He smiled winningly.

"Ha ha, sir. I should hope not. Not on a lovely evening like this." He was quite a one.

Enderby went out with a bottle of a hundred. He had exactly twopence left in the world. "Good," he thought, "timing."

Two

"A queer year," reflected Enderby, potential death in his pocket, turning off the warm gay beery candy-flossy promenade into Boggart Road. It had been a queer empty year, or near-year.

June had been the month of marriage, honeymoon, desertion. He had drawn out from his London bank ninety pictures of clavigerous lions. He had bought a sponge-bag, stuffed the lions into it, wound the string of the bag round a trouser-button, then hung the bag inside his trousers. There it had walked and sat with him, a big comforting scrotum. Every man's fly his own bank; cheerful disbursements at all hours; no interest (though, of course, no overdrafts); frugal needs met without formality. He had travelled to this Northern resort once mentioned with approval by Arry (far from South, London, Vesta). He had found a homely attic with a gas-ring (share lavatory and bathroom) at Mrs Bamber's, Butterworth Avenue, a permanent apex above the transient holiday guests.

In July and August he had put together laboriously a volume of fifty lyric poems (the fair copies and late drafts had fortunately been in his suitcase taken to and from Rome; a mass of other, rougher, material was still in, or else had been thrown out of, the Gloucester Road flat and was, presumably, no longer recoverable). The title of the volume was *The Circular Pavane*. Having been turned into typescript by a little woman at a typing bureau in Manchester, it had been delivered to, and received with little enthusiasm by, his publisher. In public lavatory cabinets, where privacy could be bought for a penny, he had planned a long autobiographical poem in blank verse, a sort of *Prelude*. The sponge-bag inside trousers still fat, he was able to afford to wait for the torpid or sulking Muse to wake up or see sense. The few autobiographical poetic lines achieved had been destroyed, re-written, destroyed, re-written, destroyed, re-written, slept on, read, re-read, re-written, destroyed. Through August and September the resort had been big-mouthed with cheerful visitors wearing comic caps with slogans (Try Me I'm The Easy Sort; Have A Go Joe Your Mother Won't Know), sticky with kisses, brine, ale, candy, rock. There had been no news of Vesta or anyone. Sitting in a public lavatory one sunny morning, hearing the cheerful bucket-and-spade-clanking children on their way to the beach, he had savoured, like Frascati, his renewed aloneness. It was a pity he could not write anything, however. He had abandoned the idea of the long autobiographical poem; how about an epic on King Arthur or Lord Rutherford or Alcock and Brown? A verse drama, perhaps? He had spent long grubbing hours in the public library, pretending that he was really working, building foundations, gathering material. He had written nothing.

October, November, brought a whiff of foreboding. This was getting past a joke. He had money enough still, of course, but less and less to do with his time. He walked through the sea-deafening deserted streets, over-coat-collar round his ear, trying to crank up a poem, returning to hopelessness, stew, Mrs Bamber insisting on coming up to his attic, sitting there, talking about her own past redolent of oyster-bars and Yates's Wine Lodge.

If, he vowed at Christmas, if he were given some sort of token of assurance that he would be able to start writing again, then, when his money ran out, he would willingly take some futile occupation or other, becoming a part-time poet, keeping alive for his Muse.

Towards the end of January he awoke to a morning clamped in frost, a poem singing in his ears. Thank God, the relief. He wrote the gnomic telegraphic message down and spent the morning refining it to a final shape:

You being the gate
Where the army went through,
Would you renew the triumph and have them deco-
rate
The arch and stone again?
Surely those flowers are withered, the army
Now on a distant plain.

Reading it, he saw, his hair bristling, that it was a private message, a message from her to himself.

But some morning when you are washing up,
Or some afternoon, taking a cup
Of tea, possibly you will see
The heavens opening and a lot
Of saints singing, with bells swinging.
But then again, possibly not.

He had felt a clammy glair of sweat settle on him, his diaphragm start to liquefy. A poem of farewell.

In March came publication of *The Circular Pavane*. Reviews followed: "... Pleasant and lucid verse in the tradition ..."; "Mr Enderby has lost none of his old cunning; it is a pity, however, that we see no signs of new cunning, new directions. It is a cunningly blended mixture, but it is very much the mixture as before ..."; "... One remembers with a sigh the old lyrical perfection. It is a relief to turn to the work of two young Oxford poets ..." And one that was surely by Rawcliffe: "Mr Enderby is undoubtedly enough of a realist not to regret the passing of the lyric gift. It cannot last for ever, and with Mr Enderby it has lasted longer than with most. Many of his contemporaries have already elected for the dignified silence of remembered achievement, and one may predict that Mr Enderby, after this not unexpectedly disappointing volume, will join their cloistral seclusion. ..." In *Fem* there was, of course, no review.

Enderby had spent April brooding over a pain in his chest. In May, now, this month, three days ago, he had decided to go to a doctor. The doctor, after palpation and auscultation, had more or less decided that nothing was really wrong but, to be on the safe side, had sent Enderby to the hospital for radiography. But, before that, with "nothing wrong" in his ears, Enderby had sat down in his warm attic to write out a list of possible ways to die:

> Slash wrists in warm bath
> Overdose of sedative
> Hang from picture rail in dining-room
> Jump in sea from jetty

This was early summer, and Mrs Bamber's house had a fair number of early summer visitors, mostly, as far as Enderby could judge from the noise, teams of galloping children ineptly driven by whoaing but disregarded young parents. It would not be right, Enderby thought, to make his suicide a public affair. It was no way to start a holiday morning to find a corpse swinging with its tongue out at the cornflakes laid the night before, or else dreaming cold in a bath of cold red ink. Too public, of course, to upset anyone might have been the jump from the jetty at the end of Central Pier, but some swimmer, bored already with his holiday, might have splashed too swiftly to the rescue. The overdose was best: clean and quiet, clean and quiet, by something something and dreamy something. Kingsley, joscular Christian.

Enderby, non-Christian stoic, climbed the vanilla-coloured steps of 17 Butterworth Avenue. The front door was open and on the hat-stand were buckets and spades, the smell of feet and sand in the whole dark seaweedy hall. All the guests were out, perhaps at *Son of the Beast from Outer Space*, but from her kitchen Mrs Bamber sang, the merry widow of a tram-driver, a song smelling of oysters and ruby port. Mounting the stairs, Enderby was suddenly transfixed by a line from, he thought, *Ulysses*, which seemed to him, with his lethal dose in his pocket, to be the most poignant line (though it was not really a line—only, so far as he could remember, a splinter of Bloom's interior monologue), the most pregnantly regretful line he had ever heard:

... And lie no more in her warm bed.

He shook his head as images clustered round it, images he was no longer capable of translating into words and rhythms: the horses under starter's orders, the champagne tent, the sun on the back of the neck, the omelette made with a hundred eggs and a bottle of Napoleon brandy, life.

... And lie no more in her warm bed.

Enderby climbed higher, climbed to the top, where there was only a roof between him and the sun. This garret of his was, like the sea, warming up for the summer. He entered and sat on his bed, panting after the climb. Then his stomach, living its own life, decided it was hungry, so Enderby put to warm on the gas-ring the remains of a simple stew. While it bubbled, he turned over and over the sizeable bottle of aspirin he had bought: he had read, or heard, that a hundred should be enough. Mrs Bamber, he felt sure, would be efficient at coping with the unexpected corpse of Enderby: she was a Lancashire woman, and Lancashire people rather enjoyed death. It would, anyway, be a clean corpse lying, jaw dropped as in astonishment at being dead, between the sheets. (He reminded himself to effect, as far as was possible, a total evacuation of his body before making it a corpse.) The holiday guests would not be disturbed; the Chief Constable and the Town Clerk would want no publicity; everything would be done quietly at night, and then cornflakes would be shuffled on to plates for the morning. Enderby now sat down, with something like appetite, to his last supper, a thin but savoury viaticum. He felt excited, as though after supper he were going to see a film that everybody had been talking about and the critics had highly praised.

Three

Enderby was in his pyjamas. It was still light, a May evening, and he had a fugitive impression of being a child again, sent to bed while the life of day was beating strongly without. He had washed his feet and scrubbed his dentures, scoured his few pots and pans, eaten a piece of chocolate left over from some weeks back, and poured water from the jug on the wash-stand into a clean milk-bottle. (He had no tumbler, and would need a good long draught to speed the aspirin down.) Now, with the cottonwool stopper removed and the tablets clinking discreetly, the aspirin bottle began to dramatise itself, drawing evening light from all angles, becoming almost grail-like, so that the hand that held it shook. Enderby carried it over to his bed, and it made a tiny dry castanet-noise all the way. From the bed, which he now entered, he could look down on Mrs Bamber's back-yard. He dredged it hungrily, squinting, for symbols of life, but there were only a dustbin, a cardboard box full of cinders, dandelions growing up from the flag-cracks, an old bicycle discarded by Mrs Bamber's son, Tom. Beyond were three-storey houses with bathing costumes drying on window-sills, beyond again the sea, above all a primrose sky. "Now," said Enderby aloud.

One shaking hand shook out a shaking palmful of aspirin. He gave the white seeds to his mouth like a gollywog money-box feeding in a penny. He drank water from the milk-bottle, still shaking. Aspen, aspirin. Was there a connection?

An aspen hand aspiring now to death

He finished off the bottle in six or seven more handfuls, washing them down carefully. Then, sighing, he lay back. There was nothing to do now except wait. He had committed suicide. He had killed himself. Self-slaughter was of all sins the most reprehensible, being the most cowardly. What punishment awaited suicide? If Rawcliffe were there now he would be able to quote from the *Inferno*, lavishly, that man who had added to Italian art. Enderby could vaguely remember that suicide belonged to Nether Hell, the Second Ring, between those who had been violent against their neighbours and those who had been violent against God and art and nature. There, in that Third Ring, Rawcliffe rightly belonged, perhaps there already. All these were, Enderby thought, Sins of the Lion. He closed his eyes and saw, quite clearly, the bleeding trees that were the suicides, harpies fluttering about with a rattle of dry wings like the magnified noise of a shaken aspirin bottle. He frowned. All this seemed very unfair. He had, after all, chosen the way of the Second Ring to avoid the way of the Third, and yet both sins were tucked together in the same round slice of Nether Hell.

With infinite care and delicacy the day wormed itself through a continuum of darker and darker greys. The watch on his wrist ticked on healthily, the too-efficient servant that would announce death as coldly as day and breakfast. Enderby began to feel a great tiredness and to hear a loud buzzing in his ears.

A fanfare of loud farts, a cosmic swish of lavatory-flushings. The dark in front of his eyes was cut away in rough slice after rough slice, like black bread, right down to the heel of the loaf. This then began to turn slowly, brightening with each revolution until it became blinding like the sun. Enderby found it an insuperable effort to interpose blankets or hands or eyelids. The circle cracked with intolerable luminosity, and then Enderby seemed to be dragged, with hearty, though somehow archangelic, tug-of-war cries towards some ineffable hidden Presence. Suddenly this Presence, at first humorously offering Itself as a datum for mere intellection, erupted into a tingling ultimate blow at all the senses, and Enderby staggered back.

There she was, welcoming him in, farting prrrrrrp like ten thousand earthquakes, belching arrrp and og like a million volcanoes, while the whole universe roared with approving laughter. She swung tits like sagging moons at him, drew from black teeth an endless snake of bacon-rind, pelted him with balls of earwax and snuffled green snot in his direction. The thrones roared and the powers were helpless. Enderby was suffocated by smells: sulphuretted hydrogen, unwashed armpits, halitosis, faeces, standing urine, putrefying meat—all thrust into his mouth and nostrils in squelchy balls. "Help," he tried to call. "Help help help." He fell, crawled, crying, "Help, help." The black, which was solid laughter and filth, closed on him. He gave one last scream before yielding to it.

2

One

"And," said Dr Greenslade the psychiatrist, "we won't try that sort of thing again, will we? For, as we can now see, it only causes lots and lots of worry and trouble to other people." He beamed, a fat young man in a white coat not too clean, with the unhealthy complexion of a sweet-eater. "For example, it didn't do our poor old landlady's heart any good, did it? She had to run up the stairs and then down the stairs"—he illustrated this with up-and-then-down-the-air wiggling fingers—"and she was most agitated when the ambulance finally got there. We must consider others, mustn't we? The world wasn't made just for us and nobody else."

Enderby cringed from the nanny-like substitution of first plural for second singular. "Everybody gives trouble when they're dying," he mumbled. "That can't be avoided."

"Ah," pounced Dr Greenslade, "but you didn't die. When people die in the normal decent way they give a normal decent *leisurely* kind of trouble which harms no one. But you were just caught more or less in the act of sailing off. That meant rushing about and worry for everybody, particularly for your poor old landlady. Besides"—he leaned forward, hushed—"it wasn't just a matter of straightforward dying with you, was it? It was"—he whispered the dirty words—"*attempted suicide.*"

Enderby bowed his head, this being the required stock response. Then he said, "I'm sorry I made a mess of it. I don't know what came over me. Well, I do in a way, of course, but if I'd been braver, if I'd stuck it out, I think I could have sailed straight through, if you see what I mean. What I mean is that that was just a vision of Hell meant to frighten me. Bogies and so on. It wasn't real."

Dr Greenslade rubbed his hands discreetly. "I can see," he said, "that a lot of fun lies ahead. Though not for me, unfortunately. Still, I'll be getting Wapenshaw's reports. It's a lovely place," he said dreamily, "especially lovely at this time of year. You'll like it."

"Where?" said Enderby with suspicion. "What?" Dr Greenslade had sounded like some Dickens character talking about a beloved idiot-child's grave. "I thought I was being discharged."

"Oh, dear me, no," said shocked Dr Greenslade. "Healthy people don't try to commit suicide, you know. Not coldly and deliberately they don't. And you'd planned this, you know. Preston Hawkes told me you'd planned it. It wasn't just a mad impulse."

"No, it wasn't," said Enderby stoutly. "It was logical. I knew perfectly well what I was doing and I've given you perfectly logical reasons for doing it." He belched acidulously: "Greeeeekh. "This hospital food's bloody awful," he said.

"The food at Flitchley is excellent," dreamed Dr Greenslade. "Everything's excellent there. Lovely grounds to walk in. Table-tennis. Television. A library of sedative books. Congenial company. You'll be sorry to leave."

"Look," said Enderby quietly, "I'm not going, see? You've got no right to keep me here or send me anywhere. I'm perfectly all right, see? I demand my freedom."

"Now," said Dr Greenslade harshly, changing from

nanny to schoolmaster, "let's get one or two things absolutely clear, shall we? There are certain laws in this country appertaining to mental derangement, laws of restraint, certificates and so on. Those laws have, in your case, already been invoked. We can't have people wandering all over the country trying to kill themselves." Enderby closed his eyes to see England swarming, as a log swarms with woodlice, with peripatetic suicides. "You're a danger to yourself," said Dr Greenslade, "and a danger to the community. A man who doesn't respect his own life isn't likely to respect anybody else's. That's logical, isn't it?"

"No," said Enderby promptly.

"Oh, well," said Dr Greenslade sarcastically, "you, of course, are the big expert on logic."

"I don't pretend to be anything," said Enderby loudly, "except a poet whose inspiration has departed. I'm an empty eggshell."

"You are," said Dr Greenslade sternly, "a man of education and culture who can be of great value to the community. When you're made fit again, that is. Empty eggshells, indeed," he poohed. "Poets," he near-sneered. "Those days are past, those wide-eyed romantic days. We're living in a realistic age now," he said. "Science is making giant strides. And as for poets," he said, with sudden bubbling intimacy, "I met a poet once. He was a nice decent fellow with no big ideas about himself. He wrote very nice poetry, too, which was not too difficult to understand." He looked at Enderby as though Enderby's poetry was both not nice and not intelligible. "This man," said Dr Greenslade, "didn't have your advantages. No private income for him, no cosy little flat in a seaside resort. He had a wife and family, and he wasn't ashamed of working for them. He wrote his poetry at week-ends." He nodded at Enderby, week-day poet. "And there was nothing abnormal about him, nothing at all. He didn't go about with a lobster on a string or marry his own sister or eat pepper before drinking claret. He was a decent family man whom nobody would have taken for a poet at all." Enderby groaned frightfully. "And," added Dr

205

Greenslade, "he had a poem in all the anthologies."
Enderby held back a loud howl. Then he said:

"If he was so normal, why did you have anything to do with him?"

"This," smiled Dr Greenslade in large triumph, "was a purely social acquaintance. Now," he said, looking at the clock above Enderby's head, "you'd better get back to your ward." Enderby stood up. He was in hospital pyjamas, dressing-gown, slippers, and felt grey, shrunken, a pauper. He shambled out of the electro-cardiogram room into the corridor, hesitated at the stairs with their WAY OUT notice, remembered that they had locked his clothes away, and then, resigned, shuffled into the Medical Ward. He had been brought here to sleep it off after the stomach-pumping in the Emergency Ward, had lain for two days starved in a sort of big cot with iron bars at the sides, and now was allowed to pout about the ward in his dressing-gown. If a fellow-patient said, "What's wrong with you, mate?" he replied, on the ward sister's instructions, "Acetylsalicylic poisoning." But these rough men, all with impressively visible illnesses, knew better than that. This here one had had a go at doing himself in. As Enderby, hands in dressing-gown pockets, bowed towards his bed (ringworm to the left of it, to the right a broken femur), a dwarf of a working-man hopped towards him on crutches. " 'Ere," said the dwarf.

"Yes?" said Enderby. The dwarf cleared his nasopharynx via his oesophagus and said, conspiratorially:

"Trick cyclist been 'avin' a go at you, eh? I seen 'im come in. Ridin' all over you, eh?"

"That's right," said Enderby.

"Should be a law against that, I reckon. Draggin' out secrets from the back of your mind, like. Not decent, way I see it. 'Ad a go at me once. Know what that was for?"

"No," said Enderby. The dwarf hopped nearer, his eyes ashine. He said, low:

"Wife and kids was out at the pictures, see. I 'ad nowt to do, not bein' much on the telly, and I'd washed up after my supper and put the kitchen straight. I'd read the paper too, see, and there wasn't much in that, all murders and suchlike and these 'ere summit conferences. Anyway, know what I'd got in my overall pocket?"

"No," said Enderby.

"One of these big nuts," said the dwarf. "Don't know 'ow it got there, but there it was. Big one," he insisted, making an illustrative ring with thumb and finger. "A nut, you know. Not a nut you can eat, but one of these nuts you put a bolt through." He showed, with the index-finger of his other hand, how exactly this was done. "Do you see my meaning?" he asked.

"Yes," said Enderby.

"Well," said the dwarf, "I got to lookin' at it and thinkin' about it, and then an idea come into me 'ead. Know what the idea was?"

"No," said Enderby.

The dwarf came very close, awkward on his crutches, and seemed about to eat Enderby's ear. "Put it in," he said. "Wife was out, see, and there was nowt else to do. It fitted real snug, too, you'd be surprised. Anyway, there it was, and you know what 'appened then?"

"No," said Enderby.

"Wouldn't come out," said the dwarf, reliving the horror in his eyes. "There it was, stuck in, and it wouldn't come out. Right bloody fool I must have looked to the cat when it come in through the window. A 'ot night, see, and the window was open. There I was, with this thing of mine stuck in this nut, and it wouldn't come out. I tries all sort of things—puttin' it under the cold water tap and gettin' a file at it, but it wasn't no good. Then the wife comes back from the pictures and she sees what I've done and she sends the kids straight upstairs. Bad enough the cat seein' it, but it wasn't right the kids should know what was goin' on. So you know what she does?"

"No," said Enderby.

"She sends for the ambulance and they takes me to 'ospital. Not this one, though. We was livin' somewhere else at the time. Well, they tries and tries, but it's no good. All sorts of things they tries. Know what they 'as to do at the finish?"

"No," said Enderby.

"Send for the fire brigade. I'm not tellin' you a word of a lie, but they 'as to do that. On my God's honour, they send for the fire brigade, and you know what the fire brigade 'as to do?"

"No," said Enderby.

"They gets one of their special saws to saw through metal and they 'as a 'ose-pipe playin' on it all the time. Know why that was?"

"To keep it cool," said Enderby.

"You've got it," said the dwarf. "There's not many as would give the right answer like you done. To keep it cool. Anyway, they gets it off, and that's when they ask me to see this trick cyclist like what you've seen. Didn't do no good, though." He looked gloomy.

"Is that why you're back in again?" said Enderby.

"Naw," said the working-dwarf with scorn. "Broke my leg at work this time. Always somethin' though, int there?"

From this moment Enderby thought that, with a certain measure of help and encouragement, he might conceivably decide that it might be possible for him to want, with certain inevitable reservations, to go on living. He woke up in the middle of the night laughing at some dream-joke. The sister had to give him a sedative.

Two

Flitchley, surrounded by the pink snow of apple-blossom, cuckoo-(appropriately)-echoing, green, quiet with a quiet that the clack and clock of table-tennis only emphasised the more, Flitchley was all that Dr Greenslade had said it would be. Several weeks later Enderby sat on a bird-loud terrace reading a harmless boy's book of violence ("... The Chink, with a sinister Oriental smile on his inscrutable yellow countenance, wrenched the knife from the back of his dead companion and threw it straight at Colonel Bill. Bill ducked, hearing the evil weapon twang in the door. He had ducked only just in time. 'Now,' he said, a cold smile on his clean-cut features, 'I think I've had more than enough of your treachery for one day, Mr John Chinaman.' He advanced on the Chink, who now gibbered in his own outlandish language what was evidently a prayer for mercy....") In the day-room was the cheerful music of the table being set for luncheon. Beyond the haha a gardener bent at work. Fellow-patients of Enderby walked the grounds or, like himself, sat at rest with sedative literature. Occasionally Enderby would lower his book to his lap, close his eyes and say softly to himself, many times over, "My name is Enderby-Hogg, my name is Enderby-Hogg." It was part of the process of his cure: a gently contrived change of identity. Hogg had been his mother's maiden name; soon, the Enderby silenced, it would be altogether his.

The bell rang for luncheon and, from the day-room radio, news refinedly boomed. Enderby-Hogg sat down, one of a mess of six, having first shaken hands with a Mr Barnaby. Mr Barnaby, like a dog, insisted on shaking hands with everybody at all hours of the day and sometimes, waking everybody gently up for the purpose, in the night. He had a sweet wrinkled face and, like that Enderby soon to disappear, was something of a poet. He had written verses on the Medical Superintendent beginning:

You have certainly got it in for me and no
Question about that, you fierce-eyed man.
Your wife no more loves you than that black crow
Up in the tree loves you, or that can
Which whilom held baked beans of the brand of
    Heinz,
Or that dog belonging to the lodge-keeper which so
    sorely whines.

At the same table was Mr Trill, one of the symptoms of whose derangement was an ability to name the winner of any major horse-race run in the last sixty years. He was a man of venerable appearance who, he swore, hated racing. Enderby-Hogg now said to him, in automatic greeting. "Thousand Guineas, 1910." Mr Trill looked up mournfully from his soup and said, "Winkipop, owned Astor, trained W. Waugh, ridden Lynham. Starting price five to two." There was Mr Beecham, a master plumber who, on psychiatric instructions, spent all his day painting pictures: black snakes, red murder, his wife with three heads. Mr. Shap, insurance agent, with dark glasses and a black hole for a mouth, said nothing, did nothing, but at times would scream one word: PASTE. Finally there was Mr Killick who preached, in an undertone, to the birds. He had the look of a successful butcher.

This company of six drank its soup and then was served, by two cheerful nurses of radiant complexion, with slabs of meat pie and scooped spuds. There were spoons and forks, but no knives. The meal chewed itself by pleasantly and quietly, except that at one point a dressing-gowned man at another table cried to the ceiling:

"Sink her, Number One!"

He was soothed quickly by one of the nurses, a homely Lancashire lass with a strong sense of humour. She said, "You sink that meat pie quick, my lad. Treacle duff's coming alongside." Enderby-Hogg laughed with the rest at this typical bit of Lancashire badinage. The treacle duff, with liberal custard, was then wheeled in, and Mr Killick, hungry after a morning preaching to the birds, had three helpings. After the meal some went back to bed, while Enderby-Hogg and others sat in the solarium. Enderby-Hogg had no money, but some obscure chairtable fund invoked by the almoner supplied him with a sufficiency of cigarettes. A nurse came round with matches to light up for the smokers: no patient was allowed matches of his own, not since one Jehova-minded G.P.I. sufferer had called Flitchley Sodom and set fire to it.

After a quiet smoke and lazy rambling chat, Enderby-Hogg went to the lavatory. The little cabinets, without doors, could be looked in on from the corridor through a thick glass wall: even here there was no sense of aloneness. After an ample healthy movement, Enderby-Hogg went to the ward he shared with eleven others, there to lie on his bed till summoned for his afternoon session with Dr Wapenshaw. He finished his boy's book ("... 'And,' grinned Colonel Bill, 'despite all the dangers and hazards, it was a jolly good adventure which I'd be happy to undertake again.' But, as he pulled the throttle and the mixture exploded sweet and strong, little did he think that adventure of an even more thrilling kind awaited him. That adventure, chaps, we shall learn about in our next story—the ninety-seventh!—of Colonel Bill and the faithful Spike."). Enderby-Hogg looked forward, without undue excitement, to reading that story.

At three o'clock a smiling nurse summoned him to Dr Wapenshaw. Dr Wapenshaw said, "Ah, hallo there, old man. Things going all right, eh? Jolly good, jolly good," for all the world like Colonel Bill or his creator. Dr Wapenshaw was a big man whose superfluous fat proclaimed, like medals, his former Rugby football triumphs. He had large feet and a moustache and a voice like Christmas pudding. But he was a clever and original psychiatrist. "Sit down," he invited. "Smoke if you want to." Enderby-Hogg sat down, smiling shyly. He adored Dr Wapenshaw.

"Enderby-Hogg, Enderby-Hogg," said Dr Wapenshaw, as though beginning a nursery rhyme. A thick file was open on the desk before him. "Enderby-Hogg. Bit of a mouthful, isn't it? I think we might drop the Enderby, don't you? Keep it, of course, in the background as an optional extra if you like. How do you feel about the Hogg?"

"Oh, fine," said Hogg. "Perfectly all right."

"What do you associate the name with? Pigs? Filth?" smiling. "Gluttony?" Humorously, Dr Wapenshaw pig-snorted.

"Of course not," said Hogg, smiling too. "Roses. A lawn in summer. A sweet-smelling woman at the piano. A silver voice. The smoke from a Passing Cloud."

"Excellent," said Dr Wapenshaw. "That will do very well indeed." He sat back in his swivel-chair, swivelling boyishly from side to side, looking kindly at Hogg. "That beard's coming along all right," he said. "You should have a pretty good one in a couple of weeks. Oh, yes,

I've made a note about glasses. We're sending you to the oculist on Thursday."

"Thank you very much," said Hogg.

"Don't thank me, my dear fellow," said Dr Wapenshaw. "After all, it's what we're here for, isn't it? To help." Tears came into Hogg's eyes. "Now," said Dr Wapenshaw, "I've explained to you already just what it is we're trying to do and why we're trying to do it. Could you recap"—he smiled—"in your own words?"

"Enderby," said Hogg, "was the name of a prolonged adolescence. The characteristics of adolescence were well-developed and seemed likely to go on for ever. There was, for instance, this obsession with poetry. There was masturbation, liking to be shut up in the lavatory, rebelliousness towards religion and society."

"Excellent," said Dr Wapenshaw.

"The poetry was a flower of that adolescence," said Hogg. "It still remains good poetry, some of it, but it was a product of an adolescent character. I shall look back with some pride on Enderby's achievement. Life, however, has to be lived."

"Of course it has," said Dr Wapenshaw, "and you're going to live it. What's more, you're going to enjoy living it. Now, let me tell you what's going to happen to you. In a month's time—perhaps less if you continue to make the excellent progress you're already making—we're sending you to our Agriculture Station at Snorthorpe. It's really a convalescent home, you know, where you do a little gentle work—not too much, of course: just what you feel you *can* do and nothing more—and lead a very pleasant simple social life in beautiful surroundings. Snorthorpe," said Dr Wapenshaw, "is a little town on a river. There are summer visitors, swans, boating, nice little pubs. You'll love it. A group of you—under supervision, of course, if you can really call it supervision—will be allowed out to pubs and dances and cinemas. In the home itself there'll be chess competitions and sing-songs. Once a week," smiled Dr Wapenshaw, "I myself like to come down and lead a sing-song. You'll like that, won't you?"

"Oh yes," breathed Hogg.

"Thus," said Dr Wapenshaw, "you'll gradually adjust yourself to living in society. You'll even meet women, you know," he smiled. "Some day, you know, I look forward to your making a *real* go of marriage. Enderby made rather a mess of that, didn't he? Still, it's all over now. The annulment's going through, so they tell me, quite smoothly."

"I can't even remember her name," frowned Hogg.

"Don't worry about that," said Dr Wapenshaw. "That's Enderby's affair, isn't it? You'll remember it in your own good time. And, moreover, you'll remember it with amusement." Hogg smiled tentatively, as in anticipation. "Now, as far as your future generally is concerned, I don't want you to think about that at the moment. There's going to be no worry about getting a really congenial job for you—we have our own department, you know, which sees to all that, and very efficient they are. The thing for you to do at the moment is to *enjoy* being this new person we're trying to create. After all, it *is* great fun, isn't it? I'm getting no end of a kick out of it all, and I want you to share that kick with me. After all," he smiled, "we've grown very close, haven't we, these last few weeks? We've embarked on a real adventure together, and I'm enjoying every minute of it."

"Oh, me too," said Hogg eagerly. "And I'm really most awfully grateful."

"Well, it's really awfully nice of you to say that," said Dr Wapenshaw. "But you've helped no end, yourself, you know." He smiled once more and then became genially gruffly business-like. "I'll be seeing you," he said, looking at his diary, "on Friday morning. Now off you go and have your tea or whatever it is and leave me to see my next victim." He sighed humorously. "Work, work, work." He shook his head. "No end to it. Run along now," he grinned. Hogg grinned back and ran along.

For tea they had Marmite sandwiches, fish-paste sandwiches (Mr Shap cried out PASTE with such exquisite appropriateness that everybody had to laugh), fancy cakes and a small plum cake to each mess of six. After tea Hogg walked the grounds and surprised Mr Killick whispering to some bread-guzzling starlings beyond the haha, "Come on now, you birdies, be good and kind to each other and love God who made you all. He was a bird just like you." Hogg returned to the sunny solarium to find Mr Barnaby triumphantly finishing another stanza of his Ode to the Medical Superintendent. He read this aloud with great feeling, having first shaken hands heartily with Hogg:

I saw you the other night out on the field
Walking with a big stick with which you struck the
    grass
Repeatedly, but the dumb grass would not yield
To your importunities. So it will come to pass
That that piece of china standing on your shelf
Will fall on your head and give quite a shock to
    your evil-smelling self.

For dinner there were fish and a rice pudding with sultanas embedded in it. Mr Beecham, his hands vermilion from his day's work on a large symbolical canvas, slowly picked out all the sultanas from his portion and arranged them in a simple gestalt on his bread-plate. After dinner there was television: amateur boxing which excited two patients so much that one of the nurses had to switch over to the other channel. On the other channel was a simple morality of good and evil set in the West of North America in the eighteen-sixties. It was interrupted at intervals by asthenic women demonstrating washing-machines, though some patients evidently could not see these as interpolations, taking them rather as integral to the plot. Integration was the theme: the building of a new human society under the sheriff's steadfast bright star. Hogg nodded frequently, seeing all this (conquest of new territory, death to the evil antisocial) as an allegory of his own reorientation.

Three

High summer in Snorthorpe. Boats for hire by the bridge, by the bridge a hotel called the White Hart, much favoured by summer visitors. Drinkers squinting happily in noonlight on the terrace. Dogs yapping in glee, chased by children. Ducks and swans, full-fed, pampered. Willows. An old castle on a height far above the river.

A knot of men came walking, in loose formation though evidently a supervised gang, in the direction of the little town from the sunbrown fields of the Agricultural Station. They were men who looked as burnt and fit as the boating visitors, each carrying some such tool as a hoe or fork. By the bridge they halted at the cheerful command of their leader. "All right," he called. "Rest for five minutes. Old Charlie here says he's got a stone in his boot." Mr Peacock was a decent brown man, squat and upright, who treated his charges like younger brothers. Old Charlie sat on the parapet and Mr Peacock helped him off with his road-dusty boot.

"Fag?" said Piggy Hogg (as he was jocularly called) to his companion. Bob Curran took one, nodding his thanks. He pulled out a cheap cylindrical lighter and struck it, the flame invisible in noon air that was all flame. Piggy Hogg bent over, sucking his fag alight.

"Won't be long for you now," said Bob Curran.

"Won't be long," said Piggy Hogg, taking in the long receding bank of willows. "Next week, they reckon." He detached a tobacco fibre from his lower lip. The lips were framed in brown beard pied with grey; his skin was tanned; he wore steel spectacles. He had something of the look of Hemingway, but there his association with literature ended. A moderately well-spoken middle-aged man evidently not used to manual work, but a good trier, respected by his ward-mates, helpful as a letter-writer. Some had said that it was a waste of an educated man, putting him like they said they were going to as bar-tender in training at a London hotel. But Piggy Hogg knew it was no waste.

A couple of nights back he had, after lights out, slipped on his bedside headphones. Rejecting, with a click of the plastic dial on the wall, first the Light, then the Home, he had notched into the Third. A bored-sounding young man had been talking about Modern

215

Poetry: "... Enderby, before his unaccountable disappearance ... established as a good minor poet in the tradition ... perhaps little to say to our generation ... the more significant work of Jarvis, Sime and Cazalet ..." He had listened with absolutely no interest. One was used, one was thrown away; Enderby had come out of it better than many; Hogg was looking forward to being a bar-tender. A bar-tender, moreover, who would be different from most, quite a character with his odd lines of poetry thrown out over the frothing pints. Behind the words and rhythms lay the sensations. Time for those.

"What did the old sky-pilot have to say to you?" asked Bob Curran.

"Him?" said Piggy Hogg vaguely. "Oh, I thought he made out quite a reasonable case for the Church of England. It's a communion of sorts. It doesn't make too many demands. He lent me some books to read, but I told him I'm not much of a reading man. If it'll give him any pleasure, I'll join."

"I've never been much of a man for religion myself," said Bob Curran. "My dad was a tinker and all tinkers are atheists. We used to have a lot of fun, I remember, on Thursday evenings in the old days. You know, belly of pork and cider and somebody would give a talk about Causal Necessity and then there'd be one hell of a discussion afterwards. All in our front parlour, you know, with The Death of Nelson above the joanna." Bob Curran was a very lean man of fifty-seven, a radio salesman recovering from schizophrenia. "It seems to me," he said, "that people had more faith in those days. They *believed* more. Why, I do believe that my old man, who was nothing more than an ignorant old tinker, believed more in there not being a God than some of these religious sods today believe in there being one. It's a funny old world," he concluded, as he always did.

"Oh, yes," agreed Piggy Hogg, "but it's not without interest." After lunch there was to be a cricket match between the Home and the local St John's Ambulance. Piggy Hogg had been persuaded to umpire. He had always been flustered by l.b.w. but, he had decided, when in doubt over any appeal except an obvious clean bowl or catch, always to say, "Not out". That night there was to be a sing-song, led by Dr Wapenshaw, with beer from the canteen—two bottles a man. Piggy Hogg led the winning quiz-team. He had beaten Alfred Breasley at chess.

"Right, my tigers," called Mr Peacock. "Old Charlie's boot's free from stones." (Old Charlie grinned without teeth.) "God's in his heaven, all's right with the etcetera etcetera. On our merry way. Let me see, it's Saturday, isn't it? Corned beef and mashed and beetroot and treacle tart to follow. Right, Piggy old man, stop slavering at the chops. Let's march."

Piggy Hogg glanced up at the tiny clouds (cotton-wool stoppers from heavenly aspirin-bottles) and down at the sun-warmed boats on the shore that looked like chicken carcasses. A swan opened an archangelic wing. Shouldering his hoe, chucking away his fag-butt, he marched.

Book Two

Esperad todavía.
El bestial elemento se solaza
En el odio a la sacra poesía
Y se arroja baldón de raza a raza.
—Rubén Darío

I

1

One

"Ir's," said this customer at the bar, "what I personally would want to call—and anyone else can call it what the hell they like for all I care—" Hogg listened respectfully, half-bowed, wiping dry a glass from which a very noisy woman, an actress or something, had drunk and eaten a Pimm's Number One. "But it's what I, speaking for myself, would call—" Hogg burnished an indelible veronica of lipstick, waiting for some highly idiosyncratic payoff, not just the just word but the word just with just this customer's personal brand of justness. "A barefaced liberty." Hogg bowed deeper in tiny dissatisfaction. He had been a wordman himself once (nay, still—but best to lock all that up: they had said those days were past, trundled off by time's rollicking draymen, empties, and they knew best, or said they did. Still—) "A man's name's his name, all said and done." You couldn't say what this man had just said. A liberty was diabolical; it was lies that were barefaced. Hogg had learned so much during his season with the salt of the earth, ˙ərmen and suchlike. But he said, blandly:

"It's very kind of you, sir, to feel that way about it."

"That's all right," said this customer, brushing the locution towards Hogg as though it were a tip.

"But they didn't call it after me, sir, in a manner of speaking." That was good, that was: genuine barman. "They brought me in here, as you might say, because the place was already called what it is."

"There's been plenty named Hogg," said the customer sternly. "There was this man that was a saint and started these schools where all these kids were in rags. They had to be in rags or they wouldn't have them in. It was like what they call a school uniform. And there's this Hogg that was a lord and gave it up to be prime minister but he didn't get it so he goes round ringing bells and telling them all off."

"There was also James Hogg, the poet," said Hogg, unwisely.

"You leave poets out of it."

"The Ettrick shepherd he was known as, in a manner of speaking. Pope in worsted stockings."

"And religion as well." This customer, who had had no lunch except whisky, grew louder. "I might be an Arsee, for all you know. Respect a man's colour and creed and you won't go far wrong. I take a man as I find him." He spread his jacket like wings to show green braces. Hogg looked uneasily across the near-empty bar. The clock said five to three. John, the tall sardonic Spaniard who waited on, the Head Steward's nark, he was taking it all in all right. Hogg sweated gently.

"What I mean is," said flustered Hogg, "this bar was called Piggy's Sty because of the man that was here before me." John the Spaniard sneered across. "Sir," added Hogg.

"And you won't go far wrong is what I say."

"It was to do with the people that started these hotels," said Hogg urgently. "They had a Hogg over there when they started. He brought them luck and he died. Americans they were."

"I can take them or leave them. We fought side by side in both lots. They did as much good as harm, and I hope they'll say as much about you." He slid his empty glass towards Hogg, impelling it as though it were a child's match-box ten-ton truck.

"Similar, sir?" asked Hogg, barman's pride pushing through the fluster.

"No, I'll try one of theirs. If the Yanks run this place then they'll likely know what's what." Hogg didn't get that. "What they call bourbon. That bottle there with the nigger on." Hogg measured out a double slug of Old Rastus. "With branch-water," said this customer. Hogg filled a little pig-shaped jug from a tap. He rang up the money and said:

"They wouldn't have false pretences, that being their policy, as you might say. They said that customers like things genuine in the States and it's got to be the same here too. So it had to be a Hogg."

The customer, as though testing his neck for fracture, swivelled his head slowly, taking in Piggy's Sty. It was one of many whimsically-named bars in this tall but thin hotel, London's new pride. This bar and the Wessex Saddleback, where at this moment there were a lot of thick-necked Rotarians sweating on to charred gristle, made up nearly the whole of the tenth floor. You could see much of autumn London from the windows of the bar (on which artificial trotter-prints were like a warning). You could see an ape-architecture of office-blocks, the pewter river, trees that had scattered order-paper leaves all about Westminster, Wren and his God like babes in the wood, the dust of shattered Whig residences thrown by the wind. But this customer looked only on the frieze of laughing tumbling porkers, the piggy-banks with broken saddles to make ashtrays, little plastic troughs with plastic chrysanthemums in them. He turned back to Hogg to nod at him in grudging admiration as though he, Hogg, had made all this.

"Closing now, sir," said Hogg. "One for the road, sir?"

"You wouldn't catch them daring to take the mike out of *my* name," said the customer. He now winked pleasantly at Hogg. "Not that I'd give them the chance. A man's name is his own." He laid his finger to his nose, as though to cool the inflammation which Hogg's stepmother had used to call Harry Syphilis, winking still. "Catch *me*." He smirked, as though his name was something he had won and was going to hug greedily to his chest till he got home. "I'll have some of our own now after that nigger stuff. A wee drappie. Och aye. There's a wee wifey waiting." Hogg daringly poured Scotch into the glass that had held bourbon. John had his eyes on his two leaving customers.

"Electric shepherds," said one of these, a man who might well be a pig-farmer and yet had not seemed really at home in Piggy's Sty. "It'll come to that, I daresay." He was with a man in clerical grey, etiolated as by a life of insurance. They both nodded at Spanish John and then went out. John showed them a baroque shrine of golden teeth and said: "Zhentilmen." Then he picked up their glasses and brought them to the counter for Hogg to wash. Hogg looked on him with hate.

"But what I say is," said the one customer left, "it's an insult to the name of your old dad. That's the way to look at it." He descended his stool with care. John bowed and bowed, his gob all bits of fractured doubloon. The customer grunted, dove into his trouser-pocket and brought up a half-crown. This he gave to John; to Hogg he gave nothing. John bowed and bowed, baring deeper and deeper gold deposits. Hogg said:

"Actually, it was my mother's."

"Eh?" The customer squinted at him.

"What I mean is, Hogg was my mum's name, not my dad's."

"I don't come in here," said the customer, "to have the piss took." A certain lowness was coming out now. "You watch it."

Hogg sulked. He had gone too far again. And this horrible John had, as before, been a witness. But Hogg had spoken truth. Hogg had been the maiden name of that barely imaginable sweet woman, singing "Passing By" to her own accompaniment, Banksia and Macartney and Wichuraiana vainly opposing their scents to hers through the open french window. His father, O-ing out the smoke of a Passing Cloud while he listened, his father had been called—

"I like a laugh same as the next one, but watch it,

that's all." And the customer left, going aaarkbrokhhh on his stomach of whisky. Hogg and Spanish John faced each other.

"*Puerco*," said John, for so he translated Hogg's mother's name. "You speak other time of poetry, not good. Get on with bloody job is right way."

"Nark," growled Hogg. "Tell Holden if you want to. A fat lot I care." Holden was the Head Steward, a big man hidden behind secretaries and banks of flowers, an American who sometimes pretended he was Canadian. He would talk of cricket. It was something to do with American trade policy.

"I say bugrall this time," promised John generously. "This time not big. Last time very big."

Well, it hadn't really been Hogg's fault. A group of young fattish television producers had been there for dinner, cramming down peanuts with the martinis, going "*Ja*" when they meant "yes." They had talked loudly of the sexual *mores* of certain prominent actresses and, by a natural transition, had been led on to a discussion of poetry. They had misquoted something by T. S. Eliot and Hogg, off his guard, had put them right. This had interested them, and they had tried him on other poets, of all of whom—Wunn, Gain, Lamis, Harkin, some such names—Hogg had never heard. The television men had seemed to sneer at him, a common barman, for knowing; now they sneered at him for not knowing. The leader of the *ja*-sayers fed himself, in the manner of a Malaysian rice-eater, with a shovel-hand loaded with salty peanuts, sneering at the same time. He said, indistinctly, "Wenggerggy."

"Who?" said Hogg. He had begun to tremble. There was a phantom girl hovering near the pig-pink (chopped-ham-and-pork-pink, to be accurate) ceiling, a scroll in her hand, queenly shoulders nacreous above a Regency ballgown. Hogg knew her all too well. Had she not deserted him a long time ago? Now she smiled encouragingly, unrolling her scroll coquettishly though, an *allumeuse*. "Did you say *Enderby?*" asked Hogg, shaking beneath his barman's white bum-freezer and frowning. The girl swooped down to just behind him,

227

flat-handed him on the nape, and then shoved the wide-open scroll in front of his eyes. He found himself reciting confidentially, as in threat:

"Bells broke in the long Sunday, a dressing-gown day.
The childless couple basked in the central heat.
The papers came on time, the enormous meat
Sang in the oven. On thick carpets lay
Thin panther kittens locked in clawless play—"

"Ah, Jesus—"
"A *sonnet* yet—"
Hogg glowered at this one, a small gesturing man, and prepared to say "For cough." But instead he went stoutly on:

"Bodies were firm, their tongues clean and their feet
Uncalloused. All their wine was new and sweet.
Recorders, unaccompanied, crooned away—"

At this moment another television man came in, one they had apparently all been waiting for. He was much like the others, very pasty. They clawed at him passionately, shouting.
"The Minetta Tavern—"
"Goody's on Sixth Avenue—"
There was a solitary man at the counter, one who had ordered by pointing; he wore dark glasses; his mouth had opened at Hogg and let cigarette smoke wander out at him. The tabled customers, aware of the intrusion of verse-rhythm into the formlessness of chat, had all been looking at Hogg. Spanish John stood shaking his head, nastily pleased.
"No more verse-fest," said the chief peanut-eater to Hogg. "More martinis."
"Wait," said Hogg, "for the bloody sestet."
"Oh, let's go in," the newcomer said, "I'm *starving.*" And so they all shouted off to the Wessex Saddleback, clawing and going *ja.* Hogg turned gloomily to the man in dark glasses and said:
"They could have waited for the bloody sestet. No

manners nowadays. It's a miracle, that's what they don't seem to realise. I tried for years to get that thing right, and only then it just came to me." He suddenly felt guilty and began to excuse himself. "Another man, though. Not really me. It's a long story. Rehabilitation they call it." The man had said:

"*Nye ponimaiu.*" That was why he had started pointing again. Hogg, sighing, had measured out a large globule of an Iron Curtain glycerine-smelling apéritif. Must watch himself. He was happy now, wasn't he? Useful citizen.

It was after that occasion that he had been summoned to see Mr Holden, a man desperately balding as though to get into *Time* magazine. Mr Holden had said:

"You were on a sticky wicket there, *ja.* A straight bat and keep your eye on the pitcher. This is a respectable hotel and you are a sort of gliding presence in white, that's your image, *ja.* You've done well to get here after so short an innings in the profession. Self-employed before, that's what it says in your dossier. Well, whatever it was is no concern of the management. Though it's beginning to sound as though it wasn't quite com eel foe. Still, the pairst is pairst. The cream of global citizenry pairsses through these portals. They don't want bar-tenders telling them to keep their tongues clean. And you said something about our cellar that was libellous, but he may have balled that up, so we'll let it pairss. It's your name that's your asset, remember that. Carry your bat, brother, or you'll find yourself no-balled PDQ."

Past, was it? The past, that is. He did something there was no law against doing shortly after. If anybody found out they would have him on television, sandwiched between a dustman who collected Meissen and a bank-clerk who had taught his dog to smoke a pipe. A curiosity at best. At worst a traitor. To what, though? To what a traitor would he be regarded as? And now, a month after, he was frowning while he compared his takings with the roll in the till that recorded each several amount rung. He would have to take the money in a little box to the huge clacking hotel treasury full of comptometers that—so Larry in the Harlequin Bar upstairs had asserted—if programmed proper could be made to see right through to your very soul. And then he had an appointment. In (his breast swelled minimally) Harley Street. To your very soul, eh? He felt uneasy. But, damn it, he had done no real wrong, surely? When John Milton clocked in to do his daily stint of translation of Cromwell into Latin, had they not perhaps used to say: "All right that was, that thing you pinned up on the wall about Fairfax and the siege of Colchester. You carry on"? He, Hogg, had not pinned anything up, though, by God, one of these days—He had merely—

"My brother," John was saying, "now he work in Tangier. At Big Fat White Doggy Wog, bloody daft name for bar. Billy Gomez, everybody know him. Good on knife if trouble, ah yes, man." He made a bloodthirsty queeeeeeking noise and drove a ghost-stiletto at Hogg's hidden puddings. "He say poetry, but now not. *Good* poetry. *Spanish* poetry. Gonzalo de Berceo, Juan Ruiz, Ferrant Sánchez Calavera, Jorge Manrique, Góngora—*good* poetry. England too fackin cold for good poetry. English man no *fuego*. Like bloody fish, *hombre*."

"I'll give you no *fuego*," said Hogg, incensed. "We gave you *mucho* bloody *fuego* in 1588, bastards, and we'll do it again. Garlicky sods. I'll give you no good poetry." A ruff went round his neck. He stroked a spade-beard, enditing. The sky was red with fireships. Then he saw himself in the gross reredos mirror, his cross reflection framed in foreign bottles, a decently shaven barman in glasses, going, like Mr. Holden, rapidly bald.

"We go eat now," said John. In the hotel's intestines steamed an employees' cafeteria, full of the noise of shovelled chips and heady with Daddies Sauce. A social organiser walked regularly between the tables, trying to get up table-tennis tournaments. John's empty stomach castanetted dully.

"I don't want to eat," sulked Hogg. "I'm full up already. Chocker, that's what I am."

Two

Hogg walked to Harley Street, much set upon by leaves and blowing bits of paper. He knew his way about these defiled streets, London Hogg as he was. His stepmother in Purgatory or wherever she was would have a fit to see how well he knew London. Bruton Street, New Bond Street, across Oxford Street, then through Cavendish Street and across Cavendish Square, then into Harley Street, knowing also that Wimpole Street was the next one, where Robert Brownng had read bits of *Sordello*, a very obscure and long poem, to that woman who had looked like and, indeed, possessed a spaniel, and under the bed there had been big spiders. Her father had made her drink very black stout. Hogg tried to pretend that he did not know these things, since they were outside his barman's province, but he knew that he knew them. He frowned and set his shoulders in defiance. A man who sold newspapers and dirty magazines said, "Cheer ap, gav."

Hogg, in working trousers and decent dogtooth—patterned sports-jacket, was soon seated in Dr Wapenshaw's waiting-room. He had received, some three days before, a curt summons from Dr Wapenshaw, chief agent of his rehabilitation from failed suicide to useful citizen. He could think of only one possible reason for the curtness, but it was a reason so unlikely that he was fain to reject it. Still, when you thought about these cybernetic triumphs and what they were capable of, and how a psychiatrist as cunning as Dr Wapenshaw would be quite likely to have banks of electronic brains working for him (and all at National Health expense), then it was just about possible that the summons might be about this particular hole-in-the-corner thing that Hogg had done, an act of recidivism, to use the fashionable jargon. Otherwise, he, Hogg, and Dr Wapenshaw had achieved a condition of mutual love and trust that, however official and Government-sponsored, had been looked on as a wonder in that green place of convalescence. Had not Dr Wapenshaw shown him, Hogg, off as en exemplary cure, inviting colleagues of all nations to prod and finger and smile and nod and ask cunning questions about Hogg's relationship with his Muse and his stepmother and his lavatory and his pseudo-wife, cooling all that turbulent past to the wan and abstract dignity of a purely clinically interesting case to be handled by fingers smelling of antiseptics? Yes, that was so. Perhaps that curtness was, after all, the official wrapping that enclosed warmth and love and protected them from the eyes of strangers. Still and nevertheless.

The waiting-room had a gas-fire, and the only other waiting patient was crouched over it, as though it were a wicket and he its keeper. The chill of autumn was reflected in the covers of copies of *Vogue* and *Vanity Fair* that lay on the polished table that turned the vase of real, not plastic, chrysanthemums into a kind of antipodeal ghost. These covers showed thin young women in mink against the falling of the leaves. Something like winter cold struck Hogg as he noticed a deck of copies of *Fem*. Those days, not so long ago, when he had actually written ghastly verses for *Fem*, set as harmless prose ("I lift my baby to the air. He gurgles because God is there") and pseudonymously signed Faith Fortitude; those incredible days when he had actually been married to its features editress, Vesta Bainbridge; those days should, officially, be striking him with little more than mild and condescending curiosity. That had been another man, one from a story read yawning. But the past was fastening its suckers on him once more, had been doing ever since that night of the goddess and the television *ja*-sayers and the unpremeditated chrysostomatic utterance. Hogg nodded, sighing heavily. Dr Wapenshaw knew; he knew everything. That was what this interview was going to be about.

"For a load of blasphemous balderdash," said the man by the gas-fire, "you ought to read this lot." He turned to Hogg, waving a thin little book. He had, then, been holding it to the gas-fire, as if, as with bread in some study feed in some school story of pre-electric days, deliberately toasting it. He was a man with wild grey

hair who spoke with a cultivated accent which made his
demotic vocabulary seem affected, which, if he was, as
he evidently was, one of Dr Wapenshaw's patients,
being rehabilitated in the same modes as Hogg himself
had been, if he really had been, it probably was. "And
they say it's *us* that are crackers," he said. "You and me,"
he clarified, "are supposed to be the barmy ones." Hogg
prepared to dissociate himself from that predication, but
he let it pass. The man launched wild fluttering wings of
paper at Hogg and Hogg deftly caught them. The man
did not say "Fielded"; that was rather for Mr Holden or
for Dr Wapenshaw himself, at least the Dr Wapenshaw
of the chummy green days with his "Good show" and
"That's the ticket." Hogg leafed through the little book,
frowning. He caught the title and further frowned: *The
Kvadrat's Kloochy*. He said, with care:

"What does it mean, then?"

"Oh," said the man, irritably, "what does *anything*
mean? It's all a *merde universelle*, as that French Irish-
man says. You read it, that's all." Hogg read, at random:

The miracle of this uncomplicated monody with its minimal
chordal accompaniment is not diminished by our hindsight
knowledge that it had been there waiting, throughout recorded history, yet unnoticed by the bearded creaking practi-
tioners of the complex. They built up their multivocal
counterpoint, their massive orchestras, their fugal and sonata
forms, seeking a perfection that, if they could have cleansed
the rheum from their old-man's eyes, they would have known
had to lie in the simple and direct rather than the periphrastic
and complicated. And yet it is in the error of the traditional
equating of age with wisdom that one may find the cause of
their blindness or, to be kind, presbyopia. The answer to all
problems, aesthetic as much as social, religious, and economic,
resides, in a word, in Youth.

"I don't see what all this is about," said Hogg. He
frowned still, turning over the page to find a photograph
of four common louts who leered up at him, one bearing
a guitar from which electrical flex sprouted, the others
poising sticks over gaudy sidedrums.

"Ah," growled the man, "don't bother *me* with it. You
stick to your world and I'll stick to mine." And then he

cried, very loud: "Mother, you've forsaken your son."
Hogg nodded without fear. Had he not spent an entire
summer among men given to sudden despairing ejaculations or, worse, quiet confident assertions about the
nature of ultimate reality, often delivered, Hogg and
other patients shaken awake for the intimation, in the
middle of the night? He read on:

Jack Cade and the Revolters established the fruitful device of
a heavy ictus on the fourth beat in their disc *Like He Done
That Time*, pressed in April, 1964. In May of the same year
this was further developed by Nap and the Bonies, who, in
their *Knee Trembler*, transferred it to the quaver between the
third beat and the fourth. Needless to say, this was achieved
instinctually, these youthful performers being unburdened
by traditional technical knowledge. In June both groups were
superseded by the Tumers who, intuitively aware of a new
shift in the *Zeitgeist*, perhaps wisely reverted to a greater
simplicity of rhythmical texture and . . .

"Ah, Hogg!" cried a voice both fierce and plummy.
Hogg looked up to see a different Dr Wapenshaw from
the one he remembered—an urban Dr Wapenshaw in a
nattty suit of charcoal grey with discreet stripes, more
formidable than the one who, in that country retreat,
had dressed for his consultations as if for outdoor games.
The chubby face was stern. Meekly Hogg went into the
consulting-room. "Sit you down," said Dr Wapenshaw.
Hogg sat on the seat nearest the door, a sort of creepy-
stool. "Here," said Dr Wapenshaw, throwing a fierce
fistful of air at a seat drawn up to the desk, a desk
massive enough to contain any number of small secret
electronic monitors. He himself went round the desk to
its window-side and stood behind his swivel-chair, grey
Harley Street framed behind him, while he watched
Hogg, who still had *The Kvadrat's Kloochy* in his hand,
shamble over. "Very well, then," said Dr Wapenshaw, in
the manner of a sour grace. Consultant and patient sat
simultaneously.

"Soon be winter now," said Hogg in a conversational
manner. "The nights are drawing in very fast. Could do
with a fire, really, in a manner of speaking." Suddenly
noticing that Dr Wapenshaw's consulting-room had a

grate conspicuously empty, he added, "Not that I meant that in any spirit of criticism, as you might say. All I meant was that it gets a bit chilly at nights." Dr Wapenshaw held him with a disgusted look; Hogg grew flustered. "What I mean is, some feel the cold more than others, so to speak. But"—and he struck hard at Dr Wapenshaw's flint, desperately seeking some of that old warmth—"nobody can deny that it's late autumn now, and after autumn, if you'll pardon the observation—"

"Shut up!" cried Dr Wapenshaw. ("No, no, don't," whimpered the patient in the waiting-room.) "I'll do all the talking." But all he did was to hurl a thick book bound in green paper across at Hogg. Hogg was already growing tired of having books hurled at him; still, he caught it deftly, just like the other one, which was now on his knee. "Look at that," ordered Dr Wapenshaw. "Page 179. Read it, man."

Hogg fingered the book rather tenderly. It was, he saw, a proof copy. He had, in the remote past when he was another man altogether, handled proof copies of his own work, very slim proof copies, poems. He flicked through the massive prose-work with a certain envy, then admired the title. "*Rehabilitations,*" he read out. "There used to be a lot like that in the old days. F. R. Leavis and such people. The New School of Criticism, they called it. But it's all changed now. They have different ideas now and more flowery titles. *The Romantic Orgasm* was one I saw in a shop. And *The Candle in the Thigh* was another. They get a lot of the titles from poor Dylan, you know, who died. It's nice to see a good old-fashioned title like this again. That," he said diffidently, though with a wisp of ancient authority, when he had lighted at last on Page 179, "isn't the right symbol for a deletion and close up, if you'll pardon the correction. It should be like a little ballon on the tip of a stick—"

"Read it, man, read it!" And Dr Wapenshaw thumped his desk thrice. Hogg read where he was ordered, wonderingly. Dr Wapenshaw tattooed the desk-top softly, as though his fingers at least were appeased—three beats in the left hand against two beats in the right, as though playing in some children's nonsense by Benjamin Britten, with tuned teacups and tin-whistles but also Peter Pears as an old man. "Well?" he said at length.

"You know," said Hogg, "this case seems pretty close to what my own was. This chap here, K you call him, was a poet, and that made him into a protracted adolescent. He spent a lot of his time writing verse in the lavatory—a kind of womb you say it is here, but that's a lot of nonsense, of course—and this woman made him marry her and it was a mess and he ran away and then he tried to go back to the old life, writing poetry in the lavatory and so on, and it didn't work so he attempted suicide and then you cured him by reorientating his personality, as it's called here, and then he became a useful citizen and forgot all about poetry and—Well," Hogg said, "that, if I may say so, is an astonishing coincidence, you might call it." He tried to beam, but Dr Wapenshaw's black look was not irradiable. Dr Wapenshaw leaned across the desk and said, with terrible quietness and control:

"You bloody fool. That *is* you."

Hogg frowned slightly. "But," he said, "it can't be. It says here that this K had delusions about other people stealing his work and making horror films out of his poetry. That's not quite the same, is it? I mean, this bloody man Rawcliffe did pinch the plot of my *Pet Beast* and make a bloody awful Italian picture out of it. I even remember the name. *L'Animal Binato* it was called in Italy—that's from Dante, you see: *The Double-Natured Animal* or something like it—and in England it was called *Son of the Beast from Outer Space*." He read more intently, frowning further. "What's all this," he said, "about a sexual fixation on this bloke K's stepmother? That can't be me, this bloke can't. I hated her, you know how much for I told you. And," he said blushing, "about masturbating in the lavatory. And about this woman being very refined and trying to make a real married man out of him." He looked up, his sternness a remote (fourth or fifth or something) carbon copy of Dr Wapenshaw's own. "That woman," he said clearly, "was *not* refined. She was a bitch. She wanted my bit of money, which she got, and she wanted a bit of my honour and glory. When I was dead, that is," he said, less assertively. "In my biography, if such should come to be written." The great expensive consulting-room tasted that, shrugged, grimaced, swallowed it.

"Can you see it?" said Dr Wapenshaw, his upper lip lifted. "Can you honestly say that you see it, man? The most elegant woman in Europe, controller of the best pop-groups in the business?" Hogg stared at this wink of evidence of knowledge of a very vulgar world (he knew it all; he read the *Daily Mirror* doggedly every morning before opening his bar) in an eminent consultant. He said:

"I've not seen her name in the papers—"

"She's married again. A *real* marriage. A man with *real* money and *real* talent, also younger than you and, moreover, *handsome*."

"—But that confirms what I always thought, what you said then, I mean. I mean *not* refined. A bitch." *The Kvadrat's Kloochy* fell off his knees, as in conscious failure to convert. Dr Wapenshaw said harshly:

"Right. Now look at this." And Hogg had hurled at him his third fluttering paper bird of the afternoon. He caught it without much skill; he was already weary; it was a journal he at once recognised; it was called *Confrontation*, a cisatlantic quarterly transatlantically financed and of, he understood, little general appeal. He nodded, unsurprised. Dr Wapenshaw knew everything, then. Hogg understood all. He knew now what it was all about. This was it. He turned to the page where the sestet of that sonnet, which the *ja*-sayers had not wished to hear, spoke to no frequenters of expensive bars, though the octave certainly had:

Coiled on the rooftree, bored, inspired, their snake
Crowed Monday in. A collar kissed the throat,
Clothes braced the body, a benignant ache
Lit up a tooth. The papers had a note:
"His death may mean an empire is at stake."
Sunday and this were equally remote.

And it was signed with that former, forbidden, name. Hogg said, stuttering:

"I can explain everything. I started that before, you see, before you got hold of me. Cured me, I mean. Of antisocial activities, that is. But I couldn't finish it. And then one night when I was working in the bar it just came. It had sort of tidied itself up behind my back. It was perfect, if you'll pardon the expression. So I sent it off and they published it. A kind of last fling, as you might term it. Or posthumous, perhaps you could even say. And then no more poetry, not never no more." That last phrase was perhaps too ingratiating, too consciously the old-time barman. Dr Wapenshaw did not fall for it. Instead, he rose in wrath and cried:

"That's right, that's right, indulge yourself at my expense." He strode across to a little table near the empty grate, picked up a human skull from it, and then waved it threateningly at Hogg. "What you won't or can't realise, *you traitor,* is that that treacherous effusion of yours has been seen, yes, seen. Shorthouse saw it, Dr Shorthouse to you. You wouldn't know who Dr Shorthouse is, in your wilful treachery, but Dr Shorthouse is the author of *The Poetic Syndrome* and *Art and the Spirochaete* and other standard clinical works. Shorthouse saw it and Shorthouse showed it to me." He crept towards Hogg, his eyes blowlamping in shame and anger, holding the skull in both hands like a pudding. "And," he cried, "I felt a fool, because I'd already discussed your case with Shorthouse."

"Dr Shorthouse," kindly emended Hogg.

"Now do you see? *Do you see?* I boast about you as a cure, and here you are again with your bloody poetry." Thumbs in skull's eye-sockets, he tore outwards in his anger, though the skull stayed firm.

"If it's the page-proofs of that thing of yours you're worried about," said Hogg, still kindly, "I'd be only too pleased to help you to correct them. What I mean is, to say that I wasn't cured after all and that my case was a failure. If that would be of any use," he added humbly. "You see," he explained, "I know all about altering things

238

when they're in proof. I was a writer by profession, you see, as you know (I mean, that's what you tried to cure me of, isn't it?), and to you, who are really a doctor, it's only a sort of hobby when all's said and done." He tried to smile at Dr Wapenshaw and then at the skull, but only the latter responded. "Or if you like," suggested Hogg, "I'll tell everybody that I'm really cured and that that sonnet was only a kind of leftover from the old days. Or that that bloke K isn't really me but somebody else. In any case, that Shorthouse man won't say anything to anybody, will he? I mean, you doctors stick together, you have to, don't you? In one of those papers of yours I could do it," expanded Hogg. "*The Lancet* and *The Scalpel* and all those things."

Dr Wapenshaw tore at the skull with his tense strong-nailed hairy fingers, but the skull, as though, it shot into Hogg's mind, remembering Housman's line about the man of bone remaining, grinned in armoured complacency. Dr Wapenshaw seemed about to weep then, as though this skull were Yoricks. After that, he made as to hurl the skull at Hogg, but Hogg got down to the floor to pick up the copy of *The Kvadrat's Kloochy*. Dr Wapenshaw put the skull back on its table, took a great breath and cried:

"Get out! Get out of my bloody consulting-room!"

"I," said Hogg, still on his knees, mildly, "only came here because you told me to."

"Go on, get out! I expended skill and time and patience and, yes, bloody love on your case, and this is the thanks I get! You want to ruin my bloody career, that's what it is!"

Hogg, who had forgotten that he was still kneeling, said with continued mildness: "You could always put what they call an erratum slip in the book, you know. I had one once. The printers had printed 'immortal' instead of 'immoral.' It'll be a great pleasure to help you, really and truly. In any case, if the worst comes to the worst, they can always take that whole section out of the book and you can put something else in. Although," he added seriously, "you'll have to make sure it's exactly the same length. You could sit down tonight and make something up."

Dr Wapenshaw now stomped over to kneeling Hogg and began to lift him by his collar. "Out!" he cried again. "Get out of here, you immoral bastard!" He thumped to the door, opened it and held it open. The patient by the gas-fire was weeping quietly. "As for you, you scrimshanker," Dr Wapenshaw cried at him, "I'll deal with you in a minute. I know you, leadswinger as you are." Hogg, in sorrowful dignity that would, he foreknew, become a brew of rage when he could get to somewhere nice and quiet, walked to the door and said:

"You take too much on yourselves, if you don't mind me saying so." He waved *The Kvadrat's Kloochy* in a kind of admonition. "I'd say it was the job of people like you to set the rest of us a good example. It's you who want a good going over, not this poor chap here."

"Out!"

"Just going," said Hogg, just going. He went, shaking his head slowly. "And," he said, turning back to Dr Wapenshaw, though from a safe distance, "I'll write what poetry I want to, thanks very much, and not you nor anybody else will stop me." He thought of adding "So there," but, before he could decide, Dr Wapenshaw slammed his consulting-room door; the patient by the gas-fire went "Oh!" as though clouted by his mother. Not a very good man after all, thought Hogg, leaving. He ought to have suspected that heartiness right at the beginning. There had always, he felt, been something a bit insincere about it.

Three

Some short time later, Hogg sat trembling in a public lavatory. He could actually see the flesh of his inner thighs jellying with rage. Up above him diesel trains kept setting off to the west, for this was Paddington Station, whither he had walked by way of Madam Tussaud's, the Planetarium, Edgware Road and so on. He had put a penny in the slot and was having more than his pennyworth of anger out. The whole poetry-loathing world had the face of Dr Wapenshaw but, he felt, having soundly and legitimately bemerded that face in imagination and micturated on it also, the world was content merely to loathe, while Dr Wapenshaw had had to go further, deliberately liquidating the poet. Or trying to. He, Hogg, was maligning the world. The world was very bad, but not as bad as Dr Wapenshaw. But then again, was not the bloody Muse bad too, withholding her gifts as she had done and then coming forward with a most ill-timed bestowal? The point was, what was the position? What precisely and the hell did she want him to do? He caught a most agonising and fragrant whiff of himself as he had once been, seated like this in the workroom of his seaside flat, scratching bared legs that were mottled by the electric fire, working away steadily at his verse, the Muse and he set in a calm and utterly professional relationship. Would she, coaxed (which meant, among other things, not calling her bad or bloody as he had done just then), be willing to return on a sort of chronic basis? An acute spasm like that one which there had just been the row about really did nobody anything but harm.

But, of course, in those days, before that bloody woman had married him and made him squander his capital, it had been possible for him to be a professional (*i.e.* non-earning, or earning very little) poet. Now he had to have a wage. Even if the gift returned properly it would have to be expended in the form of what was called a nice hobby. Of course, he had been able to save a little. He had a little bedroom in the hotel, his food, a few tips. His trousers being down, he was able to find out at once how much he had saved. He still kept his cash in a sponge-bag whose string was wound about a fly-button. He trusted neither banks nor his colleagues at the hotel. Keys there were a mockery, because of pass-keys. Once he had entered his little bedroom to find Spanish John in it, with a shirt of Hogg's in one hand and one of Hogg's razor-blades in the other, and Hogg had been quite sure he had locked his door. John had smiled falsely and said that he had found the door unlocked and had entered to borrow a razor-blade, he being out of them, and at the same time had been filled with a desire to admire Hogg's shirts, which he considered to be very good ones. Hogg did not believe that. Anyway, he kept his money in a bag in his trousers. It was also a kind of testicle-protector, for there were some dirty fighters among the Maltese and Cypriot commis waiters. He now took his roll of five-pound notes out of the bag and counted them earnestly. A crude drawing of a man, a sort of naked god of fertility, looked down without envy.

Twenty-five drawings of a clavigerous lion guarding a rather imbecilic teenage Britannia. That was not bad. That was one hundred and twenty-five pounds. And, in his trouser pocket, there was about thirty shillings in silver, made up of mostly very mean gratuities. The value of certain other gratuities, dispensed in foreign notes, he had not yet troubled to ascertain. These—dirhams, lire, newfrancs, deutschmarks and so on—he kept folded in his passport, which was in the inside pocket of his sports-jacket, now hanging from the door-hook. It was necessary, he had learned, for every employee of the hotel to keep close guard on his passport, because of the thievery and shady trade in passports that went on among the dark scullions, outcasts of the islands, creatures of obscure ethnic origin, cunning, vicious, and unscrupulous. Despite Britain's new despised status in the world, a British passport was still prized. So there it was, then. Enough to buy time to write, say, a really careful sestina or a rambling Pound-type canto, if the Muse would be willing to cooperate. He blew very faint wind. That was not, he told her, in case she were around, acting silly, meant in any spirit of acrimony or impatience: it was a legitimate efflation, paid for in advance.

He was calmer now. He looked with sympathy at the graffiti on the walls and door. Some of these must, he thought, be considered a kind of art, since they were evidently attempts to purge powerful emotion into styl-ised forms. There were also wild messages, pleas for assignations at known places, though the dates were long gone; there were boasts too extravagant to be capable of fulfilment, also succinct desiderations of sexual partners too complaisant to be of this world. Sex. Well, he, Hogg, had tried, following the rehabilitatory pattern imposed by Dr, now bloody, Wapenshaw, to go in for sex like everybody else, but it had not been very successful. In any case, you really had to be young nowadays to go in properly for sex: that had been made fairly clear to him by such of the young—Italian chambermaids and so on—as he had met, as also by some of the popular art he had, again in fulfilment of the Wapenshaw bloody pattern, tried glumly to appreciate. So there it was, then. He must stop himself saying that to himself all the time.

On the walls there were also little verses, most of them set—like those works of Faith Fortitude—as prose. They were all traditional verses, mostly on cloacal subjects, but it was somehow warming to find that verse was still in regard for its gnomic or mnemonic properties. Among the common people, that was. He could not imagine bloody Wapenshaw writing or drawing anything in a lavatory. There was, Hogg noticed, a nice little patch of naked wall by his right arm. He did not need his Muse for what he now took out his ballpoint pen to write. He wrote:

> Think, when you ease your inner gripe
> Or stand with penis in your paw,
> A face is lodged within the pipe
> And it belongs to Wapenshaw.

That, perhaps, would be learned by heart and reproduced elsewhere underground, imperfect memory blurring the sharp elegance but perhaps not wholly losing that name, in some allomorph or other. Enderby, folk poet. Enderby, not Hogg. And Wapenshaw given a proper immortality.

Hoggerby now felt hungry. He girded himself, pulled the chain, donned his jacket and went out. He nodded kindly at the wash-and-brush-up man, who was reading the *Evening Standard* by his glazed partition, then mounted to the light. He walked out of the station and found a sufficiently dirty-looking little eating-hell in a sidestreet, nearly filled with slurping men. He knew the sort of meal he wanted: a rebellious meal. From the tooth-sucking man with glasses behind the counter he ordered a mug of very strong tea, eggs and fat bacon, marged doorsteps. He was going to give himself indigestion. That would show bloody Wapenshaw.

2

One

"A GREAT honour, *ja*," said Mr Holden from behind
massed flowers of the season. In the adjoining office
typewriters clacked. Standing before Mr Holden were
Hogg and John the Spaniard, respectively flashing gold
and caries and looking dour about the great honour.
"Smallish and very select, and the Saddleback is just
about the right-sized pitch, *ja*. So it'll be cocktails in the
Sty, and this is where you, brother Hogg, show your
batting strength. We'll be having some waiters from the
Sweet Thames Run Softly bar, sort of extra cover. You'd
better start boning up on your cocktails, fella, read up
your sort of bar-tender's Wisden. Horse's necks, sidecars,
manhattans, snowballs, the lot. You reckon you can carry
your bat?"

"I know them all," said Hogg, "including some that
haven't been thought of yet."

"I show him," said John, "if he not know."

"A pop-group, you say?" said Hogg.

"You ought to know these things," said Mr Holden.
"You get plenty of time for reading the papers. A sort of
belated celebration, a kind of late cut to the off. They've

been making this movie in the Bahamas, as you should know, and only now have they been able to get this fixture organised. There's a lot to celebrate. A new golden disc, the birthday honours, and now Yod Crewsy gets this F.L.R.S. thing. *Ja,* plenty to celebrate. *Mucho,*" he added for John's benefit.

"*Usted habla bien español.*"

"F.R.S.L.?" Hogg queried. "Fellow of the Royal Society of Literature?"

"Not bad, not bad, fella. Keep on like that, eye on the ball and all that palooka. *Ja,* he got the Hangman award for some book of poems he wrote and then this F.S. thing sort of automatically followed."

"Heinemann award?" frowned Hogg. "And what do you say this lot are called?"

"Ah, Jesus, you'll never get off the reserve list," said Mr Holden. "The Crewsy Fixers. You mean to say you never heard of the Crewsy Fixers? England's best ambassadors they've been termed, a little Test team all on their own, *ja,* doing all in their power to protect the wicket of your shattered economy. Foreign earnings, that is, an export drive to the boundary, and Her Majesty the Queen" (Mr Holden bowed his head) "is no doubt dooly grateful. Hence, fella, those medals. So now you know, but I guess you should have known already."

"*Sí sí sí,*" agreed John. "Already he should know."

"I would call that a very blasphemous name," said Hogg coldly. "Not," he added hastily, "that I'm at all a religious man, you understand. What I mean is, it seems to me in very bad taste."

"To the pure," said Mr Holden, "all things are pure. There's Yod Crewsy and his Fixers, so they become the Crewsy Fixers. Right? If you're thinking it sounds like something else, then you're on a very shaky wicket yourself, fella, so far as taste goes. And they're very very religious boys, which again you should have known. *Molto religioso,*" he added to John.

"*Lei parla bene italiano.*"

"I bet," divined Hogg, "that he called himself Crewsy just so he could make up that blasphemous name. And

246

that Yod bit doesn't sound Christian to me. Yod," he told Mr Holden, "is a letter of the Hebrew alphabet."

"Now you'd better watch that," said Mr Holden very sternly. "Because that sounds to me very much like racial prejudice. And if there's one thing the policy of this hotel group says out out out to, it's racial prejudice. So watch it."

"He say too," intimated John, "about Spanish people not good."

"Right, then," said Mr Holden. "We'll have harmony, efficiency, and team spirit. A very special luncheon for very special people. The confectionary chefs are working out a very special ice pudding for the occasion. And there's going to be a very exotic dish not before served here. It's called—" he consulted a draft menu on his desk, "—*lobscowse*. Something Arabic, I guess. Those boys sure scored big in Saudi-Arabia."

Hogg stood transfixed. "Ice pudding," he said. "In Saudi-Arabia. It melts as it is made. Like time, you know."

"You feeling all right, Hogg?" While Mr Holden frowned, John the Spaniard poked his right temple with a brown finger, shaking his head in sad glee. "You sure you feel up to this, fella? If not, we can always get Juanito here to take over. I reckon he can face the bowling if you can't."

"It has to be a Hogg," said Hogg, distracted. "He may be a pig but he's not a Hogg. It's coming," he added. "There's something there all right. The gift's coming back. Something special. I'll have to go and put it down on paper."

"Ah, a cocktail," nodded Mr Holden, relieved. "That's okay, then. Something special, eh? You go right off and get it down, fella. And don't forget that we own the copyright. One more thing. Wigs. There's got to be wigs. They needn't fit too good, but there's got to be wigs. Okay. Back to the pavilion."

Hogg left in a small daze. "Useless to hope to hold off," he muttered, "the unavoidable happening." What the hell was it all about? She was there all right; she was playing silly hide-and-seek, finger in mouth, up and down the corridors. She was wearing a very short dress. John the Spaniard said:

"What you mean, *hombre?* You call me pig."

"Big, I said big," said Hogg, distracted. "Look, the bar doesn't open for another hour. I've got to go to my room."

"Big pig, you say? I hear. Not bloody daft, man."

Hogg made a dash for the staff lift which, he saw, was just about to land. It opened, and a very natty though puffy young man came out, bearing what looked like the disgorgements of one of the hotel computers. He seemed to look direly at Hogg, as though it was his character that had been programmed. Hogg got in frowning, his brain full of words that were trying to marshal themselves into an ordered, though cryptic, statement. John the Spaniard tried to follow, but the puffy young man was in the way. Hogg pressed the right button and saw the door slice fist-shaking John laterally until there was nothing left of him save the after-image of the glow of his fillings. The lift-car seemed to remain where it was, and only the flash of the floor-numbers spoke of rising to 34A, a floor not accessible to the hotel guests. A high-powered car rushing on to it, whether you will or not. Hogg nearly fainted.

He got out blindly when the door automatically opened, fumbled for his key, almost tumbled into his cheerless cell. Paper. He had a lined writing-pad, in keeping with his new image. He sat panting heavily on his cot and began to scribble. She breathed hard into his left ear; her voice had become, for some reason, a lisping child's one. He wrote:

> Unless to hope to hold off
> The unavoidable happening
> With that frail barricade
> Of week, day or hour
> Which melts as it is made,
> For time himself will bring
> You in his high-powered car,
> Rushing on to it,
> Whether you will nor not.

And then sudden silence. What was it all about? What did it mean? Too much meaning in your poetry, Enderby. Somebody had said that once. You worry, my dear Enderby, far too much about meaning. Rawcliffe, one of the special trinity of enemies. And there was Wapenshaw, trying to crush his skull. He saw the strong hairy fingers, but the skull only grinned. The consolation of bone, the bone's resignation. But what thing was going to happen that he had to resign himself to? A handshake of finality, the welcome of whole fields of empty time. No, no, it was not quite that. With a rush like blood it came:

> So, shaking hands with the grim
> Satisfactory argument,
> The consolation of bone
> Resigned to the event,
> Making a friend of him,
> He, in an access of love,
> Renders his bare acres
> Golden and wide enough.

The prophetic tingling, as of something thrilling to welcome and then to lose and not to mind losing. He could have wept. The Muse stood by his wash-basin. What, then? What was the covenant to be? He might have to wait for a dream for the full disclosure. There was a hammering on the door. She hid, sliding through its door, into his tiny clothes-cupboard.

"*Puerco, puerco!*" called John the Spaniard. "You get tonic water for bloody bar, man!"

"For cough!" cried Hogg. "Go away, you garlicky bastard!"

And then, radiating from the clothes-cupboard, it announced itself as the last stanza:

> And this last margin of leaving
> Is sheltered from the rude
> Indiscreet tugging of winds.

"*You* bastard! You pull pudding in there! I bloody *know!*" Hogg wrote, like a dying message:

> For parting, a point in time,
> Cannot have magnitude
> And cannot cast shadows about
> The final

John's thudding drowned the final whatever it was. The Muse, hidden in the cupboard, shook her sad child's head. Hogg-Enderby, enraged, got up and unlocked his door. Then he pulled it open. John almost fell in.

"Right," Hogg-Enderby clenched. "You've had this coming a long time, bloody *hombre*. You and bloody Franco and wanting bloody Gibraltar. Right." Well, Wapenshaw and the rest wished him to be involved in the world, didn't they—low, vulgar, an ordinary citizen ungiven to civilised restraints? John grinned dirty gold and put out mean claws. Hogg, as low barman, at once kicked him on the shin. While John was hopping mad, Hogg pushed him on to the bed. John sat there nursing his pain and trying to kick at the same time, mouthing the foulest bodega provincial Spanish with no refined lisp in it. Hogg looked for something to hit him with and picked up the cheap bedroom chair from near the clothes-cupboard. By the time he had raised it John was on his feet again. He leered very terribly and said:

"*Momento de verdad.*" Hogg thought he saw peasant's muscles underneath the cheap bar-waiter's clothes; his heart failed; he was too old; he shouldn't have started this. He put the chair gently down on the floor again. He said:

"All right. Here's my bloody throat." And he proffered it. John did not expect this. He said:

"You give kick on flaming leg, *hombre*. Not good."

"Listen," said Hogg, "listen." He, who had done Latin at school, who had spoken soldier's Italian in Catania but also read Dante with a crib, for some reason was now impelled to draw on this Romance equipment and create, nearly from scratch, not merely a language for

Spain but a literature as well. "*La consolación del osso,*" he suggested. John cocked an ear and said:

"*Hueso.*"

"That's right," Hogg agreed. "*La consolación del hueso resignado al evento.*" He didn't know whether that was right or not, but he felt it ought to have a place somewhere along the line of colonial deformation of Latin. In any case, John went pale. It was Orpheus with his lute, by God, who (so Hogg as schoolboy Enderby had believed, taking the first line of the song as a semantic entity) made trees. "And," said Hogg, very recklessly now, "*To say adiós, no è que un punto temporál.*"

"*Sí sí.*"

"*Y un punto* can't have a bloody *ombra.*"

"*No puede tener sombra, sí, claro.*"

"And so there can't be any *sombras* around the something *finál.*" (There was a rhyme there, wasn't there? He was actually rhyming in Spanish.)

"Ah," and as though they were both merely trying to remember a Spanish poem that actually existed, "*el beso.*"

Beso, baiser, bacio. Kiss.

> And cannot cast shadows about
> The final kiss

Tears came into Hogg's eyes. He felt unutterably wretched. He said to John, tearfully, "You can have the job any time you like. I don't want it. I want to be a poet again, that's all."

John nodded. Garlicky sod as he was, he understood. "Poetry no money," he said. "Go on National Assistance, man." Like most immigrants, he knew everything about the resources of the British Welfare State. And then he said: "No, no good. Wait is best. Wait." He knew all about destiny too, being a foreigner. "Wait for," he said, "*el acaso inevitable.*"

Hogg looked at him in wonder. The unavoidable happening.

Two

They got on a good deal better after that, though John exaggerated the limp from Hogg's shin-kick. When the day for the luncheon arrived, they were working in accord, and Mr Holden was pleased. "*Ja*," he said. "All we want here is harmony. Like a real good opening pair. Hobbs and P. G. Grace, or two guys like that." But Mr Holden fussed in nervousness at midday on the day. Everything had to be just right. Out of stereophonic speakers there excreted (Hogg could think of no other word) pseudo-music composed and performed by the guests of honour, and Mr Holden tried to adjust the volume so as to secure the correct balance between the subliminally insinuating and the overtly assertive. Furniture-music, like Erik Satie, but set cunningly for the barking of ears: that was the aim. Hogg considered that he had never in his whole life heard anything so, at the same time, obscene, noisy, and insipid. He was mixing cocktails in big crocks, selecting the ingredients aleatorically. After all, poetry was compounded of chance elements, and cocktail-making was by far the inferior art. He set out now to blend his special, intended for people he already disliked, like this blasphemous gang that was a collective guest of honour, and those he would dislike when he saw them. He threw together Scotch whisky and British port-type wine, adding flat draught bitter beer, grenadine, angostura, and some very sour canned orange juice which the management had bought up cheap some months before. As the resultant colour seemed rather subfusc for a festive drink, he broke in three eggs and electrically whisked all up to a yellowy pinkish froth. He tasted a little gingerly from a dram-measure and found it tasted of nothing. It left, however, a sickish residual gust that would do very well. Nodding, he put it in the refrigerator to keep cold with the other crocks.

"You better get your wig on, fella," said Mr Holden. Hogg looked around, seeing John the Spaniard and the three Albanian waiters from the Sweet Thames Run Softly bar downstairs all looking terrible in coarse golliwog toupees that were meant to be a kind of homage, so Hogg understood, to an enviable aspect of youth typified by these blasphemous obscenities—namely, a riotous and sickening excess of head-hair. Hogg picked up his own wig and crammed it on. He did not like what he saw in the mirrored reredos. He seemed to resemble very much his stepmother surfacing from blurred after-stout sleep, taken with her glasses on and teeth in, her head a very unsavoury Medusa-tangle.

The first man to arrive seemed to be the man who had been deputed to organise this luncheon by the various interests concerned. Hogg frowned: the face seemed familiar. It was a stormy Irish face that appeared to fight against its London sleeking. The lapelless jacket and tapering trousers were of a kind of healthy stirabout colour.

"You'll find everything in order," said Mr Parkin, a very much more important man than Mr Holden. He was British, not American, and he wore striped trousers and a short black jacket, like a member of parliament meeting his constituents in the lobby. He had obviously, considered Hogg, been cast rather than appointed. He was distinguished greying butler-talking British, which meant, thought Hogg, that he was probably a con-man reformed out of fear of another stretch. He was in charge of banquets and luncheons for the distinguished and the like. He was above knowing Hogg's name. "Barman," he said, "a drink for Mr Macnamara."

So that was who it was. Shem Macnamara, once a poet himself but now, analogously to Mr Parkin, reformed. "Scatch on the racks," said Shem Macnamara, like an American. He did not recognise Hogg. He breathed a kind of mouthwash as he opened meaty lips for his drink. Hogg remembered that luncheon long ago that had been given for him, himself, Enderby as he had been, when he had won the Goodby Gold Medal for poetry. Then Shem Macnamara had been very poor, only too ready for a free meal and a quiet sneer at the success of a fellow-poet. Then, instead of expensive

253

mouthwash, he had breathed on Hogg-Enderby bafflingly (for no banquet would serve, because of the known redolence of onions, onions) onions.

"Onions," said Hogg. He was frowned on in puzzlement. "Cocktail onions," he offered. Well, just imagine, Shem Macnamara. Shem Macnamara deepened his frown. Something in that voice saying "Onions"? He did not take any onions.

The guests began to arrive. There were ugly tall girls, very thin, showing bony knees, whom Hogg took to be photographer's models, or some such thing. He filled out tray-loads of his special cocktail for them, and told the waiters to say it was called a Crucifier. It seemed to do none of these girls any harm, blasphemous bitches as they were. There were young men who seemed to be literary men, and some of these ordered drinks that had to be freshly made up and were very complicated. Hogg cursed under his wig when one young man stood over him at the bar while some exotic nonsense called a Papa Doc was painfully put together—rum, lemon juice, vermouth, tabasco (two drops), stir with a cock's feather. "This," groused Hogg, "is a hen's feather. Does it make much difference?" Mr Holden hovered, looking black. Some very important New York Jews came in, all stroking some of the model-girls as if thereby to conjure humps of voluptuousness. A most insolent Negro in native robes was made much of; Hogg had a large helping of the Crucifier ready for him, but he asked for plain milk, and this had to be sent downstairs for, and then, when it had been handed to him, he merely carried it round unsipped, as if to demonstrate that he was not totally anti-white. Photographers struck with flashes from opposed corners, like a little war, and there were, though not practising their art today, some, so Hogg heard from John, very great photographers among the guests.

The Crucifier was, to Hogg's annoyance, rather popular. Atrophy of the gustatory sense or anaesthesia of the stomach lining, or something. He prepared a sicklier version—whiskey and port-style British wine diluted with warm water from the washing-up tap—and this too was well appreciated. It was the name, that was what it was: it was a small and unbargained-for poetic victory. Suddenly, while Hogg was sucking on the sour lozenge of an image of himself, sweating under a dyed-wool wig into the American-type martinis he was pouring from the gin bottle, there was a reverent hush. The Prime Minister had arrived. He was a little bumptious man in a baggy suit to show he had just come from work, and he was at his ease with everyone and full of little pleasantries. Hogg begged John the Spaniard to make sure he got a Crucifier, but the Prime Minister asked for orange juice. Hogg was happy to serve some of the cheap acid variety. Then he got down to a batch of champagne cocktails for a bunch of exquisite young men who grinned at his wig, himself longing for a mug of very strong, or stepmother's, tea. There was a lot of loud chatter and some giggles (as though the session were proceeding at once, without the interim of a meal, towards seduction); under it the ghastly pseudo-music swelled up, reached its sonic level, then rose above to drown it. It was a fanfare. There were cheers. The guests of honour had come at last, embraced and worshipped from their very entrance. Hogg stopped mixing to have a good look at them.

They were, he thought, about as horrible in appearance as it was possible to imagine any four young men to be. The one Hogg knew to be their leader, Yod Crewsy, received, because of his multiple success, the most homage, and he accepted this as his due, simpering out of a lopsided mouth that was too large to be properly controlled and, indeed, seemed to possess a kind of surrealist autonomy. The other three were vulgarly at home, punching each other in glee and then doing a kind of ring-a-roses round the Prime Minister. The working photographers flashed and flashed like an epidemic of sharp sneezes. With the four, Hogg now noticed, there was a clergyman. He was small, old, and vigorous, and he champed and champed, nodding at everyone and even, before he came up to Hogg at the bar, sketching a general blessing. He said, nodding:

"If there's such a thing as a Power's among that heathen army you have up there on your shelves, then

I'll have a double Power's. And I'll trouble you for a glass of fresh water."

Hogg surveyed his small stock of Irish. "Will a Mick Sullivan do?"

"Ah, well then, I'll try it. Such a big place as you are and divil a drop of Power's to bless yourself with."

"If you'd like something for a change," said Hogg, "there's this special cocktail here I've mixed in honour. A Crucifier, it's called." He at once realised that that must sound like deliberate insult to this man's cloth. "Blasphemous, I know," he said. "I apologise. But I consider that the name itself. Of these four, I mean. The guests of honour, that is. Father," he added.

"Well now, shouldn't we all be sticking to our own vocations and not stepping outside the lines to deliver judgments on what isn't our proper province at all? Perhaps you'd be willing to allow that it's myself as would be the proper and qualified judge of what's blasphemous and what isn't, me being the chaplain to those boys?" While he spoke his eyes roamed everywhere in Irish neurosis. In the corner there was the sound of someone being sick, a woman from the pitch of the retchings. Hogg showed minimal satisfaction, then swiftly shut it off. The chaplain saw. "Taking pleasure itself it is, in the misfortune of some poor body's weak and delicate stomach and it fasting from dawn maybe?" The Prime Minister was heard to say:

"Well, as long as nobody blames it on the Government." There was dutiful laughter, though one young man, standing alone by the bar, nodded seriously. He had, like the Crewsy Fixers, very long hair, but it seemed as seedy as Hogg's own wig. His suit was not new; the side-pockets bulged. The chaplain poured himself another measure from the whisky bottle. Yod Crewsy and one of his group, a guffawing youth with very white dentures, came over to the bar, bearing glasses, Hogg was glad to see, of the later version of the Crucifier. Yod Crewsy said to Hogg:

"What you on then, dad?" Before Hogg could make an evasive reply, Yod Crewsy feigned to be surprised and overjoyed by the sudden sight of the seedy-maned young man with the bulging pockets. He put on a large record-sleeve smile and then embraced him with arms whose thinness the cut of his serge jerkin did nothing to disguise, saying: "Jed Foot. Me old Jed, as ever was. Glad like you could make it, boy." Jed Foot, mouth closed, smiled with his cheek-muscles. Hogg could not remember whether Jed belonged to the same alphabet as Yod. Yod Crewsy said to his chaplain: "Look who's here, Father. We're back to the old days. Happy times them was," he said to Jed Foot. "Pity you got out when you did. What they call a miscalculation. Right?" he said to Hogg cheekily.

"A memento mori," said Hogg, with poet's acuity. The chaplain chewed darkly over that before taking more whisky, as though Hogg had revealed himself as an anti-vernacularist.

"You got your mementos," said Jed Foot to Yod Crewsy. "Them songs. Pity I never learned how to write down music."

"Every man to his own like opinion," said Yod Crewsy. "You said the groups was finished. What you been on—the Western Australia run? Dead horrible, I know. Collie and Merredin and Bullfinch. They've been working you hard, boy. I can see that."

"I've been doing the clubs. The clubs is all right."

"Have another of these," said Hogg to Yod Crewsy. "A *big* one. A Crucifier, it's called."

"What I want," said Yod Crewsy, "is me dinner. Her ladyship here yet?"

"Herself will be the last to come," said the chaplain. "'Tis a lady's privilege. You," he said to Hogg, "have the face of a man who's been a long time away from the altar. A Catholic face I said to meself as soon as I clapped eyes on it, and very guilty and shifty too with your self-knowledge of being in the presence of a priest of your Church and you with the boldness to be speaking of blasphemy and many a long year between yourself and the blessed sacrament."

"Look here," said Hogg. Swirls of toothed worshippers were about Yod Crewsy and his accomplices, but this

Jed Foot drank bitter gin alone. "You," said Hogg, "and your bloody ecumenical nonsense."

"Is it yourself as would be daring to flaunt the shame of your apostasy in the face of a priest of your Church and spitting venom on the blessed enactments of the Holy Father himself?" He took more whisky. "I'll be troubling you," he said, "for another glass of fresh water."

It had been part of Hogg's cure to attend the services of the Church of England, a means of liquidating for ever his obsession with his dead stepmother who, Dr Wapenshaw had said, was really the Catholic Church. He was about to tell this chaplain that the liturgy of traditional Anglicanism was superior to that of reformed Papistry when the chaplain turned his face towards the entrance with mouth open in joy. Everybody else turned too. A lady was entering and, with her, a handsome and knowing Jewish man in his thirties. Hogg's heart turned over several times, as on a spit. Of course, of course, blast it: he should have known. Had not bloody Wapenshaw said something about her running the best pop-groups in the business? This was too much. He said to Mr Holden, who was standing by the bar, though not drinking:

"I've got to get out of here, I've *got to*."

"You stay where you are, fella, on the crease."

"But I've got to get to a lavatory."

"Now listen," said Mr Holden, his tea-coloured eyes very hard. "I've had about enough from you, fella, that I have. Obstruction for its own sake and going against the rules. You stay in till you're given out, right? And another thing, there's too many been made sick, and hard drinkers too from the look of them. See, they're taking that poor girl off now. I reckon those drinks you've been mixing will have to be looked into. Now what in hell's name—" for Hogg had pulled his wig down over his eyes like a busby. Even so he could see her clearly enough through the coarse fringe.

"Vesta, me dear," the chaplain was saying. "Five Our Fathers and five Hail Marys for being late." She smiled from her clever green eyes. She, never behind in the fashions, was in a new long-length skirt of palest pink and a brown biki-jacket. On the shining penny-coloured hair was a halo hat of thrushes' feathers. Her purse and shoes were quilled. All the other women at once began to look dated in their bright reds and greens. Hogg moaned to himself, desperately washing a champagne-glass below the level of the counter-top.

"You know my husband, I think," Vesta said.

"And isn't it meself he's been coming to for his preliminary instruction? Well, praise be to God, as one goes out another comes in." He swivelled his long Irish neck to frown at Hogg.

"What a strange little man," Vesta said. "Is he serving only from the top of his head, or something?" And then she turned to greet the Prime Minister with every sign of ease and affection. Her chief pop-group came over whooping to kiss her cheeks extravagantly, calling her, though in evident facetiousness, "mum." The photographers opposed fresh lightnings at each other.

"Oh God God God." groaned Hogg.

"Repentance, is it?" the sharp-eared chaplain said. "Well, you have a long penance in front of you for scoffing at the True Church itself."

A man with glasses, dressed in hunting pink, came to the door to bawl that luncheon was served. There was a ragged shouting exodus towards the Wessex Saddleback. Some, though, as Hogg saw, with very little satisfaction now, on the clearing of the bar, would not be wanting any lunch. Himself included. Shem Macnamara was one of the last to leave. He turned frowning to look at Hogg, mouthing the word "onions." He had, he was sure, heard that voice somewhere before.

Three

Hogg and John the Spaniard washed glasses companionably together, Hogg in a daze though, though he responded to John's excited comments on the event still proceeding with his usual courtesy. John had been swigging from half-empty glasses and was more garrulous than usual.

"You see that bloody thing, *hombre?* All ice cream and done like big *monumento.*" It appealed to John's baroque taste and prompted memories of the victorious group-effigies erected by the Caudillo: the Crewsy Fixers, with drums and guitar, in highly compressed frozen confectioner's custard—whether really to be eaten or not was not clear, though the sound of laughing chiselling was coming through at that moment.

"Oh?" said Hogg.

"See this bloody *vaso?* One *párpado* dropped in. Daft, *hombre.*" It was not so much a false eyelid as a set of false eyelashes for one eye.

"Ah," said Hogg. Some of the glasses were very filthy.

"One thing," said John. "We not serve no *coñac* from in here. Bottles on the *mesa* already. *Vasos* too. Not bar job, *hombre.*"

"No."

John sang. It was a kind of flamenco without words. Soon he desisted. The rhythms, if not the sense, of an after-lunch speech were coming through. It was the Prime Minister. "He speak bloody good, man. But always same thing. I hear on telly." Hogg could tell exactly what the Prime Minister was saying: selling country short; legacy of misrule; determination to win through to solvency despite treacherous and frivolous opposition of opposition; teamwork of these four boys here, not unfortunately his constituents but he would be proud to have them, example to all; people's art; art of the people; the people in good art, heart; struggles to come; win through to solvency; legacy of misrule. After long clapping there was the sound of a kind of standing ovation. Suddenly the door of Piggy's Sty was burst open. It was Jed Foot lurching in, very white. He said:

"Give us something strong. Can't stand it, I tell you. The bastard's on his feet." Sympathetic, Hogg poured him a large brandy. Jed Foot downed it in one. "Taught him all he knows," he whined. "Bloody treachery. Give us another one of them." Hogg poured an even larger brandy. Jed Foot gave it, in one swig, to his gullet. John tut-tutted. He said:

"We finish now here, *hombre.* I go see."

"I'm getting out," said Hogg. "Out. Bloody fed-up, that's what I am."

"Bloody fed-up, mate?" said Jed Foot, his mouth quivering. "You don't know what bloody fed-upness is. I'll have another one of them."

"I'm off duty now," Hogg said. He had already discarded that shameful wig. Now he took off his barman's coat. His own mufti jacket was in the little storeroom at the back of the bar. He went to get it. John was just opening the door that led to the exit-corridor; the door of the Wessex Saddleback was opposite. When Hogg, decently jacketed, was making his way out, he found that that door had been thrown wide open so that hotel employees could listen and look. The whole of Europe was represented there among the chambermaids and small cooks who, with open mouths, worshipped this global myth. Jed Foot was at the back of them; John had pushed to the front. Hogg, shambling in wretchedness towards the staff lift, suddenly heard familiar noises:

"And so the car plunged in the singing green
Of sycamore and riot-running chestnut and oak
That squandered flame, cut a thousand arteries
    and bled
Flood after summer flood, spawned an obscene
Unquenched unstanchable green world sea, to choke
The fainting air, drown sun in its skywise tread."

It was being read wretchedly, as though the reader was decoding it from ill-learnt Cyrillic. Yod Crewsy now said:

"Me teeth is slipping a bit." Laughter. "I can write em but I can't say em. Anyway, here's how it finishes:

But the thin-tuning fork of one of the needs of
    men,
The squat village letter-box, approached, awoke,
Called all to order with its stump of red;
In a giant shudder, the monstrous organ then
Took shape and spoke."

There was applause. Yod Crewsy said: "Don't ask me what it means; I only wrote it." Laughter. "No, serious like, I feel very humble. But I put them poems together in this book just like to show. You know, show that we do like think a bit and the kvadrats, or squares which is what some of you squares here would like call yourselves, can't have it all their own way." Cheers.

Hogg stood frozen like an ice cream *monumento*. He had left, when he had run away from that bitch in there, several manuscript poems in her Gloucester Road flat. They had been written; later they had been written off. The holograph of *The Pet Beast* had been among them. Unable to reconstitute them from memory, he could not now be absolutely sure—But wait. A painter friend of that bitch, his name Gideon Dalgleish, had said something on some social occasion or other about driving with a friend through green summer England and being overwhelmed with its somehow, my dear, *obscene* greenness, a great proliferating green carcinoma, terrifying because shapeless and *huge*. And then the sudden patch of red from a letter-box concentrated and tamed the green and gave it a comprehensible form. Nature *needs* man, my dear. The words CURTAL SONNET had flashed before his, Hogg's, Enderby's, eyes, and the rhymes had lined up for inspection. And then—He stood gaping at nothing, unable to move. He heard Yod Crewsy's voice again, calling microphonically over loud cheers:

"Right. So much for the F.S.L.S. lot, or whatever it is. And I'd like to say a very 'artfelt *ta* to our mum here, who like encouraged me. Now we're going to do our new disc, and not mime neither. I see the lads is all ready up there. All they want is me." Ecstasy.

Hogg painfully turned himself about. Then, as against a G science-fictionally intensified twentyfold, he forced his legs to slide forward towards the open door of the Wessex Saddleback. Jed Foot was trembling. Across the smoky luncheon-room, now darkened by drawn curtains, he saw, glorious in floodlighting, the Crewsy Fixers ranged grinning on a little dais. Yod Crewsy held a flat guitar with flex sprouting from it. In front of each of the others was a high-mounted sidedrum. They poised white sticks, grinning. Then they jumped into a hell of noise belched out fourfold by speakers set at the ceiling's corners.

"You can do that, *ja*, and do this. *Ja*.
You can say that you won't go beyond a kiss. *Ja*.
But where's it goin to get ya, where's
It goin to get
Ya (*ja*), babaaah?"

Where was she, that was the point? Where was she, so that he could go in there and expose her, the whole blasphemous crew of them, before high heaven, which did not exist? Hogg squinted through the dark and thought he saw that cruel feathered halo hat. Then, in that little group by the open door, there seemed to be violent action, noise, the smell of a sudden pungent fried breakfast. A couple of chambermaids screamed and clutched each other. The sidedrums on the dais rim-shotted like mad. Yod Crewsy did a crazy drunken dance, feet uplifted as if walking through a shitten byre. His autonomous mouth did a high scream, while his eyes crossed in low comedy. The crowd clapped.

"Here yare," panted Jed Foot, and he handed something to Hogg. Hogg automatically took it, a barman used to taking things. Too heavy for a brandy glass. Jed Foot hared off down the corridor.

"Lights! Lights!" called somebody, the king in *Hamlet*. "He's shot, he's hurt!" Yod Crewsy was down, kicking. The dullest of the Crewsy Fixers still leered, singing inaudibly. But drums started to go over. Hogg was being started back from, John incredulous, the chambermaids pointing and screaming, a minor cook, like a harvest-caught rabbit, wondering whither to run, whimpering. Hogg looked down at his hand and saw a smoking gun in it. Shem Macnamara was yelling: "Him! Stop him! I knew that voice! Sworn enemy of pop! Murderer!" John the Spaniard was quick, perhaps no stranger to such southern public violence. He yapped like a dog, most unspanishly, at Hogg: "Out out out out out out!" It was

263

like a Mr Holdenish nightmare of umpires. Hogg, with an
instinct learnt from the few films he had seen, pointed
the gun at Shem Macnamara, marvelling. Some of the
guests still thought this part of the show. Others called
for a doctor. Hogg, gun in hand, ran. He ran down the
corridor to the service lift. The indicator said it was on
another floor, resting. He called it and it lazily said it was
coming. He kept the gun pointing. John was in everybody's way, but some were thinking of coming for him.
Vesta now would be weeping over her favourite client,
the impersonal and opportunist camera-lights cracking.
The lift arrived and Hogg entered, still marvelling.
Armed. Dangerous. The lift-door snapped off the sound
of running and falling feet. Drunk, that was the trouble
with them: all drunk. Hogg stood dazed in a fancied
suspension of all movement, while the lighted floor-
pointer counted down. He had pressed, for some reason,
the button marked B for basement. As low as you could
get. He landed on a stone corridor, full of men trundling
garbage bins. Useless to hope to hold off. It was a matter
of running, if he could, up a short dirty flight to a
ground-level back entrance. He remembered, near-dead
with breathlessness, to drop the gun at the top of the
stairs. It clanked down and, the safety-catch still off,
somehow managed to fire itself at nothing. *El acaso
inevitable*. With that frail barricade. Would the frozen
monument be melting now up there, Yod Crewsy dis-
solving first? Men were coming to the noise of firing. He
was out. It was a staff car-park, very unglamorous. For
time himself will bring. You in that high-powered car. A
taxi. London lay in autumn after-lunch gloom, car-horns
bellowing and yapping. Rushing on to it. Air, air. Hogg
gasped for it. "Taxi," he breathed, waving like mad,
though feebly. Amazingly, one stopped. "Air," he said.
"Air."

"Airport?" the driver wore sinister dark glasses. "Air
terminal? Cromwell Road?" Hogg's head sank to his
chest; the driver took it for a nod. "Right, gav. Hop in."
Hogg hopped in. Fell in, rather.

Four

So they were trying to go west, Gloucester Road way, despite the opposition (frivolous and treacherous) of contrary traffic and stultified red signals. There, he supposed, his days of misery had really begun, in the flat of that woman. And now the unavoidable happening was rushing him (well, hardly rushing) to the same long street to make his escape from not merely Vesta's world but Wapenshaw's as well. Well, they were the same world, they had to be the same. They were not the poet's world. Did such a world really exist? Where, anyway, did he think he was going to? He had better make up his mind. He could not say, "What planes do you have, please?" Quite calm now, iced by his wrongs, he got his five-pound notes out of their hiding-place. His passport rode in hard protectiveness over his right pap. It was decidely an ill wind. About passports, he meant. He had nothing in the way of luggage, which was a pity. Airlines, he thought, must be like hotels so far as luggage was concerned. But you had to pay in advance, didn't you? Still, there must be nothing to arouse suspicion. The newspapers would be cried around the streets shortly. Man answering to this description. May be using an alias. Was he being followed? He looked out of the rear window. There were plenty of vehicles behind, but from none of them were hands and heads broadcasting agitation. He would be all right, he was sure he would be all right. He was innocent, wasn't he? But he hadn't behaved innocent. Who would speak up for him? Nobody could. He had pointed a loaded gun at Shem Macnamara. Besides, if that ghastly yob was dead he was glad he was dead. He had desire and motive and opportunity.

The taxi was now going up the ramp that led into the air terminal, a stripped-looking and gaudy place like something from a very big trade exhibition. He paid off the driver, giving a very unmemorable tip. The driver looked at it with only moderate sourness. Would he remember when he saw the evening papers? Yus yus, I picked him ap ahtside the otel. Fought vere was summink a bit fishy. Flyin orf somewhere he was. Hogg entered the terminal. Where the hell was he going to go to? He suddenly caught the voice of John the Spaniard, talking of his brother Billy Gomez. In some bar or other, very exotic, knifing people. Where was that now? Hogg had a confused image of the Moorish Empire: dirty men in robes, kasbahs without modern sanitation, heartening smells of things the sun had got at, muezzins, cockfights, shady men in unshaven hiding, the waves slapping naughty naughty at boats full of contraband goods. Hogg noticed a raincoated man pretending to read an evening paper near an insurance-policy machine. The news would not be in yet, but it wouldn't be long. There was a crowd of people having its luggage weighed. Hogg got in there. One married man was unpacking a suitcase on the floor, almost crying. His wife was angry.

"You should have read it proper. I leave them sort of things to you. Well, it's your stuff that'll have to stay behind, not mine."

"How was I to know you couldn't take as much on a charter flight as on one of them ordinary uns?" He laid a polythene-wrapped suit, like a corpse, on the dirty floor. Hogg saw a yawning official at a desk. Above him stretched a title in neon Egyptian italic: PANMED AIRWAYS. Panmed. That would mean all over the Med or Mediterranean. He went up and said politely:

"A single to Morocco, please." Morocco was, surely, round the Mediterranean or somewhere like that. Hogg saw the raincoated paper-reader looking at him. Lack of luggage, no coat over arm, a man obviously on the run.

"Eh?" The official stopped yawning. He was young and ginger with eyes, like a dog's, set very wide apart. "Single? Oh, one person you mean."

"That's right. Just me. Rather urgent, actually." He shouldn't have said that. The young man said:

"You mean this air cruise? Is that what you mean? A last-minute decision, is that it? Couldn't stand it any longer? Had to get away?" It was as though he were rehearsing a report on the matter; he was also putting words into Hogg's mouth. Hogg said:

"That's right." And then: "I don't *have* to get away, of course. I just thought it would be a good idea, that's all."

"Charlie!" called the young official. To Hogg he said: "It looks as though you're going to be in luck. Somebody died at the last minute."

Hogg showed shock at the notion of someone dying suddenly. The man called Charlie came over. He was thin and harassed, wore a worn suit, had PANMED in metal on his left lapel. "They won't ever learn," said Charlie. "There's one couple there brought what looks like a cabin-trunk. They just don't seem able to *read,* some of them."

"The point is," said the young ginger man, "that you've had this cancellation, and there's this gentleman here anxious to fill it. Longing to get to the warmth, he is. Can't wait till the BEA flight this evening. That's about it, isn't it?" he said to Hogg. Hogg nodded very eagerly. Too eagerly, he then reflected.

Charlie surveyed Hogg all over. He didn't seem to care much for the barman's trousers. "Well," he said, "I don't know really. It's a question of him being able to pay in cash."

"I can pay in nothing else," said Hogg with some pride. He pulled out a fistful in earnest. "I just want to be taken to Morocco, that's all. I have," he said, improvising rapidly, "to get to my mother out there. She's ill, you see. Something she ate. I received a telegram just after lunch. Very urgent." *Very* urgent: the typesetters would be setting up the type now; the C.I.D. would be watching the airports.

Charlie had a fair-sized wart on his left cheek. He fiddled with it as though it activated a telegraphic device. He waited. Hogg put his money back in his trouser-pocket. A message seemed to come through. Charlie said: "Well, it all depends where in Morocco, doesn't it? And how fast you want to get there. We'll be in Seville late tonight, see, and not in Marrakesh till tomorrow dinner-time. This is an air cruise, this is. If it's Tangier you want to get to, we shan't be there for another fortnight. We go round the Canaries a bit, you see."

"Marrakesh would do very nicely," said Hogg. "What I mean is, that's where my mother is."

"You won't get anybody else, Charlie," said the young ginger official. "That seat's going begging, all paid for by the bloke who snuffed it. He's got cash." He spoke too openly; he seemed to know that Hogg was making a shady exit. "The bus," he looked at the big clock, "leaves in ten minutes."

"Shall we say fifty?" Charlie licked his lips; the young official picked up the gesture. "In cash, like I said."

"Done," said Hogg. He lick-counted the money out. A good slice of his savings. Savings. The word struck, like a thin tuning-fork (he was glad Yod Crewsy was dead, if he *was* dead), a pertinent connotation. He put the money on the counter.

"Passport in order, sir?" said the ginger official. Hogg showed him. "Luggage, sir?"

"Wait," said Hogg. "I've got it over there." He pierced the waiting crowd. That unpacking man had finished unpacking. In the big suitcase lay only a pair of Bermuda shorts, some shaving gear, and two or three paperbacks of a low sort. The unpacked garments were on his arm. "They said I could leave them in their office here," he puffed. "Collect them on the way back. Still, it's a bloody nuisance. I've practically only got what I stand up in." Hogg said:

"Saw you were in a bit of trouble over weight." He smiled at the couple as if they were going to do him a favour, which they were. "That suitcase could go with mine, if you like. I'm taking practically nothing, you see."

The couple looked at him with proper suspicion. They were decent fattish short people in late middle age, unused to kindness without a catch in it. The man groused: "It means I'll have to shove it all in again."

"That's right," said Hogg. "Shove it all in again." The man, shaking his head, once more got down heavily on his knees.

"It's very kind, Mr er," said the wife, grudgingly.

They never took their eyes off Hogg as he swung the reconstituted bag to the weighing. Charlie and the ginger official had seen nothing: they were busy doing a split on Hogg's money. The raincoated paper-reader, Hogg noticed, had gone. Perhaps to buy a later edition. Hogg was glad to be herded to the bus.

Five

This Charlie seemed to be what they called a dragoman. He counted his charges on and then, when they were on, counted them again. He frowned, as if the numbers did not tally. Hogg was seated next to a rather dowdy woman in early middle age, younger than himself, that was. She smiled at him as to a companion in adventure. She wore churchgoing clothes of sensible district-nurse-type hat and costume in a kind of underdone piecrust colour. Her stockings, of which the knees just about showed, were of some kind of lisle material, opaque gunmetal. Hogg smiled back very tentatively, and then warily surveyed the other members of the party. They were mostly unremarkable people subduedly thrilled at going off to exotic places. The men were already casting themselves for parts, as if the trip were really going to be full of enforced privations and they had somehow to make their own entertainment. One beef-necked publican-type was pointing out the sights on the way to the airport and inventing bogus historical associations, like "Queen Lizzy had a milk stout there." There was cautious fencing for the rôle of low comedian, and one man who, his teeth out, could contort his face in a rubbery manner seemed likely to win. There was a loud and serious man, a frequenter presumably of public libraries, who was giving a preliminary account of the more hurtful fauna of North Africa. Another man could reel off exchange rates. Hogg's seat-companion smiled again at him, as if with pleasure that everything was going to be so nice and cosy. Hogg closed his eyes in feigned (but was it feigned?) weariness.

When they got to the airport the news was still unbroken. Perhaps the management, on the instructions of the police, had sealed everything off, and it was no good the Prime Minister saying he had to get back to the House. Twenty minutes before take-off. Hogg spent most of that time in one of the lavatories, sitting gloomily on the seat. Could he do anything about disguising himself? With teeth out he would be expected to compete for the part of cruise comedian perhaps. Spectacles off? He tried that; he could just about see. Rearrange hair-style? Too little hair really, but he combed what he had down in a Roman emperor arrangement. Walk with a limp? Easy enough, if he could remember to keep on doing it. He heard ladylike intonations from a loudspeaker, so he pulled the chain and went to join his party. The man with the overweight luggage had suddenly woken up to the fact of Hogg's kindness; he did not seem to notice any change in Hogg's appearance. With bleary unfocused eyes, top denture out (a compromise that a sudden feeling of nausea had forced upon him on leaving the lavatory), and scant imperial coiffure, Hogg nodded and nodded that that was really quite all right, only too glad to oblige.

They all walked to the aircraft. Wind blew grit across the tarmac. Farewell, English autumn. It did not seem to Hogg to be a very elegant aircraft. There was a button missing from the stewardess's unform jacket, and she herself, though insipidly and blondly pretty, had a look of vacancy that did not inspire confidence. Things done on the cheap, that was about it. Hogg sat down next to a starboard window, taking his last look at England. Somebody sat next to him, a woman. She said, in a semi-cultured Lancashire accent:

"We seem destined, don't we?" It was the one who had sat next to him on the bus. Hogg grunted. The unavoidable happening. In the elastic-topped pocket on the back of the seat in front of him, Hogg sadly found reading-matter, very cheerful and highly coloured stuff. No need to worry if we go down into the sea. We have a fine record for air safety. Keep calm, the stewardess will tell you what to do. But who, wondered Hogg, would tell her? There were brochures about the ports of call on the air cruise.

"This is my first time," said the woman next to Hogg. "Is it yours?" Her teeth seemed to be all her own. She had taken off her hat. Her hair was prettily mousy.

"First time to do what?" said Hogg dourly.

"Oh, you know, go on one of these things. It's funny really, I suppose, but I know all about the moon yet I've never seen the Mountains of the Moon."

"A stronger telescope," said Hogg. He was leafing through a booklet, full of robes, skies of impossible blue, camels, palms, the wizened faces of professional Moorish beggars, which told him of the joys of Tangier.

"No, no, I mean the Mountains of the Moon in Africa." She giggled.

Hogg heard the door of the aircraft slam. It did not slam properly. Charlie the dragoman, who now wore a little woolly highly coloured cap, helped the stewardess to give it a good hard slam, and then it seemed to stay shut. Engines and things began to fire and backfire or something. They were going to take off. Hogg felt safe for an instant, but then realised that there was no escape. They had things like Interpol and so on, or some such things. Spanish police, with teeth all bits of gold like John, waiting for him at Seville. But perhaps not, he thought with a little rising hope. Perhaps Spain would consider the murder of a pop-singer a very nugatory crime, which of course it was. Not really a crime at all if you took the larger view. Well then, landed in Spain, let him stay in Spain, *el señor inglés*. But how live there? With his little bit of money he could not, even in that notoriously cheap (because poverty-stricken) country, find a retreat or lavatory that would accommodate him long enough to coax, like a costive bowel, the art of verse back. The Muse had still made no real sign. There was a poem still to be completed. And, besides, there was terrible repression in Spain, a big dictator up there in the Escorial or wherever it was, directing phalanges of cruel bruisers (no, not bruisers; thin sadists, rather) with steel whips. No freedom of expression, poets suspect, foreign poets arrested and eventually handed over to Interpol. No, better to go to a country full of men on the run and smugglers and (so he had heard) artistic homosexuals, where English, language of international shadiness, was spoken and understood, and where at least he might hide (even out of doors; the nights were warm, weren't they?) and work out the future. One step at a time.

"You haven't fastened your safety-belt," said the woman. Hogg grumbled, fumbling for the metal-tipped tongues of dirty webbing. The airfield, his last view of England, was speeding as a grey blur back into the past. Speed increased; they were getting off the ground. You in that high-powered car. Perhaps an old-fashioned image, really. Hogg leafed through the Tangier brochure absently noticing little box advertisements for restaurants and bars. He frowned at one of these, wondering. It said:

AL-ROKLIF
English Spoken Berber Dances
Wide Range of Exotic Delights
A Good British Cup of Tea
"IN ALL THE ANTHOLOGIES!"

He wondered, he wondered, he wondered. Artistic, which included literary, homosexuals. The name, rationalised into mock-Arabic:

الروقليف

The slogan. Well. He began to breathe hard. If they caught him, and he would surely know if they were going to catch him, he would not be punished gratuitously. There was something very just but highly punishable he would do before Interpol dragged him off in handcuffs. When you came to think of it, Tangier sounded like just the sort of place a man of Rawcliffe's type would end up in. Moorish catamites. Drinking himself to death. Drinking was too slow a process.

Hogg came to to find the woman gently unclicking his safety-belt for him. "You were miles away," she smiled.

"And we're miles up. Look." Hogg, mumbling sour thanks, surveyed without much interest a lot of clouds lying below them. He had seen such things before, travelling to Rome on his honeymoon. He gave the clouds the tribute of a look of weary sophistication. It was the Romantic poets really who should have flown; Percy Shelley would have loved to see all this lot from this angle. How did that thing go now? He chewed a line or two to himself.

"Did you say something?" asked the woman.

"Poetry," said Hogg. "A bit of poetry. About clouds." And, as if to make up for his neglect of her, kind and friendly as she was, he recited, in his woolly voice:

> "I silently laugh at my own cenotaph,
>   And out of the caverns of rain,
> Like a child from the womb, like a ghost from the
>   tomb,
>   I arise and unbuild it again."

"Oh, I do love poetry," this woman smiled over the engines. "It was a toss-up whether I did literature or astronomy, you know. But it was the moon that won."

"How do you mean," asked Hogg carefully, "it was the moon that won?"

"That's what I do," she said. "That's what I lecture in. The moon. Selenography, you know."

"Selene," said learned Hogg. "A fusion of Artemis and Hecate."

"Oh, I wouldn't know about that," she said. "Selenography is what it's called. I'd better introduce myself, I suppose. My name's Miranda Boland."

Miranda: a wonder to her parents: poor woman, all alone as she was. "Well," said Hogg cautiously, "my name—"

Charlie the dragoman suddenly boomed through a crackling speaker. "My name," he announced, "is Mr Mercer." No familiarity, then; he was no longer to be thought of as Charlie. "My job," he said, "is to look after you on this cruise, show you around and so on."

"Come wiz me to ze Kasbah," said the rubbery man.

He had made it, then. It was his début as resident comedian. "Shut up, George," his wife said, delightedly. Members of the party grinned and made their bottoms and shoulders more comfortable. The holiday was really beginning now.

"I hope you will enjoy this cruise," crackled Mr Mercer. "Lots of people do enjoy these cruises. They sometimes come again. And if there's anything you don't like about this cruise, tell me. Tell *me*. Don't bother to write a letter to Panmed. Let's have it out at once, man to man, or to woman should such be the case. But I think you'll like it. Anyway, I hope so. And so does Miss Kelly, your charming air-hostess, and Captain O'Shaughnessy up front. Now the first thing is that we can expect a bit of obstruction at Seville. It's this Gibraltar business, which you may have read about. The Spanish want it and we won't let it go. So they get a bit awkward when it comes to customs and immigration and so on. They try and delay us, which is not very friendly. Now it's quicker if I show your passports all in one lump, so I'm coming round to collect them now. And then Miss Kelly here will serve tea."

Miranda Boland (Mrs? Miss?) opened a stuffed handbag to get her passport out. She had a lot of things in her bag: tubes of antibiotics and specifics against diarrhoea and the like. Also a little Spanish dictionary. That was to help her to have a good time. Also a small writing-case. This put into Hogg's head an idea, perhaps a salvatory one. Hogg, without fear, produced his own passport.

"Miss Boland?" said Mr Mercer, coming round. Miss, then. "Quite a nice photo, isn't it?" And then: "Mr Enderby, is it?"

"That's right." Mr Mercer examined a smirking portrait of an engaged man, occupation not yet certain at that time but given as *writer;* a couple of official Roman chops: in and then, more quickly, out again.

"And what do *you* do, Mr Enderby?" asked Miss Boland.

"I," said Enderby, "am a poet. I am Enderby the Poet." The name meant nothing to this poetry-loving

274

selenographer. The clouds below, Shelley's pals, were flushed with no special radiance. "The Poet," repeated Enderby, with rather less confidence. They pushed on towards the sun. Enderby's stomach quietly announced that soon, very soon, it was going to react to all that had happened. Delayed shock said that it would not be much longer delayed. Enderby sat tense in his seat, waiting for it as for an air-crash.

3

One

"COPERNICUS," Miss Boland pointed. "And then a bit to the west there's Eratosthenes. And then further west still you get the Apennines." Her face shone, as if she were (which in a sense she really was) a satellite. Enderby looked very coldly at the moon which, for some reason to do with the clouds (Shelley's orbéd maiden and so on), he had expected to lie beneath them. But it was as high up as it usually was. "And down there, south, is Anaxagoras. Just under the Mare Frigoris."

"Very interesting," said Enderby, not very interested. He had not himself ever made much use of the moon as a poetic property, but he still thought he had more claim on it than she had. She behaved very familiarly with it.

"And Plato, just above."

"Why Plato?" They had had not only tea but also dinner, spilt around (hair fallen over her right eye and her tongue bitten in concentration) by that Miss Kelly. It had not been a very good dinner, but Enderby, to quieten his stomach, had wolfed his portion and part of (smilingly donated; she did not have a very big appetite) Miss Boland's. It had been three tepid fish fingers each, with some insufficiently warmed over crinkle-cut fresh frozen potato chips, also a sort of fish sauce served in a plastic doll's bucket with a lid hard to get off. This sauce had had a taste that, unexpectedly in view of its dolly-mixture pink and the dainty exiguity of even a double portion, was somehow like the clank of metal. And, very strangely or perhaps not strangely at all, the slab of dry *gâteau* that followed had a glutinous filling whose cold mutton fat gust clung to the palate as with small claws of rusty iron. Enderby had had to reinsert his top teeth before eating, doing this under cover of the need to cough vigorously and the bright pamphlet on Tangerine delights held to his left cheek. Now, after eating, he had to get both plates out, since they tasted very defiled and bits of cold burnt batter lodged beneath or above them, according to jaw. He should really get to the toilet to see about that, but, having first had doubts as to whether this aircraft possessed a toilet and then found these dispelled by the sight of the rubbery comedian called Mr Guthkelch coming back from it with theatrical relief, he felt then superstitiously that, once he left the cabin, even for two minutes, a stowaway newsboy might appear and distribute copies of a late edition with his photograph in it, and then they would, Mr Guthkelch suddenly very serious, truss him against the brutal arrest of the Seville police. So he stayed where he was. He would wait till Miss Boland had a little doze or they got to moonlit Seville. The moon was a very fine full one, and it burnt framed in the window to be tickled all over with classical names by Miss Boland.

"I don't know why Plato. That's what it's called, that's all. There's a lot of famous people commemorated all over the lunar surface. Archimedes, see, just above Plato, and Kepler, and right over there on the edge is Grimaldi."

"The clown Grimaldi?"

"No, silly. The Grimaldi that wrote a book on the diffraction of light. A priest I believe he was. But," she added, "I often thought it might be nice if some *newer* names could be put up there."

"There are a lot of new Russian ones at the back, aren't there?" said well-informed Enderby.

"Oh, you know what I mean. Who's interested in the Rabbi Levi and Endymion, whoever he was, any more? Names of great modern people. It's a daring idea, I know, and a lot of my colleagues have been, you know, aghast."

"The trouble is," said Enderby, "that nobody knows who's really great till they've been a long time dead. The great ones, I mean. Dead, that is." Mount Enderby. "Like some of these Russian towns. One minute they're one thing and the next another. Stalingrad, I mean. Now it's something else."

"Volgograd."

"Yes, and that's another. You'd be having pop-stars up there perhaps, and then in ten years time everybody would be wondering who the hell they were." Pop-stars. He shouldn't have mentioned that. He felt very and metallically sick. Then it passed. "Sorry I said 'hell'," he said.

"People who give pleasure to the world," said Miss Boland. And then: "There's Hell on the moon, did you know that? A bit old-fashioned really, but that's true of a lot of lunar nomenclature, as I say." And then: "Of course, you being a poet wouldn't like pop-stars much, would you? I can quite see that. Very inferior art, you'd say. I know."

Enderby wished he could get his teeth out and then back in again. But he said quickly: "No, no, no, I wouldn't say that. Some of them are very good, I'm sure. Please," he begged, "don't consider me an enemy of pop-culture."

"All right, all right," she smiled, "I won't. All these long-haired young singers. It's a matter of age, I suppose. I have a nephew and niece who are mad on that sort of thing. They call me a kvadrat."

"Because I'm not, you see."

"But I was able to say to them, you know, that this special idol of theirs seemed very unkvadrat, if that's the right expression, publishing this book of quite highbrow verse. Now that ought to change your opinion of pop-artists, if not of pop-art. I take it you saw the book? One of our junior English lecturers was quite gone on it."

"I've got to get out," said Enderby. She looked surprised. This was not, after all, a bus. "If you'll excuse me—" It wasn't just a matter of teeth any more; he really had to go. A fat beaming woman was just coming away from it now. "A matter of some urgency," Enderby explained and prepared to go into further, plausible, details. But Miss Boland got up and let him out.

The stewardess, Miss Kelly, was sitting at the back with Mr Mercer. Mr Mercer still had his woolly cap on but he was sleeping with his mouth open. Miss Kelly seemed totally content with an expression and posture of sheer vacancy. Enderby nodded grimly at her and entered the toilet. Why hadn't he known these things— kvadrats and so on and that lout publishing a book of verse, and who blasted Vesta had got married to? He had read the *Daily Mirror* every day with positively adenoidal attention. Very little had got home, then: his rehabilitation had never had a hope of being perfect. He quietened his stomach via his bowels and, the while, rinsed his clogged teeth under the tap and scrubbed them with the nailbrush. Then he reinserted them and, with hands gently folded on his bared lap, cried bitterly for a minute or two. Then he wiped his eyes and his bottom with the same pink paper and committed both lots of wrapped excreta to the slipstream, as he supposed it was called. He blinked at himself in the little mirror, very recognisable Hogg. If he had still had that beard which, in the intensive phase of personality change, he had been made to grow, he could be shaving it off now, having borrowed a razor from somebody, perhaps even Miss Boland, who must surely have one for leg-hair and so on in her crammed bag. Ha ha, you and the start of a holiday make me feel quite young again: I can't wait to divest myself of this fungus, ha ha. But that beard had had to go when he became a barman. So there was nothing between him and the urgently telegraphed photographs (straight from Holden's bloody secret-police dossier) now being handled by swarthy Interpol Spaniards. Nothing except the name.

But damnable and treacherous Wapenshaw would already be talking away, baling out what were properly secrets of the confessional. And tomorrow morning copies of the *Daily Mirror*, which was notoriously on sale before other newspapers, as if unable to wait to regale egg-crackers with the horrors of the world, would be circulating among British holidaymakers on the Costa Brava or whatever it was called. There would be a stern portrait of Hogg on the front page, under a very insulting headline. On the back page would be great air disasters and bombs in Vietnam and avalanches and things. But on the front page would be the murderer Hogg. He did not, it seemed, read the *Daily Mirror* closely enough, but he had a sufficient appreciation of its editorial philosophy.

He re-entered the long dozing cabin with its little sprays of ceiling light blessing bald and dyed heads. Miss Boland seemed to be counting moon-craters with a puzzled finger: perhaps something new had got up there since her last going-over with a telescope. Enderby said with sudden fierceness to Miss Kelly:

"This woman in charge of pop-singers and so on. Who was it she married?"

Miss Kelly seemed unsurprised by the question. It seemed that pride in her ability to answer the question overcame such surprise as she ought properly to be showing. "Vesta Wittgenstein? Oh, she married this man called Des Wittgenstein who ran the Fakers and the Lean Two, but now she runs them and a lot more besides. She'd been married before, to the racing-driver Pete Bainbridge, but he got himself killed. Very tragic, it was in all the papers. Then there was somethng about her marrying a middle-aged man and that did not bring her true happiness and it lasted less than a year, just imagine. But now she's found true happiness with Des Wittgenstein and they've both got pots of money. You ought to see her clothes. I was on an aircraft she flew on once, coming back from Rome. That's when she was very ill with this unhappiness, but she was still terribly smart."

Enderby nodded a casual thank-you, as if for some

pedestrian information about time of arrival. Miss Kelly smiled conventionally and went into a vacant relapse. Enderby thought he would now write a letter on some of Miss Boland's stationery, so he went back to his seat purposefully, like a man with something other to do than merely be flown to Seville. She welcomed him as if he had been a long time away and even said: "Feeling all right now?"

"I've got to write," said Enderby at once. "A matter of some urgency." He felt he had perhaps used those words before. "If you could oblige me with the wherewithal."

"A poem? How thrilling. What do you mean by the where-withal? You want me to pay you for it? I will if you like. This is the first time anybody's ever said they'd write a poem for me." Enderby looked sternly at her. She seemed to be teasing. It was possible she did not believe that he was a poet. Her eyes were, he noted with gloom, what might be termed merry.

"Paper is what I want," he said. "And an envelope, if you can spare it. Two envelopes," he amended.

"Dear, dear, you do want a lot." She took out her writing materials gaily. Enderby said:

"I'll write you a poem tonight. When we get there."

"I'll hold you to that."

Enderby took out his ballpoint and wrote to John the Spaniard: "You know I didn't do it. Pass this note on to you-know-who. I shall be in you-know-where. Your brother. That fat dog place you mentioned. Keep in touch. Yours—" He didn't know how to sign himself. At last he wrote PUERCO. Then he took another piece of paper and addressed it from In The Air. He wrote: "To Whomsoever It May Concern. It was not me who shot that pop-singer, as he is called. It was—" He was damned if he could remember the name. To Miss Boland he said once more: "I've got to get out. I've forgotten something." She let him out, mock-sighing and smiling. He kept paper and ballpoint in his hands. He went back to Miss Kelly, still in a trance of vacancy. Mr Mercer was lip-smacking, ready to surface. A monitor in his sleep had perhaps warned him that soon they would be starting to drop towards Seville. Enderby said:

"That one that used to be with Mrs Einstein's lot—"

"Mrs Wittgenstein."

"That's right. The one that got out and became unsuccessful and goes round the clubs now."

"Jed Foot, you mean."

"That's it." He wrote the name in standing. He might forget it again if he waited till he got back to his seat. Might spill it on the way. He nodded thanks and went back now, and Miss Boland, letting him in, said:

"You *are* a busy little bee."

Enderby wrote: "He handed me the gun and I took it without thinking. I panicked and ran. Pick him up and get him to confess. I am innocent." Then he signed that abandoned pseudonym. He addressed one envelope to The Authorities and the other to Mr John Gomez, Piggy's Bar, Tyburn Towers Hotel, W.1. He licked and folded and arranged. Then he sighed. Finished. He could do no more. He thought he had better shut his eyes and get ready for Seville. That would stop Miss Boland teasing him further. Miss Boland, he noticed, was looking something up in her little Spanish dictionary. She was grinning. He didn't like that. It was too small a dictionary to have anything to grin at in it. He killed her grin with his eyelids.

Two

Enderby slept, though without dreaming, as though the recent materials made available for dreams were far too shocking to be processed into fantasy. He was shaken awake by Miss Boland, who smiled on him and said, for some reason, "Dirty." He said:

"Eh?"

"We're there," she said. "Sunny Spain, though it's the middle of the night and it's been raining. The rain in Spain," she giggled.

"What do you mean, dirty? Did I do something I shouldn't? In my sleep, that is?" He wondered what incontinent act might have overtaken him.

"That's what it says. Come on, we're to get out."

People were passing down the aisle, some yawning as after a boring sermon. Miss Boland smiled as if she were some relative of the vicar. "Also," she said over her shoulder, "it says nasty and foul." Enderby saw wet-gleaming tarmac under dim lamps. There was something he had to worry about. He said:

"What does?"

"Oh, come on." She was getting her raincoat and overnight satchel from the rack. Enderby had nothing to get. Feeling naked, he said:

"I'll carry that if you like." And then his fear smote him and his hand shook.

"That's sweet of you. Take it then." He could hardly get his hand through the strap of the bag, but she didn't notice: she had arrived in non-sunny, not even moony, Spain. Mr Mercer seemed as nervous as Enderby himself; it was as though he had to introduce Seville like his wife and, perhaps being on the menopause, she might do something embarrassing. This was it, Enderby thought, this was it. He was cold and sober and ready and he would bluff it out to the end. He looked coldly and soberly on Miss Boland and decided that she must, in a manner, help him. He would laugh down the steps with her, linked, as if she were his wife. They were looking for a single desperate fugitive, not a laughing married man. But, as they smiled and Enderby nodded at Miss Kelly, standing at the aircraft exit, he saw that the stairway was very narrow and that he must go down unlinked. Miss Kelly beamed at everybody as if they had all just arrived at her party, which was being held in the cellar. Enderby heard Mr Guthkelch ahead, singing "The Spaniard who blighted my life," doing his job.

"He shall die! He shall die! He shall die tiddly iddly eye tie tie eye tie tie tie!"

In very bad taste, Enderby thought. Stepping out into moist velvet warmth, he saw at the stair-bottom only Mr Mercer with an armful of passports chatting quite amiably, though in the loud and slow English needful when speaking to a foreigner, to a foreigner. It was a uniformed Spaniard in dark glasses. He had both hands in his trousers pockets and seemed to Enderby to be playing the solitaire game known as pocket billards. He looked up at Miss Kelly, blowing up sparks from his cigarette at her like impotent signals of desire. He was not, Enderby was sure, from Interpol.

Miss Boland descended before him. As soon as he had reached damp tarmac, Enderby skipped up to her and took her arm. She seemed surprised but not displeased; she pressed Enderby's arm into her warm side. There seemed, and Enderby's knees liquefied in relief as he saw that there seemed, to be no raincoated men waiting anywhere for him on the passage over the tarmac to the airport building. There seemed to be only very lowly workmen, thin and in blue, leaning against walls, smoking vigorously, and eyeing the tourists with the hungry look of the very poor. The airport itself, despite its being very late at night, was busy. There was an aircraft with Arabic letters on it preparing to take off and there was one called IBERIA taxiing in. There were men in overalls pulling carts around and chugging about in little tractors. Enderby approved of all this bustle, especially the passenger-bustle that was evident in the building they now approached. He saw himself being chased and hiding behind people. But no, he was safe for the time being. Miss Boland said:

"There's no *luna*. That's what it's called, isn't it? *Luna*. Better than 'moon.' Lunar. Lunation. Endo-lunar. I thought the *luna* would be here to meet me. Never mind."

"You've had plenty on the way," said Enderby in a slightly chiding tone. "You'll get plenty while you're here. On holiday, I mean. But I thought perhaps you'd want to get away from it." A fellow-tourist walking near them gave Enderby a suspicious look. "The *luna*, I mean," Enderby said.

"You can't get away from it," said Miss Boland. "Not if you've given your whole life to it, as I have." And she squeezed Enderby's arm with hers. She was very warm. "Where did you learn Spanish?" she asked.

"I never did. I don't know any Spanish. Italian, yes, a bit. But not Spanish. They're similar, though."

"You're very mysterious," said Miss Boland mysteriously. "You intrigue me rather. There seems to be a lot you're holding back. Why, you haven't even brought a raincoat. But I suppose that's your business, not mine. And no overnight bag of your own. You give me the impression of a man who had to get away in a hurry."

"Oh, I had to," palpitated Enderby. "What I mean is, I'm a man of impulse. I think of a thing and then I do it." She squeezed his arm again and said:

"You can call me Miranda if you like."

"A very poetical name," said Enderby in duty. He couldn't quite remember who wrote that poem. A big Catholic winy man in a cloak. "The fleas that tease in high Pyrenees," he quoted. And then: "Never more, Miranda, never more. Only the something whore."

"Pardon?"

"And something something something at the door." They had now entered the airport building. It was small, dark, and smelt faintly of men's urinals, specifically foreign ones, a garlic-scented effluent. There was a big photograph of General Franco, dressed as a civilian, a bald man with jowls and parvenu lifted eyebrows. There were also yellowing notices, probably forbidding things. Mr Mercer was already there, having perhaps been given a lift in one of those tractors. All the cruise members clustered round him, as for protection. Enderby saw that his arm was still in Miss Boland's. He disengaged it by saying he had to post a letter.

"Mysterious again," she said. "You're no sooner here than you have to post a mysterious letter. Signed with a mysterious name."

"What?" squawked Enderby.

"I'm sorry. I couldn't help seeing it. You left it on the seat. Do forgive me. It was with those brochures and things, and I picked them up to look at them and there was your letter. But it's no good my pretending that I don't know your first name now, is it? Or nickname it must be."

"Oh, no."

"It *must* be. I've never seen the name Puerco before." She pronounced it *Pure co*. "And then, since it looked foreign, I looked it up in my Spanish dictionary, and, lo and behold, there it was. Meaning 'dirty'."

"Actually," Enderby improvised in delirium, "it's an old border name. Welsh border, I mean. My family came from near Shrewsbury. That's a coincidence, that is, the Spanish business, I mean. Look, I've *got* to post this letter. I'll be back." As soon as he had clumsily pushed his way through the crowd that was round woolly-capped Mr Mercer, he realised he had behaved foolishly in being willing to leave her if only for five minutes. She wouldn't believe that story about Puerco being an old border name; she'd look it up again in her Spanish dictionary and she'd find more than dirty and filthy and so on. She was bound to. He hesitated at a door that led on to a dismal wet garden, beyond it a kind of restaurant all made of big dirty windows. He would have to get that dictionary away from her, tear out the dangerous page or lose the whole book. Or should he now, with his five-pound notes and anthology of exotic *pourboires*, get out there into the great rainy windy peninsula, lose himself in cork-woods, later become dried up like a raisin tramping the hot white country roads? He thought not. A lean poor man was standing by the door, opposing cigarette-sparks to the dull damp night. It was possible, thought Enderby, that Spanish John's hispaniolising of his mother's maiden name represented a historical phase of the word, long superseded. But if, of course, it was the same as Italian and—Enderby said to this man:

"*Amigo.*" The man responded with a benison of sparks. Enderby said: "In *español. L'animal.* What's the *español* for it?" He snorted and snuffed the air all around at chest-level as though rooting for truffles. Then he saw that a man in smart uniform, just behind him, was watching with some interest. The lean poor man said:

"*Entiendo. Un puerco.*"

That was it then, Enderby thought grimly. He stood wavering, letter in hand. The thin poor man seemed to be awaiting further charades from Enderby. The uniformed man frowned, very puzzled. The thin poor one whinnied and said, "*Un caballo.*" Enderby said, "*Sí,*" then tripped over the uniformed man's left boot as he went in again, letter unposted.

"My goodness, you were quick," said Miss Boland.

"It's the language," Enderby said. "I don't know the language, as I said. Perhaps if I could borrow your little dictionary—"

"Right," Mr Mercer was now saying. "Everybody please stand round there where the baggage is." They'd got it out pretty quickly, Enderby thought distractedly: no spirit of *mañana* here. "As you know, they have customs here same as everywhere else—"

"Old Spanish customs," cried Mr Guthkelch.

"—But only a few of you have to open your bags—"

"As long as nobody has to drop 'em," cried Mr Guthkelch, perhaps going too far.

"—It's a sample, you see, what you might call a sample check-up."

"I don't suppose," said Miss Boland to Enderby, "that you've got anything so bourgeois as luggage, have you? I suppose you'll be sleeping in your shirt or in the altogether." Her eyes glistened when she said that, as though excited by it. Enderby was disgusted; he said:

"You'll soon see whether I've got anything or not. I'm no different from anybody else." The man who had looked at him suspiciously on the way across the tarmac now did the same thing again. "In the sense, that is," expanded Enderby, "of personal possessions and the like."

"This is a bit like an identification parade, isn't it?" giggled Miss Boland. "Very thrilling." They were all there near the pile of luggage, and an official with a peaked cap did a caged-tiger walk up and down in front of this squad of pleasure-seekers, hands folded behind his back. Enderby saw who it was: that man out there who had frowned at his pig-snorting. The man now halted and faced them. He had jowls not unlike those of his Caudillo and even allomorphs of those eyebrows; perhaps a lowly relative for whom the régime had had to find a job. He sternly pointed at people. He pointed at Enderby. Enderby at once looked round for the man with the overweight luggage. He found him and said:

"Where is it?"

"What? That? Why can't you show him your own?"

"Reasons," Enderby said. "Things nobody must see."

"Thought there was a catch in it. Right liberty, I call it. Anyway, I've got nothing to fear." And he showed where the super-numerary bag was. Enderby lugged it to the customs-counter. The official was already delicately rooting in a pair of very clean white cotton gloves. He was perfunctory about most passengers' luggage; with Enderby's supposed he was thorough. At the bottom of the bag he found, under that man's Bermuda shorts, the three garish paperbacks that had looked quite harmless in the London air terminal. Here, in a repressed and repressive Catholic country that discharged its extramarital lust in bullfights, they suddenly seemed to flare into the promise of outrageous obscenity. Miss Boland, though not of the luggage-opening elect, was nevertheless by Enderby's side. She saw; "Dirty," she said, grinning. The official held up the three books very nearly to the level of the portrait of the Caudillo, as if for his curse. Mr Guthkelch said: "Who'll start the bidding?" The covers blared three allotropes of mindless generic blonde, in shock and undress. The official pronounced: "*Pornográficos.*" Everybody nooded, pleased that they could understand Spanish. And then, straight at Enderby, he snorted and gave back Enderby's own mime of snout-truffling, adding: "*Puerco.*"

"I see, I see," said Miss Boland, quietly gratified, pressing into Enderby's flank. "So that's how you pronounce it. And it means "pig" too. Stupid of me, I should have seen that. They know you here then. You *are* a dark horse. Pig, I mean, a dark pig."

From one of the upheld books two flat square little packets dropped out. They fell on to the exposure of somebody's sensible white underwear. All the men at once knew what they were, but one elderly woman, evidently sheltered from the world, said: "Sort of rings. What are they for then?" The man who could best tell her was heard groaning: those objects were obviously ferial, not marital, equipment. The official wiped one cotton-gloved hand against another, made an extravagant gesture of disgust and dismissal, and turned his back on the lot of them. *"Ipocritico,"* murmured Enderby. The official did not hear, or else the Spanish was different from the Italian.

"It pays to be straight," the overweight man was whining. "I've learned my lesson, that I have." His wife looked out, dissociated from him but there would be hell tonight in a foreign bedroom, into wet dark Seville, Don Juan's town. "Let me down, you have," he said unreasonably to Enderby. Everybody else frowned, puzzled, not quick on the uptake. Even Miss Boland. Miss Boland took Enderby's arm, saying: "Come on, Piggy." A very liberalising influence the moon, Enderby bitterly thought. Mr Mercer called them, in a fatigued voice, to the waiting bus.

Three

An hour later, Enderby lay exhausted on his hotel bed. He had posted that letter in the box in the hotel lobby, having found some pesetas in his little treasury of tips and been able to buy stamps from the moustached duenna yawning with dignity at the reception desk. None of the hotel staff, admittedly tired and proudly resentful of the late-arriving guests, seemed even minimally agitated by news of the death of a British pop-singer. So things were all right so far. But soon they would not be. A lot of course depended on the chief guardian of the true identity of Hogg, namely bloody Wapenshaw; much depended on the Hogg-photograph in tomorrow's newspapers; a little depended on Miss Boland's semantic investigations into the word *puerco*.

Soon, when he was less exhausted, he would go and see Miss Boland. She was on this floor of the hotel, which was called the Hotel Marruecos; she was just a couple of doors down. Soon. Enderby had had sent up a bottle of Fundador and a glass. He knew Fundador from Piggy's Sty: it was a kind of parody of Armagnac. He was drinking it now for his nerves. He lay on the bed, whose coverlet was the colour of boiled liver. The wallpaper was cochineal. There were no pictures on the walls. It was all very bare, and he had done nothing to mitigate that bareness. Nothing in the wardrobe, no suitcase on the luggage-stand at the bed's bottom. The window was open, and a hot wind had started blowing up, one which seemed to match the cochineal walls. This hot wind had scattered the clouds and disclosed what was now a Spanish moon, a Don Juan stage property. Miss Boland, in a sensible dressing-gown, would now be putting curlers in her hair, looking at the moon. *Luna.* Perhaps she would be checking the word in her handbag dictionary.

Painfully Enderby got up and went to the bathroom. He could hear, through the wall, in the adjoining bathroom, the man with overweight luggage being rebuked bitterly by his wife. Libidinous wretch. Condom-carrier. Thought he'd have a nasty sly go at the *señoritas* or *bintim* did he? Words to that effect, anyway. Best years of her life slaving away for him. Enderby, sighing, micturated briefly, pulled the chain and left his room buttoning, sighing. Leaving his room, he met Miss Boland coming to his room. Quite a coincidence, really.

"I've come," she said, "for my poem." She looked rather like a woman who was coming to collect a poem, not a bit the lecturer in selenography. Her dressing-gown was far from sensible: it was diaphanous black, billowing in the hot wind from the window at the corridor's end, and under it was a peach-coloured nightdress. Her pretty mousy hair had been brushed; it crackled in the hot wind; a peach-coloured fillet was binding it. She had put on cochineal lipstick, matching the hot wind. Enderby gulped. Gulping, he bowed her in. He said:

"I haven't had time yet. To write a poem, that is. I've been unpacking, as you can see."

"You've unpacked *everything*? Goodness. A bit pointless, isn't it? We're only here for the night. What's left of it, that is. Ah," she said, billowing in the hot wind over to the window, "you have the *luna* too. My *luna* and yours."

"We must," Enderby said reasonably, "be on the same

side of the corridor. The same view, you see." And then: "Have a drink."

"Well," she said, "I don't usually. Especially at this hour of the morning. But I am on holiday after all, aren't I?"

"You most certainly are," Enderby said gravely. "I'll get a glass from the bathroom." He went to get it. The row was still going on next door. Uncontrollable lust in middle age. Comic if it was not disgusting. Or something like that. He brought back the glass and found Miss Boland sitting on his bed. "Mare Imbrium," she was saying. "Seleucus. Aristarchus." He poured her a very healthy slug. He would make her drunk and have a hangover, and that would distract her tomorrow morning from *puerco* business. Soon he would go to her room and steal her dictionary. Everything was going to be all right.

"You've been thorough," she said, taking the glass from him. "You've even packed your suitcase away."

"Oh, yes," he said. "It's a sort of mania with me. Tidiness, that is." Then he saw himself in the dressing-table mirror—unshaven since early this morning in London (he had written *Londra* on the envelope; was that right?) and with shirt very crumpled and trousers proclaiming cheapness and jacket thin at the elbows. He gave himself a grim smile full of teeth. They looked clean enough, anyway. He transferred the smile to Miss Boland. "You poor man," she said. "You're lonely, aren't you? I could see that when you got on the bus in London. Still, you've no need to be lonely now. Not for this holiday, anyhow." She took a sip of the Fundador without grimacing. "Hm. Fiery but nice."

"*Mucho fuego*," said Enderby. English man no *fuego*: he remembered that.

Miss Boland leaned back. She wore feathery slippers with heels. Leaning back, she kicked them off. Her feet were long and clean and the toes were unpainted. She closed her eyes, frowned, then said: "Let me see if I can remember. A *cada puerco* something-or-other *su San Martín*. That means: Every dog has his day. But it should be 'every hog' really, shouldn't it? The dictionary says hog, not pig."

Enderby sat down heavily on the other side of the bed. Then he looked with heavy apprehension at Miss Boland. She seemed to have lost about two stone and fifteen years since embarking at London. He tried to see himself imposing upon her a complex of subtle but vigorous amation which should have an effect of drowsy enslavement, rendering her, for instance, totally indifferent to tomorrow's news. Then he thought he had perhaps better get out of here and find his own way to North Africa: there must surely be something hopping over there at this hour. But no. Despite everything, he was safer in Mr Mercer's party—a supernumerary, fiddled in with a wink, no name on the manifest, waved through by officials who were waved back at by Mr Guthkelch. Moreover, Mr Mercer had returned everybody's passport, and Enderby's was snug once more in its inside pocket. He was not going to let it go again, unless, in final desperate abandonment of identity, to the fire of some Moorish kebabvendor. He saw this man quite clearly, crying his kebabs against the sun, brown and lined and toothless, opposing his call to the muezzin's. That was the poetic imagination, that was.

"And," Miss Boland was now saying, having helped herself to more Fundador, "Mother and Dad used to take me and Charles, that was my brother, to see Uncle Herbert when he lived in Wellington—Wellington, Salop, I mean; why do they call it Salop? Oh, the Latin name I suppose—and we went up Bredon Hill several times—"

"The coloured counties," Enderby said, doing an estimate of her for seduction purposes and realising at the same time how purely academic such a notion was, "and hear the larks on high. Young men hanging themselves and ending up in Shrewsbury jail. For love, as they call it."

"How cynical you are. But I suppose I've every right to be cynical too, really. Toby his name was—a silly name for a man, isn't it?—and he said I had to choose between him and my career—I mean, more the name for a dog, isn't it, really?—and of course there was no question of me abandoning my vocation for the sake of anything he said he had to give. And he said something about a brainy wife being a bad wife and he wasn't going to have the moon lying in bed between us."

"A bit of a poet," said Enderby, feeling himself grow drowsy. The hot wind puppeteered the window-curtains and plastered Miss Boland's nightdress against her shin.

"A bit of a liar," Miss Boland said. "He lied about his father. His father wasn't a solicitor, only a solicitor's clerk. He lied about his rank in the Royal Corps of Signals. He lied about his car. It wasn't his, it was one he borrowed from a friend. Not that he had many friends. Men," she said, "tend to be liars. Look at you, for instance."

"Me?" said Enderby.

"Saying you're a poet. Talking about your old Shropshire name."

"Listen," said Enderby. And he began to recite.

"Shrewsbury, Shrewsbury, rounded by river,
    The envious Severn like a sleeping dog
That wakes at whiles to snarl and slaver
    Or growls in its dream its snores of fog."

"That's yours, is it?"

"Lover-haunted in the casual summer:
    A monstrous aphrodisiac,
The sun excites in the noonday shimmer,
    When Jack is sweating, Joan on her back."

"I was always taught that you can't make poetry with long words."

"Sick and sinless in the anaemic winter:
    The nymphs have danced off the summer rout,
The boats jog on the fraying painter,
    The School is hacking its statesmen out."

293

"Oh, I see what you mean. Shrewsbury School. That's where Darwin went to, isn't it?"

"The pubs dispense their weak solution,
    The unfructified waitresses bring their bills,
While Darwin broods upon evolution,
    Under the pall of a night that chills—"

"Sorry, I shouldn't have interrupted."

"—But smooths out the acne of adolescence
    As the god appears in the fourteenth glass
And the urgent promptings of tumescence
    Lead to the tumbled patch of grass."

"A lot of sex in it, isn't there? Sorry, I won't interrupt again."

"This is the last bloody stanza," Enderby said sternly. "Coming up now."

"Time and the town go round like the river,
    But Darwin thinks in a line that is straight.
A sort of selection goes on for ever,
    But no new species originate."

They were silent. Enderby felt a spurt of poet's pride, and then exhaustion. It had been a terrible day. Miss Boland was impressed. She said: "Well, you *are* a poet, after all. If that *is* yours, that is."

"Of course it's mine. Give me some more from that bottle." And she glugged some out for him gladly, hand-maiden to a poet. "That's from my early volume, *Fish and Heroes*. Which you haven't read. Which nobody's read. But, by God," said Enderby, "I'll show them all. I'm not finished yet, not by a long chalk."

"That's right. Don't you think you'd be more comfortable with your shoes off? Don't bother—leave it to me." Enderby closed his eyes. "And your jacket too?" Enderby soon lay on one half of the bed in shirt and trousers; she had had his socks off too and also his tie, which was in the hotel colours of red, white, and blue.

The hot wind was still there, but he felt cooler. She lay next to him. They had a cigarette apiece.

"Associations," Enderby found himself saying. "Mind you, everybody's done it, from that Spanish priest right up to Albert Camus, with Kierkegaard somewhere in the middle."

"Who's Kierke-whatever-it-is?"

"This philosopher who made out it was really like God and the soul. Don Juan using women and God using man. Anyway, this is his town. And I was going to write a poetic drama about a Don Juan who bribed women to pretend that he'd done it to them because really he couldn't do it, not with anybody. And then poetic drama went out of fashion." His toenails, he decided, could really do with cutting. The big toenails, however, would have to be attacked with a chisel or something. Very hard. He had not changed all that much, after all. A bath, after all, was a tank for poetic drafts. He felt a new poem twitching inside him like a sneeze. A poem about a statue. He looked rather warmly on Miss Boland. *The final kiss and final*—If only he could get that one finished first.

"And who was this barber of Seville?"

"Oh, a Frenchman invented that one, and there's a French newspaper named after him. A sort of general factotum, getting things for people and so on." Enderby nodded off.

"Wake up." She was quite rough with him; that would be the Fundador. "You could have a play in which this barber was really Don Juan, and he did horrible things with his razor. In revenge, you know."

"What do you mean? What revenge?"

"I said nothing about revenge. You dropped off again. Wake up! I don't see why the moon couldn't be a proper *scientific* subject for a poem instead of what it is for most poets—you know, a sort of lamp, or a what-do-you-call-it aphrodisiac like the sun in your poem. Then you could have as many nice long words as you wanted. Apogee and perigee and the sidereal day and ecto-craters and the ejecta hypothesis."

"What did you say about ejectors?"

She hadn't heard him. Or perhaps he'd said nothing. "And the months," she was now saying. "Synodic and nodical and sidereal and anomalistic. And isostasy. And grabens and horsts. And the lunar maria, not seas at all but huge plains of lava covered in dust. Your body is a horst and mine a graben, because horst is the opposite of graben. Come on, let's get out of here and wander the streets of Seville as we are, in our night clothes I mean. But your night clothes are the altogether, aren't they? Still, it's a lovely night though the moon's setting now. Feel that warm wind on your flesh?" That was not true about the moon setting. When they were walking down the *calle* outside the hotel, Enderby totally bare, his little bags aswing, the moon was full and huge and very near. It was so near that an odour came off it—like the odour of cachous from old evening bags, of yellowing dance-programmes, of fox-fur long laid in mothballs. Miss Boland said: "Mare Tranquillitatis. Fracastorius. Hipparchus. Mare Nectaris." She had brought the moon right down to the Seville housetops so that she could go burrowing into its maria. She disappeared temporarily into one of those, and then her head, its mousy hair become golden Berenice's and flying about, popped through the northern polar membrane. She seemed to be agitating this hollow moon from the inside, impelling it towards Enderby. He ran from her and it down the *calle*, back into the hotel. The old hall-porter yawned out of his *hidalgo* lantern jaws at Enderby's twinkling naked-ness. Enderby panted up the stairs, once getting his toe caught in a carpet-hole, then cursing as a tack lodged in his calloused left heel. He found his room blindly and fell flat on the bed, desperate for air. There was not much coming from the open window. What was coming in by that window was the moon, much shrunken but evidently of considerable mass, for the window-frame creaked, four unwilling tangents to the straining globe, bits of lunar substance flaking off like plaster at the four points of engagement. Miss Boland's head now pro-truded at a pole which had become a navel, her hair still flying in fire. Enderby was stuck to that bed. With one lunge she and the moon were on him.

"No," he grunted, waking up. "No, you can't do that, it isn't right." But she and her heavy lunar body held him down. That left heel was fluked by one of her toenails; the staircarpet-hole turned out to be a minute gap between the fabric of her dressing-gown and its lacy border. There was no real nakedness, then: only exposure, things riding up and pulled down.

"Show me then, show me what's right. *You* do it."

He rolled her off, so that she lay expectant on her back now, and with desperate agility he trampolined his buttocks away from the punished mattress. This was springier than he had thought, for he found himself on his feet looking sternly down at her. "If," he said, "you want that sort of a holiday there'll be plenty to provide it. Gigolos and whatnot. Little dark-skinned boys and so on. Why pick on me?"

She started to whimper. "I thought we were going to be friends. You're unnatural, that's what you are."

"I'm *not* unnatural. Just very very tired. It's been a terrible day."

"Yes." She wrapped her dressing-gown round her body and looked up at him, hard but tearfully. "Yes, I'm sure it has. There's something not quite right about you. You've got things on your mind. You've done something you shouldn't have done. You've got away in a hurry from something or other, I can tell that."

This wouldn't do at all. "Darling," creaked Enderby, holding out his arms and advanced, smirking.

"You can't get round me that way."

"Darling." Enderby frowned now, but with his arms still out.

"Oh, take your non-pyjamas out of your non-suitcase and get to bed after your terrible terrible day. There's something very fishy about you," said Miss Boland. And she started to get up from the bed.

Enderby advanced and pushed her back again somewhat roughly, saying: "You're right. I *have* run away. From her. From that woman. I couldn't stand it any longer. I got out. Just like that. She was horrible to me." A back cinder in Enderby's raked-out brain spurted up an instant to ask what was truth and niggle a bit about situation contexts and so on. Enderby deferred to it and made an emendation: "I ran away."

"What woman? Which woman?" Woman's curiosity had dried her tears.

"It was never really a marriage. Oh, let me get to bed. Make room there. I'm so desperately tired."

"Tell me all about it first. I want to know what happened. Come on, wake up. Have some more of this brandy stuff here."

"No no no no. Tell you in the morning." He was flat on his back again, ready to drop off. Desperately.

"I want to know." She jerked him as roughly as he had pushed her. "Whose fault was it? Why was it never really a marriage? Oh, *do come on.*"

"Hex," said Enderby *in extremis.* And then he was merrily driving the rear car of the three, a red sports job, and arms waved jollily from the Mercedes in front. It was a long way to this roadhouse type pub they were all going to, but they were all well tanked-up already though the men drove with steely concentration and insolent speed. The girls were awfully pretty and full of fun. Brenda had red hair and Lucy was dark and small and Bunty was pleasantly plump and wore a turquoise-coloured twin-set. Enderby had a college scarf flying from his neck and a pipe clenched in his strong white smiling teeth. "You wait, Bunty old girl," he gritted indistinctly. "You'll get what's coming to you." The girls yelled with mirth. Urged on by them hilariously, he fed ever greater speed with his highly-polished toecap to the growling road-eating red job, and he passed with ease the other two. Waves of mock rage and mock contempt, laughter on the spring English wind. And so he got to the pub first. It was a nice little pub with a bald smiling barman presiding in a cocktail bar smelling of furniture polish. He wore a white bum-freezer with claret lapels. Enderby ordered for everybody, telling the barman, called Jack, to put a wiggle on so that the drinks could be all lined up waiting when the laggards arrived. Bitter in tankards, gin and things, an advocaat for Bunty. "That'll make you bright-eyed and bushy-tailed, old girl," winked Enderby. And then the watery signal from within. As Frank and Nigel and Betty and Ethel and the others roared into the bar, Enderby at once had to say: "Sorry, all. Got to see a man about a dog." Bunty giggled: "Wet your boots, you mean." At once the urgency roared in his bladder, drowning the roaring of his pals, but he did not run to the gents: he walked confidently, though he had never been in this pub before. But, seeing it at the end of a corridor, he had to run. Damn, he would only just make it.

He would only just make it. He jumped out of bed and made for the toilet, fumbling cursing for the light-switch. Pounding his stream out, he grumbled at the prodigality of dreams, which could go to all this trouble—characters, décor and all, even an advertisement for a beer (Jason's Golden Fleece) which didn't exist—just so that he would get out of bed and micturate in the proper place. He pulled the chain, went back to bed and saw, by the bathroom light he had not bothered to put out, that there was a woman lying in it. He remembered roughly who it was, that lunar woman he'd been flying with (why flying?) and also that this was some foreign town, and then the whole lot came back. He was somewhat frightened that he wasn't as frightened as he should be.

"What, eh, who?" she said. And then: "Oh. I must have dropped off. Come on, get in. It's got a bit chilly now."

"What time is it?" Enderby wondered. His wrist-watch had stopped, he noticed, squinting in the light from the bathroom. Somewhere outside a big bell banged a single stroke. "That's a lot of help," said Enderby. Funny, he hadn't noticed that bell before. They must be near a cathedral or town hall or something. Seville, that was where they were. Don Juan's town. A strange woman in bed.

"So," she said. "Her name was Bunty, was it? And she let you down. Never mind, everybody gets let down sometime or other. I got let down by Toby. And that was a silly name, too."

"We were in this car, you see. I was driving."

"Come back to bed. *I* won't let you down. Come and cuddle up a bit. It's chilly. There aren't many clothes on the bed."

It was quite pleasant cuddling up. *I've been so cold at night.* Who was it who had said that? That blasted Vesta, bloody evil woman. "Bloody evil woman," muttered Enderby.

"Yes, yes, but it's all over now. You're a bit wet."

"Sorry," Enderby said. "Careless of me." He wiped himself with the sheet. "I wonder what the time is."

"Why? Why are you so eager to know what the time is? Do you want to be up and about so soon? A night in Seville. We both ought to have something to remember about a night in Seville."

"They lit the sun," said Enderby, "and then their day began."

"What do you mean? Why did you say that?"

"It just came to me. Out of the blue." It seemed as though rhymes were going to start lining up. Began, plan, man, scan, ban. But this other thing had to be done now. She was not a bit like that blasted Vesta, spare-fleshed in bed so that she could be elegant out of it. There was plenty to get hold of here. He saw one of his bar-customers leering, saying that. Very vulgar. Enderby started to summon up old memories of what to do (it had been a long time). The Don himself seemed to hover above the bed, picking his teeth for some reason, nodding, pointing. Moderately satisfied, he flew off on an insubstantial hell-horse and, not far from the hotel, waved a greeting with a doffed insolent feathered *sombrero* at a statue of a man.

"They hoisted up a statue of a man," mumbled Enderby.

"Yes, yes, darling, I love you too."

Enderby now gently, shyly, and with some blushing, began to insinuate, that is to say squashily attempt to insert, that is to say. A long time. And now. Quite pleasant, really. He paused after five. And again. And again. Pentameters. And now came an ejaculation of words.

300

What prodigies that eye of light revealed!
What dusty parchment statutes they repealed,
Pulling up blinds and lifting every

A sonnet, a sonnet, one for a new set of *Revolutionary Sonnets,* the first of which was the one that bloody Wapenshaw had raged at. The words began to flood. He drew the thing out, excited.

"Sorry," he said. "I've got to get this thing down. I've got to get some paper. A sonnet, that's what it is." There was, he thought, a hanging bulby switch-thing over the bed-head. He felt for it, trembling. Seville's velvet dark was jeered out by a sudden coming of light. She was incredulous. She lay there with her mouth open, shocked and staring. "I'll just get it down on paper," promised Enderby, "and then back on the job again. What I mean is—" He was out of bed, searching. Barman's pencil in his jacket-pocket. Paper? Damn. He dragged open drawers, looking for that white lining-stuff. It was all old Spanish newspaper, bullfighters or something. Damn.

She wailed from the bed. Enderby dashed into the bathroom, inspired, and came out swathed in toilet-paper. "This will do fine," he smiled. "Shan't be long. Darling," he added. Then he sat at the dressing-table, horridly undressed, and began to write.

Pulling up blinds and lifting every ban.
The galaxies revolving to their plan,
They made the coin, the conch, the cortex yield
Their keys

"You're hateful, you're disgusting. I've never in my whole life been so insulted. No wonder she—"

"Look," said Enderby, without turning round, "this is important. The gift's definitely come back, thank God. I knew it would. Just give me a couple of minutes. Then I'll be in there again." In the bed, he meant, raising his eyes to the dressing-table mirror as to make them tell her, if she was in that mirror, precisely that. He saw her all right. He ought, he knew, to be shocked by what he saw, but there was no time for that now. Hell has no fury. Better not let other poems get in the way. Besides, that quotation was wrong, everybody always got it wrong.

> And in a garden, once a field,
> They hoisted up a statue of a man.

"Finished the octave," he sang out. "Shan't be long now."

"You filthy thing. You sexless rotter."

"Really. Such language." Mirror, terror, error. Pity there was no true thyme for *mirror*, except that bloody Sir Launcelot thing Tennyson pinched from the pincher Autolycus. "And you a seleno-whatever-it-is."

"You won't get away with this. You wait." And, dressing-gown decently about her, she was out through that door, to Enderby's mild surprise, and was gone, slamming it.

"Look here," Enderby said feebly. And then the mirror, holding out its English name, told him to get on with the sestet.

Four

The sestet. It was all right, he thought. He told the Spanish dawn he thought it was all right. Then he had a swig of Fundador. Not all that much left. She'd put her name into it, that one, Miss whoever-it-was, moon-woman. He told the sestet to his reflection like an elocutionist:

> "Of man, rather. To most it seemed a mirror:
> They strained their necks with gazing in the air,
> Proud of those stony eyes unglazed by terror.
> Though marble is not glass, why should they care?
> There would be time for coughing up the error.
> Someone was bound to find his portrait there."

And the meaning? It seemed pretty clear, really. This was what happened in a humanist society. The Garden of Eden (and that was in the other sonnet, the one that had rendered bloody Wapenshaw violent) was turned into a field where men built or fought or ploughed or something. They worshipped themselves for being so clever, but then they were all personified in an autocratic leader, like this Franco up there in Madrid. Humanism always led to totalitarianism. Something like that, anyway.

Enderby was moderately pleased with the poem, but he was more pleased with the prospect of a bigger structure, a sequence. Some years before he had published the volume called *Revolutionary Sonnets*. The book had contained things other than sonnets, but the title had derived from that opening group of twenty, each of which had tried to encapsulate—exploiting the theme and countertheme paradigm of the Petrarchan form—some phase of history in which a revolution had taken place. He felt now that it might be possible to wrest those twenty sonnets from that volume and, by adding twenty more with the cooperation of the Muse, build a sizeable sequence which would make a book on its own. A new title would be needed—something more imaginative than the old one, something like *Conch and Cortex* or something. So far he had these two sonnets—the Garden of Eden one and the new one about man building his own world outside the Garden. Somewhere at the back of his mind there pricked the memory of his having started and then abandoned, in a very rough state, another sonnet that, nicely worked up and carefully polished, would make a third. It was, he thought, really an anterior sonnet to these two, an image of the primal revolution in heaven—Satan revolting, that sort of thing. Lucifer, Adam, Adam's children. Those would make the first three. He felt that, with a certain amount of drunkenness followed by crapulous meditation, that sonnet could be teased back to life. He was pretty sure that the rhymes, at least, would come marchng back, in U.S. Army soft-soled boots, if he left the gate open. Octave: Lucifer fed up with the dead order and unity of heaven. Wants action, so has to conceive idea of duality. Sestet: he dives, creates hell to oppose heaven. Enderby saw him diving. An eagle dropping from a mountain-top in sunlight. Out of Tennyson, that. The wrinkled sea beneath him crawls. Alls, balls, calls. Was that one of the sestet rhymes?

He felt excited. He toasted himself in the last of the Fundador. That bloody woman. But there was time for shame now and for the desire to make amends. He thought he had better go now to her room and apologise. He saw that it was not perhaps really all that polite to get out of bed and so on with a woman in order to write down a poem. Especially on toilet-paper brought in like triumphal streamers. Women had their own peculiar notion of priorities, and this had to be respected. But he had no doubt that she would see his point if properly explained. Suppose, he might say, she had suddenly spotted a new lunar crater while so engaged, would she not herself have leapt up as he had done? And then he could read his sonnet to her. He wondered whether it was worth while to dress properly for his visit. The dawn was mounting and soon the hotel would stir with insolent waiters coming to bedrooms with most inadequte breakfasts. But she might, thoroughly mollified by the sonnet, bid him back to bed again, her bed now, to resume what had, so to speak, that is to say. He blushed. He would go, as a film Don Juan he had once seen had gone, in open-necked shirt and trousers.

He went out on to the corridor, his sonnet wrapped round his wrist and one end secured with his thumb. Her room was just down there, on the same side as his own. When they had all, with Mr Mercer leading and Mr Guthkelch crying: "Keep in step there, you horrible lot," marched up together, he had definitely seen her allotted that room there. He went up to it now and stood before it, taking deep breaths and trying out a plenidental smile. Then he grasped the door-handle and boldly entered. Dawn-lit, the curtains drawn back, a room much like his own though containing luggage. She was lying in bed, possibly asleep, possibly—for every woman was supposed to be able to tell at once when there was an intruder, something to do with the protection of honour—pretending to be asleep. Enderby coughed loudly and said:

"I came to tell you I'm sorry. I didn't mean it. It just came over me, as I said."

She started awake at once, more surprised, it seemed, than angry. She had changed her nightdress to demure cotton, also the colour of her hair. It was the aircraft's stewardess. Miss Kelly was the name. Enderby frowned on her. She had no right—But perhaps he had entered the wrong room. She said:

"Did you want something? I'm not really supposed to be available to passengers, you know, except on the flight."

"No, no," frowned Enderby. "Sorry. I was after that other woman. The moon one. Miss Boolan."

"Miss Boland. Oh, I see. It's your wrist, is it? You've got that thing round your wrist. You've cut your wrist, is that it? All the first-aid stuff's on the aircraft. The hotel people might be able to help you."

"Oh, no, no, no," Enderby laughed now. "This is a poem, not an improvised bandage. I had to get up and write this poem, you understand, and I fear I annoyed Miss Boland, as you say her name is. I was going to apologise to her and perhaps read out this poem as a kind of peace-offering, so to speak. It's what's known as a sonnet."

"It's a bit early, isn't it?" She slid down into her bed again, leaving just her head and eyes showing. "I mean, everybody's supposed to be still asleep."

"Oh," Enderby smiled kindly, "it's not that sort of poem, you know. You're thinking of an aubade—a good-morning song. The Elizabethans were very fond of these. Hark hark the lark, and so on. When all the birds have matins said, and so forth. A sonnet is a poem in fourteen lines. For any occasion, I suppose."

"I know what a sonnet is," her voice said, muffled but sharp. "There's a sonnet in that book by Yod Crewsy."

Enderby stood paralysed, his own sonnet held forward like a knuckleduster. "Eh?" Thought fell in at a great distance and, in British tommies' clodhoppers, advanced steadily at a light infantry pace.

"You know. You were asking about pop-singers on the

plane. Vesta Wittgenstein you were asking about too, remember. Yod Crewsy did this book of poems that won the prize. There's one in it he calls a sonnet. I couldn't make head nor tail of it really, but one of the BOAC ground-hostesses, educated you see, she said it was very clever."

"Can you," faltered Enderby, "can you remember anything about it?" Like Macbeth, he began to see that it might be necessary to kill everybody.

"Oh, it's so early. And," she said, a girl slow on the uptake, sitting up again, things dawning on her, "you shouldn't be in here really at this hour. Not at any hour you shouldn't. Nobody asked you to come in here. I'll call Captain O'Shaughnessy." Her voice was growing louder.

"One line, one word," begged Enderby. "Just tell me what it was about."

"You're not supposed to be in here. It's taking advantage of being a passenger. I'm not supposed to be rude to passengers. Oh, why don't you go?"

"About the devil and hell and so on? Was that it?"

"I've had enough. I'm going to call Captain O'Shaughnessy."

"Oh, don't bother," groaned Enderby. "I'm just going. But it's liberty after liberty."

"You telling *me* it's taking a liberty."

"First one thing and then another. If he's dead I'm glad he's dead. But there'll be other heads rolling, I can tell you that. Did it have something about an eagle in it? You know, dropping from a great height?"

Miss Kelly seemed to be taking a very deep breath, as though in preparation for shouting. Enderby went, nodding balefully, closing the door. In the circumstances, he did not much feel like calling on Miss Boland. Women were highly unpredictable creatures. No, that was stupid. You could predict them all right. He had thought he would never have to see blasted treacherous Vesta again, but he obviously had to confront her before he did her in. The future was filling itself up horribly. Things both monstrously necessary and sickeningly irrelevant. He wanted to get on with his poetry again.

4

One

CALM, calm. Enderby reflected that it was morning and he was up and there was nothing to prevent his engaging Seville in the doing of what had to be done. First, a question of pesetas. Unshaven, dirty-shirted, otherwise respectable, he asked the day-porter of the hotel, yawning to his duty, where sterling might be changed. He asked in Italian, which, thanks to the Roman Empire, the porter clearly understood. Enderby had some idea that it was forbidden by the British government, treacherously in league with foreign bankers (even Franco's fiscal thugs), to present naked pounds in any Continental place of official monetary transaction. They found you had more pound-notes on you than you ought, by law, to have, and then, by various uncompassionate channels, they reported you to the Chancellor of the Exchequer, an insincerely smiling man Enderby had once seen with a woman in Piggy's Sty. In Italy that time, on his brief and dummy honeymoon, it had been traveller's cheques, which were all right. The porter, in mime and basic Romance, told Enderby that there was a barber round the corner who gave a very good rate of exchange. Enderby felt a little ice cube of pleasure, soon to be pounced on and demolished by the hot water he was in. He needed a shave, anyway. A barber of Seville, eh? "Figaro?" he asked, momentarily forgetting his actual, and other people's proleptic, trouble. Not Figaro, said the unliterary and literal porter. He was called Pepe.

This barber breathed hard on Enderby as he shaved him, a sour young man smelling of very fresh garlic. He seemed not unwilling to change fifty pounds of Enderby's money, and Enderby wondered if the suspiciously clean pesetas he got were genuine. The world was terrible really, full of cheating and shadiness, as much in low as in high places. He tested his pesetas in a dirty eating-den full of loud dialogue (the participants as far away from each other as possible: one man tooth-picking at the door, another hidden in the kitchen, for instance). Enderby asked for *ovos* which turned out to be *huevos,* and for *prosciutto,* not cognate with *jamón.* He was learning essential words: he would not starve. He changed a big note with no trouble, receiving back a fistful of small dirty rags. Then, on the counter, he saw a copy of a newspaper called *Diario Pueblo.*

How often had he, on the day of publication of a volume of his verse (or the day before, if publication day had been Monday), gone to the quality papers as to a condemned cell, his stomach sick and his legs pure angelica. Usually there was no review, poetry being left to accumulate in literary editors' offices until there was enough of it for one expert to do a single clean sweep in a grudging brief article, everybody—Enderby, po-etesses, poetasters, Sir George Goodby—all fluffed up together. But once, surprisingly, there had been a prompt solus of condemnation, all for Enderby, in a very reputable paper. Since then, the smell of newsprint had always made him feel slightly giddy. The fear he felt now was strong enough, since it was to do with his appearance in a context of action, but it was mitigated somewhat by the fact of the newspaper's foreignness. It seemed a very badly put together newspaper, with a lot of news items boxed in thick black, as though they were all obituaries. "*Scusa,*" he said to the curled dark youth who took his money. And then he looked for news of himself.

He did not have far to look. It was on the front page. There was, thank God, no photograph, but there were frightful succinct words, as though from some sensational foreign novel. *Chocante. Horroroso.* Come, that was going too far. *Delante del Primer Ministro Británico.* They had to bring that in, make it political. *Banquete para celebrar* something or other. And then *Yod Crewsy, cuadrillero de los Fixers.* Was he dead, then? What was "Dead"—*morto?* No, Enderby concluded from both his Spanish pseudonym and his eggs, now repeating violently, it must be *muerto.* References to a *revólver,* very clear that, and to a *tiro* and—what the hell was this?— an *escopetazo.* And then it said: *El víctima, en grave estado, fué conducido al* some *hospital* or other, English name of it all messed up. Not *muerto* yet, then. Enderby was horrified at feeling cheated. All this upset for just *en grave estado.* Still, that might be pretty bad. Then it said something about *Scotland Yard buscando* something something *un camarero.* He knew what that was: Spanish John had once or twice been hailed by that title facetiously by men and women who had been to the Costa del Sol. John had always responded readily, gleaming in complaisant dentition, all of gold. And now it was he, Enderby, who was the *camarero.* He was wanted, the paper said, to *ayudar* the *policía* in their *investigación.* Well, he'd already helped, hadn't he? He'd sent them the name of the true attempted *matador,* or whatever it was. And now the newspaper gave Enderby's own abandoned other name, or a version of it. *Hagg.* That was hardly fair to that barely imaginable sweet woman.

Un camarero quien se llama Hagg. He now felt somewhat better, the eggs settling down, the reality of the thing confirmed, no bad dream. So he went out now, nodding politely to various walnut-skinned early-morning coffee-suckers, and looked on the *calle* for a general outfitter's shop. The cathedral bell banged once at him, as to announce that the fight was on. So he went and bought himself a drip-dry green *camisa,* a pair of cheap grey *pantalones*, and a very light *americana* or jacket of fawn Moygashel. Also a tie or *corbata* of rather mouth-watering lime. He changed into these in a dark bread-crumby cubbyhole at the rear of the shop. He also bought a black Basque beret (ah, that took him back, back to the old gusty seaside days when he had fed the ungrateful gulls every perishing morning; happy days, before the horrible outside world's impinging, pressing, overpowering). Also a little overnight bag to put his Hogg clothes in. *Hagg*, indeed. He couldn't help laughing. Also a razor and blades. And a kind of superstructure of plain anti-sun lenses to clip on to his spectacles. Then he sat outside a café and drank Spanish gin and tonic while a shoeblack blacked his shoes. He counted what money he had left in sterling and pesetas. Not a lot, really, though the shoeblack seemed to think so: his hands performing busily away, he gave money-counting Enderby close attention, as if he were a conductor. And then Enderby saw her, Miss Boland, walking down the *calle* with arms full of little toys and dolls bought from street-vendors.

Of course, she had as much right to be here as he had, if not more. And so had various other members of the tour who were walking down this main street (the hotel just around the corner), probably newly released from breakfast. There was even Mr. Guthkelch over there on the pavement opposite, full of gummy fun though inaudible because of the traffic. Enderby stood up, one foot still on the cleaner's box, and shyly waved at her with both arms. She recognised him, despite his new smartness, and looked grim. She seemed fifteen years older than last night, also very thin, as though wasting away. Her summer dress was suitable for the warm southern autumn, but very dowdy—a blue flowery sack with a string defining her waist. Having given Enderby a filthy look, she was prepared to walk on, but Enderby cried:

"It was inspiration, that's what it was, inspiration. Can't you see that? That hadn't happened to me for years. And I came round to your room, but the door was locked, and I—"

"Don't shout," she hissed. "Don't shout at me. For that

matter, don't speak to me. Do you understand? I don't want to see you again. Ever. I want to make that clear, here and now. I don't know you and I don't want to know you." She prepared to move on. Enderby put pesetas on the table, leaving their apportionment to waiter and shoeblack, and then grabbed her arm. He said:

"I know precisely how you must feel." He found he had left his overnight bag on the table, so he went back to get it. "How you must feel," he panted, "but just think," panting to keep up with her long strides. "It was you who brought the gift back. You. The excitement. I didn't dare lose that poem. It meant so much. It was you. The poem was you." He marvelled at himself. "I knew you'd understand." She shook her body impatiently, as to shake him, Enderby, away, and a small clockwork goose, with articulated neck, fell from her arm to the pavement. Enderby picked it up and the beak came off. He panted worse than ever. He said: "In my bag. Put those things in my bag. See, I bought this bag this morning. I got up early and bought things, including this bag. But I'll take my things out, if you like, and you can use the bag for putting your things in."

She began to cry, still walking down the *calle*. A swarthy man saw her tears and looked with distaste on Enderby. "Oh, you're horrible," she said.

"I'll buy you another goose," promised Enderby. "Though it wasn't my fault it broke," he added, justly. "Look, give me those dolls and things and they can all go in my bag."

She wanted to dry her eyes but couldn't, her arms being full of toys. Who were they for? Perhaps a maternal lust had welled up in her suddenly, thought Enderby with fear. Perhaps she was looking ahead. Perhaps any man would do. He had read of such matters. She was buying playthings for children yet unborn. Enderby said eagerly:

"I wanted to read you the poem, but I couldn't get in." Then he saw that that particular poem, with its tabloid history, would not have done. He was slow in learning about women. Only a love poem could placate

311

her. Had he anything in stock? "See," he said, "look. There's a horse and carriage thing." A *coche* was creaking along, drawn by a glossy sugar-fed mare. "We'll go for a drive in that, and you can tell me how horrible I am."

"Oh, leave me alone, go away." But she wanted to wipe her cheeks. The coachman, a lined, knowing, very old man, had stopped in response to Enderby's eager look.

"Get in," Enderby said, pushing her. A small tin tortoise prepared to dive from her arm. Enderby saved it and made it nest in his bag, along with the goose. Life was terrible, really. "Go on, get in," he said, more roughly. And then: "I've told you I'm sorry. But you can't get in the way of a poem. Nobody can." So then, sniffing, she got in. "The way of a poem," Enderby said, "passes all human understanding." The cathedral bell clanged a sort of amen. And so they were trotted off gently, and she was able to dry her eyes.

"It could have waited," she said. She began to look plumper again; she was becoming near-mollified. They turned right down a narrow street of pleasant yellow houses with balconies, empty, at this hour, of coy serenaded señoritas.

"A kind of sprung rhythm," said Enderby. He now thanked God, or *Dios* as He was here, that some crude lines from an apprentice poem came wriggling back. "Listen." He gave her them in counterpoint to the jaunty bouncing crupper with its blue-ribboned tail:

"I sought scent, and found it in your hair;
Looked for light, and it lodged in your eyes;
So for sound: it held your breath dear;
And I met movement in your ways."

"I see what you mean." She was quick to forgive, a bit too quick. She was thinking of her holiday; Enderby was primarily for holiday use. And on holiday my dear I met this poet. Really? A poet, just imagine. "But even so."

"That time will come again, often." Oh no, it bloody well wouldn't. The ghost of Juan was in the sunlit streets, approving his proposed desertion. "Whereas the time for paying homage—to your beauty, that is—"

"Oh, you *are* a pig, aren't you?" She came up close to him. "A dirty pig, a *puerco puerco*. Piggy."

"Don't call me that."

"Hog, then. Hoggy." Enderby sweated. "Perhaps," she said, "we could get off soon and have a drink. I'm terribly thirsty."

"It's the crying that does it. A big thirst-maker is crying." He remembered his stepmother jeering at him when she'd clouted his earhole and made him howl: *Go on, cry more and you'll pee less.* "A loss of liquid, you see. It needs replacing."

Two

They had lunch at an open-air café place, and of course it had to be paella. She had read about this in some coloured supplement as being one of the glories of the Spanish cuisine, but Enderby considered that never in his life had he been served with anything so insolent. It was warm sticky rice pudding embedded with strips of latex and small gritty seashells. Before it they had cold tomato soup full of garlic. She giggled and said: "It's a good thing we're both having garlic." Enderby choked on that, but later he choked harder on both a seashell and her saying: "Oh, look, there's a little man selling newspapers. Do let's have a Spanish newspaper. I've got my little dictionary with me." He choked so frightfully at the vendor that the vendor went off.

"Has something gone the wrong way? Have a drink of your nice wine." It was *not* nice wine: it tasted of ink and alum and eels and catarrh. "Oh, I did so want a newspaper."

"Lies," snarled Enderby. "Spanish bloody lies. All propaganda and censorship. You're not to have one, do you hear?"

"Darling Hoggy. Quite the heavy husband, aren't you? Perhaps there was fault on both sides."

"What do you mean?"

"Your wife."

"Oh, her." He sourly tongued wine-lees from his palate. "She's got a lot to answer for. Plagiarism, apart from anything else." As soon as he got to Morocco he would get hold of that book. Some effete expatriate writer would probably have it.

"Plagiarism?"

"Oh, never mind." He had gone too far, or nearly had. "I don't want to talk about it."

"Perhaps she didn't like your poem-writing habits." Miss Boland had had too much of this adenoidal wine-substitute. Enderby scowled at her. "No poems tonight, hm?"

"That," said Enderby, with a kind of reproving leer, "I can promise."

"Oh, good heavens, look at the time. There won't be any tonight at all if we don't get back to the hotel. The coach leaves at one-thirty."

Enderby paid the bill, leaving no tip. It had been a horrible meal and it was a horrible place, full of eroded statues and stunted trees. She squeezed his arm, linking him, as he went to the pavement's edge to call at any vehicle that looked like a taxi. One taxi already had Miss Kelly and two uniformed men, pilot and co-pilot probably, in it. Miss Kelly clearly recognised Enderby but did not smile or wave. A damned silly girl. Enderby thought he would mention that business of the wrong room to Miss Boland, but then he decided not. The female temperament was a strange one.

At last a taxi took them to the Hotel Marruecos, where tour-members were already assembling at the entrance, luggage all about them. Miss Boland had to rush to her room to see about hers, not quite finished packing. Enderby saw another newspaper-seller hovering and gave him a five-peseta note to go away. Things would be all right, but for God's sake let things be hurried up. Mr Guthkelch had bought a pair of castanets and was fandangoing clumsily, clumsily clacking them. The man with the condoms in his luggage looked very tired, but his wife was erect, in rude health. Mr Mercer counted and re-counted and stopped counting when Miss Boland appeared, flushed and panting, a porter bearing her bags. And then the coach came and then they were off.

The airport was full of gloomy British travellers from Gibraltar, and they were being punished for that by being made to wait a long time for customs clearance. So, anyway, their courier whined to Mr Mercer, whom he seemed to know as an old pal in the game. And then Mr Mercer's lot marched across the tarmac and Miss Boland, God be praised, was a little sleepy after the wine. There was Miss Kelly waiting to welcome them all aboard again, but she had no welcome for Enderby. Mr Mercer came round with immigration forms, and they took off. It was a lovely golden Spanish afternoon.

Courteously, Enderby gave Miss Boland the window-seat he had had on the first leg of the journey. She slept. Enderby slept. Enderby was awakened. A uniformed man, pilot or co-pilot, was bending over him. He was a thick man, not old, jowled with good living, hangover-ishly bloodshot. "Is your name," he said, his rather hairy hand on Enderby's shoulder, "Enderby?"

Enderby could do no more than feebly nod. So, then, radio messages were crackling all over the world's air. Wapenshaw had talked, killing in childish spite his own handiwork.

"I'm the pilot of this aircraft. You'll appreciate I have certain responsibilities." O'Shaughnessy then, but it was not an Irish voice. Enderby said, voicelessly:

"I'll come quietly. But I didn't do it. I just took his gun without thinking."

"Well, perhaps it might be better if you *did* think a bit, man of your age. She's my responsibility as a member of my crew. I won't have passengers taking advantage."

"Oh, that. You mean that." Enderby's relief was vented in a cough of laughter.

"It may be just a bit of a holiday lark to you, but this is our work. This is what we do for a living. We take our work seriously, but you don't help much with that sort of liberty-taking."

"I took no liberty," Enderby said with heat. "I made a mistake. I went to the wrong room. The room I meant to go to was the room of this lady here." He jerked his eyes and thumb at Miss Boland and saw she was awake.

"Make a habit of going to ladies' rooms, do you? Well, if it was a mistake you took long enough apologising for your mistake. She said something about you spouting poetry about putting the devil in hell and whatnot. Now, I may be only an ignorant pilot, as you'd think me I suppose, but I've read that thing about putting the devil in hell. The Cameron it's called." There were many passengers straining to listen, but the engines were loud. But Captain O'Shaughnessy was becoming loud too.

"The Dee Cameron," said Enderby. "Look, she's been telling you lies."

"We've never had any complaints before about passengers' behaviour. I don't want to be nasty, but it's my duty as pilot of this aircraft to give you fair warning. Any more of this interfering with Miss Kelly and I must ask you to leave the tour. I'm sorry, but there it is."

"It's a tissue of lies," said flushed Enderby. "I demand an apology."

"There it is. I take full responsibility. So no more messing about. Is that clear?"

"I'll give you messing about," cried Enderby. "If I could get off now I would. But I'm getting off at Marrakesh anyway. It's an insult and an injustice, that's what it is." Captain O'Shaughnessy jerked a salute at Miss Boland and went back to his engines. "That's what one's up against all the time," said Enderby to Miss Boland. "It makes me sick."

"All the time," said Miss Boland. "It makes you sick."

"That's right. It was the wrong room, as I said."

"As you said. And now would you kindly sit somewhere else? Otherwise I shall scream. I shall scream and scream and scream. I shall scream and scream and scream and scream and scream."

"Don't do that," said Enderby, very concerned. "Darling," he added.

"How dare you. *How dare you!*" She pressed the little bell-push up above.

"What did you do that for?" asked Enderby.

"If you won't go you must be made to go. I'm defiled

just by sitting next to you." Miss Kelly, wisely, did not come to the summons. Mr Mercer came, sad and troubled in his woolly cap. "You," said Miss Boland. "Make this man sit somewhere else. I didn't come on this tour to be insulted."

"Look," said Mr Mercer to Enderby. "I didn't say anything about that other business. It's the captain's responsibility, not mine. But this sort of thing is something that I'm not supposed to let happen. I made a big mistake having you on this, I did that. Now will you be told?"

"If you won't do something," said Miss Boland, "I'll scream."

"Don't worry," said Enderby. "I'll go. I'll go into that lavatory there." He got up and took his bag and beret from the rack. There were toys still in the bag. Enderby gravely dropped them into Miss Boland's lap—tortoise, beakless goose, flamenco doll, cymbal-pawed clockwork brown bear. She at once became thin and evil and ready to throw these things at Enderby, crying:

"He's hateful. No woman is safe with him. Throw him out." Many of the passengers looked on with interest, though not well able to understand, or even hear, what was proceeding. Behind, the condom overweight man and his wife sat stiffly, still not on speaking terms. They refused to be interested in the Miss Boland-Enderby trouble, though it was just in front of them, since showing interest would have drawn them into a common area of attention, which would have been rather like, or indeed might have led to, being on speaking terms again. Enderby stood stony in the corridor, swaying with the plane in a slight air turbulence (the Mountains of the Moon perhaps, or something), waiting for instructions. To the condom man's wife, who was in the outer seat, Mr Mercer said:

"I wonder if you'd mind, Mrs er, changing places with this er. It's only for a short while, really. We're not all that far from Marrakesh now."

"Men on holiday. Brings the beast out as you might call it. *I know.* I have no objection if she there hasn't." And, getting up, she gave Enderby a murderous look

317

which he considered unfair, since he had, after all, been the instrument of disclosure of her husband's beastliness, meaning the truth. As she sat down grunting next to Miss Boland, Enderby saw that she had an English newspaper folded to what looked like a simple cross-word puzzle. She had a ballpoint, but she did not seem to have filled anything in yet. He leaned across her bosom to squint at the date and saw that, as far as he could judge, it was yesterday's. That was all right, then. Before that lot happened. And then he saw that it was the *Evening Standard* and it was not all right. He said to this woman, leaning over more deeply:

"Where did you get that? Give it me, quick. I must have it. Something I've got to see."

"Right," said Mr Mercer. "Go and sit down quietly behind next to this lady's husband. We don't want any more trouble, do we now?"

"Cheek," said the woman. "It was left in the ladies at the airport by one of them Gibraltar people. I've as much right to it as what he has."

"Oh, please go on now," said Mr Mercer in distress. "If you can't hold it you shouldn't take it. A lot of this foreign stuff's stronger than what many are used to."

"*She* may be drunk," said Enderby, shoulder-jerking towards Miss Boland, "but I'm not, thank you very much. All I want to see is that paper. Something in it. A book review, very important. And then I'll go to that lavatory and sit in there quietly." Seeing Miss Boland gasp in a lot of air to revile him further, he made a grab for the newspaper. The condom man's wife strengthened her hold.

"For God's sake," said Mr Mercer, uncourierlike, "let him see what he wants to see and then let's get him out of the way."

"I want to find it myself," said Enderby. "I don't need her to show it me."

"And who's *her* when she's at home?" said the woman. Miss Boland looked cunning and said:

"Let *me* see. There's something very fishy about all this. Running away from his wife, so he said."

"Really? Told you, did he?"

"Let *me* see." And Miss Boland, unhandily in the manner of all women with a newspaper, unfolded the *Evening Standard,* and the safe backwater of small ads and cartoons and crossword gave place, after a rustling tussle, to the horrid starkness of front page news. There it was, then. Enderby gulped it all in like ozone.

"Oh," said the woman, "I never seen that. Oh terrible, that, oh my word."

"Yes," said Miss Boland. "Terrible."

A screaming banner announced the shooting of Yod Crewsy. In hour of triumph. In Premier's presence. Waiter believed assailant. There was a large blurred photograph of Yod Crewsy with stretched gob or cake-hole, but whether shot or just singing was not indicated. There was also a still photograph of the Prime Minister looking aghast, probably taken from stock. No picture, thank God, of waiter believed assailant. But Miss Boland was reading avidly on. Enderby had to now or never. He leaned over the condom man's wife and grabbed. The paper did not tear: he got the thing whole. He said:

"Very important review. Book page, book page," rustling tremulously through. "Oh, stupid of me. Wrong day for book page." And then, as though an issue without the book page were an insult to the literate, he crumpled the *Evening Standard* into a ball.

"That's going too far," said Mr Mercer.

"You mannerless thing," said the woman. "And that poor lad dead, too."

"Not yet," said Enderby unwisely. "Not dead yet."

"Hogg." That was Miss Boland.

"Eh?" Enderby looked at her with bitter admiration. He had been right, then; he had known all along this would happen.

"Hogg. *Puerco.* That's why you're on the run."

"She's mad," Enderby told Mr Mercer. "I'm going to the lavatory." He began to unball the paper and smooth it out. She had seen the name Hogg; the only thing to do now was to insist that he was not Hogg. There was no point in hiding the fact that Hogg was wanted to assist in a police enquiry. If, that is, one were oneself not Hogg. And one was not, as one's passport clearly showed. Enderby nearly drew out his passport, but that would look too suspiciously eager to prove that he was not Hogg. A lot of people were not Hogg, and they did not have to keep presenting their passports to prove it.

"The police," said Miss Boland. "Send a radio message to the airport. He did it. That's why he's run away."

"I don't have to put up with all this, do I?" said Enderby with a fine show of weariness.

"He said all the time that he hated pop-singers."

"That's not true," said Enderby. "All I said was that you mustn't necessarily regard me as an enemy of pop-culture."

"Jealousy," said Miss Boland. "A bad poet jealous of a good one. And what was that you said just then about a gun? I'm quite sure I didn't dream it." She seemed very calm now, glinting, though breathing heavily.

"I'll give you bad poet," said Enderby, preparing to shout. "If there's any good in that book of his, it's because it's been pinched from me. That bitch. Plagiarism. I hope he dies, because he deserves to die."

"Look," said Mr Mercer, "we don't want any trouble, right? This is supposed to be for pleasure, this cruise is. Will you both stop shouting the odds? If there's anything to be seen to I'll see to it, right?"

"If you don't," said Miss Boland, "I will. I will in any case. He killed him, no doubt about it. He's as good as admitted it."

"Who's a bitch?" said the condom wife, belatedly. "Who was he saying was a bitch? Because if he was meaning me—"

"I'm going to the lavatory," said Enderby. Mr Mercer did not attempt to stop him; indeed, he followed him. The crumpled *Evening Standard* had somehow reached Miss Kelly. She was spelling all that front page out, reserving her reaction till she had taken everything in. Just by the lavatory door Mr Mercer said:

"What's going on with her down there? Is she potty or what?"

"A matter of sex," Enderby said. "I spurned her advances. I don't think it's decent the way she carries on, and me with my mother dying in Marrakesh."

"Look," said Mr Mercer without sympathy. "You shouldn't rightly be on this plane at all, as you well know, and I'm bloody sorry I let you come on it. It was a bit of a fiddle, and I think I've learned my lesson now about that sort of thing. Now she's going on about you being a dangerous criminal, which sounds to me like a load of balls. You've not been killing anybody, have you?"

"I have enough on my hands," said Enderby gravely, "with a dying mother."

"Right then. I'll get her calmed down and I'll tell her that I'm doing whatever has to be done. The police and that. The customers have got to be satisfied, that's laid down in the rules. Now it won't be long to Marrakesh now, so I'll tell you what I'll do with you. You nip off before everybody else, see, because I'll let you."

"Thanks very much," said Enderby.

"I'll keep them all back till you have time to get away. I don't want her on the job again, howling murder and upsetting the other mugs," said Mr Mercer frankly. "So you'll find three taxis laid on specially for the tour. They take one lot to the Hotel Maroc and then keep coming back for the rest. Well, you get into one and get the driver to drop you wherever it is you want to be dropped and then send him back to the airport, right? How far is it you have to go?"

"Near that place where Winston Churchill used to stay," said Enderby with sudden inspiration.

"Not too far then, that isn't. And then," said Mr Mercer, "that'll be the end as far as you and me and everybody else is concerned. Got that?"

"That suits me well enough," said Enderby.

"You'd better get in there, then. Look, she looks like getting up to start asking for immediate action. Summary execution and that. You thrown out into the bleeding slipstream. You sure you done nothing wrong?"

"Me," said Enderby, "with a dying mother?"

"You don't look the type, anyway. Get in there. If anybody else wants to go I'll have to tell them to let it bake till we get to Marrakesh. I wish," said Mr Mercer with large sincerity, "I'd never bloody well set eyes on

321

you." Enderby bowed his head. "Mysterious fascination for women, eh? Now get yourself locked in there."

It was better in the lavatory, an interim of most delectable peace and quiet. All Enderby could hear was the engines except for a brief phase of shock and howling from Miss Kelly. She was, it seemed, sorry that Yod Crewsy had been shot. Then she appeared to have got over it.

Three

Mint, mint, mint. It was too easy to think that, though the immigration official waved him through when he cried: *"Ma mère est mortellement malade,"* though the leading taxi opened up smartly for him when he mentioned *Monsieur Mercer*, he was destined for the butcher's block. The sun was about half way down the sky, but it was still up to Regulo Mark 4 and there was all this mint. The memory fumed in of his once trying out a small leg of fatty New Zealand in Mrs Meldrum's gas oven. It had emerged not well-cooked, and he had made a stew out of it. You could not really go wrong with a stew. There had been a lot of grease to skim off, though. The driver, a Moor as Enderby took him to be, was stewy in the armpits—no, more like a tin of Scotch Broth. But he was fumigating himself and his cab with a home-rolled cigarette that reeked of decent herbs, though possibly hallucinogenic. He also rolled his eyes. Soon, Enderby considered, the time must come for jettisoning his Enderby passport. Miss Boland would soon be uncovering aliases to the police. He could not be Hogg, he could not be Enderby. The nasty world outside had suceeded in taking pretty well everything away from him. Except his talent, except that.

A well-made road with trees, probably bougainvillea and eucalyptus and things. And plenty of mint. Also people in turbans, caftans, nightgowns with stripes, and what-you-call-them djebalas. The driver drove with the automatism of a pony pulling a trap, though much faster, his being not to reason why Enderby had to reach the tour hotel before everyone else. It was time to tell him some other place to go. Enderby said:

"*Je veux aller à Tanger.*"

"*Demain?*"

"*Maintenant.*"

"*Impossible.*"

"*Regardez*," Enderby said, "I'm not going to that bloody hotel. *Une femme. Une question d'une femme. Il faut que j'évite une certaine femme.*"

With care the driver steered his cab round the next corner and stopped by the kerb. His hand-brake ground painfully. "*Une femme?*" It was a pleasant little residential avenue full of mint. But down it a bare-legged man in Sancho Panza hat and loose brown clouts urged a laden donkey. "*Tu veux une femme?*"

"Just the opposite," said Enderby, frowning at the familiarity. "*J'essaie à éviter une femme, comme j'ai déjà dit.*"

"*Tu veux garçon?*"

"Let's get this straight," cried Enderby. "I want to get away. *Comment puis-je* get to bloody Tangier?"

The driver thought about that. "*Avion parti*," he said. "*Chemin de fer—*" He shrugged. Then he said, "You got money, Charlie?"

"I thought it would come to that," said Enderby. He brought out his small bundle of old international tips. What was the currency here? There were a couple of notes with a bland capped and robed ruler on them. *Banque du Maroc* and a lot of Arabic. What were these? Dirhams. He had, it seemed, ten dirhams. He didn't know how much they were worth. Still, resourceful Enderby. Ready cash for all emergencies of travel. The driver was quick to grab the ten dirhams. He pushed them, as if he were a woman, into his unbuttoned hair-whorled brown breast. Then he cheerfully started up his cab again. "Where are we going?" Enderby wanted to know. The driver didn't answer; he just drove.

Enderby was past being uneasy, though. After all, what was he trying to do except borrow time against the inevitable? If Yod Crewsy died, well then, he, his supposed murderer, could only be put in jail for a long period, the death penalty having kindly been abolished. And in jail poetry could be written. There would be ghastly stews, but he knew all about those. Great things had been written in jail—*Pilgrim's Progress, De Profundis,* even *Don Quixote.* Nothing to worry about there. Slops out. Here's your skilly, you horrible murderer, you. Snout-barons. What you in for, matey? I murdered a practitioner of foul and immoral art. You done a good job, then, you did. But, sheep for a lamb (all this mint, mint everywhere), he had things to do first. They had to catch him first, and it was up to him, rules of the game, to make things difficult. They drove down a great smooth highway, then turned right. It was all French colonialism, with decent official buildings, green lawns, palms. Little Moroccan girls were coming out of school, gaily shrieking, and some were sped off home to their mint tea, as Enderby supposed, in haughty squat automobiles. But soon the road changed its character. Instead of shooting cleanly along an artery, the cab began to engage a capillary that was pure, and dirty, Moorish.

"Where are we going?" asked Enderby again.

"*Djemaa el Fna,*" said the driver. This meant nothing to Enderby. They were now honking among fruit-barrows, donkey-whippers, brown and black vociferators in pointed hoods and barmcake turbans and even little woolly caps like Mr Mercer's. The faecal-coloured houses and windowless shops (loaves, strangled fowls, beads, eggplants) bowed in towards each other at the top. Somebody wailed about Allah in the near distance. It was what was known as very picturesque, all laid on for Winston Churchill as amateur painter. Then, shouted at through gold or no teeth, the cab-flanks resonantly fisted, they drove into a great square which was full of robed people and very loud. There seemed to be native shows going on: Enderby glimpsed a fire-swallower and a man who let snakes crawl all over his person. Then, above the heads of the crowd, a small black boy went up into the air, wiggled his fingers from his ears, then sailed down again. Enderby did not really like any of this. The driver stopped and, with a vulgar thumb, pointed to where Enderby should go. It seemed to be a

324

soft-drink stall, one of many set all about the square. He shooed Enderby out. Enderby got out, bag on arm, groaning. The driver did an urgent and insolent turn, butting bare shins with deformed fenders and, cursed at by some but greeted toothily and, Enderby presumed, with ribaldry by others, probed the crammed barefoot alley whence he had come. He honked slowly among thudded drums and weak pipe-skirls, fowl-squawks and ass-brays, then was smothered by night-shirts and most animated robes, pushing his way back to a world where an airport, complete with waiting Miss Boland, might be possible. Enderby encountered blind men howling for baksheesh. He brutally ignored them and made his shoes pick their way among great splay brown feet towards this soft-drink stall that had been thumbed at him. He would have a soft drink, anyway. No harm in that. And that climbed hill of an act would show the next one. But just by the stall, newly disclosed by a small mob that came away chewing things, probably nasty, he saw a patriarch tending a small fire. A little boy, his head shaven as for ringworm, was threading rubbery gobs of what Enderby took to be goat meat on to skewers. Enderby nodded in awed satisfaction. His imagination had not failed him, then. It was time to get rid of that passport.

He stood by the fire, the passport in his hands open, mumbling to himself the liturgy of its shards of autobiography. There were still so many blank pages of travelling Enderby to be filled, and they would not now be filled. He must appear, he thought, like some Zoroastrian missionary to these who skirted him warily in robes and yashmaks: murmuring a late afternoon office to the fire. And then, as he prepared to drop the well-bound document in, the act was, as by an Oriental miracle, arrested. A bony tanned wrist gripped his chubbier whiter one, pulled, saved. Enderby looked from wrist to shoulder, meekly surprised. Then up to face above that. A white man, though brown. Lined, crafty, the eyes blue but punished. The straight hair as though bleached.

"I was," said Enderby with care, "just getting rid of it. No further use, if you catch my meaning."

"You cracked? You skirted? You got the big drop on? Grandmother of Jesus, I never seen." The man was not old. His accent and vernacular were hard to place. It was a sort of British colonial English. One hand still gripped Enderby's wrist; the other hand snatched the passport. The man then let go of Enderby and began to pant over the passport as if it were a small erotic book. "Holy consecrated grandad of Christ Jesus Amen," he said. "And this is you too on it and the whole thing donk and not one little bit gritty. The genuine, and you ready to ash it up. If you don't want it, others as do. A right donk passy. Feel his uncle, O bastard daughters of Jerusalem."

Enderby almost smiled, then felt cunning creeping along his arteries. "I tried to sell it," he said. "But I could find no buyers. All I wanted was a trip to Tangier. No money, you see. Or not very much."

"You better come over," said the man. "Ariff's got a swizer of that-there at the back." And he led Enderby across to the very soft-drink stall that had been thumbed to him by that driver.

"Funny," Enderby said. "This man who brought me wanted me to wait there or something. I wondered what for."

"Who? One of the cab-nogs? Ahmed, was it?"

"Don't know his name," said Enderby. "But I told him I had to get away."

"You on the out, then? How did he know it was tonight? Some shitsack's been on the jabber." He mumbled strange oaths to himself as he led Enderby over. The drink-stall was a square wooden structure covered in striped canvas. There was a counter with cloudy glasses and bottles of highly coloured liquids. There were oil-lamps, blind at the moment, since the sun had not yet gone down. A few Moors or Berbers or something were downing some sticky yellow horror. Behind the counter stood a lithe brown man in an undervest, snakes of veins embossed on his arms. Crinkled hair rayed out, as in shock, all over his bullethead. "Right," said this British colonial man, "swing us two bulgies of arry-arry."

"Where do you come from?" asked Enderby. "I can't

quite place the accent. No offence," he added hurriedly.

"None took. Name of Easy Walker. Call me Easy. Your name I know but I won't blart it. Never know who's flapping. Well now, you'll have heard of West Rothgar in New Sunderland. Fifty or so miles from the capital, boojie little rathole. Had to blow, see the great wide open. And that. And other things." As if to symbolise the other things, he stretched his left mouth-corner, as also the left tendon of his neck, and held the pose tremulously. This, Enderby seemed to remember, was known as the ki-yike. Easy Walker then scratched his right ear with Enderby's passport and said: "You sound to me like from back." Enderby stared. Easy Walker snarled a full set in impatience. "Great Dirty Mum," he explained. "How shall we extol thee?"

"I beg your pardon?"

"Who were born of thee," danced Easy Walker. "Here it is, then. Down the upbum or," he said, in a finicking uncolonial accent, "the superior arsehole." There were on the counter two tumblers of what looked like oily water. Easy Walker seemed to wrap his lips round the glass-rim and, with a finger-thud on the glass-bottom, drive the substance down as though it were corned beef hard to prise from its container. He smacked in loving relish. Enderby tasted what tasted of aniseed, lubricator, meths and the medicinal root his stepmother called ikey-pikey. "Similar," Easy Walker told the barman. "And now," to Enderby, "what's on? Why you on the out, brad?"

"You can't really say 'similar' if it's the same again you want. 'Similar' means something different. Oh, as for that," Enderby recalled himself from pedantry that reminded him poignantly of those good seaside days among the decrepit, "it's partly a matter of a woman."

"Ark." Easy Walker was not impressed.

"And," Enderby bid further, "the police are after me for suspected murder of a pop-star."

"You do it?"

"Well," said Enderby, "I had the means and the motive. But I want to get to Tangier to see off an old enemy. Time is of the essence."

This seemed reasonable to Easy Walker. He said: "See

that. Right right. Gobblers watching at the airport and on the shemmy. Clever bastard that cab-nog, then. Ahmed, must have been. Well," he said, fanning Enderby with Enderby's passport, "give me this and you can come on the lemon-pip by the long road. Fix you up in Tangey up the hill. No questions, get it? The gobblers leave it strictly on the old antonio. Wash me ends, though. Right up to you, brad. Never clapped mincers on you, get it?"

"Oh, yes," Enderby said. "Thank you very much. But," he added, "what are you on then, eh?"

"Well," said Easy Walker, rolling his refilled tumbler. "It's mostly Yank camps, junkies, had-no-lucks. See what I mean?"

"American troops in Morocco?" Enderby asked.

"Riddled," said Easy Walker. "All off the main, though. Forts, you could call them. Very hush. Moscow gold in Nigeria I mean Algeria. PX stuff—fridges mainly—for Casablanca and Tangey. That's why I've got this three-ton."

"A lorry? Where?"

"Up the road. Never you mind."

"But," said Enderby with care, "what are you doing here, then?"

"Well, that's the real soft centre," Easy Walker said. "See these niggers here? Not the Marockers, more brown they are than the others, the others being from more like *real* blackland."

"The heart of darkness," said Enderby.

"Call it what you like, brad. Berbers or Barbars. Barbar black shit, but no offence is what I tell them. They bring the stuff up with them for this here racketytoo."

"What stuff? What is all this, anyway?"

"Everything," said Easy Walker, with sudden lucidity, "the heart of darkness could desire. Tales of Ali Baba and Sinbad the whatnot, and snake-charmers and all. Suffering arsehole of J. Collins, the sprids they get up to in this lot. Hear them drums?"

"Go on," said Enderby.

Easy Walker did a mime of sucking in dangerous smoke and then staggered against the flimsy counter.

The barman was lighting the lamps. "Pounds and pounds of it, brad. I'm like telling you this because you won't gob. Daren't, more like, in your state of you-know-what. They grind up the seeds and nuts and it burns cold, real cold, like sucking ice-lollies. The Yank junks go bonko for it."

"Drug addicts," questioned Enderby, "in army camps?"

"Drag too," said Easy Walker calmly. "Human like you and I, aren't they? Loving Aunt Flo of our bleeding Saviour, ain't you seen the world? What you on normal, brad? What you do?"

"I," said Enderby, "am a poet. I am Enderby the poet."

"Poetry. You know the poetry of Arthur Sugden, called Ricker Sugden because he played on the old rickers?"

"I don't think so," said Enderby.

"I know him all off. You can have the whole sewn-up boogong tonight on the road."

"Thank you very much," Enderby said. "What time do we start?"

"Moon-up. Crounch first. You crounch with me. Little stoshny I got up this street of a thousand arseholes. Up above Hassan the hundred delights. Know what those are? Glycerine like toffees with popseeds, stickjaw that'll stick to your jaw, shishcakes and marhum. And I mean a thousand arseholes. Not my creed. Yours?"

"I don't like anything any more," Enderby said. "I just want to get on with the job."

"Right, too. Ah, here comes the old jalooty." A sly black man came in. He grinned first then peered behind as though he feared he was being followed. He had a woolly cap on, a knee-length clout done up like a diaper, a stiff embroidered coat with food stains on it. He carried a grey darned gunnysack. Easy Walker tucked away Enderby's passport in the breast-pocket of his shirt, then from the back-pocket of his long but crease-less canvas trousers he pulled out a wallet. "This," he told Enderby, "is as it might be like my agent. Abu." The

black man responded to his name with a kind of saliva-
tion. "Mazooma for pozzy, as my dad used to say. Died
at Gallipoli, poor old reticule. It's my Aunt Polly as told
me he used to say that. Never clapped mincers on him
myself. Abu grabs what per cent he has a fishhook on.
Leave it to him." To this Abu Easy Walker told out what
appeared to Enderby to be no more than fifty dirhams.
Then he took the gunnysack and shushed Abu off like a
fly. "Now then," he said, his hand on Enderby's arm,
leading him out to the flared and oil-lamped sinister
gaiety of the evening, "time for the old couscous. You
like couscous?"

"Never had it," said Enderby.

"The best one of Ricker Sugden's," said Easy Walker,
as they walked among baskets and moonfruit in the reek
of lights, "is 'The Song of the Dunnygasper.' You not
know that one, brad?"

"What," asked Enderby, "is a dunnygasper?" A youngish woman raised her yashmak and spat a fair gob
among chicken-innards. Two children, one with no left
leg, punched each other bitterly.

"A dunnygasper is a bert that cleans out a dunny.
Now, the pongalorum of a dunny is that bad that you'd
lay out a yard in full view if you drew it in in the way of
normality. So he has to like under water hold his zook
shut then surface for a gasp. You see that then?" An old
man with a bashed-in turban tottered by, crying some
prayer to the enskied archangels of Islam. Easy Walker
started to recite:

"Gasping in the dunny in the dead of dark,
    I dream of my boola-bush, sunning in the south,
And the scriking of the ballbird and Mitcham's lark,
    And bags of the sugarwasp, sweet in my mouth."

"That's not bad," said Enderby. "Not much meaning,
though." Meaning? Too much meaning in your poetry,
Enderby. Arch-devil of the maceration of good art for
pop-art. Kill, kill, kill. He could be calm at soul, whatever
justice said.

"For here in the city is the dalth of coves,
      Their stuff and their slart and the fell of sin,
The beerlout's spew where the nightmort roves
      And the festered craw of the filth within."

A moustached man, the veins of his head visible under a dark nap, called hoarsely at Enderby and, with flapping hands, showed small boys in little shirts lined up behind the lamp in his shop-front. A woman squatted on a step and scooped with a wooden spatula the scum from a seething pot on a pungent wood-fire.

"That drink," belched Enderby, "whatever it was, was not a good idea."

"Feel like a sack of tabbies when you've gooled up a pompey of couscous."

Graaarch, went Enderby. Perfwhitt.

"God's own grass for this porrow in my pail,
      Surrawa's lake for this puke and niff,
Prettytit's chirp for the plonky's nipper's wail,
      And the rawgreen growler under Bellamy's Cliff."

"Rawcliffe," growled green Enderby. "It won't (errrrgh) be long now."

Easy Walker stopped in his tracks. A beggar clawed at him and he cleaned the beggar off his shirt like tobacco ash. "You say Rawcliffe, brad? Rawcliffe the jarvey you bid to chop?"

"Plagiarist, traitor (orrrph), enemy."

"Runs a little beacho. Called the Acantilado something-or-the-next thing. Not far from the Rif. Not there now, though. Very crookidy. Quacks pawing him all over on the Rock."

"In Gibraltar? Rawcliffe? Ill?"

"Crookidy dook. He'll be back, though. Says if he's going to snuff he'll snuff in his own dung."

"Rawcliffe," said Enderby, "is (orrrfff) for me."

"We're there," said Easy Walker. "Up that rickety ladder. Niff that juicy couscous. Yummiyum. Then we hit it. Moon's up, shufti." Enderby saw it with bitterness. Miss Boland seemed to rage down from it.

"This jarvey Rawcliffe," said Easy Walker, leading the way up the ladder, "is some kind of a big jarvey. Big in films and that. You sure you know what you're on, brad?"

"I (arrrrp) know," said Enderby, following him up. A fresh beggar, wall-eyed, embraced his left leg passionately, shrieking for alms. Enderby kicked him off.

II

1

One

ALI FATHI sat on the other bed and pared his foot-soles with a table-knife honed to lethal sharpness on the window-sill. He was on the run from Alexandria, which he called Iskindiriyya, and was scornful of the Moors, whose language he considered debased. He himself spoke a sort of radio announcer's Arabic, full of assertive fishbone-in-the-throat noises and glottal checks that sounded like a disease. He was very thin, seemed to grow more and more teeth as time went on, and was always talking about food. "*Beed madruub,*" he said to Enderby now. He had a passion for eggs. "*Beeda masluugha.*" Enderby said, from his own bed:

"*Mumtaaz.*" He was learning, though not very quickly. It was hardly worth while to learn anything new. Soon, he saw, he must give up giving money to Wahab to buy the English newspapers that were sold on the Boulevard Pasteur. They were a terrible price, and money was fast running out. When the hell was Rawcliffe going to come back to be killed? He read once more the latest Yod Crewsy news. It could not be long now, they reckoned. Yod Crewsy was in a coma. Day and night vigils of

335

weeping fans outside the hospital. Stones hurled at windows of No. 10 Downing Street. Probability of National Day of Prayer. Mass of Intercession at Westminster Cathedral. In Trafalgar Square protest songs, some of them concerned with the Vietnam war. Attempted suttee of desperate girls in a Comprehensive School.

"*Khanzür.*" That was not right, Ali Fathi being a Muslim, but Enderby himself would not have minded a nice plate of crisply grilled ham. His diet, and that of Ali Fathi and the other two men, Wahab and Souris, was very monotonous: soup of kitchen scraps and rice, boiled up by fat Napo in the snack-bar below, the odd platter of fried sardines, bread of the day before yesterday. Enderby was now sorry that he had exchanged his passport for a mere jolting trip from Marrakesh to Tangier. He had discovered that British passports fetched a very high price on the international market. Why, this Ali Fathi here had looked at Enderby as if he were mad when he had been told, in French, what small and uncomfortable (as well as to him hazardous) service in lieu of money Enderby had been willing to take in exchange for a valuable document. If he, Ali Fathi, had it he would not be here now. He would be in Marseilles, pretending to be an Arabic-speaking Englishman.

"*Beed maghli.*" He was back on eggs again. Well, that valuable document, with its old identity razor-bladed and bleached out and new substituted, was now at its charitable work in the world of crime and shadiness. It was saving somebody from what was called justice. It could not, nor could its former guardian (Her Majesty's Government being the avowed owner, though it had not paid for it) ask better than that. Enderby nodded several times. Encouraged, Ali Fathi said:

"*Bataatis mahammara.*" That meant, Enderby knew now, potato crisps. An inept term, soggy-sounding. It had been, Enderby admitted to himself, a boring trip on the move under the moon (courtesy of Miss treacherous bloody Boland), with Easy Walker reciting the collected works of Arthur Sugden, called Ricker Sugden because he had used, when composing his verses, to clash out the rhythm with the castanetting bones once a percussive

336

staple of nigger, christy rather, minstrel shows. Easy Walker had given Enderby not only a reprise of "The Song of the Dunnygasper" but also "The Ballad of Red Mick the Prancerprigger," "The Shotgun Wedding of Tom Dodge," "Willie Maugham's Visit to Port Butters," "My Pipe and Snout and Teasycan," and other specimens of the demotic literature of an apparently vigorous but certainly obscure British settlement.

"*Kurumba.*" Some vegetable or other, that. Cabbage, probably. And then these American camps, off the main north-south motor route, with torches flashing through the Moorish dark, a rustling in the shadows and whispers as of love (money and goods changing hands), the loading—Enderby cajoled to help—of refrigerators, huge cans of butter, nitrited meatloaf, even military uniforms, all on to Easy Walker's truck. And then more of Ricker Sugden—"The Ditty of the Merry Poddyman," "Wallop for Me Tomorrow Boys," "Ma Willis's Knocking Shop (Knock Twice and Wink for Alice)"—till the next call and, finally, what Easy Walker knew as Dear Old Tangey. Well, Easy Walker had at least found him what seemed a safe enough retreat off the Rue El Greco (many of the streets here were named for the great dead, as though Tangier were a figure of heaven)—no passports needed, no questions asked of guests or tolerated of casual visitors to bar below or brothel above, but, on the other hand, too much cash demanded in advance, too little to eat, the bedclothes never changed, not enough beds.

"*Shurbit tamaatim,*" watered Ali Fathi, still slicing thin shives, as of restaurant smoked salmon, from a foot-sole. At once, as though he had spoken of the source of gingili or benne oil, the door-handle began to turn. He poised that knife at the ready. The door opened and Wahab came in. Smiling teeth popped and rattled as the two men embraced, full of loud throaty crooning greeting, yum yum yum and the voiced clearing of phlegm from pharyngeal tracts. Enderby looked with distaste on this, not caring much for sex of any kind these days really, for himself or for anybody else. Ali Fathi hugged his friend, knife still clutched in a hand that knuckled his friend's vertebrae, all his teeth displayed in glee to Enderby. Enderby said coldly:

"Le patron de l'Acantilado Verde, est-il revenu?"

"Pas encore," said Wahab's back. Wahab was a Moor, hence his mind was despised by Ali Fathi, but his body was apparently loved. He had fled from trouble in Tetuan and was lying low till things cooled. He spent much of the day trying to steal things. Now, as evening prepared to thud in, tally-hoed on by the punctual muezzin, he grinningly pushed Ali Fathi temporarily away, then took off his long striped nightshirt with hood attached. He was dressed underneath in blue jeans and khaki (probably American army) shirt. He has a marsupial bag knotted round his waist, and from this he produced his spoils, neither choice nor lavish, holding them up for Ali Fathi to admire. He was not a very good thief; it was evident that he was not on the run for thievery; perhaps he had merely spat on the King's picture. On the bed he placed, with a smile that was meant to be modest, a couple of gritty cakes of the kind dumped with the coffee on outside café tables, also a single Seville. Then he produced a small round tin labelled in English. Enderby could read that it was tan boot-polish, but Ali Fathi seized it with a kind of gastronome's croon, probably believing it to be a rare (hence the exiguity of the tinned portion) pâté.

"Pour les bottines," said Enderby helpfully. *"Ou pour les souliers. Pas pour manger, vous comprenez."* Soon Ali Fathi and Wahab saw that this was so, and then they started a kind of married wrangle. Enderby sighed. He hated these public homosexual carryings-on. Shortly Ali Fathi would have Wahab down on the bed, and they would perhaps indulge in the erotic refinement they called *soixante-neuf*, which reminded Enderby of the Pisces sign on newspaper horoscope pages. Or else there would be plain howling sodomy. And to them Enderby was only a piece of insentient furniture—the only piece indeed, save for the two beds, in the whole room. Soursi, the other man, would not come in till very much later, often when Ali Fathi and Wahab were already in bed, and then what took place took place, mercifully, in the

dark. The bed was not big enough for three of them, so there was a lot of crying and writhing on the floor and, if a synchronised triple crisis was reached, which happened occasionally, the window rattled and the beds, one of them with tired but sleep-deprived Enderby in it, shook from the legs up. Souris was not a murine man. He was very gross and he sweated what looked like crude oil. He had hurt somebody very badly on the outskirts of Casablanca—a totally unwilled act, he swore frequently, an ineluctable side-issue of a process designed mainly for pleasure. When the three of them had completed their Laocoon performance, they would sometimes (Enderby had seen this in the moonlight, Miss Boland also grimly seeming to look down from the moon) shake hands, though not heartily: it was like the end of a round in a wrestling bout, which in a sense it was, though three were involved and there was no purse. Once or twice, Souris had then tried to get into bed with Enderby, but Enderby would have none of that. So Wahab, the youngest, was often made to sleep in his robe on the floor, as though it were the desert. He would sometimes cry out in his uneasy sleep, seeming to roar like a camel. This was no life for anyone.

"*Moi*," said Enderby, pocketing the tan boot-polish, "*j'essayerai à le vendre ou, au moins, à l'échanger pour quelquechose de comestible.*"

"*Tu sors?*" said Ali Fathi, who already had Wahab round the neck.

Enderby did not like this familiarity. He nodded frowning. Yes, he was going out. The time had come to find out what was going on with respect to himself as regards the impending death of Yod Crewsy. For nobody back there in Scotland Yard seemed to be doing anything. There was the usual odd statement about investigations still proceeding, but most of the newspaper concentration now seemed to be on Yod Crewsy as a dying god, not one of the daily victims of common murderous assault. The butcher had become somehow shadowy and august, a predestined and impersonal agent of the dark forces, proud and silent in a Frazerian grove. But the police back there in England were brought up on Moriarty, not Frazer, and Enderby felt sure they were slyly about something. They might be grilling Jed Foot in under-river cellars. Or they might be here, raincoated, holding on to their hats in the Tangerine sea-wind. It was time to go to this Fat White Doggy Wog Place and see if John the Spaniard had sent a letter to Enderby through his brother Billy Gomez, if Enderby had remembered the name right.

There were two other bedrooms on this floor, and these comprised the brothel part of the establishment, though, on busy nights, cubicles in the bar below were curtained off for the more urgent and perfunctory clients, and fat Napo's kitchen had once or twice been used, since it had a stout table for table-corner specialists. The room that Enderby shared with Ali Fathi, Wahab, and Souris had not, so far as Enderby knew, ever been desecrated by acts of a heterosexual nature, but it was understood that, normally in the late morning, an occasional sharp act of commercial pederasty might be consummated there, Enderby and Ali Fathi (who were not supposed to leave the premises, Napo apparently not trusting them not to be caught) going into the backyard with the scrawny hens, there to smoke a soothing marijuana fag or two, given to them by Napo as a little reward for temporarily and gratuitously leasing lodgings for which they had paid in advance.

Out now on the landing, which had a naked light-bulb and a portrait of the King of Morocco, Enderby saw disgustedly that one of these other bedrooms had its door open. A couple of laughing male friends, both of a Mediterranean complexion, were preparing to engage houris—whose giggles agitated their yashmaks—on adjacent beds. Enderby angrily slammed their door on them, then went down the carpetless stair grumbling to himself. A scratchy record of popular Egyptian music was playing in the bar—the same theme over and over again in unison on a large and wasted orchestra. Peering through a hole in the worn curtain of dirty Muslim pink, Enderby saw Napo behind his counter. A man grosser than Souris, he had modelled himself on the Winston Churchill he had once, he alleged, seen painting in

Marrakesh, but the baby-scowl sat obscenely on a face bred by centuries of Maghreb dishonesty. He was now arguing about the magical properties of certain numbers with a customer Enderby could not see: something to do with a lottery ticket.

Enderby went loudly to the lavatory by the kitchen, then tip-toed through the kitchen to the back door. It was a blue evening but rather gusty. In the little yard the hens had gone to roost in the branches of a stunted tree that Enderby could not identify. They laid on a quiet crooning protest chorus, all for Enderby, and their feathers ruffled minimally in the wind. Enderby frowned up at the moon, then climbed to the top of the low wall by means of an empty Coca-Cola crate and a couple of broken-brick toeholds. He dropped easily, though panting, over the other side. It was an alley he was in now, and this led to a street. The street went downhill and led to other streets. If you kept going down all the time you eventually came to the Avenue d'Espagne, which looked at the plage. That dog place was down there, not far from the Hotel Rif.

It was very steep and not very well lighted. Enderby teetered past a crumbling theatre called the Miguel de Cervantes then, finding that the next turning seemed to take him some way uphill again, tried a dark and leafy passage which went unequivocally down. Here a little Moorish girl cried when she saw him, and a number of house-dogs started to bark. But he went gamely on, supporting himself by grasping at broken fences. Precipitous: that was the word. At last he emerged from the barking dark, finding himself on a street where a knot of Moorish boys in smart suits called to him:

"You want boy, Charlie?"

"You very hot want nice beer."

"For cough," said Enderby, in no mood for foreign nonsense, and a boy riposted with:

"You fuck off too, English fuckpig." Enderby didn't like that. He knew that this place had once belonged to the English, part of Charles II's Portuguese queen's dowry. It was not right that he should be addressed like that. But another boy cried:

"You fucking German. Kaput heilhitler." And another: "Fucking Yankee motherfucker. You stick chewing-gum up fucking ass." That showed a certain ingenuity of invective. They were very rude boys, but their apparently indifferent despication of foreigners was perhaps a healthy sign, stirring in sympathy a limp G-string in his own nature. He nodded at them and, more kindly, said once more:

"For cough." They seemed to recognise his change of tone, for they merely pronged two fingers each in his direction, one or two of them emitting a lip-fart. Then they started to playfight, yelping, among themselves. Enderby continued his descent, coming soon to a hotel-and-bar on his left called *Al-Djenina*. The forecourt had bird cages in it, the birds all tucked up for the night and Enderby could distinctly see, through the long bar-window, middle-aged men drunk and embracing each other. Those would, he thought, be expatriate writers. He was, of course, one of those himself now, but he was indifferent to the duties and pleasures of sodality. He was on his own, waiting. He had written, though. He was working on things. The wind from the sea upheld him as he tottered to level ground. Here it was then: the Avenue d'Espagne, as they called it.

He turned left. A fezzed man outside a shop hailed him, showing rugs and saddles and firearms. Enderby gravely shook his head, saying truthfully: "*No tengo bastante dinero, hombre.*" He was becoming quite the linguist. A gormless-looking boy, thin and exhibiting diastemata in the shop-front lights, offered him English newspapers. This was different. Enderby drew out dirhams. He tried to control his heavy breathing as he looked for news. The wind breathed more heavily, seeming to leap on the paper from all four quarters, as though it was all the news Enderby could possibly want. Enderby took his paper into the doorway of the rug-and-saddle shop. The fezzed man said:

"You man like good gun. I see." That was not a discreet thing to say, and Enderby looked sharply at him. "Bang bang bang," added the man, indicating his rusty Rif arsenal of Crimean rifles and stage-highwayman

pistols. Enderby read. *All Hope Abandoned*, a headline
said Dantesquely. The end was very near now a few days
off at most. He was in a coma. Where the hell then,
Enderby wondered, had that bullet struck him? Police
would be treating case as murder, the paper said. Re-
doubling efforts, acting on valuable information, Interpol
on job, arrest expected very soon. The wind pushed,
with a sudden whoosh, those words into Enderby's open
mouth. Enderby pushed back and then looked at the
date of the newspaper. Yesterday's. He might be dead
already, his gob, money-coining but not golden, shut for
ever. The shopkeeper now showed a real golden mouth,
like Spanish John's (and, there again, how far was *he* to
be trusted?) as he softly placed, on the newsprint Enderby held tautly at chin-level like a communion cloth, a
specimen pistol for his inspection and admiration. Enderby started and let it drop in the doorway. One of its
fittings clattered free and the shopman got ready to
revile Enderby. "*No quiero*," Enderby said. "I said that
before, bloody fool as you are." And then he entered the
wind, looking troubled at flickering lights on head-
lands. He didn't need his newspaper any more, so he
threw it into the wind's bosom. The wind, like a woman,
was clumsy with it.

The sea. *La belle mer*. Why had he never realised
that that was the same as *la belle-mère*, which—with
some kind of French irony—had been forced into meaning "Stepmother"? Well, he had come back to her for a
brief time, belching and grousing over there, brewing
strong green tea all day long, groaning in her bed at
night. She had seen him taken off by a woman, and soon
it would be by the police. Which was Rawcliffe's place?
Street-lamps showed the Sun Trap, with a kosher in-
scription, and the Well Come. They were in the dark;
people moved inland with the night, to fat belly-dancers
and bottles of alum Valpierre. There it was: *El Acantilado Verde*, a tatty yellowish place. Rawcliffe had had,
apparently, several little Tangerine bars and tea-shops.
This would be his last.

Enderby mastered his breathing before entering the
bar-restaurant that had a shagged dog sign swinging,

with its lamp of low wattage, in the paper-ravaging wind. The crossword, pathetically unsolved, rode and span briefly on the air at Enderby's eye-level as he made for the closed door. There were deserted metal tables with chairs on top of them stretching along the pavement. From within came piano music. He pushed the door open.

The piano was an upright, in tone tinny, scarred in appearance, on a platform made of old beer-crates, and the man who played seemed to be a North European. He played slow jazz with sad authority, sadly chewing his lips. He had suffered, his blank face said, but had now passed beyond suffering. An American, Enderby decided. All Americans, he thought, looking shyly round: it was to do with sitting postures of insolent relaxedness. There was an herbal smell on the air, an autumn smell. *Herbst* was the German for autumn, was it not? A poem, like the transient randiness felt when coming upon a gratuitous near-nude set in the pages of a magazine article one finds absorbing, twitched. These Americans would call it the fall. A fall of herbs, of grace, herb of grace. No, there were other things to think of and do, and he already had a poem on the forge. Still, he sniffed. Drugs, he tingled; something stronger than that harmless marijuana (Mary Jane, that meant: a mere kitchenmaid of narcotics) he had been given to smoke. A very thin young man in dark glasses mouthed and mouthed in a trance. A white-haired cropped man, also young, sat reading a thin, or slim, volume. "Shit," he kept judging. Nobody took any notice; nobody took any notice of Enderby. There was a man in the corner in a skin-tight costume as for ballet practice writing words shakily on a blackboard. *Braingoose*, he wrote, and, under it, *Rape of Lesion*. Enderby nodded with tiny approval. Literary exiles of a different sort. Which reminded him: that bloody book of that dying yob; here might they know? "Shit," said the white-haired man, turning a page, then laughed.

There seemed to be no waiter about. There was a wooden bar in the distant corner, its lower paint ruined by feet, and three bar-stools were empty before it. To

344

get to it Enderby had to get past a dangerous-looking literary man who had arranged three tables about himself like an ambo. He had shears with which he seemed to be busy cutting strips out of newspaper-sheets, and he looked frowning at Enderby while he pasted some of these, apparently at random, on a pawed and sticky piece of foolscap. He looked like an undertaker, mortician rather; his suit was black and his spectacles had near-square black rims, like the frames of obituary notices in old volumes of *Punch*. Enderby approached diffidently, saying: "Pardon me—" (good American touch there) "—but can anybody?"

"If," said the man, "you mean aleatoric, that only applies to the muzz you embed the datum in." He sounded not unkind, but his voice was tired and lacked nuances totally.

"What I meant really was a drink, really." But Enderby didn't want to seem impolite; besides, this man seemed engaged on a kind of literature, correcting the sheet as he started to now with a felt-tipped inkpencil; he was a sort of fellow-writer. "But I think I see what you mean."

"There," said the man, and he mumbled what he had stuck and written down, something like: "Balance of slow masturbate payments enquiries in opal spunk shapes notice of that question green ass penetration phantoms adjourn." He shook his head. "Rhythm all balled up, I guess."

"I'm really looking," Enderby said, "for the waiter you have here. Gomez his name is, I believe." A man came out, somewhat dandyishly tripping, from behind a curtain of plastic strips in various primary colours. He had a greenish shirt glazed with never having been, for quite a time anyway, taken off, and thin bare legs that were peppered with tiny holes, as with woodworm. His face was worn to the bone and his hair was filthy and elflocked. To the scissored man he said:

"He reckons he's through on the hot line now."

"Any message?"

"Fly's writing it down. May I enquire whom you are?" he then said to Enderby.

"Something about Gomez, I guess," said the mortician.

"Later." The other dabbled his fingers in air as in water. "He's off till *un poco mas tarde*." The pianist was now working on some high-placed old-time discords, school of Scriabin. "Crazy," the dabbler said.

"I'll have a drink," said Enderby, "if I may."

"British," nodded the mortician. "Guessed so. God-damn town's lousy with British. Out here to write about tea with Miss Mitford, rose gardens in rectory closes, all that crap."

"Not me." Enderby made a noise which he at once realised was like what the cheaper novels called a gay laugh. He must be very ill-at-ease then. "I'll have a Bloody Mary, if you have it, that is." He clanked out a few dirhams. The tomato-juice would be nourishing; he needed nourishment.

"*Sangre de Maria*," shrugged the filthy-haired man, who seemed to own this place, going to behind the bar. Enderby went to climb a stool.

"Very baroque, that is," he pronounced. "They all call it that, I believe. They lack a knowledge of English history, naturally, the Spaniards, I mean, so they make a kind of Crashaw conceit out of it, though, of course, the Crashavian style derives, so they tell me, from Spanish models. Or that statue of St Teresa, I think it is, with the dart going through her. But this, of course, is the Virgin Mary, bleeding. A virgin, you see: blood. The same sort of thing, though. Professor Empson was very interested in that line of Crashaw—you know: "He'll have his teat ere long, a bloody one. The mother then must suck the son." Two lines, I mean. Baroque, anyway." All who were not in a drug-trance looked at Enderby. He wondered why his nerves babbled like that; he must be careful; he would start blurting everything out if he wasn't. "And your Gomez," he said, "is, I am credibly informed, something of an expert on Spanish poetry."

"Gomez," said the mortician, "is an expert only on the involutions of his own rectum."

The man with the blackboard shakily wrote *Comings in the skull*. The white-haired reader said, very seriously:

"Now, this, I reckon, is *not* shit. Listen." And he read out:

> "Society of solitary children—
> Stilyagi, provo, beat, mafada,
> Nadaista, energumeno, mod and rocker—
> Attend to the slovos of your psychedelic guides—
> Swamis, yogins and yoginis,
> Amerindian peyote chiefs, Zen roshis.
> Proclaim inner space, jolting the soft machine
> Out of its hypnosis conditioned by
> The revealed intention of the Senders—"

"But," said Enderby unwisely, dancing the bloody drink in his hand, smiling. "we don't have mods and rockers any more." He had read his *Daily Mirror,* after all, to some purpose. "That's the danger, you see, of trying to make poetry out of the ephemeral. If you'll forgive me, that sounded to me very old-fashioned. Of course, it isn't really clear whether it *is* actually poetry. Back to the old days," he smiled, "of *vers libre.* There were a lot of tricks played by people, you know. Seed catalogues set out in stanzas. Oh, a lot of the *soi-disant avant-garde* were taken in."

There were low growls of anger, including, it appeared, one from a man who was supposed to be in a trance. The white-haired reader seemed to calm himself through a technique of rhythmic shallow breathing. Then he said:

"All right, buster. Let's hear from you."

"How? Me? You mean—?" They were all waiting.

"You know the whole shitting works," went the mortician. "You've not quit talking since you came in. Who asked you to come in, anyway?"

"It's a bar, isn't it?" said Enderby. "Not private, I mean. Besides, there's this matter of Gomez."

"The hell with Gomez. Crap out with your own."

The atmosphere was hostile. The owner air-dabbled from behind the bar, sneering. The pianist was playing something deliberately silly in six-eight time. Enderby said:

347

"Well, I didn't really come prepared. But I'm working on something in the form of an Horatian ode. I've not got very far, only a couple of stanzas or so. I don't think you'd want to hear it." He felt doubt itching like piles. All that stuff about swamis and inner space. A sonnet, yet. Horatian ode, yet. He was not very modern, perhaps. A critic had once written: "Enderby's addiction to the sonnet-form proclaims that the 'thirties are his true home." He did not like the young very much and he did not want to take drugs. He was supposed to have killed a quintessential voice of the new age. But that voice had not been above garbling Enderby's own work and getting a fellowship of the Royal Society of Literature for it. Enderby now recited stoutly:

> "The urgent temper of the laws,
> That clips proliferation's claws,
>   Shines from the eye that sees
>   A growth is a disease.
>
> Only the infant will admire
> The vulgar opulence of fire
>   To tyrannise the dumb
>   Patient continuum
>
> And, while the buds burst, hug and hold
> A cancer that must be controlled
>   And moulded till it fit
>   These forms not made for it."

Out of a trance somebody farted. "That last couplet," Enderby said trembling, "needs a bit of a going over, I see that, but I think you'll get the general idea." In confusion he swigged his Bloody Mary and presented the flecked glass (splash of some small slaughtered animal on a windscreen) for another. When Enderby had been a boy he had gone to sleep on the upper deck of the last tram of the night and had wakened in the tramshed. Leaving in shame he had noticed uniformed men looking at him in the quiet wonder which was the proper tribute to an act of an imbecile. He seemed to be getting that same look now. He said: "I stand for form and denseness. The seventeenth-century tradition modified. When is this man Gomez coming in?" The mortician resumed snipping and gumming, shaking his head, grinning like a clown. The white-headed cropped man hid his own grin in a new slim volume. The entranced offered the loudest criticism, great lip-farts competing through inner space. "Well," said Enderby, growing angry, "what about that bloody act of plagiarism of bloody Yod Crewsy?"

A man came limping from behind the blackboard (which now had, very vulgar, *My cuntry is the yoniverse* scrawled on it) and said: "I'll tell you about that, friend." He was totally bald but luxuriantly bearded and spoke in an accent Enderby had hitherto associated with cowboy films on television. "That was pure camp. Is, I guess. A new frame of awareness. It's not the poems as such so much as how he looks at them. Like you get these good pictures with shitty Victoriana in them, a frame inside a frame. Man, it's called the Process."

"I'd very much like to see—" Enderby's nausea was complicated. And if that sonnet-draft was in there, the Satan one. And, whether it was there or not, could he control himself, handling richly rewarded flagrant sneering theft?

"You can learn any place," said the bald bearded man. "You'll find it in the john library." He pointed beyond the curtain of many-coloured plastic strips with a finger that seemed half-eaten, a kindly man really. "And as for plagiarism, everything belongs to everybody. Man, that's called the Lesson." He returned to behind the blackboard, limping. On the blackboard was now written *Vinegar strokes through magnified sebacities.* Enderby went, his heart fainting, towards the john. There was a dark passage, sibilant with the wind, and crunchy rubbish underfoot. In a kind of alcove a man lay on a camp-bed under a dull bulb, another man beside him with a notebook. The supine man, on a drugged trip, sent reports up from the unconscious. Down there ghostly scissors were at work on newspapers out of eternity. It was a lot of nonsense.

349

The lavatory was small and dirty, but there was a red light of the kind used in electric log-fires. There were a lot of books, many of them eaten by mould. Enderby sat heavily on the hollow seat and disturbed the books with a paddling right hand, panting. That sinful volume was not too far from the top. The title was *Fixes;* there was a bold leering protrait of the pseudo-author. The sixteenth impression, Enderby noted with gloom. He noted too that many of the poems were not his own; it was a case of multiple theft, perhaps, unless bloody Vesta or that Wittgenstein man had written some of them. Enderby found six unpublished poems by himself and, a small mercy in a world of filth, not one of them was that sonnet. There was, as Miss Kelly had said, a poem entitled "Sonnet," but that had twelve bad unrhyming lines and might well be something that Yod Crewsy himself had composed at his secondary modern school. Enderby read it shuddering:

My mum plonks them on the table for Susie
    and Dad and I
Plonk plonk and dull clanks the sauce bottles
And Susie reads their names to herself
Her mouth is open but that is not for reading
    aloud
The fact is that her nose is stopped up like
    those sauce bottles are
Like OK and HP and Al and FU and CK and O
I mean oh red red tomato
And I dream while the frying goes on and Dad
    has his mouth open too at the TV
How I would like catsup or ketchup splattering
All over the walls and it would be shaken from
    these open mouths
And hers in the kitchen all her open mouths
And it would be red enough but not taste of
    tomato

"God," said Enderby to his shrinking bowels. "God God God." So they had come to this, had they? And his own finely wrought little pieces desecrated by contact.

He dropped the book on the floor; it remained open, but a sharp draught from under the far from snugly fitting door pushed at the erect fan of its middle pages and disclosed a brief poem that Enderby, squinting in the dim red light, seemed thumped on the back into looking at. Something or somebody thumped him: an admonitory goblin that perhaps lived wetly in the lavatory cistern. He had not noticed this poem before, but, by God, he knew the poem. He felt a terrible excitement mounting. He grabbed the book with both hands.

Then the door opened. Enderby looked, expecting to see the wind, but it was a man. Excited though he was, he began to deliver a standard protest against invasion of privacy. The man waved it away and said: "Gomez."

"The fact that the door isn't locked is neither here nor there. All right then, I've finished anyway." Something in the spread sound of his words seemed to tell him that he was smiling. He felt his mouth, surprised. It was the excitement, it was the first rehearsal of triumph. Because, by God, he had them now. By the short hairs, as they said. But was he sure, could he be sure? Yes, surely he was sure. Or was it just a memory of having foreseen it in print? He could check, he was bound to be able to check, even in this bloody heathen place. There might be some really cultivated man here among the expatriate scribblers.

"Gomez. Billy Gomez." He was a bit rodent-like and, so Enderby twitched at once, might be dangerous. But in what context? Gomez finned out his paws in a kind of cartoon-mouse self-depreciation. He had a dirty white barman's jacket on but no tie. He seemed also to be wearing tennis-shoes.

"Ah." That other structure of urgency was suddenly reilluminated. Heavy as an ivied tower, it crashed the blackness, decolated, to the sound of brass, like something in *son et lumière*. "*Sí,*" Enderby said. "*Su hermano*. In London, this is. *Mi amigo*. Or colleague, shall I say. Has he sent anything for me?" That sonnet by Wordsworth, on the sonnet. Key becomes lute becomes trumpet. This book he now thrust into his side-pocket.

Load of filthy treachery becomes, quite as improbably, sharp weapon of revenge.

"You come." He led Enderby out of the lavatory down a passage that took them to stacked crates of empties and then to a garlicky kind of still-room, brightly lighted with one bare bulb. Enderby now saw Gomez very clearly. He had red hair. Could he possibly be the true brother of swarthy John? Gomez was a Goth or perhaps even a Visigoth: they had had them in Spain quite a lot, finishing off the Iberian part of the Roman Empire: they had had a bishop who translated bits of the Bible, but that was much later: coarse people but very vigorous and with a language quite as complicated as Latin: they were perhaps not less trustworthy than, say, the Moors. Still, Enderby was determined to be very careful.

In this still-room a small brown boy in a striped night-shirt was cutting bread. Gomez cuffed him without malice, then he took a piece of this bread, went over to a stove maculate with burnt fat, sloshed the bread in a pan of what looked like sardine-oil, folded it into a sandwich and, drippingly, ate. He took in many aspects of Enderby with darting pale eyes. The boy, still cutting bread, as it were clicked his eyes into twin slots that held them blazing on to Enderby's left ear. Enderby, embarrassed, changed his position. The eyes stayed where they were. Drugs or something. Gomez said to Enderby:

"You say your name." Enderby told him what he had been called in his regenerate, barman's, capacity, but only in the Spanish version. Enderby said:

"He said he'd send a letter through you. *Una carta.* He promised. Have you got it?" Gomez nodded. "Well," said Enderby, "how about handing it over, then, eh? Very urgent information."

"Not here," dripmunched Gomez. "You say where you stay. I come with letter."

"Ah," Enderby said, with something like satisfaction. "I see your little game." He smiled, it seemed to him, and to his astonishment, brilliantly: it was that triumph pushing up. "Perhaps it would be more convenient if we could go to your place and pick up the letter there. It would be quicker, wouldn't it?"

Gomez, who had eaten all his oiled bread and licked some fingers, now took an onion from a small sack. He looked at the boy, who still cut bread but whose eyes had now clicked back down to the operation, and seemed to relent of cuffing him, however unmaliciously. He stroked the boy's griskin, grinning. Spanish poetry, thought Enderby. This man was supposed to know all about it. Was a knowledge of poetry, even a nominal one, a sort of visa for entry into the small world of Enderby-betrayal? Gomez topped and tailed the onion with his teeth (*tunthus*, Enderby suddenly remembered for some reason, was the Gothic for a tooth, but this man would know nothing of his ancestral language), then, having spat the tufts on to the floor, he tore off the onion's scarf-skin and some of the subcutaneous flesh and started to crunch what was pearlily revealed. There was a faint spray of zest. It smelt delicious, just as chunks of grilled human flesh might smell delicious. Enderby knew he had to get out. Fast. Gomez said:

"Tonight I work. You say where you live."

The boy left off bread-cutting (who the hell would want all that bread, anyway?) and ran the knife-blade across his brown thumb. Enderby said:

"It doesn't matter, after all. Thanks for your help. Or not help, as the case may be. *Muchas gracias*, anyway." And he got out of the room, clanking loose bottles on the floor of the dark corridor. Gomez called after him something ending with *hombre*. Enderby passed the man on the couch and in the next world and the amanuensis who sat by him. Then he breasted the plastic strips and blinked into the bar. There was a new man there, a Scot apparently, for he talked of "a wee bit fixie." The man at the blackboard had just finished writing *Hot kitchens of his ass*. Salami, Enderby thought in his confusion, salami was made of donkeys. The white-cropped man was reciting:

"Archangels blasting from inner space,
Pertofran, Tryptizol, Majeptil,
Parstelin and Librium.
And a serenace for all his tangled strings."

Romantic, thought Enderby distractedly, better than that other stuff. Remembering that he had stolen a book from their john, he clapped his hand to his pocket. A dithery young man in dark glasses recoiled, pushing out his palms against the expected gunshot. Enderby smiled at everybody, thinking that he had ample cause to smile, even when carted off. But not yet, not just yet. He yearned towards solitary confinement as to a lavatory, but duty, like an *engaged* sign, clicked its message. The mortician did not smile back. The dithering young man had recovered: all a joke, his manic leer seemed to say. Enderby held that book in, as if it might leap out. Out, out. Into the windy Moroccan night.

It was a slow and panting climb, and Enderby had to keep stopping suddenly, holding himself in shadow against whatever wall offered, listening and watching to find out if he was being followed. It was hard to tell. There were plenty of little Moorish boys about, any one of whom could be that bread-cutting lad, but none seemed furtive: indeed, one pissed frankly in the gutter (but that might be his cunning) and another hailed a smartly dressed elderly Moor who was going downhill, running after him then, crying unheeded certain complicated wrongs. Enderby passed dirty coffee-shops and then came to a hotly arguing group of what seemed beggars at a street corner. They had thin though strong bare legs under swaddling bands and ragged European jackets, and all were turbaned. Enderby stood with them a space, peering as best he could between their powerful gestures. Things seemed to be all right; there was nobody following; he had given that treacherous Gomez the slip. Two treacherous Gomezes. That bloody John in London was, after all, the rotten bastard Enderby had always known him to be. Enderby, filling his lungs first like a dog running to the door in order to bark, turned left for a steeper hill. Half way up was a very loud cinema with what he took from posters to be an Egyptian film showing (an insincerely smiling hero like Colonel Nasser). He felt somehow protected by all that row, which was mostly the audience. A tooth-picking dark-suited young man by the paydesk looked at

Enderby. The manager probably. *"Alors, Ça marche, hein?"* Enderby panted. If anybody asked that man if he had seen an Englishman going that way he would say no, only a Frenchman. Now he said nothing, merely looked, tooth-picked. Enderby climbed on.

When, dying and very wet, he came to the Rue El Greco, he realised he was not too sure what would be the right back wall. Fowls, stunted trees: they all probably had them round here. He should have chalked a sign: he was new to this business. He would have to risk going in the front way. After all, there would be a lot of customers at this hour and fat Napo would be too busy hitting the rotten ancient coffee-machine to notice. Enderby caught a sudden image of El Greco himself, transformed into his own Salvador, peering down in astigmatic woe at the deplorable street that bore his name. There were some very nasty-looking places called snack-bars, as well as upper windows from which small boys thrust their bottoms, either in invitation or contempt. You could also hear very raucous female laughter—wrong, wrong; should not Islam's daughters be demure?—from down dark passageways. An old man sat by deserted and boarded-up premises. Inside, Enderby saw with poetic insight, would be rats and the memories of foul practices, the last fleshly evidence of outrage being gnawed, gnawed; the man cried his wares of tiny toy camels with here and there a dromedary.

Enderby gave his sweated spectacles a good wipe with his tie before approaching *El Snack-Bar Albricias.* By conceiving an image of fat Napo waiting for him on the doorstep, as a tyrannical father his precocious debauched son, he was able to forestall any such reality. Indeed, scratched Cairo music was coming out very loud, but not so loud as the noise of customers. Enderby peered before entering and was satisfied to see Napo fighting the coffee-machine before a thick and applauding bar-audience. *"Pardon,"* said a bulky fezzed would-be entrant to Enderby, Enderby being in the way ."*Avec plaisir,"* Enderby said, and was happy to use this man as a shield for his own ingress. To be on the safe side, he tried to make himself look Moorish, flattening his feet,

imagining his nose bigger, widening his eyes behind
their glasses. There were girls, giggling, yashmaks up
like beavers, drinking the local bottled beer with real
Moorish men. Enderby tut-tutted like one in whom the
faith burned hot. Then he noticed something he had not
seen before—little verse couplets hanging on the wall
behind the bar. He had time to read one only before
going to the lavatory before going upstairs. It said:

> *Si bebes para olvidar,*
> *Paga antes de empezar.*

That, thought Enderby, meant that if you drank to
forget you'd better pay before you began. Drinking and
forgetting, that was. Enderby felt a bit cold. Verse and
treachery went together. He hadn't thought of it before,
but Napo had, in the nature of things, to be a traitor.
Fugitives had sooner or later to be kicked out from
upstairs; no criminal could afford to stay for ever; the
quickest way of getting rid of a guest who'd outstayed
his welcome was to—But no, no. There had to be someone you could trust. Wasn't Napo, especially when a
customer gave him a cigar, an admirer of Winston Churchill? But when you thought of political coat-turning and
the guns pointing the wrong way at Singapore and some
rumour of ultimate perfidy in the Straits of Gibraltar—
No, no, no. Napo was all right. Well in with the police,
too. Enderby felt colder.

Two

He came to full wakefulness in the middle of the night,
the Boland moon looking grimly in on him. He had gone
to sleep early, so that his eyes could avoid a very complicated and laborious (with hand-spitting beforehand)
bout of triple sodomy on the floor. He had had enough
sleep, then, but his room-mates were hard at it, snoring,
Wahab on his back, mouth open to the spiders, in his
robe on the bare boards. But what really seemed to have

jolted him awake was the Muse, pushing lines at him. It was a bit more of that Horatian Ode·

> And something something something can
> Take partners for a plonk pavane,
> The blinded giant's staff
> Tracing a seismograph.

Accompanying this was a burbling of unhappy tomato-juice, together with, in the throat, a metallic suspicion that it had not been all that fresh. And then. And then. The derision of that bloody merry crowd (ha) in that place at what had seemed to him, Enderby, and still seemed very respectable verses. Was it then possible that art that was good for one time was not good for another, the laughter justified, himself out of date? There was a Canadian professor who had once been in Piggy's Sty with fawning hosts, going on burringly about new modes of communication and how words were all finished or something and everybody was too much bemused by Gutenberg and not wide enough awake to the revolution in electronics, whatever that was. And there were also these people who, by taking drugs, were vouchsafed visions of the *noumenon*, and this made them scornful of art that used merely phenomenal subject matter. But what could you do about a noumenal medium, mused Enderby, putting his glasses on. The moon defined itself in sharper craters and ridges, as though the spectacles themselves were in the service of Miss bloody Boland. And, while bloody came into things, that Bloody Mary was dancing about very obscenely inside, and that vodka had probably not been vodka at all but something merely sold as vodka. Enderby winced on a sour vague image of the *noumenon* behind the label. Diluted surgical spirit, homemade potato-fire, meths. He had better get up and go to the lavatory.

He was fully dressed, except for his shoes, which he now painfully put on. It seemed to him to be cold tonight, and he shivered. He also, despite the shattering evidence that had been granted him this evening, felt depressed. Was anything he could now do as a poet of any value to the world or God the ultimate *noumenon?* Graaarp, answered his stomach, like some new mode of communication. Behind the door on a nail was hanging the hooded nightshirt garment, djebala or whatever they called it, that Souris, now snoring on top of Ali Fathi, wore when he essayed the streets. Enderby took it and wrapped it round himself, but he saw that his shivering came from the expense of body-fuel in the service of the visceral bubbling that oppressed him. He went downstairs to the lavatory, hearing nothing from either brothel-dormitory, calm of brerrrrgh mind all aaaaarfph passion gockle spent.

But from below he heard quiet but somehow urgent talking, and he saw that a dim lamp, apt for furtive colloquy, was on. He tiptoed down, suppressing his inner noises by some obscure action of the epiglottis and diaphragm. When he got to the bottom of the stairs, he saw, from shadow, that Napo was with a couple of men in the pretentious uniform of the local police. These men, lean, moustached, mafia-swarthy, crafty-eyed, were each taking from Napo a glass of something gold and viscid in the lamplight. Alcohol, against the tenets of the faith, they ought to be had up for that, police and upholders of Islamic law as they were supposed to be. Enderby, flat against his dark wall, listened, but the language was Moghrabi Arabic. It was a serious discourse, though, evidently, and Napo's part in it sounded a bit breathy, even whining. Enderby listened for certain illuminative international or crassly onomatopoeic words, but the only word that was made much of was something sounding like *khogh*. It was, as Enderby's viscera quietly attested, parroting and nipping him like a parrot, a very visceral sound. *Khogh*, the viscera went. And then, somewhat louder, *Genggergy*. Enderby suddenly saw, and then he panicked.

The police and Napo had heard. Enderby saw, in addition to who *Khogh* was, opened mouths and wide eyes turned on to his patch of dark. He thought he heard a safety-catch clicking off. His first instinct was to run to the lavatory, but they would, he knew, soon have that

door shot open. Still, his insides, like spoilt cats demanding milk as lava begins to engulf the town and the cats
with it, complained and switched on a kind of small
avant-garde chamber piece for muted brass. Enderby,
like, with that gown on his shoulders, a student late for a
lecture, ran through the kitchen, sufficiently lighted by
Miss bloody Boland, and out into the yard. The roosting
fowls crooned at him, and the stunted tree raised, like
some outworn Maeterlinck property, a gnarled fist. He
got over the wall with agility he marvelled at and then
panted a second or two in the alleyway. They were after
him all right, though they seemed first to be, from a
sudden meagre uprush of lunated feathers and a
squawked track of conventional gallinaceous protest,
abusing the fowls for letting him get away. Enderby ran
a yard or two downhill and tried a back door on the
opposite side of the alley. It was locked, so he padded,
in frightful borborygms and breathlessness, to the next.
This was open. He got in, finding himself alone with a
tethered white ruminating goat who surveyed Enderby
with no surprise, and closed the door, a very warped
one, gently. Very usefully, a dog next door made a deep
chest-bay once only, as though Enderby had entered a
frame or two of his dream, and this sparked off a small
violent yapper further up the hill and, further up again,
what, very improbable, could only be a pet hyena.
Towards these noises, Enderby could tell, four feet were
now, with a sketch of urgency, proceeding. The voice of
Napo, back at base, made a brief speech with elements
of controlled Churchillian outrage in it, then turned into
grumbling coughs going back to the kitchen. Good. This
would do very well.

Enderby was, in a sense, pleased that a new phase
was beginning, perhaps the last phase of the fugitive. It
was all a question now of how long Rawcliffe would be
in rendering himself available for death. And that was
absurd, when one came to think of it, he, Enderby,
killing Rawcliffe. But, if one accepted that killing was a
legitimate and sempiternal human activity, authorised
by the Bible, was there any better motive than Enderby's own? The State made no provisions for the punish-

ment of the perversion of art; indeed, it countenanced such perversion. God, whose name had so often been invoked in the name of bad art, was, at bottom, a Philistine. So it was up to him, Enderby, to strike a blow for art. Was he not perhaps by some considered to have done so already? The popular press might be against him, but surely some letters, suppressed by editors, must have been written on his behalf? There might even be a fund started by Earl Russell or somebody to provide cates and art for him in prison and set him up on his distant release. He was, he was convinced, not alone. His stomach felt easier.

Watched by the chewing goat, Enderby put the djebala or whatever it was on properly, so that, what with the hood, he became a kind of capuchin. He had slept in his teeth as usual, fearing their theft if he did not, but now he removed and stowed them. Remembering the tin of boot-polish in his pocket, he allowed his heart to leap in awe at the poetry which existence itself sometimes contrived: the fusion, or at least meaningful collocation, of disparates—as, for example, a tin of tan boot-polish and himself, Enderby. He removed his spectacles and bedded them with his teeth. Now he disposed his hood in the academic position, pushed up all available sleeves too near the elbow, got out the tin and his handkerchief, then began to dye himself, all that was likely to be visible, by dipping his handkerchief in the tin and thinly spreading the polish. He did not forget nape and ear-crevices. The smell of the stuff was not unpleasant—astringent, vaguely military. Why, there had been that man Lawrence, colonel and scholar, got up like this. He had been viciously debauched by Turks, but his country had honoured him. He too, like Enderby, had had to change his name. He had died in lowly circumstances, riding a motorcycle.

What, when he had finished, he now looked like there was no means of finding out. In the moonlight his hands seemed of a richer colour than nature herself might allow, a richness that suggested dye, or perhaps thinly spread tan boot-polish. Still, it would serve, sleeves well down, hood well over. The goat, with the blessed impartiality granted to animals, saw no difference between the two Enderbys. It took without gratitude the empty polish tin and began to crunch it up roundly, its goatee wagging. Enderby took his leave, Ali bin Enderbi or some such name.

Whither? The Boland moon, asked, would not answer. His true place was that Kasbah, high up at the end of the town, where beggars slept at night in the doorways of shark shops, all Rif rifles from the iron-founding Midlands. But it was necessary that he stay near Rawcliffe's beach-place, not to let his quarry slip out of his tan-polished hand. It was not windy now, but it was not warm. Autumnal Morocco. He could doze, all hunched up, in the shadow of the *Acantilado Verde*. In the morning he could drink coffee and eat a piece of bread (there was a dirham or so still in his pocket) and then, an eye open for Rawcliffe, get down to begging. There was a lot of begging here: no shame in it. There were a couple of rich hotels near the *Acantilado Verde*—the Rif and the Miramar: good begging pitches.

He padded gently down the hill-alley, silently rehearsing the Koranic name of God. Properly enunciated, it could serve for many things—disgust, gratitude, awe, admiration, pain. Enderby had heard the name several times a day in his hideout: he thought he could manage the gymnastics of its articulation. You had to try to swallow the tip of your tongue, growling, then pretend you had to give up the attempt because you had to expel a fragment of matter lodged in your glottis. Easy: *Allah*. He allahed quietly towards the sea under a frowning moon.

2

One

HEART. He let himself get upset about something. Blowing his top. Ranting and raving. Carrying too much weight, of course. That's what comes of building up rugger-muscle in youth."

"Where's he been sent?"

"That place of Otto Langsam's. Out in the wilds. Cut off from the great world. Not even a daily newspaper."

"They say he was going on about some piece of pottery. Abusive. Lines written in a public lavatory. Obviously needed a rest. Good job they got him in time."

"Oh, very good job. Look, *emshi emshi* or whatever the word is. All right, take this. Now bugger off and buy yourself a shave."

"*Allah.*"

President of the moon's waning, Enderby was not too cold at night. He slept uncertainly, however, in the lee provided by the suntrap arena of *El Acantilado Verde*, a sandyard for torso-bronzing with a couple of umbrella-topped tables. The seaward-looking gate was easily climbed over. Crouched in an angle, he would see at first light two walls made of bathers' changing-cubicles, a corner of the kitchen, the back door of the bar-restaurant. Mercifully, so far, there had been no night rain. Rawcliffe could bring the rain with him if he wished. Nobody seemed to be sleeping on the premises, and Enderby moved away at dawn. Dawn brought the diamond weather of a fine autumn. Skirring his fast-growing grey face-bristles with a tanned hand, Enderby would gum-suck his way to a small dirty shop off the esplanade, sticking out the other hand for alms. (*Allah*) if any untimely European were about, and then take breakfast of coffee-in-a-glass and a fatty Moorish pastry. He feigned mostly dumb, except for the holy name. A holy man perhaps, above dirt and toothlessness, once granted a vision of the ultimate garden (houris, nectar-sherbet, a crystal stream) and then struck speechless except for the author's signature.

Up the cobbled street tottered the saint-eyed don-keys, most cruelly panniered, driven by bare-legged Moors in clouts, ponchos, and immense straw sombreros. Biblical women with ancient hard eyes and no yashmaks carried hashish-dreaming fowls in upside-down bundles, scaly legs faggoted together. They climbed, in a whirl of wind-blown feathers, up to the dirty small hotels for long haggling on the pavement outside, then the leisurely *halal* slaughter, blood sluggishly rolling downhill, the chickens dying on a psychedelic vision. And just along there was that treacherous White Doggy Wog place. Were its denizens right? Was it right that art should mirror chaos? What kind of art would it be proper for him to produce in his coming cell?

His brain, aloof from his begging hand, worked away at one poem or another. Was it perhaps a kind of holiness that gathered the disparate arbitrarily together, assuming that God or Allah—at the bottom of the mind's well, a toad with truth's jewel in its brow—could take care of the unifying pattern, that it was blasphemy for the shaping human mind to impose one of its own? Shatter syntax also, and with it time and the relation-ships of space. That Canadian pundit had said some-thing about the planet itself, earth, becoming, as per-ceived by a new medium which would be no more than heightened consciousness, a kind of work of art, so that every aspect would be relevant to every other aspect. Fish, spit, toe, antenna, cognac, spider, perspex, keyboard, grass, helmet. Helmeted in grass, the perspex spider spits with toed antenna, a noise like fish, the cognac keyboard. Too elegant that, too much like Mallarmé or somebody. Old-fashioned too, really. Surrealist.

Allah.

Up there the white huddled Medina on the hill, once watchful of the sea-invaders. Blood and buggery, the Koranic cry of teeth as the scimitar slashed. And now a pretty cram of stucco for the visiting painter. Donkeys, palms, the odd insolent Cadillac with a sneering wealthy young Moor in dark glasses. This bilious sea. There were not, thank Allah, many police about and, in any case, they did not greatly molest beggars.

"Give him something, George, go on. Poor old man."

And the plebeian tourist, in open-necked shirt and double-breasted town suit, handed Enderby a tiny clank of centimes. His wife, growing a lobster colour that was vulgarly Blackpool, smiled in pity. Enderby bowed and allahed. It was really surprising what you could pick up on this game—handfuls of small tinkle that often added up to well over a dirham, filthy torn notes that the donors probably thought carried plague, the absurd largesse of holiday drunks. He was eating, if not sleeping, well on it all. Arab bread with melon-and-ginger *confiture,* yummiyum couscous (better than Easy Walker's), fowl-hunks done with saffron, thin veal-shives in a caraway sauce—all at a quiet fly-buzzing incurious shop near the little Souk or Succo, one that had, moreover, a Western WC instead of a hazardous wog crouch-hole. He was also drinking a fair quantity of mint-tea, good for his stomach.

"*Pauvre petit bonhomme. Georges, donne-lui quelque chose.*"

It was a living. For occupation he had the working-out, though not on paper (there would be paper in prison), of a sonnet concerned with the relationship of the Age of Reason and the so-called Romantic Revival:

> Augustus on a guinea sat in state—
>> The sun no proper study but each shaft
>> Of filtered light a column: classic craft
> Abhorred the arc or arch. To circulate
> (Blood or ideas) meant pipes, and pipes were
>> straight.
>> As loaves were gifts from Ceres when she
>> laughed—

A difficult form, most exigent. Those drug-takers in the Doggy Wog place didn't have all that to worry about: no octaves and sestets in the free wide-open unconscious. A load of bloody rubbish, of course, but he couldn't quell his new self-doubt. As for reading, he would glance shyly at foreign papers left on outdoor café tables: there seemed to be nothing about Yod Crewsy.

And then, outside the Rif, he had heard these two men, talking loudly about someone who could only be Wapenshaw. The Turkish Delight commercial doorman was whistling a taxi to come over for them from the taxi-stand opposite the Miramar. And one of the two men, his belly pushed out to keep up his unbelted long shorts, had said to the other (both had spatulate scrubbed and shaven-looking fingers): "Heart. He let himself get upset about something." It was as they were climbing into their *petit taxi* or *taxi chico* that the other one, oldish but thin and strong like a surgical instrument, had said: "Now bugger off and buy yourself a shave," handing Enderby a fifty-centime piece.

"*Allah.*"

Retribution, justice: that was what it was. Serve Wapenshaw right. He had grinned and then seen his grin reflected in the glass door of the Rif, the back of a fat woman in black rompers making a temporary mirror-back. He had looked pretty horrible—a face without margins peering from the cave of the capuchin hood, toothless. He could not see his grey whiskers, but he felt them: skirr skirr. He grinned in horror.

At this moment another beggar, sturdy and genuine, had come up to remonstrate loudly. He had been crouched in the entrance to the hotel garage, but now, seeing the grin, he had risen, it seemed, in reproach of one not taking the business seriously enough. He was darker than Enderby, more of a Berber, and had plenty of teeth. He gnashed these in execration, starting to push Enderby in the chest. "Take your hands off," Enderby cried, and a visitor in a Palm Beach suit turned in surprise at the British accent. "For cough," Enderby added, preparing to push back. But careful, careful; respectable beggary only: the police might conceivably come. He saw then what the trouble was: pitch queering. "*Iblis*," he swore mildly at this colleague or rival. "*Shaitan. Afrit.*" He had learned these words from Ali Fathi. And then, the real beggar calling terms less theological after him, he began to cross the road rather briskly. Perhaps he ought, anyway, to haunt the beach more, specifically that segment near *El Acantilado Verde*, even though so many people on it had their clothes off and locked away, able with a good conscience to grin (more kindly than Enderby had grinned) and show empty hands and armpits filled only, in the case of the men, with hair.

The restaurant part of Rawcliffe's establishment was glassed like an observatory. The rare eaters sweated on to their food, brought to them by an amiable-looking negroid boy in an apron and tarboosh. Windows were open, and Enderby would shyly squint in, but Rawcliffe did not seem to be about yet. He would justify the peering by shoving in a hand for alms, and, on the first day of this new pitch, he had had a squashy egg-and-salad sandwich plopped on to his paw. Palms, alms. Was there a poem there? But he gained also the odd bit of small change when customers—mostly German, needing a substantial bever between meals—paid their bills.

These last two days had yielded a sufficiency, and the fine weather held. Padding the sand, on which the sea, clever green child but never clever at more than a child's level, had sculpted its own waves, he breathed in salt, iodine, the sea's childish gift of an extra oxygen molecule, and thought in quiet sadness of old days—bucket and spade, feet screaming away from jellyfish,

Sam Brownes of seaweed and the imperial decoration of a starfish (belly thrust out like that Wapenshaw-talking man, chest sloped to keep it on). And *El Acantilado Verde* reminded him of later days by the sea, betrayed and ruined by so many. "*Baksheesh*," he suggested now to a mild German-looking couple who, in heavy walking dress except for bare feet, drank the wind, strolling. They shook their heads regretfully. "German bastards," Enderby said quietly to their well-fed backs. The light was thicker, less heat was coming today from the piecrust cloud. There might be rain soon.

Here was a family that looked British. The wife was thin as from a long illness, the husband wore stern glasses, a boy and girl undressed for water-play chased and tried to hit each other.

"Daft old Jennifer!"

"Silly stupid Godfrey! You've got all sand in your tummy-button!"

Enderby addressed the father, saying, with begging hand: "*Allah allah. Baksheesh, effendi.*"

"Here," said the man to his wife, "is an example of what I mean. You have a good look at him and what do you see? You see a wog layabout in the prime of life. He ought to be able to do a decent day's work like I do."

"*Allah*," with less confidence.

"They should be made to work. If I had the running of this tinpot little dictatorship I'd make sure that they did." He had a cheap-looking plastic-bodied camera dangling from a cord. His stare was bold and without humour.

"He's only a poor old man," said his wife. She was, Enderby could tell, a woman much put upon; the children too would be insolent to her, asking *why* all the time.

"Old? He's not much older than what I am. Are you? Eh? Speak English do you? Old."

"No mash Ingrish," Enderby said.

"Well, you should learn it, shouldn't you? Improve yourself. Go to night-classes and that. Learn something, anyway. This is the modern world, no room for people that won't work, unless, that is, they've been thrown out

367

of it through no fault of their own. Don't understand a blind bit of what I'm saying, do you? Trade, eh? Learn a trade. If you want money, do something for it."

"Come on, Jack," said the wife. "There's a man there keeps looking at our Godfrey."

Enderby had not previously met a response to mendicancy as hard-hearted and utilitarian as this. He looked grimly at this man of the modern world: a trade-union man, without doubt; perhaps a shop steward. He wore a dark suit with, concession to holiday, wings of open-necked shirt apparently ironed on to lapels. "Trade," Enderby said. "I got trade." The sky seemed to be getting darker.

"Oh, understand more than you let on you're able to, eh? Well, what trade have you got, then?"

"*Bulbul*," Enderby said. But that might not be the right word. "*Je suis*," he said "*poète*."

"Poet? You said poet?" The man's mouth had opened into a square of small derision. He took from a side-pocket a ten-centime piece. "You say some poetry, then. Listen to this, Alice."

"Oh, let him alone, Jack."

It might have been the word *bulbul* that did it. Suddenly Enderby, in a kind of scorn, found himself reciting a mock *ruba'iy*. Would those debauchees of the Doggy Wog laugh less at this than at his Horatian Ode?

> "*Kazwana ghishri fana kholamabu*
> *Bolloka wombon vurkelrada slabu,*
> *Ga farthouse wopwop yairgang offalflow*
> *Untera merb—*"

A voice behind him said: "Better, Enderby. Much better. Not quite so obsessed with meaning as you used to be." It was an eroded dyspneal voice. Enderby turned in shock to see Rawcliffe being helped, by two Moorish youths in new black trousers and white shirts, up the three steps that led to the door of his bar-restaurant. Rawcliffe paused at the top, waiting for the door to be opened. He panted down ghastily at Enderby, his palsied grey head ashake. "Thou art translated," he wavered, "but not so much." The door opened, and its glass panels mirrored momentarily the thickening sea-clouds. "*Gracias,*" Rawcliffe said to the two Moors and trembled from his trouser-pocket a ten-dirham note for them. They hand-waved and grinned off. Then, to Enderby: "Come and drink with one about to die."

"All right," said the trade-union man. "You win. Take your ackers." But Enderby ignored him and followed, with his own shaking, the broken frame of Rawcliffe from which an Edwardian suit bagged and hung. About to die, death, dying. That man Easy Walker had said something about his being crookidy dook. But was it rather that Rawcliffe, out of the vatic residuum of a failed poet's career, knew that he was going to be killed? Enderby then realised that he'd done nothing, despite this long wait, about getting hold of a weapon. God knew the shops had offered him enough. Not cut out for murder perhaps really. Not really his trade.

Two

Enderby climbed those three steps like a whole flight, shaking and panting. When he entered the bar he found that Rawcliffe, helped now by a dark and curly pudding of a young man, had not yet arrived at the place he was groaning and yearning towards—a fireside-type chair at the end of the room, facing the main door, with the back door near it open for air. There was too much glass here altogether: it was to bake the summer customers and make them drink more. But now, in the expected pathetic fallacy, the sky was darkening fast, rain on its way. The bar-counter was to the right, facing the doorless entrance to the eating-conservatory. The pudding young man got behind the bar before starting to shoo Enderby out. Rawcliffe, now heavily sitting, said: "*Oqué, oqué, Manuel. Es un amigo.*"

"That's not," Enderby said, "quite what I'd call myself." There was an aloof interested inner observer, he was concerned to be interested to note, noting all this as possible material for a future poem, including the notation of the interest. That was not right: it was that inner observer, also creator, that had primarily been wronged. "The enemy," Enderby said. "Come to get you. You know what for." The inner observer tut-tutted.

"I knew you'd give it up, Enderby," Rawcliffe said. "You did bloody well, really. All those years writing verse when, by rights, you should have flitted to the tatty Olympus of remembered potency." He wavered all this like an ancient don pickled in the carbon dioxide of his college rooms. Then he coughed bitterly, cursing with little breath. Recovering, he gasped: "Brandy, Manuel. Large."

"Doctor he say—"

"Curse the bloody doctor and you and every bloody body. Who's master here, God blast you? Brandy. Very very large." Manuel, his eyes on Rawcliffe, slopped much Cordon Bleu into a lemonade glass. "Bring it over, Enderby. Have one yourself."

"How did you know it was me?" Enderby asked, interest much too active.

"I can see through things. Poetic clairvoyance. Bring that brandy over."

"I'm not here—"

"To be a bloody waiter. I know, I know. Bring it over just the same." Enderby shambled to where Rawcliffe was and splashed the glass down on a small table by the chair. This table had a mass of personal trash on it, as, Enderby thought, in that poem by Coventry Patmore: to comfort his sad heart. A pile of old newspapers, a Woolworth watch, a couple of stones (ha) abraded by the beach, an empty bottle, no bluebells, cigarette packets. Beware of pity, however. Pity spareth many an evil thing. Rawcliffe took the glass and, in an aromatic brandy tempest, put it to his starved lips. Bleeding to death, Enderby saw; he was near the end of his blood. Pity causeth the forests to fail.

"Swine," Enderby said as Rawcliffe drank. "Filthy traitor and pervert."

Rawcliffe surfaced from drinking. His face started to mottle. He looked up at Enderby from behind his Beetle goggles, his eyes bloodless like his mouth, and said: "I grant the latter imputation, Enderby," he said, "if you call a search for pure love perversion." As on cue, the negroid waiter in the tarboosh appeared from the kitchen, posed against the door-post, and looked in a sort of loving horror at Rawcliffe. "There, my black beauty," cooed Rawcliffe's abraded larynx. "Anybody noshing in there? *Quién está comiendo?*" His head twitched towards the dining-room.

"*Nadie.*"

"Shut up bloody shop, Manuel," coughed Rawcliffe. "We're closed till further notice. The bloody *baigneurs* and *baigneuses*—and a fat pustular lot they are, Enderby—can do key-business at the scullery door." Manuel began to cry. "Stop that," said Rawcliffe with a ghost of sharpness. "As for," he turned back to Enderby, "being a filthy traitor, I've done nothing to contravene the Official Secrets Act. The beastly stupid irony of sending you out here as a spy or whatever it is you are. That *maquillage* is ridiculous. It looks like boot-polish. Get it off, man. You'll find turps in the kitchen."

"To me," Enderby said. "A traitor to me, bastard. You grew fat on the theft and travesty of my art." Pity slayeth my nymphs. "I mean metaphorically fat."

"Of course you do, my dear Enderby." Rawcliffe finished his brandy, tried to cough and couldn't. "Better. A mere palliative, though. And that's why you got yourself up like that, eh? My brain's fuddled, such of it as has not yet been eaten away by this encroaching angel. I fail to see why you should dress up as whatever it is you're supposed to be in order to tell me I've grown metaphorically fat on your whatever it is." He grew suddenly drowsy and then shook himself awake. "Have you locked those bloody doors yet, Manuel?" he tried to shout.

"*Pronto, pronto.*"

"It's a bit of a long story." Enderby saw no way out of seeming to make an excuse. "I'm hiding from the police, you see. Interpol and so on." He sat down on a stackable chair.

"Make yourself comfortable, my dear old Enderby. Help yourself to a drink. You look sunken and hungry.

There's Antonio sleeping in his kitchen, a very passable pastmaster of short-order cookery. We'll shout him awake and he will, singing his not altogether trustworthy Andalusian heart out, knock you up his own idiosyncratic version of a mixed grill." He probed his throat for a cough but none came. "Better. I feel better. It must be your presence, my dear old Enderby."

"Murder," Enderby said. "Wanted for murder. Me, I mean." He couldn't help a minimal smirk. The Woolworth watch ticked loudly. As in a last desperate gasp, the sun slashed the shelves of bottles behind the bar with fire and crystal, then retired. The clouds hunched closer. Bathers were running into Rawcliffe's arena, after keys and clothes. Manuel was there shouting at them, jangling keys. "*Cerrado. Fermé. Geschlossen.* Shut up bloody shop."

"Like something from poor dear dead Tom Eliot," said Rawcliffe. "He always liked that little poem of mine. The one, you may remember, that is in all the anthologies. And now the rain laying our dust. No more shelter in the colonnade and sun in the Hofgarten." He seemed ready to snivel.

"Murder," Enderby said, "is what we were talking about. I mean me being wanted for murder."

"Be absolute for life or death," said Rawcliffe, fumbling a dirty handkerchief from one of the many pockets of his jacket-face. He gave the handkerchief to his mouth with both hands, coughed loosely, then showed Enderby a gout of blood. "Better up than down, out than in. So, Enderby," he said, folding in the blood like a ruby and stowing it with care, "you've opted for the fantasy life. The defence of pretence. I can't say I blame you. The real world's pretty horrible when the gift goes. I should know, God help me."

"It went but it came back. The gift, I mean. And now," Enderby said, "I shall write in prison." He crossed one leg over the other, disclosing much of his European trousers, and, for some reason, felt like beaming at Rawcliffe. "They don't have the death penalty any more," he added.

Rawcliffe shook and shook. It was with anger, Enderby saw with surprise. "Don't talk to me about the bloody death penalty," Rawcliffe shook. "Nature exacts her own punishments. I'm dying, Enderby, dying, and you burble away about writing verse in prison. It's not the dying I mind so much as the bloody indignity. My underpants filling with bloody cack, and the agony of pissing, and the smell. The smell, Enderby. Can you smell the smell?"

"I've got used to smells," Enderby apologised, "living as I've been doing. You don't smell any different," he smelled, "than that time in Rome. You bloody traitor," he then said hotly. "You stole my bloody poem and crucified it."

"Yes yes yes yes." Rawcliffe seemed to have grown tired again. "I suppose the decay was always with me. Well, it won't be long now. And I shall infect neither earth nor air. Let the sea take me. The sea, Enderby, *thalassa, la belle mer.* Providence, in whatever guise, sent you, in whatever guise. Because, delightful though these boys could often be in my violet-enough-smelling though really Indian summer, days, they can't altogether be trusted. With me gone, a mere parcel of organic sludge yumyumyummed away at by boring phagocytes, Enderby, the posthumous memory of my request will not move them to fulfil it. Oh, dear me, no. So that can be handed over to you with total confidence, a fellow-Englishman, a fellow-poet." The boys could be heard in the kitchen, hearty Mediterranean lip-smacking, the rarer and more sophisticated ping of a fork on a plate, Moghrabi conversation, laughter escaping from munches. Not altogether to be trusted. The rain now came down, and Rawcliffe, as if pleased that a complicated experimental process were under way, nodded. Enderby suddenly realised that that was who he'd got his own nod from: Rawcliffe.

"Rawcliffe," he said, "bastard. I'm not here to do anything for you, bastard as you are. You've got to be killed. As a defiler of art and a bloody traitor." He noticed that he still had one leg comfortably crossed over the other. He disposed himself more aggressively, hands tensely gripping knees, though still seated. That tan polish

373

seemed to be sweating off, a bit streaky. He'd better do something about that before killing Rawcliffe.

"If you killed me," Rawcliffe said, "you'd be doing me a very large favour. There might be a small obituary in *The Times*. The triumph of that early poem might be recalled, the poem itself reproduced, who knows? As for a weapon, there's a till-protecting service revolver in that cupboard behind the bar. Or our steak-knives are pretty sharp. Or you could feed me, say, fifty sleeping-capsules, pellet by pellet. Oh, my dear Enderby, don't be a bloody bore. Let me expiate in nature's way, blast you."

"That's not right," Enderby started to mumble. "Justice. What I mean is." What he meant was that he'd been quite looking forward to a life sentence, a bit of peace and quiet, get on with his. "I mean that if they're going to get me it'd better be for something real." Then: "I didn't mean that. What I meant to say was for a sheep as well as a lamb. Look, I will have a drink after all."

"Better, Enderby, much better. There's a nice bottle of Strega behind the bar. Remember those brief sunny Strega-drinking days by the Tiber? Days of betrayal, you will say. Was I the only betrayer?" He sat up with sudden alertness. "Do pass me that bottle of life-surrogate there, my dear Enderby. Cordon Bleu, a blue cordon to keep out that scrabbling crowd of clawers hungry for my blood. They must wait, must they not? We have things to see to, you and I, first." Enderby went to the bar, handed shaking Rawcliffe his bottle, unwilling anyway to pour for the sod, then looked at all the other bottles, embarrassed for choice. "Didn't go well, that marriage, did it, Enderby? Not cut out for marriage, not cut out for murder. Tell me all about that. No, wait. Dear Auntie Vesta. Married now to some sharp Levantine with very good suits. But she failed really, you know, failed despite everything. She'll never be in anybody's biography, poor bitch. You're a remarkable man, Enderby. It was in all the papers, you know, that marriage. There was a pop nuptial mass or something. Choreography round the altar, brought downstage for the occasion. A lot of bloody ecumenical nonsense."

"That," grudgemumbled Enderby, "is just what I said. Not in that connection. I mean in the other one. That priest, I mean. The day it happened." Fundador. Not too bad a drink, despite that blasted moon woman. Rawcliffe clanked and clanked out his slug, then drank. Enderby, ashamed at his quieter co-ordination, did a real professional barman's pour of his own. "What happened was this," he said, before drinking. "This yob got shot, Crewsy that is, was, and someone put the gun in my hand. I ran, you see. You'd have done the same."

Rawcliffe frowned, made a shot at his lips with his glass, sprayed and dribbled cognac, sucked in a fair amount, gasped. "Let's get all this straight, Enderby," he gasped. "I read the papers. I read nothing else. I've been hanging on to life, you know. The ephemeral, I mean, the sad, pretty, awful, tragic everyday, not the transcendencies of great art. I shall meet the eternal soon enough. I shall get my chamber music without the trouble of having to attend to profundities squeezed sweating from sheepgut. Or there will be nothing, like Sam Beckett. I read the papers—the pipe-smoking dogs, the topless weddings, the assassinations of pop-singers. Yod Crewsy I know all about. Dying, soon to die. Perhaps we shall die on the same day, he and I. That will be fitting, somehow. A barman shot him. I don't remember the name. Wait: something porcine."

"Hogg," said Enderby with impatience. "Hogg, Hogg." There was a young wall-eyed man in a dirty apron, the cook Antonio probably, standing by the kitchen door, picking his teeth with a quill and frowning puzzled at Enderby's get-up. "Hogg."

"That's it. So you read the papers too. A poetical name, that I did know. A very Jacobitical poet, that one. Charlie he's my darling. Wha the deil hae we goten for a King but a wee wee German lairdie. I like that weewee bit. He spoke out, Enderby. He didn't give a worsted-stocking damn."

"Listen," Enderby hissed, coming from behind the bar with his glass of Fundador. "That was me. Hogg. That was my mother's name. They turned me into a barman, Wapenshaw and the rest of them. Yes, yes, they did. A useful citizen, they said, poet no longer. You didn't know, nobody knew. *That* was never in the papers." Rawcliffe was all rigidity now, staring. "But," Enderby said, "I got away. As Enderby. I'd got my passport. And then that bloody woman found out that Enderby and Hogg were the same. So I had to get rid of the passport. It's a long story really." He drank some Fundador and tasted again that night of the bloody woman. Bloody women.

"It must be, it must be. But," said Rawcliffe, "it's a man called Hogg they were looking for." Enderby borrowed Rawcliffe's rigidity, staring. "Oh yes. Nothing about may be travelling under an alias. Ill-known minor poet who mysteriously disappeared, nothing like that. Nobody blew the gaff, my dear Enderby."

"She must have done. Selenographer, she called herself. The police scouring Morocco. Me in hiding. And then there's John the Spaniard."

"Yes yes yes." Rawcliffe spoke soothingly. "The world's full of traitors, isn't it? But tell me, Enderby, why did you shoot him?"

"He deserved to be shot. Plagiarism. A travesty of art. He stole my poems. The same as you."

"Oh, for God's sake," said Rawcliffe with emphatic weariness, "get it over with. Shoot everybody. Shoot the whole damned treacherous world, then get behind bars and write your bloody self-pitying doggerel."

"Doggerel," Enderby sneered. "You're a right bastard to talk about me writing doggerel."

"Wait, though, wait. Didn't you say something about not having shot him at all? About someone putting the smoking gun in your innocent paw? That figures, as the smoking gun films put it. Spaghetti Westerns. They had me writing those, Enderby. But I got out. I didn't do too badly out of *L'Animal Binato*. That was a bloody good idea of yours." He shook himself back to the immediate topic. "You're no killer, be sure of that. You're not even the predestined victim. You wriggle out of the real striking of the blow by the operation of a time-warp or space-woof or something. You fall on your feet. You'll have to rename the *Acantilado Verde*, of course."

"Eh?"

"Green cliff, raw cliff. You're got somebody on your side. Who? There you stand, absurd but vigorous. And Auntie Vesta is vanquished and poor Rawcliffe is dying. Is there anything more you want? Oh, yes. I shall dictate a letter to Scotland Yard—there's an old office Oliver in my bedroom behind the bar—and confess all. After all, Enderby, I could quite easily have done it. I even had an invitation. After all, I have been one of the great diluters, worthy to be asked. And I was in London, seeing the last of my head-shaking consultants. Very grave he was. Prepare to meet thy God. My Goddess, rather. Yes yes yes, the mockers and diluters and travestists deserve to die." Enderby frowned, unsure whether this was all drunkenness or the start of terminal delirium. Rawcliffe closed his eyes, his head lolled, his trouser-fly darkened and then his crotch dripped. Enderby saw barman and waiter and cook all crammed in the kitchen doorway, open-mouthed.

"Get him to bed," he ordered. "Come on, jump to it." Antonio crossed himself, quill still in his teeth. They did not exactly jump to it, but Manuel and the tarbooshed waiter grabbed each an oxter of Rawcliffe. Rawcliffe was dimly roaring. Enderby took the legs. He had done that before for Rawcliffe, he remembered. In Rome, honeymooning. Rawcliffe was lighter now than then. Antonio pointed where the bedroom was. The rain was easing a bit.

Three

"You one of his *friends*, then?" asked the doctor. "Didn't know he had any *British* ones." He looked at Enderby with little favour, despite the restored teeth and shaved pinkness (that tan stuff had been hard to get off, the solvents painful), hair scant but washed and brushed, serious spectacles catching the pale after-rain Tangerine light. He was also wearing one of Rawcliffe's neo-Georgian suits, grey and hairy and not too tight in the armpits. The three boys, who were growing pimples and mannerisms as Enderby got to know them better (the tarbooshed waiter had also grown a name—Tetuani, after his hometown Tetuan), had been helpful with the restoration. They had even made up a sort of bed for him with the fireside-type chair and two or three stackable ones. It seemed to them to be a relief to have an Englishman around who was not dying.

"Not in that sense," Enderby said sternly. "A sort of friend, but not in the sense you mean."

"What do you mean, in what sense I mean?" The doctor was an upright tall man in his hale sixties, with a lot of wavy silver hair; he looked like a military medical officer who, on the repatriation of a superior garrison, had elected to stay behind. I liked the place or something. But probably secrets of his own; shadiness. He was a bit too sharp with his "What do you mean?"

"You know what I mean," Enderby said, blushing. "I'm finished with sex, anyway," he blabbed, ill at ease, unhappy with doctors. As if this declaration were a clue to identity, the doctor said:

"Seen you before somewhere, haven't I?"

"My picture in the papers perhaps. Or rather," Enderby emended with haste, "the picture of a man who looks very much like me, or so I'm told. A man called Hogg."

"I wouldn't know. Never read the papers. A lot of lies mostly. As for that sex business, I'm not all that interested in what people do in that line so long as they don't come moaning to me about the consequences. This one," he said, shouldering towards Rawcliffe, who lay feebly snorting under a blanket, "has favoured the dirty and diseased. But you know that, of course, being his *friend*. *Nostalgie de la boue*, if you know what that means. But what he's dying of could happen to anybody. To you," he said. "To your maiden aunt in Chichester or wherever it is."

"I haven't got—"

"He's riddled with it, no respecter of persons. All we can do is to ease the end. You can pay me for the hypodermic and the morphine now if you like. And for this and two previous consultations. Call me in again when you think he's gone. I'll have to sign the death certificate."

"The body," said Enderby. "There's the question of—"

"He should have done what most of the British do out here. Fifty quid or thereabouts for a patch at St Andrew's. Burial service, resurrection and the life, the lot. Told me once he was a conscientious hedonist, though. Pleasure the end of life, that means. Very unwise, look where it's got him."

"But you said it could happen to—"

"He'll have to be interred at Bubana. I daresay they'll say a few words over the grave. Somebody from the consulate usually turns up. Leave all that to you."

"Look here—"

"I usually get paid in cash. Out of the till." He marched ahead of Enderby into the bar and, nodding at Antonio and Manuel, who were playing Spanish Scrabble, helped himself to what looked like forty-five dirhams.

"ELLA."

"ELLAS."

"He says," Enderby said, "that he wants to be dropped into the sea. It's in writing, signed and witnessed. That he's to be dropped into the sea. Is there any law against that?"

"Damned irregular," the doctor said, helping himself to a snifter of Bell's. "The thing ought to be done properly. What must they think of the white man here, I often ask myself. Pederasty, if you know the term, and drunkenness. Also drugs and writing. You're new here so you wouldn't know half that goes on. Keep away from that stupidly-named Dog place across the road. Americans of the worst type. Still, *autres temps autres moeurs.* I need not, I hope, translate. I leave everything to you, his *friend.* Don't neglect to get me on the blower when the time comes."

"Enby." It was Rawcliffe, very feeble.

"You'd better go in and see what he wants. Don't excite him. He's in your hands now."

"Look here—"

"DIOS."

"ADIOS."

"Little poem in itself, that, you could call it I suppose," said the doctor. He smacked off the last of his Bell's. "Still, I leave poetry to you and your kind. I must be off now."

"What do you mean by—"

"Enby." Rawcliffe had pumped up a few extra teaspoonsful of painful air to strengthen his call. No compassion in his march, the doctor let himself out. Bgr you Enby. Comere." Enderby went back into the sickroom. It was small but cool. Rawcliffe's bed was a double mattress laid on a worn Bokhara; thrown about all over the floor were local goat-skins, of different degrees of off-whiteness; there were cheap ornaments from the bazaar—a hand of Fatma, a cobra which was really an iron spring—it throbbed and jumped and burred on the Moorish coffee table if you touched it, a Rif saddle, a hubble-bubble, scimitars and daggers on the walls. One wall was all books in army cartridge-boxes disposed like shelf-units. Enderby had not yet had time to look through those books: there might conceivably be a copy of—The smell of dying Rawcliffe fought against an incense-burner and an aerosol lavender spray. Rawcliffe, naked under his blanket, said: "Brandy. Vry lrge."

"He said you're to have morphine," Enderby said uneasily. "Alcohol won't help the pain, he said."

"Bgrim. Wanna talk. Bndy." Enderby tried to harden his heart against him, traitor, traducer, diluter, sinner against literature. He went to get a new bottle of Cordon Bleu. Could Rawcliffe cope with a lemonade glass?

"CACA."

"CACAO."

There was a china feeding-cup next to the iron cobra. Enderby poured cognac in, sat on Rawcliffe's bed and helped him to drink. Rawcliffe spluttered, coughed, tried to say *Christ*, but he got down what Enderby estimated to be about a bar quintuple. He had once, in Piggy's Sty, had to serve one of those to a Cabinet Minister: it had come to thirty shillings, taxpayers' money.

"Better, Enderby, much better. Taken that letter to the post, has he? Loiters on the way sometimes, wayward. Good fundamentally, though. A bottom of good sense. Dr Johnson or somebody said that, Enderby."

"It was about a woman."

"Woman, was it? Well, of course, that's more your line, isn't it? God God God God, the bloody pain. The thing to do is to try to see the bloody pain as working in something out there. The body is not me. No transubstan. But Christ Christ, there's a hot line to the brain. Snip the nerve-endings, is there a me still there when all have been snipped? Psychoneural paral paral parallelism ism. Very popular that, before the war. The new immortality."

"There's this morphine here," Enderby said.

"More your line. Two lines there, though, hot and cold. Sun and moon. Moon's no power over you, Enderby. Me, I sinned against the Muse, all woman, and she took her revenge. And now to be sacrificed to her. But she'll be partly cheated, Enderby. New moon coming up about now. But eastward there are tideless waters. Drop this exterior thing in the tideless waters, Enderby. More brandy."

"Do you think you—"

"Yes, I do. Got to tell you. Give instructions." Enderby poured more cognac into the feeding-cup. Obscene, somehow, that festive gold and heady vapour in bland invalid china. Rawcliffe sucked more in avidly. "There's a man called Walker, Enderby. Useful sort of man, British colonial. His precise terry territory uncertain. He's in Casablanca now. Get in touch with him, his phone number's behind the bar. He knows how to get a small aircraft, borrows it from Abdul Krim or somebody, bloody rogue whoever he is. Bloody rogue. What was I saying? Tight, a bit, that's the trouble. Empty stomach, that's the trouble."

"I know this Walker. Easy Walker he calls himself." And then: "Can you eat something? An egg or something?"

"It's not your job to keep me alive, is it, Enderby? What's the bloody use of nutriment to me? Listen. The money's in this mattress. For Christ's sake don't let anybody burn it. It's not that I don't trust the banks. It's the buggers in the banks I don't trust, Enderby. Tattle tattle tattle about how much he's got, then coming along for a loan, then beat you up in a back-alley if they can't have it. I know them all too well. You know them all too well. You know Easy Walker. Always said you'd fall on your feet, Enderby. Get that bloody Antonio in here."

"What for?"

"Tell him to bring his guitar. Want to hear. To hear. In all the anthol. He sings it."

Enderby went out to the bar and said: *"Antonio. Señor Rawcliffe quiere que tu, usted canta, cante,* subjunctive there somewhere, whatever it is. *Su canción, él dice."* Antonio and Manuel both looked up from a Scrabble board now nearly full of words, their eyes ready to brim. Enderby went back to Rawcliffe. "That letter to Scotland Yard," he said. "It won't do any good. There must be a lot who send in letters like that." And where was he to go, where? He had reconciled himself, hadn't he? But that was when it had seemed possible to be able to murder Rawcliffe. Rawcliffe's eyes were closed. He had started snorting again. His body writhed feebly. And then he started violently awake.

"You've no bloody idea," he said with slow seriousness, "of the bloody agony. You wouldn't think it possible. Don't leave it too long, Enderby."

"Morphine?"

"Brandy. Insult to the brain. Poor Dylan. Kill me with bloody kindness." Enderby sighed, then recharged the feeding-cup. Antonio came in, trying his strings, crying. "Sing, blast you," said Rawcliffe, spluttering out cognac. The smell of it was fast overcoming his own. Antonio sat on the Rif saddle and twanged his thumb from E to e, sniffing his tears back. It was a well-worn guitar; Enderby could see the abrasions of fingers that, in Andalusian style, had drummed its body. Antonio gave out a thrummed major chord that, with the smell of cognac, seemed to affirm life (sun, zapateados, death in the afternoon). He wailed:

"Per ap sa yamna tuonti diri seyed,
    Per ap sayid beter go,

382

Ji seyed. Mocionles jer ayis, jer jeyed,
     Seyin not yes, not no."

"In all the anthologies," Rawliffe cried, then coughed and coughed. Antonio did not go on. "Put that, death, in your bloody pipe," said Rawcliffe more weakly when the racking had subsided. "*Exegi monumentum.* And what of yours, Enderby?" He was so faint that Enderby had to drop his ear towards him. "Better to be the one-poem man. But she left me then. Opened up heaven of creativity and then closed it. All right, Antonio. Later, later. *Muchas gracias.*" Antonio blew his nose on his cook's apron. "Read me something of yours, Enderby. They're there, your slender volumes, somewhere. I bought your books at least. Least I could do. I am not all badness."

"Well, really, this is hardly—What I mean is—"

"Something appropriate. Something to one about to die or one dead."

Enderby felt grimly in his left jacket pocket. He had transferred that stolen horror thither. "I can," he said, "without going to your shelves." But there was here at last, and his heart began to climb as with muscular pseudopodia, the chance of checking. Auntie Vesta. He strode over Rawcliffe's hidden feet towards the wall of books. A lot of cheap nasty stuff there: *Bumboy, Mr Wigg's Fancy, Lashmaster.* He thought, from the shape and size, he saw a copy of his own *Fish and Heroes,* but it turned out to be a small collection of glossy photographs: men and boys complicatedly on the job, with idiot eyes. But here it was, that other volume, the one the critics had trounced: *The Circular Pavane.* He flicked and flicked through the pages. There weren't many. And then. "Right," he said. Rawcliffe's eyes were closed again but he could tell Enderby was smiling. He said:

"Glee, eh? The creator's glee? You've found something that recalls the actual ecstasy of its making. Don't exass exacerbate my agony. Read it."

"Listen." Enderby tried to be gruff, but his reading made the poem sound sneering, as though the emotions of the mature were being mocked by some clever green child:

"They thought they'd see it as parenthesis—
   Only the naked statement to remember,
Cleaving no logic in their sentences,
   Putting no feelers out to the waking dreamer—

So they might reassume untaken seats,
   Finish their coffee and their arguments,
From the familiar hooks redeem their hats
   And leave, with the complacency of friends.

But strand is locked with strand, like the weave of bread,
   And this is part of them and part of time—"

"Oh God God," Rawcliffe suddenly cried. "Ugly hell gape not come not Lucifer." He began to babble. "And if the eternal finds its figures in the temporal then they can find their inferno here." He screamed and then collapsed, his head lolling, his tongue out, blood coming from his left nostril. Antonio's guitar clanged gently superposed fourths and my-dog-has-fleas as he put it down. He made the sign of the cross and prayed weeping. "A shot, Enderby, for Christ's sake." Enderby stared: a test; see if he could really kill? "A lot of shots." He saw then and went over to the coffee-table and the syringe and the morphine ampoules in their box. He hoped he could cope. Those Doggy Wog people would be able to cope all right.

Four

Rawcliffe did not stay under for long. There was a powerful life-urge there, despite everything. "Brandy," he said. "I'll beat them all yet, Enderby." Enderby filled the cup: the bottle was near its end. Rawcliffe sucked it all in like water. "What news?" he asked. "What irrelevancies are proceeding in the big world?"

"There's nothing as far as I can see," Enderby said. "But we've only got the Spanish paper, and I can't read Spanish very well."

Enough, though. When Tetuani came back from posting that air-letter, he brought with him a copy of *España*, which Enderby took with him to a bar-table. Rawcliffe unconscious, though roaring terribly from deep in his cortex, Enderby sat with a large whisky, breathing the prophylactic of fresh air from an open window. *"Quiere comer?"* Antonio asked. Enderby shook his head: he couldn't eat anything just yet, not just yet, *gracias* all the same. He drank his drink and looked at the paper. It was better that he read what he was undoubtedly going to read not in English: he needed the cushioning of a foreign tongue, with all its associations of literature and tourism, despite his foreknowledge. Words had power of their own: *dead* would always be a horrible word. On the front page the Caudillo still howled for the Rock, and some Arab leader called vainly for the extermination of Israel. When, on the second page, he came to the headline YOD CREWSY MUERTO, his response was that of a printer who had set the type himself. The score was, say, 10-2, and you had to wait ten minutes, say, for the anticlimax of the final whistle. What it said under the headline was brief. It said, as far as Enderby could tell, that he had passed into a terminal coma after a moment of flickering his eyes open and that soon there were no further indications of cardiac activity. There would be a sort of lying in state somewhere and then a requiem mass at the Catholic Cathedral in London (they meant Westminster). Fr O'Malley would deliver the panegyric. Nothing about girls weeping, as over Osiris or Adonis or somebody. Nothing about Scotland Yard expecting immediate arrest.

"Nothing at all," Enderby said.

What would Scotland Yard do about Rawcliffe's letter? Enderby had two-fingered it himself to Rawcliffe's dictation. It would do no good, Enderby had said, but Rawcliffe had insisted. Repentance, seeing the light, symbolic blow against anti-art. A guest (check guest-

385

list) who had come with full cold-blooded intention of killing and then being arrested—dying of those encroaching claws, what had he to lose?—he had succumbed in reflex to panic and handed gun to an anonymous waiter. He was not sorry, oh no, far from it: so perish all art's enemies, including (but with him it was the fullest blackest knowledge: he knew what he did) himself. Rawcliffe's scrawl, two witnesses: Antonio Alarcón and Manuel Pardo Palma. Well, Enderby thought, it might resolve things one way or the other. It would welcome the police to one terminus or another. And your name, sir, *señor?* Enderby. Your passport, please, *por favor.* Well, a slight problem there, officer. Whispered consultation, sergeant calling inspector over, comparing photograph with. All right, Hogg then. I recognised the true murderer and pursued him. Doing the job of the police for them, really, in best fictional tradition. I say no more. All right, arrest me then. Obviously I say no more. No warning necessary.

He was indifferent, really. All he wanted was a small room and a table to write verse on and freedom from the necessity to earn a living. But there remained self-doubt. Was the Muse so generous now only because she was dispensing rubbish? The future, perhaps, lay with those Doggy Wog people. He didn't really know; he wanted to be told, shown. But was he being reserved for something? Why did not everybody know that Hogg was Enderby? Why had that moon-bitch been silent? If John the Spaniard had blown the gaff, why was Tangier not milling with Interpol, demanding to see all foreign passports, combing? What force had struck down Wapenshaw, if it was Wapenshaw they'd been talking about, and rendered him dumb?

Enderby wondered now, sitting on the Rif saddle, keeping away from the putridity, whether he should ask Rawcliffe (meaning the still not foundered intelligence in the penthouse above the demolition squads), as a dying man who had nothing to gain by mendacity, what he thought of his, Enderby's work and (what he really meant) whether he should go on with it. But heaving and groaning Rawcliffe gave him an answer without being asked, without speaking. Go on with anything so long as you're alive; nothing matters except staying alive. Enderby could see that now, but had not always thought so. Rawcliffe said:

"Get on to Walker. It's going to be *it* soon, Enderby. Never mind what he asks. Money money money. All money these days. Fortunately it's stuffed in here, mine I mean, by my feet. No danger, Enderby, of ultimate incontinence fouling it. Clean money, most. The dirty part did not really harm my country. Hashish a harmless enough drug. More brandy."

"I'll have to get a new bottle."

"Get it then, blast you. What are those bloody boys doing?"

"The siesta."

"Something in the Bible about that. What, could ye not watch with me one hour? This night, before the cock crow." Rawcliffe took breath, rattling, and went feebly cocorico. Then he coughed and coughed. Blood bubbled from both nostrils and some trickled from his right mouth-corner. "God Christ," he panted, "I won't have this. Bewrayed, beshitten. Die in one's own bloody dung." He tried to shift his body away from the new foulness but rolled back on to it. "I'm getting up," he said. "I'm going to die on my feet. Help me, blast you, Enderby."

"You can't, you mustn't, you—"

"Best to be shot, knifed, standing." He threw his blanket off. He was naked except for a safety-pinned towel like a baby's diaper. "I insist, Enderby, you bastard. I'll drink my terminal liquor in a bar, like a man. My viaticum, you swine." He started, cursing, to get up. Enderby had to help, no way out of it. He went further than he'd gone for anybody. He pulled off Rawcliffe's diaper and wiped him clean with the clean part of it. He forgave his stepmother everything. There was a bathrobe on a nail behind the door. He put his arm round bare shivering Rawcliffe and shuffled-danced him towards it. "Better, Enderby, better," as he was clothed in gay yellow and blue. "Take me to the bar. Wake those bloody boys. They must be my crutch."

Pushing Rawcliffe before him, Enderby yelled. Antonio peered out from the kitchen first, startled, naked as Rawcliffe had been. He went back in to get the others, himself yelling. Rawcliffe tried to yell but collapsed into coughing. He collapsed against the bar-counter coughing, trying to curse. Soon Antonio and Manuel were holding him up, an arm each about him, in dirty white shirts; Manuel's trousers were already black. "Now, Enderby," Rawcliffe gasped at last. "You say you've been a bloody barman. Mix me something. A cocktail called *Muerte*. Stop that blasted snivelling, you two." Tetuani, tarboosh on, came out, frightened.

And I will, thought Enderby. "Leave it to me," he said, adding, in desperate facetiousness, "sir." He took a large beer-glass and slopped brandy in, then white rum, gin, whisky, vodka. The bottles flashed in the fair afternoon light. It was like celebrating something.

"No need for ice," Rawcliffe gasped. "Get that, maybe, soon. That thing in bloody Shakespeare. Measure for measure, eh? Altogether fitting. Thrilling regions of ribbed ice. Top it, Enderby, with something spumous. Asti, memories of Rome. Add, for old time's sake, a dollop of Strega. Strega, a witch. Witchbitch. That bloody man in Mallorca, Enderby, says the day of the moon goddess is done. The sun goddess takes over." Enderby found a bottle of Asti on the shelf, very warm, favoured of the sun. He cracked its neck against the counter-edge. "Good, Enderby." There was a fine gush. The stench of Rawcliffe was now well overlaid with powerful yea-saying aromas. But, admired Enderby, those boys' stomachs were strong. He gave the full spuming glass to both Rawcliffe's claws. "A toast," Rawcliffe said. "What shall it be, eh? *La sacra poesia?* The sun goddess? The survival of the spirit? To the," he began to droop, "impending dissolution," to snivel; the strong-handed boys began to snivel with him, "of this, of this—" Enderby became stern: he didn't like this snivelling. He cried:

"Ah, shut up. Get that bloody drink down and shut up." It was strong fatherly talk; the medicine was wholesome; had not he, Enderby, once dared death, though dragged gurgling back? "Get on with it, Rawcliffe. Bloody traitor."

"Good, Enderby, good, good. No false compassion there. Excellent." Rawcliffe braced himself, pumped air into his lungs like a parody of a dog's panting, then took his medicine. It spilled and rilled, the *mousse* got up his nose, he coughed some back into the glass, but he went gamely on to the dregs. Antonio put the flecked glass down for him. Rawcliffe gasped and gasped. "Put. That. On. The." He coughed, like payment, a coin of bloody sputum on the counter. "I mean. *Muerte*. The. Ult. Ult. Ultmte. Cktl." He yearned towards his chair, feebly turning. The boys took him over, only his bare toes touching the floor. Rawcliffe collapsed next to his chairside table, full of toys. Coventry Patmore. "Lil slp now." He at once began to snore. The boys put his feet up on a stackable. Enderby thought he had better now telephone Casablanca.

Five

It was growing dark when Rawcliffe surfaced for the last time. Enderby had sent the boys out, sick of the hand-wringing and snivelling. He sat at the other side of Rawcliffe's chair, smoking the local cigarettes that were called *Sport*, not drinking. The thought of drink made him shudder. When Rawcliffe surfaced, it was with an accession—that condemned man's supper—of clarity and calm. He said:

"Who's that there?"

"Me. Enderby."

"Ah yes, Enderby. Know your poetry well. Stole one of your ideas once, a bloody good one. No regrets. Now I give you something in return. My last poem. It came to me in sleep. Listen." He cleared his throat like an elocutionist and intoned slowly but with vigour:

> "The benison of lights and the
> Hides of asses and the
> Milk of the tide's churns.

> She should not have
> Rejected me like any copulative
> Of the commonalty.

Too much light, Enderby. Turn one of those lights off."
There were no lights on. "I've done that," Enderby
said.

"Good, Now where was I? Ah, I know. Listen.

> At length I heard a ragged noise and mirth
> Of thieves and murderers. There I him espied,
> Who straight, *Your suit is granted*, said, and died."

"That," Enderby said, "is George Herbert."
Rawcliffe suddenly began to rage. "It's not it's not it's
not you fucking swine. It's me. Me." In the dusk his
head rolled. Quietly, "Your suit is granted," he said, and
died. With the conventional accompaniment of rattle
and postlude of rictus and liquidity.

3

One

"And," Easy Walker cried above the engine, "real donk dirt-bibles. Got a jarvey, brad, all towsermouth for that variety of how's your Auntie-Doris-and-little-Nora-and-the-twins. So we'll march on markers when this lot's dooby-dooed."

The physical assumption of Rawcliffe. His body, in clean pyjamas and wrapped in a Union Jack that Manuel had bought for a few dirhams in, of all places, the Big Fat White Doggy Wog, sat next to Easy Walker in what Enderby took to be the co-pilot's seat. At least a kind of half-eaten steering-wheel or joy-stick in front of Rawcliffe twitched and turned in sympathy with Easy Walker's. And also dead Rawcliffe had his share of very lively dials and meters and emergency instructions, exclamation-pointed. His arms were pinioned beneath the flag, and he was corded at neck, waist, thighs, and ankles. No danger of his, its, flailing around if it-he came back to life.

"You sure he's footed the old garbage-can proper?" Easy Walker had asked while they had been bundling him in. "Because there's been cases. There's this case

now, brad. Tell you after. Maybe you minced it all mas-
terman."

Enderby sat behind Rawcliffe, an empty seat next to
him. It was a small but neat aircraft, American-made,
though there was a spelling mistake, Enderby noted, in
one of the instructions on the instrument-panel: *jetison*.
That did not make him doubt the airworthiness of the
craft, for it was always a matter of every man to his own
trade. This one of piloting seemed as much a trade of
Easy Walker's as any of the others he professed. He had
cried conversationally above the engine even as, tearing
down the runway, he brought the speed up to air-speed:

"A real donk passy too, there'll be there. Left the
whole bimbang kadoozer to you then, has he, brad?"

"There's the question of," Enderby had shouted. "That
one of mine, I mean."

"Welcome to Bird County," Easy Walker had yelled as
the craft nosed into the old-gold Moroccan air. The late
afternoon sky to themselves, except for rare gulls and,
far to port, a migrant exaltation of brownish birds that,
after a rest on the top of Gibraltar, were crossing the
Straits for their African wintering. No Air Maroc flight
till very much later. Below on the cabochon-cut Mediterranean very few boats, though what looked like a rich
man's yacht gleamed to starboard. It was still the sun's
time. The moon, thin last night, was not watching over
Rawcliffe's ascension into heaven. Fattened, she would
draw at him vainly from the deep, gnawed by fishes, his
flag defiled. Over the air-craft wireless strange English
crackled from Tangier control tower. Easy Walker ignored it. Aft lay Ceuta.

"There was one," he yelled without effort, "Ricker
Sugden did for like his booze brad when he kicked. Do
too for this jarvey, I reckon." He recited, drowning the
engine:

"Dragged from his doings in the roar of youth,
   Snipped like the stem of a caldicot flower,
   Snarled time's up ere he'd quaffed his hour,
Tossed to the tearing of the dour dog's tooth."

"That's not quite right for Rawcliffe," Enderby shouted. It wasn't, either. The right one was in all the anthologies, but Enderby's calling of it would never prevail against this of Ricker Sugden's. It was the right one only because it was the only one.

"Bye, my brad, let the bright booze pour
  That is suds of stars in the Milky Way,
  And its door swing open all the joylit day
And the heavenlord landlord cry you time no more."

"Not one of his best," called Enderby, but he was not heard. Not obscure enough, too much meaning. Poor Rawcliffe. Traitor Rawcliffe rather, but he had paid. Your suit is granted. What suit? To be granted a cell, smallest unit of life. Enderby feebly tried to give out to sea, sky and Easy Walker that last stanza ("His salts have long drained into alien soil"), and then saw how inappropriate it really was. His soil would drain soon into alien salt. There was nothing for Rawcliffe. But it was something to rest in bones, rags of flag fluttering, at the sea's bottom between two continents. It was a kind of poem. Easy Walker cried:

"Nowsy wowsy. You right for the shove, brad?" Enderby nodded, forgetting that Easy Walker's eyes were ahead and there was no driving mirror. The corpse of Rawcliffe had lolled to rest against the perspex of the starboard door. Enderby roughly pushed it so that it began to topple gracefully against Easy Walker. "Watch it, watch it, brad." Leaning over, Enderby turned the door-handle, panting. It was rather stiff. Suddenly it opened and swung, and the huge roaring air without seemed to pull at him, but he dug his nails into Rawcliffe's seat-back. "Nowsy wowsy powsy." Easy Walker made the craft list hard to starboard. A torrent of frozen air was rushing in up diagonally now. Enderby clawed at the corpse through its flag-shroud, heaving it out, but, falling to the air, it seemed to be merely buoyed up by it. "Blast you, Rawcliffe," went Enderby for the last time. "Righty right," Easy Walker sang, and he kicked out at a dead shin. Then he listed further.

Enderby pounded and pushed. As it were reluctantly, Rawcliffe's body launched itself into this quite inferior region of the sky, lower, surely, than Parnassus. "Got him, brad," meaning space had. The tricolor, crude in this sapphire and turquoise ambience, span slowly down. "Gone." Without sound, and with lips parted only as for a cigarette, the sea took him. Here lies one whose name was *not* writ in water, he had once said in his cups.

It was hard to get that door, which had swung open to its limit, back in place. But Easy Walker lurched violently to port and the door hurtled in and, on a lurch that brought them both lying on their sides as at a Roman supper, it slammed to. Then he righted the craft and, widely circling in the air, its nose sniffed round towards home. Home: what else could you call it? Green Africa ahead, then the geometry of the little airport, then a sudden urgent love for the runway. A three-point landing of the kind called insolently skilled, a taxiing towards Easy Walker's waiting Volkswagen.

"Talking about passports," Enderby said as they sped through the brown country outside town, "I'd like that back if you've still got it. I let it go too soon."

"Not poss, brad. Swallowed up, that, in the great dirty passy-hungry what-does-your-dad-do. Have his, though, your need being greater than. Dead jarveys help the living from their heart of darkness. Still. A pig of a pity."

"What I mean is," said Enderby, "I'm entitled to an official identity of some sort." But was he? And, if so, why? He might yet be taken somewhere, but he had no intention of making a move of his own. And, anyway, did bearing a name matter? Rawcliffe would be glad to be called anything or nothing if he could be alive again.

"There was the time I got this passy just as the jarvey as todded it seemed like as to take off. But he came to, yes he did, when it was already swapping fumblers. Well, you're all right, I'd say, with this Rawcliffe jarvey. He won't come up, no, not never no more. Different from this jarvey back in Great Dirty Mum."

When they arrived back at *El Acantilado Verde*,

Rawcliffe's other verbal monument, Easy Walker was eager to see what shady treasures there might be to buy cheap and sell dear. The three boys sat, in clean white, at a table by the bar-counter, playing some game which involved the linking of little fingers. They had some difficulty in composing their faces to a funeral look. "All finished," Enderby said. *"Finito."* But there must be a better Spanish word than that. *Consommado?* It sounded soupish. *"Consummatum,"* he said, pushing down to the roots.

"March on markers," said Easy Walker. He was very deft. The amount of pornography he uncovered was shocking. It was mostly in the cartridge-box book-shelves, though previously—because of the austerity of the binding—unsuspected by Enderby. "Here," said Easy Walker, "is some right donk fladge for such as takes a swizzle to it," showing Enderby Victorian steel-engravings of bloody wounds, lovingly detailed, and knobbed whips and knotted thongs. "And here's them shoving up the old kazerzy with it, very painful for my shekels and sherbet. And here," Easy Walker said, shock on his unshockable, "is what I would not have if it was my own Aunt Ada as did it, brad. Cause there's limita-tions to all bozzles, has to be, stands." In his hands trembled a leather-bound folio of what, to squinting Enderby, seemed at first to be illustrations to the Bible. But they were very perverted illustrations, and there was one that made Enderby feel sick. "I mean," Easy Walker said, slamming the book shut, "that was bad enough in itself without making it worse and dirty sex-ual." It was the first time Enderby had heard him use plain language. "Making a mock of it like that jarvey I said. When a jarvey snuffs it's not up to him to come back, up-your-piping and that. All right for him in here," he bowed his head, "because he was what he was and no up-my-tickle. But this jarvey like I said. And there was like that saucepan-lid, Lazarus his all-the-same. And crucifixions too in this one, very dirty. Very clear that came off."

"What?" said Enderby. "Who?" Time himself will bring you in his high-powered car. And supposing the car doesn't go on to pick someone else up but, instead, goes back to the garage. Things as they were before, or as near as you could get them. He would not be surprised, he would not be surprised at anything. "You mean," said Enderby, "Yod Crewsy. You mean he's not dead after all."

Easy Walker nodded and nodded. "Laid out, brad, in some arsee plum-and-apple in the Smoke. Then all them teens brooping round, going sniff sniff. Turn-the-handles lighted all about him in his best whistle. And his three brads keeping double-scotch, two at his toots and one behind his uncle. Then he flicks open and says "Where am I?" Got it this morning on the talkbox, in the near-and-far, coming here."

Enderby nodded and nodded. Bitch. Blasphemous bitch. Very clever. Easily done, bribed doctors or not even that. Genuine error. Clinical death and real death. And now sermons about miracles and popsters flocking to give thanks. Our Thammuz, Adonis, Christ for that matter. "And," Enderby said, "I suppose there was one sly pseudo-mourner, come to see, his only chance, his handiwork, lurking in the shadows of the chapel, and, when this body rose from the dead, he screamed. Screamed that the times have been that, when the brains were out, the man would die, and there an end, but now they rise again, this is more strange than such a murder is."

Easy Walker shook his head, baffled. "Don't get that at all, brad. Forked me on the cobbles and no rare-with-Worcester. Have to mince the papers when they come out, not out yet, not with that, pennywise."

Enderby shook his head, not baffled. "No more papers. Bugger the outside world," he said violently. "If not that way, some other. I'll hear about it, only a question of waiting. No resurrection for Rawcliffe, not of any kind. They'll crumple his letter up at Scotland Yard, another crank."

"I'll ghoul these off now," Easy Walker said, "dirt-bibles." He showed new shock on the realisation that his slang had, for once, slung at the gold and pierced it. Enderby then had an intuition that he was going to throw off what must be a home-stitched patchwork of patois and, strayed sheep or remittance-man, speak a true language that was far more middle-class than his, Enderby's. "It's all dirt and cheating," he said, and only on the last word (*cheadn*) did the innominate colonial really sound out. He seemed for an instant as feeble as in a plonk hangover. Enderby nodded. He said kindly:

"Come back tomorrow or the next day for the rest of the stuff. Except for what I want, that is. Any heterosexual pornography I'll keep. I've finished with women."

"Finish with them." It was clear and bitter. And then: "What's all them there sling-your-hooks there, brad?" He headed at a set of cartridge-boxes set aside, special.

"Those," said Enderby, "are all the anthologies."

When Easy Walker had left, Enderby ripped open Rawcliffe's mattress with a tarnished curved dagger. There were bundles of dirty notes, high and low in denomination: about, he reckoned, fifteen thousand dirhams. He would buy a new mattress tomorrow; tonight he would make a dog's bed of rugs and cushions. Then he went thoughtfully to examine Rawcliffe's bath and lavatory, rather well-appointed; for the customers there was only a stark, though regularly sluiced, WC off the dining-conservatory. Then he went to the bar. All three boys looked at him in expectation, a composition, as for an early Picasso, of coffee-mug handlers: Antonio sipped wide-eyed; Tetuani warmed both dark brown hands on the mug's belly; Manuel, finished drinking, swung his gently, handle on little finger. "No," Enderby said firmly. "I sleep alone. *Yo duermo solo.*" They nodded with degrees of vigour: they had merely wanted to know. Manuel said:

"Open up bloody shop?"

"*Mañana.*"

"*Quiere café?*" asked Antonio.

Enderby did not resist his yearning towards a resumption of chronic self-imposed dyspepsia. He had convinced himself that he could be healthy enough if he wanted to be. "Make," he said slowly, "very strong tea. *Muy fuerte.* Not tea-bags but spoonfuls of the real stuff. *Comprendido?* Tinned milk, *Leche condensada.*" And later he

397

would eat—What? Something stepmotherly gross—a corned beef stew with bacon added to make floating flowers of grease, a grumbling huddle of boiled spuds, pickled onions. He nodded with relaxed kindness then went for his first for a hell of a long time leisurely session in the lavatory.

Two

"What I say is," said the oldest of the men, his skin of broken veins and capillaries like an enlargement of a microscopic picture of motor oil, "there couldn't have been any conspiracy. They choose crack shots. A political assassination is, in our country at least, a rather serious undertaking."

"It's altogether possible," said a dried ancient, goitrous thyroid colloidally distended, eyes popping, voice hoarse, "that it was the act of a private entrepreneur. More enthusiasm than skill. They should never have got rid of National Service."

"Well, that's just what I said, isn't it?"

"Implied, if you will. Hardly said."

"He too," said a brisk barking small ex-major, the youngest, about seventy-five, "might have been resurrected. Wouldn't put anything past them. An everlasting premier."

"Or he was just a liar." This was a dithering man with twittering toothless mouth. "Jealousy of the bug for the flea. Shot at him. Failed to kill. Now tries to make himself a political hero. What do you think, Rawcliffe?"

"I really have no opinion on the matter," said Enderby. He sat in the fireside-type chair, the table in front of him, paper and ballpoint on the table, not a line added to the lines already there:

As loaves were gifts from Ceres when she laughed,
Thyrsis was Jack, but Crousseau on a raft
Sought Johnjack's rational island—

The sun was weakish, what Tangier called winter inching up. The bottles behind the bar caught that meagre light as if to store anew what was already long stored. Manuel measured out whisky for the old men, retired here for the warmth and fancied cheapness. Manuel was cheerful and honest, to be trusted with the till. Honesty was a Tangerine luxury, to be enjoyed. There were bright pin-up calendars, promising, after the mild though windy winter, torrid abandon renewed, golden flesh, the heart-breaking wagging cruppers of the bikinied young over the golden beaches. And there were plaques advertising Byrrh, Rivoli, Royal Anjou, Carlier, a British beer called Golden Fleece. The Coca-Cola ice-box had been freshly polished by Tetuani. Marie Brizard's name was on the water-jugs, Picon's on the ashtrays. Antonio sang, preparing *tapas* in the kitchen. "Both politicians and pop-singers," Enderby said, "are boils on the bottom of the communal body." The oldest elder went aaaaargh. He liked that. Writer fellow this Rawcliffe. The apt phrase.

Enderby was not pushing on with the sonnet, nor with the letter he still had to write. The question was, he was thinking, how he was to address her. When he wrote. If he wrote. Dear Vesta: never. Dear Mrs—He'd forgotten her new name. (The address was easy: the publisher of this filthy volume.) An abusive salutation, that would be letting himself down. He had written to his own publisher, for he thought he might need him, them, again. Tiny royalties had accrued: they had been keeping them for him [£5. 7. 9.]; they were glad, they said, to know where he was at last. As for this business of plagiarism, that was his affair, since he owned copyright. They themselves were not willing to take action, since they were in the bidding for resurrected Yod Crewsy's next book—a brief prose volume, they understood, humorous, inspirational, even religious. And they enclosed a personal letter, still in its envelope, only recently arrived at the office. Enderby had frowned over the handwriting, female. You and your female hadmirers. With a thudding heart he had opened it up.

Dear Piggy or Hoggy or Dirty (for I don't know what else to call you, do I?),

I was sorry about things and still am. And now this is the only way I can get in touch with you. Because I got it out of that silly girl on the plane that it was all really a mistake and you *had* gone to the wrong room without meaning to do what that silly captain of the plane thought (you know what I'm talking about, don't you). They choose too many of these air-hostesses for their looks, though hers weren't much to write home about really, and not their intelligence, and that silly captain was a bit too quick to draw conclusions, and I certainly shan't fly with them again, that courier with the stupid woolly cap on was also very rude, I thought. The number of wrongs that seem to have been done you! I was stupid too, wasn't I, thinking you could have anything to do with that shooting, it must have been my inflamed holiday imagination. I've been thinking about you a lot and am sure you must have been thinking very bad thoughts about me. But could you blame me really? I mean, you were a bit mysterious, no luggage and all. What I *had* to do to try and make amends was to get some of your poems from the library —very difficult, the library had to send off for them—and I found some of them rather obscure and others very sad. Very modern, of course. I can't make up my mind yet about whether I really like them—that sounds ungrateful, doesn't it, but I do like to think of myself as an Honest Person, but one of our junior English lecturers—did I tell you about him? Harold Pritchard, he's trying to get a little book of criticism published—was quite gone on them. He said there were curious resemblances to the poems of Yod Crewsy (the more I think of this whole scandalous business the more convinced I am it was a big publicity stunt and in the presence of the Prime Minister as well and that makes me think less of *him*). Then Harold found the same poem in both books, and that gave him an unholy thrill, he loves anything like a literary scandal. There was no doubt, he said, who stole from whom. So he's written a letter to the Times Literary Supplement and thinks the sparks will fly. Where are you, dear Piggy? I wish I could make proper amends. Looking back I see that despite everything that Seville night was really romantic—love and your sudden inspiration and my dear moon and even your mistake when, bless you, you were looking for me. Write to me and accept my love if you will and forgive me.

Your
Miranda

Sitting here on this quiet week-day, the train from royal Rabat just going by on the single-tracked line that separated the Spanish Avenue from the beach cafés, the ink-paint congealing in his ballpoint, the harmless winter approaching, he thought that, despite the luck that had been granted (*said, and died*) the autumn should, for the sake of justice, flame out with a last act of vengeance. But he could not write the letter and, the letter unwritten, the poem would never flood into the estuary of its sestet. What did he really want from her? His money back? No, this place made enough, even in winter. Her humiliation, her smartness wrecked once more but by more devastating waters than the rain of Castel whatever-it-was, the snivelling, the running eye-shadow, the smooth face collapsed into that of a weary crone? No, not that either. Rawcliffe had taught him pity, that maketh the forests to fail.

"It will die down," said the goitrous old man, "and new sensations will come up. That new shiftless generation must be fed with fresh novelties." He took some Wilson's snuff, then hawked, carked and shivered with the dour pleasure of it.

"Not a religious man," said the snapping ex-major. "But when I see a central tenet of my father's faith—he held it, poor devil, through all his suffering—when I see that, I say, turned to a trick or gimmick or whatever the fashionable word is, then I wonder. I wonder what new blasphemy they can devise." He shuddered his whisky down in one.

"No morals," said the twittering man. "No loyalty. They will turn on their friends as if they were enemies. It was at a private party that this youth with the gun boasted in his cups. Isn't that so, Rawcliffe?"

"I don't really know," said Enderby. "I don't read the papers."

"Very wise too," said the senior elder. "Stay away from that world. Get on with your job, whatever it is."

"Sam Foot," said the goitrous old man. "A ridiculous name. Probably made up."

"Samuel Foot," said Enderby, "was an eighteenth-century actor and playwright. He was also an agent for small beer. *And they all fell to playing the game of catch as catch can, till the gun-powder ran out at the heels of their boots.*"

There was a silence. "They did, eh?" said the senior. "Well suppose I'd better be thinking about getting home for lunch. Takes me longer and longer. Walking, that is."

"He wrote that," said Enderby. "It was a test-piece. This other man said that he could recite anything after hearing it once only."

"On my way too," said the ex-major. "Bit of a blow on the prom."

The door opened and a girl came in, very tanned. She wore, as for high summer, a simple green frock well above her knees, deep-cut at her young bosom, her golden arms totally bare. She carried a beach-bag. She smiled shyly and went up to Manuel at the bar. "I understand," she said, "that I can hire a changing-cubicle or whatever it's called." Her voice was low in pitch, the accent classless. Susannah among the elders, Enderby thought. The ex-major said quietly:

"Susannah among the elders." Enderby could see them feeling old, impotent, lust too tired within to rage at so many opportunities lost, the time gone, perhaps death to be their next season. And himself? He got up and said to the girl:

"Well, you *can* actually, but—" She looked at him from green eyes sprinkled, like a *sireh* quid, with gold. They were set wide apart but not too much: enough for beauty, perhaps honesty; not enough for the panic mindless world of the animals. Hair? Enderby at once, to his surprise, thought of the flower called montbretia. "What I mean is that, surely, it's getting a bit cold now. This time of the year I mean."

"I don't feel the cold. A cold sea doesn't frighten me." As in an allegory or *Punch* title-page, the aged trundled off—winter or war, industrial depression or an all-around bad year—from the presence of youth as peace, spring, a change of government. They creaked and groaned, snorted, limped, winced at arterio-sclerotic calf-ache, went. One or two waved tiredly at Enderby from beyond the closed glass door, a safe distance. "Could I have one of then? For a couple of days. Do I pay in advance?"

"No, no, no need—Certainly. *Un llave*, Manuel."

"*Numero ocho*," Manuel smiled.

They all—Tetuani clearing the old men's whisky-glasses, Antonio at the kitchen-door, Manuel from the arena with its furled umbrellas, Enderby turned in his chair—watched her prancing seawards over the deserted sand, in scanty crimson, her hair loose. Enderby turned back in rage to his table. He took paper and wrote fiercely: "You bitch, you know you ruined my life. You also stole my verse to give to that blasphemous false commercial Lazarus of yours. Well, you won't get away with it. One of the stolen poems had already been published in one of my volumes. I'm going to sue, you're all going to suffer." And then he could see Vesta standing there, cool, smart in spotless dacron, unperturbed, saying that *she* wouldn't suffer, only that mouthing creature of hers, and he was going to be abandoned anyway, past his peak, the time for the chaotopoeic groups coming, or the duo called Lyserge and Diethyl, or Big D and the Cube and the Hawk and the Blue Acid. Or worse. Enderby took another sheet of paper and wrote:

Smell and fearful and incorrigible knackers
With the crouched pole under
And strings of his inner testes strewn
Over curried pancreas and where the
Hollowed afternoon vomits
Semen of ennui and

And and and. Send it round, signed, to the bloody Doggy Wog, showing that I can beat them at their own game if I want to, but the game isn't worth the, in Walkerian locution, turn-the-handle. And, *amigo* with the onion, I know what's in the *carta* you wanted to bring round to my lodgings where my razor and antisolar spectacle clip-on and few dirty handkerchiefs have been long snapped up by those who had not, that night, yet been betrayed to the police by fat Napo. *Khogh.* It was some word of their language, no deformed proper name from another. And the letter surely says that he saw who did it, *hombre*, and told Scotland Yard as much. A curious and perhaps suspicious lack of treach-

403

ery from treacherous Spain. Enderby felt ungratefully gloomy. All was set for writing and yet he could not write. Draft after unfinished draft. Gloomily he read through his sonnet octave again.

Augustus on a guinea sat in state. This is the eighteenth century, the Augustan age, and that guinea is a reduction of the sun. *The sun no proper study.* Exactly, the real sun being God and that urban life essentially a product of reason, which the sun melts. And no more sun-kings, only Hanoverians. *But each shaft of filtered light a column.* Meaning that you can't really do without the sun, which gives life, so filter it through smoked glass, using its energy to erect neo-classic structures in architecture or literature (well, *The Rambler,* say, or *The Spectator,* and there's a nuance in "shaft" suggesting wit). *Classic craft abhorred the arc or arch.* Yes, and those ships sailed a known world, unfloodable by a rational God, and the *arc-en-ciel* covenant is rejected. Something like that. *To circulate (blood or ideas) meant pipes, and pipes were straight.* Clear enough. You need the roundness of the guinea only so that it can roll along the straight streets or something of commercial enterprise. The round bores of the pipes are not seen on the surface, the pipes in essence being means of linking points by the shortest or most syllogistical way. And, to return to that guinea, impress on it the straight line of royal descent. And, to return to that pipe business, remember that pipes were smoked in coffee-houses and that news and ideas circulated there. And that craft business ties up with Lloyd's coffee-house. *As loaves were gifts from Ceres when she laughed, Thyrsis was Jack.* A bit fill-in for rhyme's sake, but, rejecting the sun, you reject life and can only accept it in stylised mythological or eclogue forms. But Jack leads us to Jean-Jacques. *Crousseau on a raft sought Johnjack's rational island—* The pivot coming with the volta. Defoe started it off: overcome Nature with reason. But the hearer will just hear *Crusoe.* Jack is dignified to John, glorification of common, or natural, man. Then make Nature reason and you start to topple into reason's antithesis, you become romantic. Why? A very awkward job, the continuation.

"Lovely." She had come running in, wet. She wrung a hank of hair, wetting the floor. Fat drops broke on her gold limbs. Her high-arched foot left Man Friday spoors. Seeing her round jigging nates, Enderby could have died with regret and rage. "Like a fool I brought everything except a towel. Could you possibly—" She smiled, her chin dripping as from a crunching of grapes.

"Just a minute." He puffed to his bedroom and brought out a bath towel, not yet, if ever to be, used by him, and also the gaudy robe, not greatly stained, that Rawcliffe had died in. He put it round her shoulders. Clear gold skin without a blemish and a flue of ridiculous delicacy. She rubbed her hair dry with vigour, smiling her thanks. Manuel hovered, smiling. She smiled back. Enderby tried to smile.

"Could I," she smiled, "have a drink? Something a bit astringent. Let me see—" The bottles smiled. No, they bloody well didn't: Enderby was not going to have that. "A whisky sour."

"Weeskee—?"

"I'll do it," said Enderby. "Fetch some white of egg. *Clara de huevo.*" Manuel ran into the kitchen. She rubbed herself all over in, with, dead Rawcliffe's brilliant robe. "A difficult art," blabbed Enderby, "making a whisky sour." That sounded like boasting. "Americans are very fond of them." An egg cracked loudly off. She rubbed and rubbed. Enderby got behind the bar and looked for the plastic lemon that contained lemon-juice. Manuel, having brought a tea-cup with egg-white in it and some minute embedded triangles of shell, watched her rub instead of his master mix. "There," said Enderby, quite soon.

She took it and sipped. "Hm. Is nobody else drinking?"

"About time," Enderby said, "I had my preprandial, if that's the right word." He seemed to himself to simper, pouring out straight Scotch.

"Do I pay now or do you give me a bill afterwards? And can I get lunch here, talking about preprandials?"

"Oh," said Enderby, "have this one on me. It's a kind of custom here, the first drink of a new customer on the house." And "Oh, yes. You can have steak and salad or something like that. Or spaghetti with something or other. Anything you like, really. Within reason, that is." Reason. That brought him back to that bloody poem. To his shock, he saw her bending over his table, looking openly at his papers.

"Hm," she said, having sipped again. "You've certainly got it in for this person, bitch rather."

"That," went flustered Enderby, coming round from the counter, "is of no consequence. I'm not sending it. It was just an idea, that's all. Really," he said, "you shouldn't, you know. Private." But it was your privates you were only too ready to expose, wasn't that so, when you— He felt a kind of tepid pleasure promising warmth, not outrage at all. She sat down in his fireside-type chair. She started reading his octave, frowning a little. A curiously tutorial aura seemed to be forming. Enderby went to sit down on one of the stackable chairs near his table.

"Bring it closer," she said. "What's all this about?"

"Well," babbled Enderby, "it's a sonnet, very strict. It's an attempt, really, to tie up the Age of Reason with the French Revolution. Or, on another level, the rational and the romantic can be regarded as aspects of each other, if you see what I mean." Sitting, he moved towards her without getting up, as though this were an invalid chair. "What I have to do is to show that romantic curves are made out of classical straightnesses. Do you see what I mean?" And then, gloomily, to himself: Probably not. She was young. She had perhaps mourned Yod Crewsy's death, gone to some open-air evangelical meeting on his resurrection.

She closed her eyes tight. "Keep a triplet pattern in your sestet," she said. "A breath between your cdc and your dcd. How will the classical pillars become Gothic arches? The sun will melt them, I suppose. And then you ought to have the guillotine. A very rational machine—sorry about the rhyme, but it's rhymes you're after, isn't it?"

"What," Enderby asked gravely, "would you like for lunch? There's Antonio, you see, waiting there ready to cook it." Antonio stood at the kitchen-door, trying to smile while chewing something. She nodded, not smiling but puckered charmingly, thoughtful. Guillotine, machine, seen, scene.

"What are you going to eat?" she asked. "I'll eat what you eat. Not fish, though. I can't stand fish."

"Well," Enderby mumbled, "I don't normally till— We close for the siesta, you see, and then I usually have—"

"I hate eating on my own. Besides, we've got to work this thing out. Is it something with meat in it?"

"Well," Enderby said, "I have a sort of stew going most of the time. Beef and potatoes and turnips and things. I don't know whether you'd like it, really."

"With pickled onions," she said. "And Worcestershire sauce, plenty of it. I like gross things sometimes." Enderby blushed. "I like to come down to earth sometimes."

"Here with your family?" She didn't answer. Monied, probably. "Where are you staying? The Rif? The El Greco?"

"Oh," vaguely. "It's right up the hill. Now, then. Try it."

"Eh?" And, while Tetuani set places in the conservatory, he tried it.

> Sought Johnjack's rational island, loath to wait
>   Till the sun, slighted, took revenge so that
> The pillars nodded, melted, and were seen
>   As Gothic shadows where a goddess sat—

"Volta not strong enough. The rhyme-words are far too weak. That *that* is shocking."

Then, over the thick stew, grossly over-sauced, with pickled onions crunched whole on the side and a bottle of thick red eely alumy local wine, they, he rather, literally sweated over the rest of the sestet.

> For, after all, that rational machine,
>   Imposed on all men by the technocrat,
> Was patented by Dr Guillotine.

"This is terrible," she said. "Such bloody clumsiness." She breathed on him (though a young lady should not eat, because of the known redolence of onions, onions) onions. "I'd like a bit of cheese now," she crunched. "Have you any Black Diamond cheddar? Not too fresh, if that's possible. I like it a bit hard."

"Would you also like," asked Enderby humbly, "some very strong tea? We do a very good line in that."

"It must be really strong, though. I'm glad there's something you do a very good line in. These lines are a bloody disgrace. And you call yourself a poet."

"I didn't—I never—" But she smiled when she said it.

Three

Enderby dreamt about her that night. It was a nightmare really. She was playing the piano in her scanty green dress for a gang of near-closing-time pot-swinging male singers. But it was not a pub so much as a long dark gymnasium. On top of the piano lay a yawning black dog, and Enderby, knowing it was evil, tried to warn her against it, but she and the singers only laughed. At last, though, he dragged her out protesting into the winter night (but she did not seem to feel the cold) of a grimy Northern industrial town. They had to get away quickly, by bus or tram or cab, or the dog would be out after her. He rushed her, still protesting, to a main road, and he stopped, with no difficulty, a southbound truck. She began to think the adventure funny and she made jokes to the driver. But she did not see that the driver was the dog. Enderby had to open the truck cabin-door while the vehicle was in motion and get her on to the road again to thumb a new lift. Again it was the dog. And again. And again. The new drivers were always the old dog and, moreover, though they barked they were southbound, they would almost at once turn left and left again, taking their passengers back north. Finally Enderby lost her and found himself in a town very much like Tangier, though in a summer too scorching for North Africa. He had a room but it was at the top of a high stair. Entering, he met with no surprise this girl and her mother, an older Miss Boland.

His heart pounded, he was pale, they kindly gave him a glass of water. But then, though there was no wind, the shutters of the window began to vibrate, and he heard a distant rather silly voice that somehow resembled his own. "I'm coming," it said. The girl screamed now, saying that it was the dog. But he swam up through leagues of ocean, gasping for air. Then he awoke.

He had foul dyspepsia, and, switching on the bedside lamp, he took ten Bisodol tablets. But the word *love*, he noticed, was in his mouth in the form of a remotish pickled-onion aftertaste, and he resented that. The moon was dim. Some Moorish drunks quarrelled in the distance and, more distant, real dogs started a chain of barking. He was not having it, it was all over. He drank from a bottle of Vittel, went brarrgh (and she had done that too, just once and with no excuse-me), then padded in his pyjama top to the bathroom. The striplight above the mirror suddenly granted him a grousing image of The Poet. He sat down on the lavatory seat and, a big heterosexual pornographic volume on his knees as writing-board, he tried to get the dream into a poem, see what it was all about. It was a slow job.

> At the end of the dark hall he found his love
> Who, flushed and gay,
> Pounded with a walking hand and flying fingers
> The grinning stained teeth for a wassail of singers
> That drooped around, while on the lid above
> The dog unnoticed, waiting, lolling lay.

She had been unwilling to give her name, saying it was not relevant. She had gone off about three o'clock, back in green, swinging her towelless beach-bag, giving no clue where she was going. Manuel, out later to pick up the cigarette order, said he had seen her coming out of the Doggy Wog. Enderby was jealous about that: was she helping those filthy drug-takers with their filthy drugged verses? Who was she, what did she want? Was she an anonymous agent of the British Arts Council, sent out to help with culture in, in Blake's phrase, minute particulars?

He noticed, cried, dragged her away from laughter.
   Lifts on the frantic road
      From loaded lorries helpful to seek safe south
      Slyly sidestreeted north. Each driver's mouth,
Answering her silly jokes, he gasped at after
The cabin-door slammed shut: the dogteeth showed.

She had better stop being a dream of boyhood, for it
was all too late. He had reached haven, hadn't he? He
would not be in the bar tomorrow morning (this morning really); he would be out taking a walk.

At last, weary, out of the hot noon's humming,
   Mounting his own stair,
      It was no surprise to find a mother and daughter,
      The daughter she. Hospitable, she gave him water.
Windless, the shutters shook.

This was all messed up. The story wouldn't run to another stanza, and this stanza was going to be too long. And
the rhythm was atrocious.

      A quiet voice said: "I'm coming."
   "Oh God God it's the dog," screamed the daughter,
      But he, up the miles of leaden water,
      Frantically beat for air.

A good discussion about that with somebody, over
whisky or stepmother's tea: that was what was needful.
The realisation suddenly shocked him. Had not the poet
to be alone? He converted that into bowel language and
noised it grimly in the still night, clenching the appropriate muscles, but the noise was hollow.

And so she was there again in the lemony Tangerine
sunlight of near-winter, this time bringing her towel.
The old men, perhaps frightened of the gunpowder
running out of the heels of their boots, had stayed away,
but there were other customers. Two youngish film-men,
in Morocco to choose locations that might serve for
Arizona, kept going *ja* at each other and greedily
scoffing Antonio's *tapas*—fat black olives; hot fried liver

410

on bread; Spanish salad of onion, tomato, vinegar, chopped peppers. An Englishman, in fluent but very English Spanish, expressed to Manuel his love of baseball, a game he had followed passionately when he lived three miles outside Havana. A quiet man, perhaps a Russian, sat at the corner of the counter, steadily and to no effect downing raw Spanish gin.

"Not worth writing," she said, "a poem like that." She had changed back into a crimson dress even briefer than the green one. The baseball *aficionado*, greying vapidly handsome, kept giving her frank glances, but she did not seem to notice. "You yourself may be moved by it," she said, "because of the emotional impact of the dream itself. But it's dreary old sex images, isn't it, no more. The dog, I mean. North for tumescence. And you're trying to protect me from yourself, or yourself from me—both silly." Enderby looked at her bitterly, desirable and businesslike as she was. He said:

"That *love* in the first line. I'm sorry about that. I don't mean it, of course. It was just in the dream."

"All right, we're scrapping it anyway." And she crumpled the work of three hours of darkness and threw it on the floor. Tetuani gladly picked it up and bore it off to nest with other garbage. "I think," she said, "we'll go for a walk. There's another sonnet we have to work out, isn't there?"

"Another?"

"One you mentioned yesterday. About the Revolt of the Angels or something."

"I'm not sure that I—" He frowned. She punched him vigorously on the arm, saying:

"Oh, don't dither so. We haven't much time." She led him out of the bar, stronger than she looked, and the customers, all of whom were new, assumed that Enderby was an old customer who had had enough.

"Look," Enderby said, when they stood on the esplanade, "I don't understand anything about this at all. Who are you? What right have you? Not," he added, "that I don't appreciate— But really, when you come to consider it—"

The wind whipped rather coldly, but she felt no cold,

arms akimbo in her ridiculously brief dress. "You do waste time, don't you? Now how does it begin?"

They walked in the direction of the Medina, and he managed to hit some of it out into the wind. It was as though she were telling him to get it all up, better up than down.

Sick of the sycophantic singing, sick
    Of every afternoon's compulsory games—

Sturdy palms set all along the sea-front, the fronds stirred by that wind. The donkeys with loaded panniers, an odd sneering camel.

"That's the general idea, isn't it? Heaven as a minor public school. Did you go to a minor public school?"

"I went," said Enderby, "to a Catholic day-school."

It was Friday, and the devout were shuffling to mosque. The imam or bilal or whatever he was was gargling over a loud-speaker. Brown men, of Rif or Berber stock, followed the voice, looking at her legs, though, with bright-eyed frank but hopeless desire. "It's a lot of superstitious nonsense," she said. "Don't, whatever the temptation, go back to it. Use it as mythology, pluck it bare of images, but don't ever believe in it again. Take the cash in hand and waive the rest."

"An indifferent poet, Fitzgerald." Enderby loved her for saying what she had said.

"Very well, let's have something better."

Sick of the little cliques of county names,
    The timebomb in his brain began to tick—

Luncheon in a little restaurant crammed with camp military gear, not too far from the Hotel El Greco. It was run by two men in love with each other, one American, the other English. A handsome Moorish boy who waited on seemed himself in love with the Englishman, who was flaxen, bronzed, petulant and given to shouting at the cook. The Moor was not adept at hiding emotion: his big lower lip trembled and his eyes swam. Enderby and she had a thin dull goulash which she said loudly was bloody terrible. The English lover tossed his head and affricated petulantly against his alveolum, then turned up the music—a sexy cocksure American male voice singing, against a Mahlerian orchestra, thin dull café society songs of the 'thirties. She prepared to shout that the bloody noise must be turned off: it was interfering with their rhythm. Enderby said:

"Don't. Please. I've got to live in this town."

"Yes," she said, her green eyes, their gold very much metal, hard on him. "You lack courage. You've been softened by somebody or something. You're frightened of the young and the experimental and the way-out and the black dog. When Shelley said what he said about poets being the unacknowledged legislators of the world, he wasn't really using fancy language. It's only by the exact use of words that people can begin to understand themselves. Poetry isn't a silly little hobby to be practised in the smallest room of the house."

He blushed. "What can I do?"

She sighed. "Get all these old things out of your system first. Then push on."

Beating out number. As arithmetic,
    As short division not divided aims,
    Resentment flared. But then, carved out in flames,
He read: *That flower is not for you to pick.*

"It's time," she said, "you started work on a long poem."

"I tried that once. That bastard stole it and vulgarised it. But," and he looked downhill, seaward, "he's paid. Wrapped in a Union Jack, being gently gnawed."

"You can get something here. This is a junction. Deucalion's flood and Noah's. Africa and Europe. Christianity and Islam. Past and future. The black and the white. Two rocks looking across at each other. The Straits may have a submarine tunnel. But it was Mallarmé who said that poetry is made with words, not ideas."

"How do you know all this? You're so *young.*"

She spat out breath very nastily. "There you go again. More interested in the false divisions than the true ones. Come on, let's have that sestet."

The sestet ended in a drinking-shop not far from the Souk or Socco, over glasses of warmish pastis. Drab long robes, hoods, ponchos, ass-beaters, loud gargling Moghrabi, nose-picking children who used the other hand to beg. Sympathetic, Enderby gave them little coins.

> Therefore he picked it. All things thawed to action,
>   Sound, colour. A shrill electric bell
> Summoned the guard. He gathered up his faction,
>   Poised on the brink, thought and created hell.
> Light shimmered in miraculous refraction
>   As, like a bloody thunderbolt, he fell.

"That *bloody*," Enderby said. "It's meant really to express grudging admiration. But that only works if the reader knows I've taken the line from Tennyson's poem about the eagle."

"To hell with the reader. Good. That needs a lot of going over, of course, but you can do that at leisure. When I'm gone, I mean. Now we'd better take a look at that Horatian Ode thing. Can we have dinner at your place?"

"I'd like to take you *out* to dinner," Enderby said. And, "When you're gone, you said. When are you going?"

"I'm flying off tomorrow evening. About six."

Enderby gulped. "It's been a short stay. You can get a very good dinner at a place called the *Parade*. I could get a taxi and pick you up about—"

"Still curious, aren't you? Bit of a change for you, isn't it, this curiosity about people? You've never cared much for people, have you? From what you've told me, anyway. Your father let you down by marrying your stepmother, and your mother let you down by dying too young. And these others you've mentioned, men and women."

"My father was all right," Enderby said. "I never had anything against him." He frowned, though ungrudgingly.

"Many years ago," she said, "you published a little

volume at your own expense. Inevitably it was very badly printed. You had a poem in it called "Independence Day." '

"I'm damned if I remember."

"A rather bad poem. It started:

> Anciently the man who showed
> Hate to his father with the sword
> Was bundled up in a coarse sack
> With a frantic ape to tear his back
> And the squawking talk of a parrot to mock
> Time's terror of air-and-light's lack
> Black
> And the creeping torpor of a snake."

"I can't possibly have written that," went Enderby, worried now. "I could never possibly have written anything as bad as that."

"No?" she said. "Listen.

> Then he was swirled into the sea.
> But that was all balls and talk.
> Nowadays we have changed all that,
> Into a cleaner light to walk
> And wipe that mire off on the mat.
> So when I knew his end was near
> My mind was freer
> And snapped its thumb and finger then
> At the irrelevance of birth,
> And I had a better right to the earth
> And knew myself more of a man,
> Shedding the last squamour of the old skin."

"That's somebody else," said Enderby urgently. "Honestly, it's not me."

"And you love your mother because you never knew her. For all you know she might have been like your stepmother."

"It's different now," pleaded Enderby. "I forgive my stepmother, I forgive her everything."

"That's very generous of you. And who do you love?"

415

"I was just coming to that," said Enderby with approaching banners of wretchedness. "What I wanted to say was—"

"All right, all right. Don't pick me up in a taxi. You can't anyway, because you don't know where I am. *I'll* pick *you* up about eight. Now go home and work on your bloody Horatian Ode. No, leave me here. I go in a different direction." She seemed needlessly irritable, and Enderby, having once, though briefly, lived with a woman, wondered if it was possibly— She was old enough, wasn't she, to have—

"Gin and hot water," he suggested kindly, "are said to work wonders." But she didn't seem to hear. She seemed to have switched off Enderby like a television image, looking blankly at him as if he had become a blank screen. A very strange girl altogether. But he thought that, having got the better of the moon, he could perhaps this time live with his fear.

Four

She was smartly dressed for the evening in bronze stockings and a brief, but not too brief, gold dress, a gold stole round her tanned shoulders, her hair up at the back. On her left wrist she had a gold chain from which miniscule figurines depended. It was a restaurant of subdued lights, and Enderby could not see what the figurines were or meant. She was perfumed, and the perfume suggested something baked—a delicate but aphrodisiacal soufflé seasoned with rare liqueurs. Enderby was wearing one of Rawcliffe's Edwardian suits—it did not fit too badly—and even Rawcliffe's gold watch and chain. One thing Enderby did not like about this place was that the mortician *collage* man from the Doggy Wog was in it and was obviously a respected and regular customer. He sat at a table opposite and was eating with his fingers a brace of roast game-birds. He had greeted this girl with a growl of familiarity but now, picking the meat from a backbone, he kept his eyes sternly on her. He did not apparently remember Enderby. She had returned his greeting with an American air-hostess's "Hi."

Tonight she was not going to have greasy stew and pickled onions and stepmother's tea. She read the menu intently, as though it contained a Nabokovian cryptogram, and ordered a young hare of the kind called a capuchin, marinated in *marc*, stuffed with its own and some pig's liver as well as breadcrumbs, truffle, and a little preserved turkey-meat, and served with a sauce full of red wine and double cream. Before it she had a small helping of jellied boar. Enderby, confused, said he would have sheep's tongue *en papillotes*, whatever they were, that was. And, after dry martinis which she sent back as neither dry nor cold enough, they had champagne—Bollinger '53. She said it was not very exciting, but it seemed to be the best they had, so they put, at her demand, another bottle on ice while they were drinking this one. Enderby uneasily saw signs of a deliberate intention to get tight. Soon, clanking down her fork, she said:

"A fancied superiority to women. Despise their brains so pretend to despise their bodies as well. Just because you can't have their bodies."

"I beg your pardon?"

"Juvenilia. One of your," she belched gently, "juvenilia."

"Juvenilia? But I never published any of my juvenilia." Several bar-customers were interested in the repeated word: a gland injection, a sexual posture, a synthetic holiday resort. She began to recite with mocking intensity:

> "They fear and hate
> the Donne and Dante in him, this
> cold
> gift to turn heat to a flame, a kiss
> to the gate
> of a mons-
> ter's labyrinth. They hold
> and anchor a thin thread—"

417

"Not so loud," went Enderby with quiet force, blushing. The mortician was looking sardonic over a large dish of blood-coloured ice cream.

> "—the tennis party, the parish dance:
> stale pus out of dead
> pores."

Someone at the bar, unseen in the dimness, applauded. "I didn't write that," said Enderby. "You're getting me mixed up with somebody else."

"Am I? Am I? I suppose that's possible. There's so much minor poetry about."

"What do you mean—minor?"

She downed a long draught of Bollinger, as though the recitation had made her thirsty, belched with no excuse-me, and said: "There was that other nasty little thing about meeting a girl at a dance, wasn't there? Juvenilia, again." Or a disease perhaps, one of those gruesomely pleasant-sounding ones like salmonella. She took more champagne and, with world-weary tone and over-sharp articulation, recited:

> "Semitic violins by the wailing wall
> Gnash their threnody
> For the buried jungle, the tangle of lianas—"

"I think," Enderby said sternly, "that I have some right to know—"

> "Or say that was before, in the first flush,
> And say that now
> A handful of coins, image and milled edge worn,
> Is spilled abroad to determine
> Our trade of emotions."

"I mean, apart from how you know all that, and I don't believe it's mine anyway—"

> "On this background are imposed
> Urges, whose precise nature it is difficult to define:
> Shells shaped by forgotten surges."

418

"I'm not having any more of this," and Enderby grasped her thin wrist firmly. She shook herself free with little effort and said:

"Too rich for you, is it?" She sniffed at his half-eaten sheep's tongue *en papillotes*. "A lot of things are too rich for you, aren't they? Never mind, mumsy will ook after him den. Let me finish." Enderby, very wretched, let her.

> "One understands so little, having no words
> To body forth thoughts, no axe
> To reach flagged soil, no drills
> To pierce to living wells. It would tax
> My energies overmuch now to garner you
> Out of worn coins, worn shells."

She took another bumper of fuming wine, belched like an elfin trumpet of triumph, then waved smiling across to the mortician. He said:

"That's telling him."

"You're being bloody unfair," said Enderby loudly and, to the mortician, more loudly, "You keep your nose out of this, sod." The mortician looked at Enderby with very small interest and went on eating ice cream.

"Big untrue postures," she delivered. "Pretence. You can't make major poetry out of pretence."

"I tell you," said Enderby, "it was my stepmother's fault, but that's all over now. Pretence, you say," he added cunningly, "but very memorable pretence. Not," he super-added, "that I wrote that. I'm sure I didn't." He was pretty sure, anyway.

"I can remember anything," she said smugly. "It's a gift." Then she went *phew*. "God, it's warm in here." And she pulled her stole off roughly, showing her glowing young shoulders.

"It's not really warm, you know," said Enderby. And, hopefully: "Perhaps it's all that champagne. Perhaps you're not feeling too well."

"I feel fine," she said. "It's the sun within me. I'm a beaker full of the warm south. Nice tension of opposites there: cooled a long age in the deep-delved earth." She had drunk most of the first bottle and was now doing very well with the second. "I won't pretend that you wrote that, because you didn't. Poor boy. But his name was *not* writ in water." Enderby felt chilled when he heard that. "Posterity," she then said. "The poet addresses posterity. And what is posterity? Schoolmarms with snotty kids trailing round the monuments. The poet's tea-mug with an ingrained ring of tannin-stain. The poet's love-letters. The poet's falling hair, trapped in brush-bristles rarely washed. The poet's little failings—well-hidden, but not for ever. And the kids are bored, and the texts are covered with thumb-marks and dirty little marginalia. They've read the poems, oh yes. They're posterity. Do you never think of posterity?"

Enderby looked warily at her. "Well, like everybody else—"

"Minor poets hope that posterity will turn them into major ones. A great man, my dear, who suffered the critics' sneers and the public's neglect. Halitotic breathing over your corpse. Reverent treading through the poet's cottage, fingering the pots and pans."

Enderby started. "That's brought back a dream. I think it was a dream. The pots and pans fell, and I woke."

"Oh, come on, let's finish this champagne and go. I can't eat any more of this muck. Creamed leveret's bones, ugh. Let's go and swim."

"At this hour? And it's very cold, the sea I mean. And besides—"

"You don't swim. I know. You're preparing your body for honoured corpsedom. You don't do anything with it. All right, you can watch *me swim.*" She filled both their flutes and downed hers, re-filled and downed again.

"What I meant to say was—It's a bit difficult, I know, but—" He called for the bill. "*Cuenta, por favor.*" Quite the little Tangerine, he was thinking. Settling here for corpsedom. No, not that. He had his work, hadn't he? And there was this other matter, and he'd better blurt it out now before the bill came. "I know," he said stiffly but urgently, "there's a great disparity of age. But if you could see your way—I mean, we get on all right together. I would leave it to you to decide on the precise nature of the relationship. I ask nothing." The bill came: another flame-haired Goth of a Spanish waiter, flashing a gold tunthus. It was a lot of dirhams. Enderby counted out note after note after note, all from Rawcliffe's mattress.

"You only ask *me*," she said. The champagne was done, and she upturned the bottle to hold it like a thyrsus. "Come on, I'm burning."

The mortician growled something about that being okay then. She smiled and nodded. "What do you do over there?" asked Enderby jealously. "You go over there. The dog place, I mean. I know you do."

"I go to a lot of places. I'm a beezy leetle girl. The world's bigger than you could ever imagine."

The doorman whistled a *petit taxi* or *taxi chico*. It was a windy night in a hilly street, no more. But a dirty old Moor shuffled to them to offer a small parcel of marijuana for five dirhams. "Shit," she said. "Dilutions for the tourists. All teased out of fag-ends collected from the gutters." She gave the old man a brief mouthful of what sounded like fluent Arabic. He seemed shocked. Enderby was past being surprised. In the taxi he said:

"What do you say then? The precise nature of the relationship—"

"You leave to me. Right. I heard you the first time." They rolled seawards. The driver, a moustached thin Moor with a skullcap, kept turning round to have a look at her. She banged him on the shoulder, saying: "Keep your fucking eyes on the road." And to Enderby: "All I want at the moment is my swim. I don't want avowals and the precise nature of the relationship." She was silent then, and Enderby thought it prudent also to be silent. They came to near the gate, only the single track to cross, which opened on to the beach steps and the— But *El Acantilado Verde* had been painted out and the new name as yet only lightly stencilled. Manuel had a brother who did that sort of thing.

The bar looked grim and functional under the plain lights. "Come in here," Enderby invited, leading her to his own room. There were table-lamps, shaded in warm

421

colours, that all came on together when he clicked the switch by the door. Many of Rawcliffe's Moorish curiosa were still around, but there was now a lot of naked shelf-space to be clothed. But with what? He didn't read much. Perhaps he ought to read more, keep in touch with the posterity of which she, all said and done, was very nearly a member. Read about media and the opening up of the psyche with drugs. All sorts of things. Enderby had bought a bedspread of camel-hair, its design undistinguished, as well as new sheets and a new mattress. There was still something raffish, riffish, Rawcliffesque about the bed on the floor, in the middle of the floor. Enderby had not yet sufficiently breathed on things.

"Hm," she said. "How about calling that cook-boy of yours to see about some coffee? I'd like some coffee afterwards."

"Oh, he's not here. They all sleep out. *Yo,*" Enderby said, with painful roguery, "*duermo solo.*" And then: "Of course, you can't swim, can you? You forgot, I forgot. You've nothing to swim in." He smiled.

"That's right," she said. "Nothing. I shall swim in nothing." And, before Enderby could say anything, she darted over to his book-shelves and picked on a gilt-backed folio.

"That," said Enderby, "isn't mine. It was left by him. Don't look at it, please." Fool, he should have thought. "And don't swim with nothing on. It's too cold, there are laws against it, the police will come along, this is a Muslim country, very strict about indecency."

"Indecency," she said, looking through the volume. "Yes. Dear dear dear. That seems more painful than pleasurable."

"Please don't." He meant two things. He felt he wanted to wring his hands. But she dropped the book on the floor and then started to take her dress off. "I'll make coffee myself," he said, "and there's some rather good cognac. Please don't."

"Good, we'll have that afterwards." And she kicked off her spiky shoes and began to peel down her stockings, sitting on Enderby's bedside chair to do it more easily.

And then. He gulped, wondering whether to turn his back, but that somehow, after that book, might seem hypocritical. Bold Enderby, unmoved, watching. But:

"Go in as you are, by all means, but—" But going in as she was now meant going in very nearly as she wanted to go in. And now entirely. Oh God. Enderby saw her totally naked, all gold, with no shocking leprous bands where they might, beach decency being observed, be expected to be. He just stood there, a butler called in by her eccentric ladyship. She looked him hard, though soft, in the eyes. He gnashed his teeth at her ghastly young beauty, all revealed. She said:

"Time enough." Huskily. Then she lay on the camel-hair, eyes not leaving his, and said: "Love. You meant to say love. Come on, take me. Darling. I'm yours, all yours. When I give I give. You know that." He did know it. And she held out gold blades of arms, gold foil gleaming in her oxters. And gold below on the mount. "You said," she said, "I must decide on the precise nature of the relationship. Well, I'm deciding. Darling, darling. Come on."

"No," gasped Enderby. "You know I can't. That isn't what I meant."

"Just like Mr Prufrock. Darling, darling, you can do anything you like. Come, don't keep me waiting."

"It won't do," said Enderby, dying. He saw himself there with her, puffing in his slack whiteness. "I'm sorry I said what I said."

She suddenly drew her knees up to her chin, embracing her shins, and laughed, not unkindly. "Minor poet," she said. "We know now where we stand, don't we? Never mind. Be thankful for what you've got. Don't ask too much, that's all." And she leapt from the bed, brushing his hand with the smoothness of her gold flank, just for a fraction of time, as she ran past him to the door, out of the door, out of the building, out of the arena, towards the sea.

Enderby sat on the bed, blood forming patterns in his eyes. His heart growled as it thumped. Off to the bloody sea, where Rawcliffe was. But no. Rawcliffe was in the Mediterranean, east of here. She was out in the fringes of the Atlantic, a bigger sea. One sometimes forgot that it was the Atlantic here, the Atlantic and Africa and all the big stuff. Minor poet in Africa, facing the Atlantic. There would undoubtedly be phosphorescence all round her as she plunged further into the Atlantic.

Five

She didn't come in the following morning, and he didn't expect her. Yet there had been no good-bye, not yet. She had high-heeled into the kitchen, glowing, clothed, even perfumed (yet smelling somehow, to his fancy, of drowned poets) to see him watching the bubbling coffee as if it were an alchemical experiment. And she hadn't liked the coffee: too weak, too minor-poetic. Well, he had never been good at coffee. Tea, now, was altogether a different matter. Anyway, she had to fly: so much to see to before really flying. And then, lightly and without satire, a kiss on each cheek for him, as at the award of some *prix* for minor poetry. And off.

Tossing in his bed, he had wondered about minor poets. There was T.E. Brown, three legs of Man, who had said: "O blackbird, what a boy you are, how you do go it," and given to British gardens pot or plastic godwottery. And Leigh Hunt, whom Jenny had kissed. And the woman who'd seen Faunus in Flush, later married to a poet deemed major. *Minor Poets of the Twentieth Century* (OUP, 84's) with a couple or three of his separated, because of the alphabetical order, from that one of Rawcliffe. But once they had thought *Aurora Leigh* the greatest thing since Shakespeare, and Hopkins to be just jesuitical hysteria. It all depended on posterity. One kiss, two kisses. And he saw that her name didn't matter.

He sighed, but not hopelessly. He had gone back to the Horatian Ode this morning, in a rather crowded bar.

> So will the flux of time and fire,
> The process and the pain, expire,

And history can bow
To one eternal now.

He had to get behind the counter, expert, Hogg of the Sty
(When you say gin, Piggy knows you mean Yeoman
Warder. False smile flashing over the shaker in some
glossy advertisement), to mix a Manhattan for a dour
Kansan who believed the drink was named for the university town in his own state. And a young but archaic
what-what haw-haw Englishman, doggy scarf in his
open shirt, had brought in two girls, one of them called
Bunty, and said that nobody in this town knew how to
mix a hangman's blood. But he, Enderby, Hogg, knew,
and the man was discomfited. Three old men had been
in, the fourth, the one with skin like microscope slides,
not being too well, confined to his room. Doubt if he'll
see another spring. Won the Bisley shoot in, let me see,
when was it? MC and bar, but never talked about it
much.

What was emerging, Enderby saw, was a long poem
based on the characters in *Hamlet*. The Horatian Ode
was for the King, type of the absolute ruler who would
seal a timeless Denmark off from the flux of history. An
epithalamium for him and Gertrude, the passion of the
mature. He'd written a good deal of that in Gloucester
Road, when Vesta went off to work for the day, bitch.

The greenstick snaps, the slender goldenrod
Here cannot probe or enter. Thin spring winds
Freeze blue lovers in unprotected hollows, but
Summer chimes heavy bells and flesh is fed
Where fruit bursts, the ground is crawling with
    berries.

Something like that. It would come back to him in time.
A long soliloquy for Hamlet. Marsyas, was he, he Enderby, risking a minor poet's flaying? Never mind. On with
bloody job is best way, *hombre*.

She came in when he was ready for his stew, followed
by tea and siesta. She was dressed rather demurely, not
unlike Miss Boland, beige suit, skirt to her knees, stock-

425

ings of a gunmetal colour, shoes sensible and well-polished. There were blue rings, half-rings really, under her eyes. She wore a hat like a Victorian sailor's. She said:

"I've got a cab waiting outside." Meaning over the sand, up the steps, across the railway line and pavement, by the kerb with a palm strongly clashing above. The wind was high. "You're not to worry too much about anything," she said. "Do what you can do. Don't try and tame dogs or enter a world of visions and no syntax." This was very sybilline talk.

"I'm doing a long poem based on the characters in *Hamlet*. I don't quite know yet what the overall theme is, but I daresay it'll come out in time. Could I make you a cup of tea? Antonio's got the day off. He's gone to see a man in Rabat."

"Good. No, thanks. I'll be back to visit you. Next year perhaps. I suppose I should have come before, but I have so much to do." Enderby was aware now that there was no point in asking further questions: taking your degree in English, are you; doing a thesis on contemporary poetry, is that it? These things didn't apply, no more than curiosity, which he no longer felt, about her identity or origin or age. All things to all poets, but to this poet perhaps less than to some others. No envy. Posterity would sort things out. But, of course, posterity was only those snotnosed schoolkids.

"I'm grateful," he said, though, out of habit, grudgingly. "You know I am."

"You can't be blamed," she said, "if you've opted to live without love. Something went wrong early. Your juvenilia days." Enderby frowned slightly. "Look," she said, "I really must rush now. I only came to say good-bye. But not good-bye really," grimacing at her watch. Enderby stood up, wincing a bit. A spasm in the right calf, altogether appropriate to middle age. "So," she said, and she walked the three paces up to him and gave him one brief kiss on the lips. His share, his quota, what he was worth. Her mouth was very warm. *The final kiss and final—* As if she knew, she gave him the referent, leaving the words to him, very briefly grasping

426

his writing fingers, pressing them. Her gloves were beige, of some kind of soft and expensive skin. *Tight pressure of hands.* That was it then, the poem finished. But the whole thing was a lie (opted to live without love), though it would not be a lie to anybody who could use it, somebody young and in love, saying an enforced good-bye to the beloved. Poets, even minor ones, donated the right words, and the small pride might swallow the large envy.

"Right, then," she said. They went together to the door, almost with the formality of distinguished customer and bowing *patron*. He watched her climb up to her taxi, feeling a spasm of hopeless rage, briefer than a borborygm, at the last sight of her neatly moving buttocks. But he had no right to that feeling, so the feeling quickly modulated, as a nettle-sting modulates to warmth (the bare-legged legionaries had kept themselves warm in British winters by lashing themselves with nettles: might there not be a poem there?), to something which had, as one of its upper partials, that very pride. She waved before getting in, and then called something that sounded a bit like *all the anthologies, anyway,* but a passing coach, full of sightseers collected from the Rif, roared at it. The gear ground, *for time himself will bring,* but this was only a decrepit Moroccan taxi. The wind blew hard. She was gone; like a hypodermic injection it was all over. He wondered if it might not be a pius duty to find out more about Rawcliffe's slender and thwarted *oeuvre,* edit, reprint at expense of mattress. There might be odd things, juvenilia even, concealed about the place, perhaps even in those tomes of pornography. But no, best keep away. He had enough work of his own to do, the duty of at least being better than T. E. Brown or Henley or Leigh Hunt or Sir George Goodby or Shem Macnamara. Whatever the future was going to be about, things ought to be all right, namely not too good, with enough scope for guilt, creation's true dynamo. It would be polite to reply to Miss Boland's letter, perhaps. If she proposed visiting him he could, if he wished, always put her off. He would go in now to his gross stew and stewed tea, then sleep for a while. The C major of this life. Was Browning minor? He turned to face the Atlantic but, going brrrrrr, was glad to be able to hurry in to escape from it.

Six

This, children, is Morocco. Does it not give you a thrill, seeing what you have all heard or read about so often? Pashas and the Beni-Quarain and camels. Mulai Hafid and Abd-el-Kadir. The light-coloured Sherifians, who claim descent from the Prophet. Palmetto and sandarach and argan and tizra. You say it does *not give* you a thrill, Sandra? Well, child, you were never strong on imagination, were you? And I do not wish to hear any of these silly giggly whispers about what *does* give you a thrill. Some of you girls have very few thoughts in your heads. Yes, I mean you too, Andrea. And, Geoffrey, because that elderly Berber is picking his nose you need not feel impelled to do the same. Lions, Bertrand? Lions are much much further south. Leopards here, bears, hyenas and wild pigs. Bustard, partridge and water-fowl. Dromedaries and dashing Barbary horses.

This is Tangier, which, you may not know this, once actually belonged to the British. Part of the dowry of Catherine of Braganza, Portuguese queen of a merry monarch. A pleasant enough town, no longer very distinguished, with some deplorable specimens of architecture. The beach is deserted. This is not the tourist season and, besides, it is the hour of the siesta. The beach cafés are garish, the paint peeling on many, but some of their names are rather charming. The Winston Churchill, the Sun Trap, the Cuppa, the Well Come. Those Hebrew letters there mean *kosher* (it is three consonants, the Semitic languages not greatly favouring the alphabetisation of vowels. Yes, Donald, Arabic too is a Semitic language and is similarly vowel-shy. Why then do not the Jews and Arabs, aware of a common origin in speech and alphabetic method as well as genes, taboos and mythology, get on better together? There, child, you have the eternal mystery of brotherhood. As Blake might have said, Let me hate him, or let me be his brother. But a good question, Donald, and thank you for asking it) which means, of food, not forbidden by religion. A holiday, you see, condones no relaxations of fundamental covenants. Stop grinning, Andrea. I shall lose my temper in a minute.

That one there is having its name repainted. You can see what it will be, in tasteful ultramarine. *La Belle Mer.* Very pretty. Some Frenchman probably, offering a most delicate cuisine, but now neatly sleeping. Listen, you can hear them sleep. Zrrrzzz. Ghraaaaaakh. Ong. Sleep possesses so many of the better sort, and it is sleep that sustains our visitation, to be fractured and fantasticated on waking, perhaps even totally forgotten.

Why are we here? A fair question, Pamela. What has all this to do with literature? I am very glad you asked that. Well, let me say this. Here you have expatriates of Northern stock, water to the oil of the Moors and Berbers and Spanish. Many of them have fled their native lands to escape the rigour of the law. Yes, alas, crimes. Expropriation of funds, common theft, sexual inversion. I thought you would ask that, Sandra. That term *sexual* effects, in your case, an almost voltaic connection. The term means nothing more than philoprogenitive urges deflected into channels that possess no generative significance. What's all that when it's at home? I expected that remark from you, ignorant girl. I shall ignore it. Ignoration is the only rational response to ignorance. Think that one over, you over-developed little flesh-pot.

And among the exiles from the North are artists, musicians, writers. They have sinned, but they have talent. Desperately they exercise their talent here, dreaming of bitter ale and meadowsweet but cut off for ever, yes for ever, from the Piccadilly flyover and the Hyde Park State Museum and the Communal Beerhall on Hammersmith Broadway. Those are the British. The Americans weep too nightly into their highballs for the happy shopping evenings in the Dupermarket, the drive-in colour stereovideo, the nuclear throb of the fully automated roadglobe. But they practise their arts. It is writers mostly. Up that hill lives a man who has already produced twenty-five volumes of autobiography: he tears at each instant of his pre-exilic past as though it were a prawn. Another man, on the Calle Larache, eats into his unconscious heart and mounts the regurgitated fragments on fragments of old newspaper. Another man again writes sneering satire, in sub-Popean couplets, on an England already dead. They are small artists, all. Here there is a *rue* Beethoven, also an *avenida* Leonardo da Vinci, a *plaza* de Sade. But no artist here will have a square or thoroughfare named for him. They are nothing.

And yet think what, on three sides, surrounds them, though the fierce Atlantic will give a right orchestration to the muscularity of what, to the sun's own surprise, has sprung out of sunbaked Africa and Iberia. The glory of the Lusiad (George, you will please not yawn) and the stoic bravery and heartbreak of the Cid, and the myth of Juan and the chronicle of the gaunter Don on the gaunt horse. Clash of guitars up there and the drum-roll of hammering heels in the dance, and down there the fever of native timpani. And, east, the tales told to the cruel Sultan Shahriyar, and the delicate verse-traceries of Omar this and Abdul that (all right, Benedict, there is no need to snigger: Islamic poetry is not my subject) and Sayid the other thing.

Yawwwwww. Ogre. Uuuuuugh.

The pain of their awakening, not all of them alone, to the coming of the Tangerine evening. All right, we all know that a tangerine is a small orange, much flattened at the poles. Very funny, Geoffrey. But perhaps now you will consider why it is called what it is called. The calligraphic neons will glow—*fa* and *kaf* and *kaf* and *nun* and *tok*—and the shops resume their oil-lit trades. Ladies in yashmaks and caftans will stroll the *rues* or *calles*, and the boys will jeer and giggle at the few male tourists and point at their younger brothers as if they were carcasses of tender lamb. And the writers will groan at their words of the forenoon and despair.

So away! Our camels sniff the evening and are glad. A quotation, if you *must* know, Benedict. Let us leave them, for men must be left to, each, the dreeing of his own weird. A man must contrive such happiness as he can. So must we all. So must we all, Geoffrey and Benedict and George and Donald and Andrea and Pamela and that horrid Sandra and— Oh, get into line there. We take off, into the Atlantic wind. The moon, sickle of Islam, has risen. The planets Marikh and Zuhrah and Zuhal shine. The stars, in American issue army boots, slide silently to their allotted posts. And the words slide into the slots ordained by syntax and glitter, as with atmospheric dust, with those impurities which we call meaning. Away, children! Leave them to it.

> Until the final glacier grips
> Each island, with its dream of ships

And and and and. Keep on. It will come out right, given time and application. You can, when depressed, pluck your own sweet bay or *laurus nobilis*. It grows here. Nobody will pluck it for you. The aromatic leaves are useful in cookery, and you can cure your sick cat with the berries.

Appendix

Some uncollected early poems by F. X. Enderby.

The poems that follow have not, for some reason, appeared in any of the published volumes of Enderby's verse, and the last poem has not previously been published at all. The poems beginning "Anciently the man who showed . . .", "They fear and hate the Donne and Dante in him . . ." and "Semitic violins, by the wailing wall . . .", allegedly from Enderby's juvenile productions, cannot be traced either in published or manuscript form. It may be of interest to note, however, that the catalogue of the ill-fated Gorgon Press, which specialised in verse printed at the author's own expense, lists a volume by one A. Rawcliffe—*Balls and Talk: Poems 1936.* No copies of this volume have as yet come to light.

A.B.

September, 1938

There arose those winning life between two wars,
Born out of one, doomed food for the other,
Floodroars ever in the ears.

Slothlovers hardly, hardly fighters:
Resentment spent against stone, long beaten out of
Minds resigned to the new:
Useless to queue for respirators.

Besides, what worse chaos to come back to.
Home, limbs heavy with mud and work, to sleep
To sweep out a house days deep in dirt.

Knowing finally man would limbs loin face
Efface utterly, leaving in his place
Engines rusting to world's end, heirs to warfare
Fonctionnant d'une manière automatique.

Summer, 1940

Summer swamps the land, the sun imprisons us,
The pen slithers in the examinee's fingers,
And colliding lips of lovers slide on sweat
When, blind, they inherit their tactile world.

Spectacles mist, handveins show blue, the urge to undress
Breeds passion in unexpected places. Barrage balloons
Soar silver in silver ether. Lying on grass,
We watch them, docile monsters, unwind to the zenith.

Drops of that flood out of France, with mud and work
Stained, loll in the trams, drinking their cigarettes,
Their presence defiling the flannels and summer frocks,
The hunters to hound our safety, spoil the summer.

Spring in Camp, 1941

War becomes time, and long logic
On buried premises; spring supervenes
With the circle as badge which, pun and profundity,
Vast, appears line and logical,
But, small, shows travel returning.
Circle is circle, proves nothing, makes nothing,
Swallows up process and end in no argument,
Brings new picture of old time.

Here in barracks is intake of birds,
The sun holds early his orderly room,
The pale company clerk is uneasy
As spring brings odour of other springs.
The truckdriver sings, free of the road,
The load of winter and war becomes
Embarrassing as a younger self.
Words disintegrate; war is words.

The Excursion

The blue of summer morning begs
The country journey to be made,
The sun that gilds the breakfast eggs
Illuminates the marmalade.

A cheque is smiling on the desk.
Remembered smells upon the lane
Breed hunger for the picaresque
To blood the buried springs again.

Here is the pub and here the church
And there our thirty miles of sun,
The river and the rod and the perch,
The noonday drinking just begun.

Let beer beneath the neighbour trees
Swill all that afternoon away,
And onions, crisp to sullen cheese,
Yield the sharp succulence of today.

Today remembers breaking out
The fire that burned the hayfield black.
An army that was grey with drought
Shows to my stick its fossil track.

Returning evening rose on rose
Or pomegranate rouge and ripe;
The lamp upon the pavement throws
The ectoplasm of my pipe.

Eden

History was not just what you learned that scorching day
Of ink and wood and sweat in the classroom, when mention
Of the Duke of Burgundy lost you in a voluptuous dream
Of thirst and Christmas, but that day was part of history.

There were other times, misunderstood by the family,
When you, at fifteen, on your summer evening bed
Believed there were ancient towns you might anciently visit.
There might be a neglected platform on some terminus

And a ticket bought when the clock was off its guard.
Oh, who can dismember the past? The boy on the friendly
      bed
Lay on the unpossessed mother, the bosom of history,
And is gathered to her at last. And tears I suppose

Still thirst for that reeking unwashed pillow,
That bed ingrained with all the dirt of the past,
The mess and lice and stupidity of the Golden Age,
But a mother and loving, ultimately Eden.

One looks for Eden in history, best left unvisited,
For the primal sin is always a present sin,
The thin hand held in the river which can never
Clean off the blood, and so remains bloodless.

And this very moment, this very word will be Eden,
As that boy was already, or is already, in Eden,
While the delicate filthy hand dabbles and dabbles
But leaves the river clean, heartbreakingly clean.

About the Author

ANTHONY BURGESS was born in Manchester, England, in 1917. After studying music and languages in Manchester (during this period he wrote a symphony), he joined the Army in October, 1940, and served for six years.

Mr. Burgess did not take seriously to writing until his late thirties. His main ambition was to be known as a composer, and he has produced and had performed works of widely differing types. In 1954, he accepted a post as Education Officer in the Federation of Malaya, where he remained until the coming of independence in 1957.

Returning to England, Mr. Burgess took up writing as a full-time career. Among his works are sixteen published novels (including his three Malayan novels, recently published here under the collected title, *The Long Day Wanes*), an introduction to linguistics, and *Re Joyce,* an explication of the aims and techniques of the author of *Ulysses* and *Finnegans Wake*.

A frequent guest on the B.B.C. and contributor of articles and reviews to *The Spectator* and *The Manchester Guardian,* Mr. Burgess has travelled extensively in Europe, Asia and America, and lives in Malta. He is married and has no children.

The Devil Drives

A Life of Sir Richard Burton

FAWN M. BRODIE

Swordsman, archaeologist, sexologist, translator of The Arabian Nights and many volumes of oriental erotics, Burton shocked his Victorian contemporaries. Acclaimed as one of the best biographies in years, this is the full-scale portrait of a brilliant and fascinating man —explorer of the unknown places of the earth and the unspeakable secrets of the human heart.

"Brilliant . . . a first class biography of an exceptional man."—New York Times

480 pages   16 pages of photos $1.25

To order by mail, write to: Dept. CS, Ballantine Books, 36 West 20th Street, New York, N.Y. 10003